EXVASCIA

THE ADRALACK TRILOGY

Beauford E. Averette

BEAUFORD E. AVERETTE

EXVASCIA - THE ADRALACK TRILOGY

Library of Congress Control Number:	2015943432
ISBN 13: Paperback	978-1-943483-27-3
PDF	978-1-943483-28-0
ePub	978-1-943483-29-7
Kindle	978-1-943483-30-3

This is a work of fiction. Names, characters, places and incidents either are the product of the author's imagination or are used fictitiously, and any resemblance to any actual persons, living or dead, events, or locales is entirely coincidental.

Printed in the United States of America.

LitFire
PUBLISHING

Contents

Acknowledgement

I want to thank my wife of 52 years, Marie, for her encouragement and for giving me time to complete this second novel. For without her support and motivation this would probably not happen.

I thank my friend Rick Roemer for the beautiful cover photo of "Punchbowl Falls" in the Columbia River George.

I also would like to thank the people who read the book and gave me their two cents, it was truly helpful.

To my high school classmate, Jim Palmquist, who had read the first of the trilogy, "The Adralack Crack on Mt. Baker". He eagerly read an early version of this novel and offered suggestions and input.

My niece, Annette Scott, for providing both critical and constructive comments that greatly helped with the outcome of the story.

My friend, Esther Bell, who by thinking outside the box was able to offer suggestions that influenced many necessary changes to improve the flow and understanding of the plot.

Not to be forgotten is the critical review by LitFire's staff. It is only through the acceptance of criticism that blinds us to our weakness that we can ever improve anything we write or attempt to do.

I am eagerly anticipating the writing of the final book of the trilogy "Creatures From Spark Stone Mountain" I trust it will be even more suspenseful, full of many surprises and end with a dramatic conclusion.

Chapter 1

A New Start

Art did not speak as the two women approached his hospital bed. He would like to but he couldn't. In fact, other than looking from one to the other, he was not able to move any part of the body he had possessed. It had been less than a week since the incident on Mt. Baker that had caused his condition. On the previous weekend Art had walked into a shallow rocky overhang on Mt. Baker in Washington State. Upon entering the area his body had been disintegrated by a powerful, unknown, alien force.

Before he entered the area he and his mountain-climbing friends had come to call the "Adralack Crack", he knew about the possible danger of disintegrating. However, he chose to enter it and trust his scientific friend Adrian's teletransporter to bring him back out. Adrian Adralack had perfected a teletransporter that could temporarily disintegrate items or people before returning them to their original state at a later time and in a different place. It had worked perfectly on him when he wasn't under the control of the alien's power in the "Adralack Crack".

Regardless of how it had worked hundreds of miles away, it was not able to overcome the power of the "Adralack Crack" and he was left stranded in the Crack without a body that he could use in the outside world.

The whole purpose of the expedition to the "Adralack Crack" was to try to pull their friend Larry Hoyle from the grasp of the alien force. He had been pulled into the Crack and disintegrated by the alien power a year and a half earlier, when he entered it for shelter after being injured in an avalanche. Adrian's teletransporter didn't have enough power to pull Larry from the grasp of the alien force and blew up. Larry resisted because he didn't want to leave Exvascia.

When Adrian's machine failed him, he walked into the Crack to join his friend Larry, who had entered the alien world earlier. Now Art was stranded without any way to escape the alien force of the Crack. Delbert, Art's friend, had started to walk into the Crack but his body fell, when he only allowed his psyche, spirit and personality to enter the Crack, leaving his body for Art to use. For a moment, Larry who was happy to see Delbert and Adrian ready to enter his world, lost his concentration and left Delbert's body outside the Crack. During those few seconds Art was able to enter Delbert's abandoned body, but he was unable to make it move or speak. Fortunately, Delbert's friend, Myrna, Art's wife, and Carol Hensley, his graduate teaching assistant, were able to pull Delbert's body beyond the power of the Crack.

Art had achieved his goal of getting back into his world in a body but appeared to be paralyzed from the neck down. He was the only person on Earth who knew he wasn't Delbert Tinsley and he wasn't able to tell anyone about it. Even now, the visitors to his room hadn't come to see him as Art, but as Delbert. What else could he expect them to think, his new body had always belonged to his friend Delbert?

Even though he knew the body he was in would be recognized as Delbert, it was hard to get used to being called Delbert rather than Art. He thought to himself. *If I'm going to get his body functioning properly, I had better start considering it mine. I'm sure not going to tell everyone that this body they see is Art or they'll think I've suffered brain damage or that I've become schizophrenic.*

Art recognized the visitors on either side of his hospital bed. Myrna, his wife, was on one side and Carol Hensley was on the other. *I wonder if I'll be able to teach Delbert's psychology course or my own geology courses in the future.* He tried to think about specific geological facts but there was nothing in his head but basic psychology knowledge. Apparently the transfer of his soul, spirit and personality had been at the conscious level and not at the subconscious level.

He didn't have any problem remembering his relationship with his wife or Carol, with whom he had slept a few nights when he had run out on his wife. He and Delbert had grown close to Carol when she had helped them work on their efforts to improve their ability to communicate telepathically. The plan was to develop their telepathic ability so Art could tell Delbert where Adrian should aim his teletransporter to withdraw both himself and Larry from the Crack. Everything was going great on Mt. Baker until Adrian's teletransporter blew up

If Larry had wanted to come back, perhaps Adrian would have been able to free him permanently rather than for just a few seconds before losing him back to the Crack's cosmic power. Art knew both Myrna and Carol were able to communicate telepathically with both he and Delbert at the Crack earlier.

If he could communicate telepathically with them now, they may be able to help the doctors and therapists with his problems. Maybe he would have been better off to stay with Larry, Delbert and Adrian and go to Exvascia with them. *I wonder what it's like on that planet. I know Delbert wanted to go to see what his son and daughters would look like after having mated with the transmutant alien, DorLetha, whose powers activated the Crack.*

After awhile he realized the two women were up to something. By trying hard he could hear what they were talking about through Delbert's ears. "Delbert, can you hear us?" It was Myrna, his wife, talking. She was standing by his right side and holding his hand. "Concentrate Delbert! I want you to squeeze my hand if you can hear me! Carol and I are going to try to find out some things about your condition. Remember how I brought you back to life when Adrian first tried his teletransporter on you and the power failed?" She bent down and kissed him on the forehead.

When Art had first decided to walk into the "Adralack Crack", Adrian was to test his teletransporter on him in his garage/workshop. All Art knew was that Adrian had tried it on Delbert first and then on Carol before he had tried it on him. He hadn't heard there was a problem so he didn't know what she was talking about. He could tell both his wife and Carol were very worried about Delbert and seemed to care deeply about him.

Art didn't mind his wife and Delbert were close because he hoped that Delbert, who was single and his best friend, would be there to take care of her if anything ever happened to him. He never knew how really close they were or that the two of them had slept together when he had run out on his wife and spent several days and nights with Carol. Here he was, appearing to be his wife's lover while being her husband at the same time. Since he couldn't relate to what she was talking about, he didn't squeeze her hand or even try to see if he could.

"Delbert its Carol, if you want to answer yes, squeeze Myrna's hand. Squeeze my hand for no! Can you hear us?"

This time Art could hear Carol, as if she was whispering, but he couldn't squeeze either of their hands.

"Do you feel anything, Carol?"

"Not yet. Delbert we can't tell what is happening with you! I see you can look at one of us or the other. Look at Myrna if you can hear me!"

That was the one body function Art had mastered. He quickly looked at Myrna. He knew Carol was sharp from her working with Delbert, Myrna and himself on their telepathic communication efforts, which she was basing her Master's thesis on.

Myrna spoke, “Delbert pull yourself together! Come on try. Look at Carol if you can hear me!”

Art's gaze quickly shifted to Carol and then back to Myrna. “Carol his eyes seem to be trying to tell me something. Delbert, both Carol and I are going to hold your hands. We want you to concentrate on squeezing your thumb against our hands as we concentrate with you. Maybe with our three minds linked we can enable you to move your thumb. We have to get some communication started with you other than eye contact. Now, try very hard as we concentrate.” The room was silent as they concentrated. The women were almost frantic because the nurse would soon be telling them their short visiting time was up.

“Myrna, he did it.”

“I feel it now too Carol. It's very weak but he's doing it. Delbert squeeze my hand for yes and Carol's for no. Can you see us?” Myrna felt a slight pressure from Delbert's thumb. “Do you know who we are?” Again she was delighted to feel a very slight pressure. “Do you hurt anywhere?” This time it was Carol's face that lit up as he responded.

That was all they were able to discover before the nurse made them leave. They located Dr. Lyons, Delbert's doctor, in the hall. They eagerly told him what they were able to find out. He knew that someone very close to Delbert would probably be able to get more cooperation from him then either he or his staff had been able to. “Ladies, let's go back into his room and see if he's tired. If he says no, let's see what else he has to tell us.” As the three of them approached Delbert's room, the nurse stopped them.

“Excuse me Dr., but these two ladies have already spent the maximum time allowed with Mr. Tinsley.”

“I understand nurse, but I need them present when I try to communicate with Mr. Tinsley. I'll see to it they leave when I do. Thank you!” With that they reentered Delbert's room. Art was glad for all the attention Delbert was being given.

“Delbert, we told the doctor what we found out. He says he can fit you with some response buttons that will only take the slightest pressure to activate. Can you hear me?” Myrna felt the response and was glad. “Do we need to talk louder Delbert?” This time Carol felt the response.

The doctor finally spoke. “Are you tired?”

“He said, ‘No’, Doctor.”

“I need to find out what feeling you have in order to tell the therapist what to do for you.” The doctor checked Delbert's reflexes and they responded. He then applied pressure on his arms and legs and asked if he felt anything.

Art answered 'No'!

"What do you think, Doctor?"

"I'm not sure, Mrs. Noack. If he can't feel the pressure I put on his arms and legs, how can he move his thumb to answer your questions? There is something very strange here!"

Art thought to himself. *If he thinks something is strange, he should try being inside someone else's body like I am! I hadn't thought about it, but somehow I'm making Delbert's body move its thumbs. If I can figure out how I do that, perhaps I can start making some progress.*

"Myrna, do you think we should tell Dr. Lyons what happened to Delbert on Mt. Baker and before, when the teletransporter lost power? Maybe that would be of help to him."

"Would you like to hear something unreal Dr. Lyons?" Myrna proceeded to tell Dr. Lyons the necessary details about Delbert's physical damage, or apparent damage, at the "Adralack Crack". She added details of the first experiment on Delbert with the teletransporter and what happened to him when the power failed.

Art listened as his wife spoke. He could now see the deep love she had for Delbert. Even now, she was squeezing Delbert's hand and kissing him while Carol continued to explain various happenings to Dr. Lyons.

To Art's surprise, he realized he had actually felt his new hand being squeezed by Myrna. He wished he could tell her how much he loved her and that he could feel the pressure she was putting on his hand.

When Dr. Lyons turned and examined his eyes, he felt his eye blink at the light and he could now feel Carol squeezing and rubbing his other hand as though she was excited. What had he or Delbert's body done to cause her to smile so? Perhaps it was the interest shown by the handsome young, single Dr. Lyons to whom she had been earnestly speaking, but that wasn't it.

"Miss Henley, I think his tear ducts are working now. Do you and Mrs. Noack think you could communicate with him telepathically and find out what he isn't able to tell us verbally that is causing him to cry?"

Dr. Lyons gently touched Carol's shoulders as he traded places with her at Art's bedside. Although he was just being careful not to trip over the intravenous feeding tube and the other monitoring equipment attached to Delbert's body, Carol noticed how strong, yet gentle, his touch was. She thought he was too young to be a Doctor. She fleetingly wondered if he was dating anyone and why he was still single.

Both Carol and Myrna moved closer to Delbert's head. Art could hear them asking him what he had wanted to tell them that made a tear come to his eye. Myrna was too emotional to receive any communication from Art even though he tried his hardest to send thoughts to her. For Carol, it was a different story. She had closed her eyes and blanked her mind so she could visualize a blank motion picture screen in her mind. She had to have some place to focus her thoughts and project the fleeting telepathic messages she might receive.

As Dr. Lyons looked on, he noticed how beautiful Carol was. She looked so peaceful with her eyes closed and her head close to Delbert's. He suddenly had the urge to plant a soft, gentle kiss on her cheek, a kiss so soft that it wouldn't distract her. However, he couldn't do that. He didn't even know her but he decided he would like to get to know her.

As Dr. Lyons looked on, he watched as Myrna got up and moved away from Delbert. He didn't know the sad feeling she had inside for Delbert or that she didn't want to pass it on to him. Myrna's leaving his side was just what Art needed to concentrate on sending Carol the message that he could now feel their touch on the hands of his newly acquired body,

Dr. Lyons then noticed a very serious expression appear on Carol's face. He wondered. *What was she feeling? What message was she receiving? How did it feel to receive a telepathic message?* He knew he would have to talk with her about that later.

The experience for Carol was the same as it had been when she was with Delbert the previous year and he had been contacted by the alien, DorLetha. Carol's whole body tensed! She had cold chills up and down her back, arms and legs. She had goose bumps everywhere and the feeling in the pit of her stomach that she always got when receiving thought from Delbert. She had to concentrate! She couldn't let him down! The message she received couldn't be right! It just couldn't be right!

She cleared her mind, the best she could and felt the feelings of a message coming through again from someone, but it didn't feel like Delbert. There it was again saying, "I can feel your touch! I can feel you holding my hand!"

Who was the message from? How could she know? She was again feeling the "Delbert feeling" coming through! He was saying, "Take care of him!" For some reason she could see Delbert looking down at her and his body. She let out a shriek, as she felt him put his hand on her shoulder and repeat, "Take good care of him!"

Carol screamed and opened her eyes to find that Delbert had reached over with his right hand and put it on her shoulder. She reached up, took hold of his lifeless hand and put it back across his chest. How was he able to do that, when all he said was, "I can feel your touch."

Dr. Lyons voice brought her back to reality. He was busy telling a nurse that everything was OK. His strong hands were gently and safely pulling her away from the bed. She turned and hugged him. Because of her previous scream and her action now, he held her violently shaking body close to his. The warmth of his body and the strength of his embrace calmed her and brought her back from her trance-like state.

As Dr. Lyons escorted Carol out of the room, Myrna said good-bye to Delbert and told him everything was OK, that she would see him again soon.Art was shaken too. For an instant it felt to him as though Delbert had reentered his own body and pushed him aside. What had he said or done to upset Carol so? He didn't like that at all. Did this mean that he wasn't free of Delbert's control? Could Delbert see all that was happening on Earth, even though he was supposedly far away on the planet Exvascia? Art felt completely helpless. Was there anything he could do?

Dr. Lyons quickly escorted Carol and Myrna to his office. He now addressed Carol by her first name. "Carol, what did he tell you?" Myrna could tell Carol wasn't ready to talk so she got her a cup of coffee. Dr. Lyons continued, "How could he reach up and put his hand on your shoulder and then not be able to take it back down? As far as that goes, how could he raise his hand at all?"

Carol took a couple of swallows of the hot coffee Myrna had brought her. What should she tell them? Should she tell Myrna about Delbert appearing not to be in his body? She wondered what Delbert had meant when he said "take care of him!" If Delbert wasn't in his body, who was? She thought back to the time at "The Adralack Crack on Mt. Baker". She knew Larry had been taken by the alien force a year and a half before. Art had become the second victim when he voluntarily walked into the shallow cave, expecting Adrian's teletransporter to pull him back out. Adrian became the third victim when he walked into the "Crack" after his teletransporter blew up.

Was Adrian, Larry or Art now in Delbert's body somehow? When Delbert fell in front of the "Crack" and the doctor said he was dead, did someone or something take over his body? Is that how he was able to stand and walk a few feet after the Army doctor pronounced him dead?

There were a lot of questions racing through Carol's mind. Although she was holding her cup of coffee to her lips, she wasn't drinking any of it. She just sat there very still, looking into space. It was Dr. Lyons gentle hand on her shoulder that helped her to speak.

"Carol I can see you've had quite an experience and I'd like to get together with you soon to talk about it. The things you've told me today and the things I've seen fascinate me. Right now, however, I'd like to find out what you can tell me about Mr. Tinsley."

"He said, 'I can feel your touch on my hand.' He seemed pleased to know that for some reason! It's as if his mind and body are somehow disconnected."

"Did he say anything else?"

"No, I don't think so."

"What do you mean by that?"

"Well, Dr. Lyons, sometimes it's hard to tell whether you're receiving a person's thought waves or your imagination's playing tricks on you. I screamed when he put his hand on my shoulder because I never thought he could do that. How could he do that Doctor?"

"I'm not sure, Carol! I just want to give the therapist all the help I can without telling her all you told me today. I can't explain what I've seen today either but I have to believe it. Maybe he somehow drew on your strength, through telepathy, to put his hand on your shoulder. Maybe that is why it got limp when he broke your concentration. I'll have him fitted for the pressure response buttons first thing in the morning. Will either of you be up tomorrow?"

"I'll be up, Dr. Lyons." Myrna said.

"What about you Carol?"

"I'm sorry, but I can't make it tomorrow."

"Is there a number where I can reach you in case I think I could use your help?"

"Sure, I'll just write it down for you. Do you think he'll get better soon, Dr. Lyons?" She studied his face intently as he thought about how he should respond. She liked what she saw, an intelligent, caring person. She liked his soft brown eyes; his pretty mouth, which complimented his relaxed smile and his well groomed hair. She thought he should be a model rather than a doctor. He was the type of man a woman likes to look at and be seen with. She wondered what he was really like.

When Dr. Lyons was paged, Myrna and Carol excused themselves so he could get back to his patients. As they waited for the elevator and later walked through the lobby, Carol's thoughts drifted back to Delbert's thoughts on soul flight, which he said was like a near death experience when one can see their own body as if they were not in it. He said this after the teletransporter accident during its first test run on him. Had his soul and spirit lingered too long before it reentered his body on Mt. Baker? Would he die, or could his mind be activated once again to operate his body? She remembered how fast he had been able to run, when the two of them went jogging. Would he ever be that way again? It was upsetting to think that someone else could have entered his body, but at the "Adralack Crack" that type of thing would have been entirely possible because of the awesome power of the alien cosmic force.

She remembered how she had been able to join in on the telepathic communications of Delbert, Adrian and Larry before they all disappeared in the "Adralack Crack" and it became inactive. W*here is Exvascia and what is life like there?*

The trip home was quiet. Neither Myrna nor Carol wished to talk. The late August sun was shining brightly and the farmers of the Willamette Valley were burning the straw left in the grain fields after the harvest was over. Myrna finally spoke. "Are you sure you can't join me tomorrow?"

"I wish I could! I think Delbert will be OK after awhile. Dr. Lyons seems like a nice person. He really wants to help Delbert. I think he and the therapist will be able to work out Delbert's problems. You'll let me know how he's coming along won't you?"

"I sure will. When are you going back east to start your new job?"

"I had planned to leave last night but I'll leave tomorrow. I hate to leave him at a time like this. If you ever need me, I could fly back here."

"I may have you do that if things don't get better." In spite of the previous relationship between Carol and her husband, Art, Myrna needed Carol's ability to communicate telepathically with Delbert.

Myrna drove over to her friend Gail Hoyle's home to pick up her son Todd and daughter Lisa. Gail enjoyed the Noack's kids. Before Larry died in the "Adralack Crack", they had thought about adopting children, since she couldn't have any but they had never gotten around to it. Gail was worried about Delbert who had been a close friend of hers and her husband Larry.

Gail felt sorry for Myrna who had lost her husband, Art, to the "Adralack Crack" and had her best friend Delbert almost killed. Now that Gail knew her husband would never return from the Crack, she was free to marry Michael Endicott, a friend of the family for many years.

When the doorbell rang, Gail was eager to talk with Myrna. "Hi, how is Delbert?"

"A little better than he was at the first of the week before he was transferred to the hospital in Portland. Carol and I were able to get him to answer some yes and no questions by having him squeezing our hands. The doctor seems encouraged, but only time will tell."

"Would you like me to watch Todd and Lisa for you again tomorrow when you go see him? If you bring them over about the same time as today,

I could drive them over to the coast? I know they would enjoy playing in the sand."

"That would be great if you could Gail, thanks."

"OK. I'll see you then."

Chapter 2

Delbert's Secret

Myrna traveled the 85 miles to Portland quite often to see Delbert. For some reason, that she couldn't put her finger on, he seemed different to her.

Art couldn't make Delbert's body do much, but he had his hopes. It was strange to be in someone else's body and even stranger for people to call you by that person's name. Would he ever be able to convince her, or anybody else, that he wasn't who he appeared to be?

"Good morning, Delbert. How are you?" Even though Dr. Lyons had wired Delbert's hands for pressure responses, yes and no was all Art was able to say at the present time. "I want you to meet your therapist, Karen Ellers. Miss Ellers will be working closely with me on your case. I want you to concentrate on learning to use your hands as soon as possible. If we can get you to the point where you can use one of your hands, even one finger, we can give you a laptop computer that will allow you to say a lot of words, even make sentences. How would you like that?"

Dr. Lyons knew Delbert couldn't answer but he wanted to give Art the feeling of being in a conversation. Art looked forward to the time when he would be able to converse. He knew the young, pleasant looking, therapist would make it easy for him to try to do his best. As he got to know her better, perhaps he could even give her telepathic suggestions on the type of therapy that would speed his progress.

"Karen, I don't know what will happen when you start to work with Delbert. If you notice anything different, unusual or have any strange feelings around him, please let me know. I think part of his problem is with his subconscious state not being in touch with his conscious level of thinking. If you can get him to concentrate on everything he does and he can make that connection again, I think he will quickly make a large initial step in his recovery. Go over everything you do three times and make sure you keep talking to him about what you are doing and what he is supposed to do. Is that clear?"

"Yes, Dr. I'll have him up and around in no time!"

Art certainly hoped she was right. He didn't want to lie in his hospital bed for very long. Delbert had kept his body in such good shape that Art knew it would be able to do just about anything, if he could get his messages across to it. He wished Carol hadn't left the area. He may need her telepathic communicative ability to get important information to either the Dr. or the therapist but she was gone and he was on his own.

It took a month for Art to learn to turn Delbert's head and to be able to sit up in a chair. He didn't feel that was much progress, especially since someone had to lift him into the wheelchair and then he had to be strapped in.

Today, as Karen worked over his body, she wanted him to raise his right hand. She repeated over and over to him, "Raise your right hand, Delbert!" Each time he failed to respond, Karen would pick it up and touch his nose with his index finger. Art tried to connect what she was doing with the subconscious level of Delbert's brain. His efforts were in vain. However, once he thought his new mind was starting to make the connection.

I've got to help myself more than this. This is my body now and I must keep reminding myself of that. It's my hand Karen wants me to move, my hand! On Karen's last try to get him to lift his arm; she felt he had assisted her a little. She told Art how he would soon be able to use that hand anytime he thought about it and to try it on his own when she wasn't around.

After lunch Karen put Art in his wheelchair and strapped him in. She then took him out on the lawn by some rosebushes where he could enjoy the view of Mt. Hood and the sunshine. Art had to laugh at himself. Here he was, having his body handled all over by Karen and he couldn't even feel it. He thought back to the time he had spent with Carol, after he had walked out on his wife. *If only Carol was here to run her soft hands over 'MY' body like Karen just did, perhaps I could feel her touch and get some control over it!*

As he sat looking at Mt. Hood, he remembered the tragic Christmas vacation climb he and his friends had made on Mt. Baker almost two years earlier. The mystifying death of his friend Larry in the "Adralack Crack", that rocky outcropping that he had entered when he was injured, haunted him. His thoughts switched to the power Larry had back in August when they had last visited the site of his death. He remembered how Larry had almost pulled Delbert's body into the Crack before Delbert gave it to him to use. What had Larry meant when he said, "We'll come back for you Art? May the cosmic force be with you until we return."

Larry had told him, when he was in the Crack, that he could see everything that was happening on Earth. Larry had even mentioned the robbery Art had been an accomplice to. *How did he know that? Did Delbert use some of the alien force to reenter his body earlier, when his hand was put on Carol's shoulder? Could or would he enter it again?*

Art's thoughts were interrupted by three things. The first was a honey bee landing on his nose. It must have flown off the nearby flowers. The second thing was his hand involuntarily slapping his nose and eye. The third thing was the cry "oh" coming from his lips.

He wasn't stung, but he would have a black eye for a while. He remembered how it felt to lift his arm. Could he do it again? He tried hard, but he could only lift his hand and forearm. He was happy about that and tried it again. Hurray, he could still do it. *Right on*! He said to himself. His efforts to say it aloud were unsuccessful. All that came out was an, "ah", sound.

"I saw that!" Karen said as she approached. "It doesn't quite look like you have control of things yet, but I see you can move your hand and arm some. I'll get you something to help heal the black eye you'll have. Can you say, "Ah", again?" Art tried and was again able to say "ah". "That's fine." That's the first sound I've heard you make. I'll tell Dr. Lyons about your adventure out here this afternoon. Now it's time for your afternoon nap. We'll see else you can do during your afternoon therapy session."

Dr. Lyons stopped by to see Art during his afternoon therapy session. He wanted to encourage him and to mention that he had talked to Carol about his condition. "Carol sends her love and said she would be thinking of you during your afternoon therapy session which is at 6:00 p.m. where she is. I told her you hadn't made much progress but we are still working with you. The next time I talk to her, I'll tell her about your experience this afternoon. I know she'll be glad to hear about it."

As Art lie there thinking about Carol, Karen continued to massage his thigh muscles. He wondered if this efficient therapist was ever sexy like Carol was. She certainly didn't have the radiant beauty Carol had. Both her build and looks were just average like most women.

His thoughts were interrupted by Karen. "Do you feel anything, Delbert? Remember, you are supposed to be trying to move your leg when I lift it."

Art pressed his "no" button in answer to her question. "What about this?" He tried to pay attention, but he didn't feel anything yet. Again he had to press the "no" button. "Do you want to know something?" Art pressed the "yes" button. "You're making some progress."

Art wished he could talk so he could ask her what she was talking about. He looked at her smiling face and wondered what she wasn't telling him. He then felt what she was talking about. He felt his face flush. What a thing to have a young lady know about. He watched her as she moved to his ankles and feet.

He thought back to the spring when Carol had driven him over to his beach condo after he had run out on his wife, Myrna, after telling her he was going to walk into the “Adralack Crack”. Carol had given him a bottle of whiskey to drink on the way over. Since he didn't usually drink, he had passed out just after they had arrived because he had drunk too much. Had she or he taken his clothes off before he got into bed. He didn't think he had undressed himself because he could only remember trying to climb the stairs. He didn't even remember entering the condo.

Karen's directions brought him back to the present. “Delbert, try to move your foot!” He tried, but he couldn't. Then he heard a loud slap and felt a tingle in his right foot. Karen had slapped the sole of his foot with the palm of her hand. That enabled him to slightly move his ankle. Karen didn't need to tell him he had moved it because he could now feel his own slight movement. Karen's persistence and efforts continually encouraged Art to do his best.

By October when Myrna, Gail and Michael visited Art, he was able to move his hands. The computer Dr. Lyons provided Art gave him a fairly comprehensive vocabulary. He was able to sit upright by himself, once someone sat him up. Karen was also working on his speech problem. So far, he could make sounds but no words.

Myrna would read Carol's letters to him when she visited and tell him everything she had been doing. The letters were great, but it would have been more fun if he could have talked with her.

Dr. Lyons had called Carol several times regarding Delbert after she had moved to Chicago and started her new job. Each evening she would take time to send messages to Delbert. Once her messages came in so loud and clear, to Delbert's brain, Art just had to send her his own message. However, he couldn't do it while Karen was giving him therapy. He would have to wait until after dinner when it would be about two hours later for Carol.

Art's thoughts were interrupted by some grunts and groans. To his surprise, it was Karen playing back the sounds he had made for her during his speech therapy session. That's what she called progress! He couldn't believe it. When Myrna arrived that evening he asked her to bring him the tape Delbert had made for her and Art some months earlier. He was fortunate his speech computer allowed him to make that request. He wasn't able to tell her exactly what he wanted, so she had to guess. She didn't know why he wanted to hear his own voice again, but she thought it might help with his speech therapy. What will my speech be like? *Will I talk like Delbert and speak in a baritone voice?*

Myrna was happy to see the progress he was finally making. His ability to move his arms and legs was coming back at their extremities first and then working their way back toward his trunk

One evening when Myrna was feeling sexy, some of the things she said surprised and enlightened him. "Delbert you've got to keep making progress so you can get back to your apartment. I know it would be great to have you hold me again. Remember how great it was making love in the moonlight?"

Art answered, "Yes", before he realized his wife was talking about Delbert and her, not him as Art. Myrna kissed Delbert on the lips and at the same time reached under his covers and aroused him. "Remember Denver? Wouldn't you like to see that again?" Art again answered "Yes" before he realized his wife was still talking about herself and Delbert. He couldn't understand her last remark about Denver. *Delbert hadn't gone to Denver with her, he had. What was their Denver secret?*

Art had been able to feel Myrna arouse him. This meant more of his feelings were coming back all the time. Maybe he would soon be able to move his whole leg. After Myrna left he was still excited, a little upset and somewhat confused. Had Myrna and Delbert had an affair while he was busy entertaining Carol? *Why should I be upset?* He thought to himself. *If it's OK for me to fool around, why couldn't she?* For the first time in his life, he could understand the hurt his wife had felt when he had stayed several days with Carol.

That additional information would make it all the harder for him to tell Myrna that he was really Art and not the Delbert she was seeing. He had to get some help from Carol on that problem. As Art lie in his hospital bed, which Myrna had cranked into a reclining position, he closed his eyes and concentrated on Carol. He wished he could speak aloud, but he wasn't able to yet. The thoughts poured from his mind. They were powered by the frustration and anxiety he felt from his condition.

Carol it's me, Art! I need your help! I'm a captive in Delbert's body. I can't make it work! Help me! During my therapy sessions, concentrate on my being able to walk. Please Carol, think of me! Art wondered if his message would be received. He decided to try tuning into Carol's thoughts. To his surprise, his ability to receive Carol's thoughts was extremely good.

Carol had just gotten into bed when she was disturbed by the feeling in the pit of her stomach that accompanied thought waves from Art. It was disturbing to her that she couldn't tune his thoughts in clearly. She tried to think about Art and the last time she had seen him. That was just before he disintegrated in the "Adralack Crack". How could she be receiving thought from him? Wasn't he whisked off to Exvascia with Adrian and Larry by the powerful alien cosmic force?

She tried to sleep; but she couldn't. She tried to get rid of the feeling that she had in the pit of her stomach. Her thoughts strayed back to the message she had gotten from Delbert, when she was beside his bed. He didn't seem to be in his body, but he wanted her to take care of whoever it was that was in it. Was that someone, Art? Maybe it was! Carol cleared her mind once again and relaxed. This time the feeling of an incoming message was accompanied not only by the feeling in the pit of her stomach, but by goose bumps on her back, arms and legs. *I must fight back my fears and receive this message even if it is from Art, or I'll never go to sleep.*

As Carol cleared her mind of all thoughts and calmed her body, Art's message came in. She could see him lying in his bed in the cranked up position. Although his lips weren't moving, she understood everything he had said. His closing statement, i*t's really me, Little Lady, Art. Believe me!"* was very clear. It just had to be Art. He was the only person who knew what his nickname for her was. She could even see he had been moved to a new room.

After receiving the message, Carol was too excited to sleep. She had to share her vision and its message with someone to relieve herself of all the pent up emotion she had inside her. *Who can I call? Myrna? No, I'd better not. She will never believe its Art. She is expecting Delbert to be the Delbert she had always known and loved. Gail and Michael are the only other people left from the Mt. Baker incident but they never were affected by the power of the cosmic alien force of the "Adralack Crack". There must be someone I can call! Maybe I should call, Dr. Lyons. He has not only heard the story, but become involved through his efforts to help Delbert, who he now knows didn't become paralyzed from any known cause.*

Carol got out of bed, put on her housecoat and then called his unlisted number, which he had given her for an emergency. It wouldn't be 9:00 p.m. yet on the west coast. Being a weekday, she might catch him at home. On the third ring the phone was answered. "Hello, this is Darrell."

"Dr. Lyons, this is Carol Henley. Do you have a few minutes to talk?" Her sweet, soft voice sounded both excited and hopeful.

"Hi Carol, it's good to hear from you. Where are you and what's on your mind?"

"I'm still in Chicago. I've received a telepathic message tonight."

"Who was the message from, Delbert?"

"Are you ready for anything I might tell you?"

"What do you mean?"

"Well, it's about your patient, Delbert, only," her voice trailed off.

"I guess so! I know his recovery is erratic. I also realize from what you told me, everything wrong with him isn't what it seems to be. I'm ready! Why don't you go ahead and tell me about it?"

"Remember what happened in Delbert's hospital room when I tried to find out what he wanted to tell us when he got that first tear in his eye? Remember what I told you?"

"Yes why?"

"Well, what I didn't tell you was that I felt Delbert's presence outside his body. He then entered it for a minute and put his hand on my shoulder and told me to take of the person in his body!"

"You mean that at the "Adralack Crack", the spirit of one of the other three men took over Delbert's body?"

"Yes, Dr. Lyons, that's exactly what I mean! The message I got tonight was from Art. He wants me to think of him during his afternoon therapy session and see if the two of us can make him walk."

"That's incredible! However, that does explain why his subconscious and conscious minds aren't working as one. Art's conscious mind must have to learn to operate at Delbert's subconscious level. That explains why Delbert's reflexes work, but Art doesn't know it!"

"Will that be of any help to you in his recovery, Dr. Lyons?"

"Possibly, Carol. I'll have someone assist Karen during his therapy sessions for the next week. Maybe with the four of you working at it you can get him on his feet."

"Dr. Lyons, do you think you could tell him what I've told you and see what he has to say? Be sure not to let Myrna know! I don't know how she would take it. You should probably ask Art if he wants you to tell her! Knowing Art, I think he would rather tell her later when his body functions have returned to normal. He's very special to both of us, as either Art or Delbert!"

"Are you positive about all this, Carol? If you are, I'll tell him, but if you have even the slightest doubt, it could be a big mistake!"

"Dr. Lyons, I'm as sure of what I've told you as I am that you are wearing a light blue, long sleeved, button sweater!"

"How do you know that?"

"I'm right aren't I?"

"Yes Carol, but how did you know that?"

"I was concentrating on you and your thoughts and I could see you sitting there in your favorite chair with a big smile on your face."

"Hey, that's no fair! I have to remember you from those few times I got to see you. Do you think you could send me a picture of yourself? What are you doing next weekend?"

"Why don't you just like me on my facebook page? Will you send me a picture?"

"Yes, but you didn't tell me what you are doing next weekend Carol?"

"Nothing Dr. Lyons. Why?"

"I could be convinced to be in Chicago for a medical conference, if I had someone to accompany me to its special functions. I might even bring that person my picture and a large corsage!"

"Are you trying to make a date with me Dr. Lyons?"

"Yes and just call me Darrell. I like you and I think it's time to get to know you before you are spoken for."

"That's always a possibility, but I'll save next weekend for you!"

"Thanks! I'll get your address off your email, if you'll send it to me."

"I'll send it. Be sure and let me know how you make out with Delbert, or I mean Art."

"OK. If I don't get involved in anything serious, I'll call you tomorrow. I'll be sure to call you by the day after tomorrow at least."

"Thanks Darrell. Good night."

"It's my pleasure! Good night Carol."

What a pleasant surprise! My handsome, young Dr. Lyons has come through! Carol was very pleased with herself and how her evening had turned out. She went to sleep with a smile on her face. All her tension and anxiety had been relieved. She had turned her problem over to Dr. Lyons and would look forward to hearing from him on Art's progress. His pleasant voice was music to her ears.

Dr. Lyons awoke the next morning with more than his normal amount of enthusiasm. Could this special girl he had met really know more about his patient than he did? If so, it would be very interesting to find out how his patient felt about this new information.

Dr. Lyons talked to Delbert's therapist about getting her some help for the afternoon session. He stopped by to see his patient on his morning rounds. "Good morning, Delbert, how are you this morning?"

Art was still not used to being called Delbert. He wasn't any more used to that than he was to being in Delbert's body. He went ahead and answered Dr. Lyons on his computer. "OK I guess!"

"I talked to Carol last night on the phone. She called me just before 9:00 p.m. She wants me to talk with you about a message you sent her last night. Was it you?"

"Yes, Doctor. She is the only person I can communicate with unless I use the computer. What did she tell you?"

"She says that she'll be trying to help you walk during your afternoon session, Art."

"She knows who I am?"

"Yes! If you can remember back to her earlier attempt to find out why a tear came to your eye, she said Delbert told her to, 'Take care of him.' The only problem was she didn't know who Delbert was talking about. She asked me not to tell Myrna yet."

"Thanks, Doctor. Does this help you understand my problem any better?"

"Not really, I've never heard of this happening before. What I think will help most is you paying very close attention to everything your body and Delbert's subconscious mind does. It's kind of like learning everything over again as a baby, except you start with an adult mind. Once you get familiar with Delbert's subconscious level of thinking, you should be OK."

"Do you have any other suggestions? How is this body physically? I know Delbert always kept it in top shape."

"It's lost a little of its edge from not being used lately, but he had it in such good shape it's still better than most people's"

"Do you have any new ideas about my therapy?"

"No, I think Karen is doing a good job. She is really interested in helping you recover. I am going to get her a helper for the next week. With the two of them holding you up and her giving you commands they should be able to hold your attention. With their efforts and the mental power of both you and Carol, concentrating on your walking, something should happen."

The next day at four o'clock, Dr. Lyons remembered Delbert would be starting his therapy session. He had an idea. *What would happen if, when everybody was concentrating on helping him, I ordered Art to walk? Would he automatically respond?* He had to try it.

Dr. Lyons went into the therapy room and called out both loud and stern, "Walk, Art, Walk!" although everyone was startled, Delbert's body didn't respond. In fact, Art didn't even notice Dr. Lyons had used his name. Because of the strange feeling he had, Dr. Lyons knew Carol must be thinking of him. He went back to his office and called Carol. "I had a feeling I should try something different today, so I called out real loud for Art to walk. It didn't help!"

"Tomorrow try the same thing, but call out to Delbert. His body and mind have always responded to that name."

"I'll try Carol. I would sure like to see him get some of his functions back so he can make more progress."

"Call me if anything happens. I'll see if I can think of anything else that you could try. Did you check my facebook page?"

"I sure did! I'm looking forward to our date this weekend."

"So am I Darrell. Thanks for calling."

"I'll let you know what happens tomorrow again Carol. Good-bye."

Dr. Lyons went back to Art's therapy session. Karen and her assistant had already helped Art from the parallel bars where he, with their help, had been trying to walk. Art was only able to give himself minimal support with his arms as he feebly grasped the bars with his hands. Every day he continued to make progress on strengthening his arms. When he was seated, he could move his feet and ankles. He could pull his knees together, but he couldn't lift his legs.

Back in Art's room Dr. Lyons talked with him and told him he would be back later. Neither of them had any new ideas. He was making progress but not as much as he could if he made an initial breakthrough.

That evening when Dr. Lyons visited Art, Myrna was visiting. "Dr. Lyons do you know what Delbert wanted the tape of his voice for?"

"I think he wanted one of his voice so he could work on his speech. Is there anything special about his speech or voice?"

"He has a beautiful baritone voice and he loves to sing!"

"Why don't you bring his tape recorder and a blank tape? It would probably be a good idea to bring a recording of him both singing and talking."

"I think he could operate his special cassette recorder. It has a toggle switch rather than two buttons to push when he wants to record."

"That should be helpful, Mrs. Noack. His speech therapist should be able to put that to good use. He can make several sounds but he is still too embarrassed to try to talk. Maybe hearing his own voice will refresh his memory as to how he used to sound."

"Have you figured out what happened to him, Dr.?"

"Not really Mrs. Noack. There must have been some brain damage. If that isn't the case it may be a psychological and/or emotional problem. How does he seem to you?" Dr. Lyons was careful not to tell her what he really knew. He noticed Delbert perspire at some of the lines of questioning.

"I don't know. It seems like his eyes are trying to tell me something. There's something wrong, but I haven't been able to put my finger on it yet." Her discerning mind was puzzled. Myrna stayed another half hour after Dr.

Lyons left. She told Delbert that Gail and Michael had set their wedding for the Saturday after Thanksgiving.

Art was glad to hear that. They really needed each other. To both his and Myrna's surprise, he said, "Good." It was a little hard to understand because it was slurred but it did show some progress. It showed that his mind was working quickly and that he understood what he heard. He looked forward to learning to speak. The more sounds he made, the better he understood how his new body worked.

Meanwhile, Gail had decided to teach fall term at the University. That meant she would have to drive 85 each way for about three weeks after she was married; which wouldn't be too bad. She felt her chances of getting a job with a college or university in the Portland area would be better if she completed fall term where she was.

Myrna was happy for Gail and Michael, but she would miss having Gail close by. Gail had put her house up for sale. She and Michael would probably rent until Michael's job situation was more stable.

The Defense Department had decided not to give Michael his TV documentary of the "Adralack Crack" teletransporter demonstration. They had several reasons. One was the damage the public may do to the environment if they were to try to examine the shallow cave involved. The other reason was their uncertainty about the active nature of the Crack, its remaining power and the possible loss of life if it suddenly became active again.

Michael often thought about what he had seen on Mt. Baker the day Delbert had been disabled. *Was what I saw real or did I just imagined the things I remember?* One thing he knew for sure was that he still had over $5,000 from his robbery after paying for Gail's wedding ring, wedding present and his new car.

When Larry died, Gail received their house free and clear, his life insurance and the $10,000 CD Adrian left her. Michael was really marrying a beautiful, intelligent and wealthy woman. Michael had previously been a good friend of the couple and now was madly in love with her. He wished Delbert would get better so he could be his best man. Unfortunately the disaster on Mt. Baker had taken many of Gail's friends, as well as his best friend, Larry, her husband.

When Michael and Gail visited Delbert, they encouraged him to get better so he could participate in their wedding. They wanted to give him one more reason to keep trying. However, the two months he had to recuperate seemed too short of a time to expect a full recovery.

During Art's therapy session the following day, Dr. Lyons stopped in to see how things were going. Art was positioned on the parallel bars with Karen on one side of him and her helper on the other. Although Art tried his best to get Delbert's body to walk, he was unsuccessful. Dr. Lyons could feel Carol telling him, "Darrel, yell out, "Walk, Delbert walk." Dr. Lyons thought to himself, *Carol, you had better be right! I can only stand to make a fool of myself so many times!*

To his surprise, he heard himself calling out, "Walk, Delbert! Walk!"

As though suddenly awakened, Art was walking.

Karen shouted, "He's walking!"

A slurred, "Hey!" came from Delbert's lips as he walked.

"Think what's happening, Art! See how your mind is working!" Dr. Lyons command helped Art concentrate. Art was surprised at how well Delbert's body did, all on its own. He walked the length of the rails he was holding onto. At the end he turned around and slowly walked back. He was excited and pleased by his sudden breakthrough. Karen helped him into his wheelchair. That was enough exercise for his first try. She knew, from now on, he would make much faster progress.

"Are you tired, Delbert?"

"Ess." That was as close as he could come to saying, "Yes", at that time. The fact that he tried to say anything aloud was encouraging to her.

"I'll have to tell your speech therapist how well you're doing!"

That evening Myrna visited Delbert again. Had he been closer than 85 miles from her home, she would have visited him more often. When she entered his room, she was surprised to see him seated in an arm chair a few feet from his bed. "Delbert, what are you doing out of bed?"

Since he could not reach his computer, Delbert resorted to sign language of sorts. He first pointed to himself and then used his index and middle finger to make a walking motion. He tried to say that he had walked, but it came out so slurred and distorted that only his sign language made it understandable. He sounded a lot like a deaf person trying to talk. As she approached, he was able to stand. He had to stand! How else could he put his arms around her? She was so happy to be able to put her arms around him she cried. Although he was standing and able to put his arms around her, he was only a mere shadow of the man who had made love to her in the moonlight.

She stepped back from Delbert and asked if he wanted to sit down. He pointed to the bed instead. She slowly and carefully helped him walk the four steps it took him to shuffle back to his bed. Once seated on the edge, she helped him get his feet in and sit in an upright position.

"I have the tapes you asked for and your cassette in this sack. I'll just set them here where you can reach them." Myrna hoped hearing his own voice would help him with his speech therapy.

The start of his recovery was now visible. Myrna continued to visit Delbert at least three times a week to encourage him.

Dr. Lyons had a very exciting report for Carol that evening and called her, as he had promised even though he would be seeing her in just 36 hours.

Darrell thoroughly enjoyed the medical conference in Chicago and the time he spent with Carol at the special functions. It gave them a chance to get to know one another better. When Carol asked Darrell how he had become a doctor so young, he told her he was a Mensa. He graduated from high school at 14 with two years of basic college course work on his record. In a year and a half he had his Bachelors Degree. He had always been fascinated by the human body and had extensive knowledge of it before he went to medical school and finished it quickly. He was glad to learn that she had a Masters in Psychology and had graduated Summa Cum Laude. They were a perfect couple with lots of other interests in common.

Once Art was able to walk, he started pushing for full recovery. His mind worked feverishly every time his new body moved or uttered a sound. Art thought to himself. *I am Delbert! I am Delbert! I look like Delbert! I must walk and talk like Delbert! I must use his mind as he did! My new body must become one with my consciousness so that I can function. Everything I know about how Delbert talked and moved must be utilized to increase my rate of progress.*

I don't have to worry about what people say about me because I can say I've had a stroke and have amnesia. His friends, who really loved him, will probably try to get to know him again. Some will like the new Delbert, others won't. Since Delbert was single, this could prove interesting. Art's adventurous nature was starting to come through.

Art worked constantly on some part of his body. If he wasn't trying to move his arms or legs, he was at least moving his fingers. He kept a complete record of all the different exercises he did and the number of repetitions he could do. To improve his speaking ability, he tried to count aloud the number of repetitions of each exercise. "One, two, three, four." It was a good thing he knew what he was saying, or even he couldn't have recognized what it was supposed to be. Although he listened carefully to Delbert's voice on the tape recorder, he wasn't able to make Delbert's speech center work. He never gave up though. *As long as I'm learning to talk, even though it's slow, I know it'll come back to me.*

Karen continued Delbert's therapy sessions with the same intensity as she had started. Art was glad for that because he was now realized she was a warm, caring individual. In fact, some of Art's old feelings started coming back to him. Even when he could walk by himself, he still liked to put his arm around Karen for support. Since Karen had never known Delbert, she didn't realize this was one of Art's traits showing through. Delbert had never been a toucher, whereas Art always had been.

Karen allowed Art to support himself on her at first because he needed to. After awhile, she could tell he was no longer supporting himself on her but just putting his arm around her shoulder. What Art didn't realize was that his strength was coming back quickly from all his effort and Karen could tell. She liked her patient and wasn't looking forward to the time when his arm would no longer hold her close as they walked.

By late October, Art had all the feeling back in his body and that speeded his recovery. He was surprised to find Delbert's body could do some things extremely well by itself. One example was tying his shoe laces. His hands just did it automatically. He wondered what else he could do automatically.

One night, as he was working on his speech program in his hospital room, he decided to listen to a couple other tapes of music that Myrna had brought him. To his surprise, he found that when he played one of the tapes, Delbert's voice started singing. His beautiful baritone voice surprised everyone on the floor and brought a nurse quickly to his room to see what had happened. That was something else! He could now sing but just barely speak. To his amazement, he could remember the words that the background music called for. Besides that, he knew the tune and was right on pitch. That was just the trigger Art needed to tie into Delbert's thinking process. From then on, he decided he no longer needed to stay in the hospital.

On the first Friday in November, Dr. Lyons released Delbert from the hospital. Myrna had kept Delbert's apartment clean for him. It hadn't taken much effort, since no one was staying there. In fact, she had enjoyed doing it for him and was looking forward to his complete recovery.

On the day she found the tapes for him, she discovered the tape of Delbert's telepathic experience when she and Art were in Denver. It aroused her and made her blush to hear Delbert explaining the vision he was having of her fully disrobed in her hotel room dressing area and thinking of him. She was glad she did it and wished she could put on a show for him again soon.

Delbert's disability insurance and medical insurance were adequately taking care of Art's needs. He wouldn't accept Myrna's personal care so she hired him a live-in caregiver to look after him until he was fully recovered. She couldn't understand why her Delbert was so different than he had been.

She didn't realize that, as Art, he didn't have the same feeling for her. Art still thought of Myrna as his wife, even though he saw Delbert's face and body every time he looked into a mirror.

He was glad that his dear friend Delbert had a picture of the four friends: Art, Delbert, Larry and Adrian; so he could see his own face once in awhile. Too, there was a lovely picture of Carol, Art's former lover. She had such radiant beauty! Her youth and touch always excited him, whereas Myrna's touch wasn't able to bring him alive anymore. *I wonder just how close Delbert and Myrna were.*

Art didn't want to commit himself to Myrna and Delbert's plans until he had a chance to see what other options Delbert had available to him. Art's opportunistic nature was surely going to change some of Delbert's girl friend's ideas about him.

There had certainly been some beautiful ladies visit him in the hospital, even though he was 85 miles from his home. They must have cared greatly for him. One problem they could see was Delbert didn't seem to remember them. To play it cool, Art hadn't spoken much as Delbert, even when he was able to. It gave him an out.

Art had an advantage over Delbert's close friends. He could read their minds and pull memories of him from them. Art knew, with Delbert's well endowed body being aroused by his adventurous mind, some of Delbert's old girl friends were certainly going to be pleased by his revitalized body and more outgoing personality.

As Art's speech rapidly improved, he was happy to be able to call and talk to Carol. He knew she would be back in three weeks for Gail and Michael's wedding. He was looking forward to talking to her about how he could explain to Myrna he wasn't her lover but her husband, Art.

His anticipation of Carol's return was dampened by her obviously new and deep feeling for Dr. Lyons. *Strange, but I seem to be happy for her! That must be the Delbert in me!* Art was right. Dr. Lyons fit into Carol's life perfectly, as Delbert would have seen it.

Art was pleased with the caregiver Myrna had hired for him. She was about eight years older than he was and the mother of an English graduate student attending the University. Since she was unattached, it gave her and her daughter an excellent opportunity to see the United States. She was a nurse by profession and had taken a year's leave of absence from her job. She could take care of Delbert through May of the following year, if he needed her. She didn't want to interfere with her daughter's life too much, so she didn't get an apartment with her. Her daughter moved into a dorm with other graduate students and was fully enjoying her year in the States.

"Nurse Liz," as Art called her, was just what he needed. First of all, she was an attractive person and very good company. Second, she was a nurse, which he still needed. Third, she liked to travel around and enjoyed being his chauffeur.

At first Art didn't think anything special about Liz, as he was busy getting ready for Gail and Michael's wedding. The university's granting him a year's sabbatical leave with half pay took care of his financial needs. Now he didn't need to explain why he couldn't teach psychology. He didn't know whether or not he would ever be able to dig that knowledge out of Delbert's brain.

He had the problem of Myrna wanting to be his lover, along with a Miss Trudy Ball, who taught algebra at the University. She had been a close friend of Delbert's and now liked him even more with his slightly different personality, although he didn't seem to remember her. Trudy thought she could use his loss of memory to her advantage to get closer to him. Art was surprised at the way Delbert's body was aroused and reacted toward her advances. She enjoyed his embarrassment and continued to push herself on him.

At times like this, it was good "Nurse Liz" was there to protect him and keep Trudy from over tiring him or forcing him to perform. *Just what would Delbert do?* He had mated with the alien, DorLetha, but that was different, she had overpowered him.

Art thought to himself. *I wonder what my friends are doing on Exvascia. Is Delbert watching me from out there?*

Chapter 3

How Exvascia Came To Be

While Art was having problems on Earth learning to use a new body; Delbert was having many of the same problems. However, Delbert's increased intelligence on Exvascia enabled him to use Art's body at about 80 percent efficiency. Art's was 36 years old and a little overweight. At 40, Delbert was in better physical shape. Adrian only had to adapt to a totally different environment and had a lot of help from Larry, who had reached Exvascia two years earlier,

Adrian had bodily walked into the "Adralack Crack" after his teletransporter blew up and failed to pull Larry from it. Delbert entered it without his body, in just his soul and spirit form, leaving his body outside for Art to use and he would use Art's.

A few seconds after they had joined their old friend, Larry, in the Crack, they arrived on a powerful transmitter station above the surface of Exvascia. During the transference process, his soul and spirit were joined with the subatomic particle state of Art's body. From there, they were instantaneously beamed to the center of the Crystal Prism Crater

Once on the surface, they regenerated into their human forms. They hadn't thought about it before but the inhabitants of Exvascia were awaiting their arrival. They definitely had the advantage over their two new human guests because Larry had lived with them for two years and they had become accustomed to the human form. They realized man's body was inflexible, inadequate and inferior but if it could adapt, it really didn't make any difference to them.

There was a rule on Exvascia that males were not to be brought to the planet except to mate with a specific female. After the mating period, they were sent back to their own planet. In fact, most of the females went to the planet of their chosen mate to breed and then returned. Larry had been brought to Exvascia by mistake. He was kept around because DorLetha needed him to find out more about Delbert, who she called Dell Bert. The ruling Matriarchal Directorate hadn't gotten around to sending Larry back. Since he was so inferior and not aggressive in any way, they had kept him around to study and learn from. He was free to move about and learn about their dwarf planet as he chose. He didn't have a harem or anything of that nature because of the structure of the females and the fact that they couldn't breed until certain changes took place a short time before their 48-hour long breeding period began. Besides, they had to be attracted to a male's aura before they mated. The few females that became fertile were very selective because of the vast number of planets they could choose to select a mate from. Because of their instantaneous transmittal powers, they weren't worried about what the physical appearance of the male creature was that they mated with. They could choose any form they wanted to when they reached the other planet.

DorLetha, like all females, desired a fertile male offspring so she would become Queen. She had originally directed a power beat to Earth to bring Delbert to her, but it missed Delbert and brought Larry to Exvascia. That's why DorLetha had to make a last minute trip to Earth to mate with Delbert.

Delbert's sperm had produced a reaction in DorLetha's egg fertilization area that told her she would have a male offspring. Her eggs were to hatch in late September. Delbert and Adrian arrived in August.

When Art, Delbert and Adrian had returned to Mt. Baker where Larry had disappeared 20 months earlier, Delbert's presence reactivated the Crack's power beam. When Art entered the "Adralack Crack," where the powerful retractor beam was focused, he found out Larry had come down from Exvascia to get him and his two friends to join him. He panicked and was only able to get back out of the Crack by willing his soul and spirit into Delbert's fallen body, which Delbert had left, at the entrance to the shallow overhang, for Art to use. He would use Art's body which had already been disintegrated in the Crack. Adrian Adralack, who the activated shallow overhang was named after, had willingly run into the Crack without hesitation.

When the three men's bodies were regenerated in the Crystal Prism Crater on Exvascia, they were met by the Matriarchal Directorate and DorLetha, as well as the other inhabitants in various shapes and forms. The reception committee had not expected Larry to bring his friends back with him. They knew from mental telemetrical viewing that he had observed the activities around the Crack when Delbert's appearance reactivated it. However, they thought he would use the opportunity to return to his people like all previous aliens had done, not bring his friends back with him. If there was any problem, the Exvascians could instantly return them. Besides, everyone wanted to meet DorLetha's mate.

DorLetha stood anxiously awaiting Delbert's arrival. To her surprise, Larry arrived with Art and Adrian. “Larry!” DorLetha yelled, as if her having communicated telepathically wasn't enough to show her astonishment, “What happened to my Dell Bert?”

Delbert answered from within Art's body, before Larry could speak. “DorLetha, it's me, Delbert!”

“No, you can't be! You don't look like my Dell Bert, or sound like him!”

“But it's me! Art was afraid to come and since his body had already been disintegrated in the Crack, I left mine for him to use and took his.”

“This isn't any good Larry, why didn't you just go back home and let Dell Bert take Art's place? You know we don't allow males here!”

“DorLetha, I know you're upset, but I didn't have enough mental power to keep Art and pull Delbert in too. I wanted them to see Exvascia with me!”

The alien's power again enabled Delbert and Adrian to understand telepathic communication. The members of the Matriarchal Directorate were discussing Delbert's fate. “DorLetha, we need to send that one back. We have used our transmutative powers in many ways, but we have never exchanged our very being with that of another with our natural form. That shouldn't be done!”

“Please, Directorates, let me find out how or why it happened!”

“Art was so afraid, DorLetha I couldn't leave him on Earth without a body. He could never have communicated with humans, touched them or taken any other form. We don't have the mental powers you do. I wanted to see you and our son, so I came ahead. I understand that I really didn't need a body here! Isn't that right?”

“Yes, that's right!”

“DorLetha, how do you know he is your Dell Bert? These humans all look alike!”

“He's mine! Look at his aura it's so bright. Art's isn't that way!”

After some discussion, the Matriarchal Directorate leaders communicated their thoughts. “They should all be sent back. Who knows what other forbidden things they may do!”

Delbert spoke up. “DorLetha, you can't let them send us back now! No telling where my body has been moved to. It certainly won't be at the Crack. All I did was try to help Art. If I could be sent back to the Crack, when he is there, then he could enter it and we could make the switch back. He would then be free to walk out of the Crack like he wanted to in the first place.”

“DorLetha, why does he worry so about the other human?”

"Madam Directorate, that's how humans are, they care about their offspring and each other."

"Why should they care about their offspring?"

"Madam Directorate, if we were on Earth, you would be proud to be the one that birthed me. You would be special, because I am special and am going to have a son!"

"Why shouldn't we all share in the joy that you are to have a male? Why should just one individual enjoy the male?"

"I can't answer that, Madam Directorate. We'll have to ask them."

Larry pulled his friends aside. "Delbert, remember that anything you say or do on Exvascia may set a precedent and give their shifting culture a strong or weak basis."

"I don't understand, Larry."

"Since there have never been any males around to form family units and no external influence because of their hyperatmospheric force field keeping aliens away; there hasn't been any need to cling to possessions or offspring."

"Thanks Larry, I'll be careful what I say. Madam Directorate, I understand your concern about your limited population. Because of your circumstances, it's good for all of you to share in the hatching of a male offspring."

Larry came to his assistance. "We live more like your scotch animals. We're responsible for ourselves and our offspring."

"What does that mean, Larry?"

"Scotches are animal families. The Kaydra make sure there are only as many males as there are females in the herds so no herd is controlled by a single dominate male. A fletch, or herd, is like a group of people. Each pair is like a family in our society. The females here keep the animal population equal as they hunt. They think their animals are like them, only able to breed once, but I don't think so."

"How do they hunt?"

"I'll tell you later, Delbert." They walked back over to DorLetha. Although the Directorate heard what had been said, it had no meaning to them.

Adrian and Delbert were startled to suddenly see, in their minds, the scene on Mt. Baker. They could see everything as clear as day. A helicopter was leaving with Delbert's body just barely alive. "Larry what are we having, a vision?"

"No Adrian, it's what they call mental telemetrical viewing. Their minds are able to look at things happening anywhere in the universe by just concentrating. It's a form of clairvoyance I think. I haven't mastered it yet even though DorLetha has tried to explain to me how to do it."

"Do you think they are looking for my body, Larry?"

"I think the Directorate wants to send you back Delbert, if DorLetha can locate your body. I think that helicopter is taking Art to a hospital somewhere."

"DorLetha tried, but she couldn't see Delbert's body anywhere!"

"They have probably taken my body to a hospital, DorLetha!"

"What's a hospital, Dell Bert?"

"It's a place where other creatures like us try to make the one not functioning properly function correctly again!"

"You sound like a politician, Delbert."

"Well, Adrian didn't Larry say we had to be careful about everything we say. Do they have any type of medical treatment here?"

"I don't think they do Delbert. I have seen a few of them die. They get too weak to make a transmutive change back from an animal form. When they disintegrate the animal form to take their primary form again, they don't seem to be able to regenerate."

"DorLetha, your Dell Bert can stay until you can locate his body. As soon as his aura is strong enough for you to locate it, the exchange should be made."

"Thank you, Madam Directorate. Did you hear that, Dell Bert? You can stay for a while."

Delbert hugged DorLetha for the first time since his arrival. To his surprise, she no longer stimulated him. The overwhelming power she had during her mating period was gone. Her Fem-Bird form was just warm and soft. His action caused her to ruffle her feathers. She asked Delbert why she felt so strange. As far as he could tell, it must have been an emotional response similar to a human blushing. The entire Directorate enjoyed observing an unusual happening, one of their own blushing, something that hadn't happened for a long time in their culture. Larry smiled because he felt Delbert was making some impressions that would be good for the dwarf planet's future.

"Why don't you tell Delbert and Adrian something about your planet, DorLetha, while I go get them some Mellow Drops to eat?"

"OK Larry. Where would you like me to start, Dell Bert?"

"Can you tell us about this dwarf planet and how your inhabitants got here and why there are no males?"

"I'll start with a battle long ago on our original home planet far from here. Our great mathematician, Canadaro, theorized that the whole of a planet, upon explosion, could be retracted to the end of a power beam, if the power beam was operating at a very high level and if the debris was not blasted apart too violently.

"Unfortunately, when the men on our planet lost the battle with the Fillatells, the entire planet was obliterated. The power beam that sent the females to Exvascia was only a local one. It only sent a portion of the planet surrounding the beams originating point, to Exvascia.

"There was a large chunk of the planet which followed the beam like the head of a mushroom would follow its stem, if it were thrown stem first. When it hit this dwarf planet, it enlarged this giant Crater which was like an extinct volcano in the mountain. The Crater, as you can see, is enormous. The tail end of the debris following the beam was molten by the time it got to where the beam stopped because it wasn't in a subatomic particle state. Therefore, it formed the Crystal dome that protects us from the atmosphere.

"Everything transported here by the beam landed in this large area and became the basis for starting our new life here. The plants and animals were from the lush portion of our planet. All the females had been hidden there to keep them from being discovered by the enemy.

"The idea of depositing the women somewhere else was to protect our society. We thought we could continue here anew, if necessary, when the war was over. When the planet's surface was drawn here by the retraction beam, its withdrawal was so accelerated it made all the females with young unable to bear males and made many others sterile.

"Even though the Crater had its own environment, we had to have a source of heat. We used our mental powers to transform the Crystal material over the entrance into a crystal prism. That provided us plenty of sunlight so the plants and animals thrived. However, this dwarf planet was thrown out of orbit by our arrival so the surface often has severe storms. As the planet's orbit changed, it wasn't long before we didn't have adequate sunlight. To solve that problem, we built and positioned a solar reflector in a stationary orbit around our planet to reflect solar light. With adequate light and warmth, we more evenly distributed the plants and animals in the Crater.

"During those early years we were occupied with various activities. Our first thought was to try and find what happened to the males of our species. We developed a power source to send our retractor beams to other planets to find males but we never found what happened to others from our former home. Another urgent problem was to develop a power source to clear our path through the universe. This dwarf planet was very hydroscopic with 95 percent of the surface covered with water. By separating the hydrogen and oxygen, we got rid of some of the water and used the hydrogen to blast our way through meteor showers and to power our protective hyperatmospheric force field. We improved the atmosphere outside the Crater by using the solar reflectors to turn some of the water into steam. We developed solar power sources so we no longer had to separate our water for hydrogen. To develop the area outside the Crater, we transplanted some of the plants and animals in a specific area and started what you would call a jungle. As the soil built up, we spread it over the surface of the planet and kept the jungle growing.

"When we decided to search for males from other planets to mate with, we decided not to bring any of them back with us because we had no way of defending ourselves. Once we were attacked by aliens from where we went to mate. They followed us here on their own power beam. We had to learn to fight for ourselves for the first time, since our males had always protected us. That's when we decided to develop our hyperatmospheric force field. We didn't know what minerals Exvascia might have that would attract additional creature, from other planets.

"It has prevented further invasions of our planet. Everything and anything that hits it is instantaneously disintegrated and dispersed into endless space without our slightest concern as to what it might have been or where it is going. Until we could find a better way to defend ourselves, we thought that solution would solve our problem.

"After much experimenting, we came up with the aura technique to find powerful male creatures to mate with. However, we haven't found any of our kind to mate with, so most of our offspring are sterile and all have been female. We have even taken different forms, such as I used on your planet, to see if we would have greater success when not in our natural form.

"Because of our lack of reason for being, over the past few centuries, we haven't even kept our original forms. We found adapting ourselves to any form, through instantaneous transmutation served our purpose very well. It provides us with both a defensive weapon and a hunting tool.

"There aren't many jobs to keep individuals occupied. We do keep a small staff tracking our solar reflectors so we have a constant source of sunlight. This gives us quite a bit of flexibility in controlling our atmosphere and the length of our nights and days, as you call them. We can direct light rays to the area outside the Crater.

"One thing we miss is the reasons males always found for the utilization of the vast storehouse of knowledge and abilities we have. Our society is almost indistinguishable from the animals because of the lack of males of our kind. Their urges and needs are not felt by our females although we enjoy physically controlling our dwarf planet. We have the ability to study the historical data of our past, through the time-exempt telepathic storage banks, but we really don't have any reason to. The Matriarchal Directorate has not tried to develop meaningless work activities. We more or less live like the animals.

"We do spend a lot of time in mental telemetrical viewing. By that method we can see the past and present activities of innumerable societies on an endless number of planets. You saw that demonstrated earlier.

"We have the facilities to take care of our newborn, but because of the number of sterile females we have, and the number of sterile newborn, we are on the verge of extinction."

When Larry returned with Mellow Drops and Marble nuts for his friends to eat, he said. "DorLetha would you like me to take care of my friends and educate them to the facts and ways of the planet, until you can locate Delbert's body on Earth?"

"Yes, Larry. Dell Bert and Adrian will have to accept a lot of attention, staring and very little privacy. Dell Bert, we are all very interested in your kind because I'm going to have a male offspring. I'm glad you're here but we never expected Larry to bring you back. We thought he would want to return to Earth.

"It doesn't seem right to have to share my having a male offspring with the entire group but we aren't very possessive on our planet. It doesn't seem right to take all the credit for it alone. It makes all the females feel sad when they find out they're sterile. Larry has seen a few die because they didn't keep eating and got too weak to function."

"We'll just stay with Larry until you decide what is to be done with us. He knows our needs and how to teach us what we need to know. Will I be seeing you much or not?"

"I'll try to spend as much time with you as I can. My job before I laid my eggs was taking care of the stationary solar reflector satellite. Now I have to train TetTrella to operate it. It's a very important task and everybody wanted to get to do it. She is very intelligent and will do a good job.

"I will become Queen, when our son is born, I will be over the Matriarchal Directorate. Therefore, I have to spend a lot of time studying the time-exempt telepathic storage banks of our history. I need to find out how to use our mental telemetrical viewing to locate hostile spots developing in the universe that might affect us. I have to confirm that the orbit our planet is in is safe for us to continue following. The leader of the Directorate will give up her position when I become Queen."

"That sounds like a lot of responsibility! Is there anything I can do to help you?"

"I don't know, Dell Bert. It would probably be good for you to learn as much as you can about our planet as soon as possible. When Larry can't teach you anything new, I'll start showing you things."

For the time being, the Directorate was finished with the men. Larry took the men to where he lived. Delbert and Adrian were very careful to get their bearings. The sooner they could get around, the better off they would all be.

Chapter 4

The Crystal Prism Crater

The Crystal Prism Crater was half a mile across. The temperature was in the 80's, with the humidity about the same. The sunlight, being directed through the prism, cast many pretty colors on the magnificent stone walls. The three men walked by a high waterfall that was crystal clear. Larry explained to the others how it was pumped through different rock formations to clean and filter it. Scavenger fish of unknown species continually cleaned the pool into which the waterfall fell.

"Larry, what are the nights like?"

"They are ten hours long. Because the area the crystal covers is so much smaller than the outside surface area, it only takes a little shift of the reflector satellite to direct the light to the jungles outside and darken the Crater. The rock formations retain the heat, so even though it's dark, it doesn't get too much cooler. With 20 hour days, the plants really grow fast.

"The Crater used to be hotter but they have changed it so I can live here. It's safe in here, which isn't the case outside. The plants and animals in here are not dangerous to you. The breeze in here is caused by the way the tunnels have been formed and how they are interconnected. Their relationship causes the hot air to rise and the cool air to fall. Some outside air is brought in and some of the excess oxygen from here escapes to help develop the atmosphere outside. The oxygen outside is equal to what it is at about 10,000 feet on Earth, so I can't hurry when I walk around outside.

"Let's go into this cave, it's my library!" The temperature in the cave was in the low 70's. As the three men entered the cave, Larry struck two flint-like rocks together and started a small pile of shale-like rocks burning in a pot for light. The oil shale was kept in shallow clay pots that had almost become ceramic because of the heat from repeated use. Larry had chiseled out shelves in the wall to put his books on. They really weren't books but individual leaves from the Mellow Drop plant with a vine running between two holes to tie them together. They had been bleached white in the sun after being cut into rectangles. Larry had then written on them with a feather quill.

"Larry, what did you use for ink?"

"I used some condensed Mellow Drop juice. Aren't they the greatest fruit? I brought you the dark blue ones. I like them best because they aren't too sweet. When I first saw them, I thought they were giant grapes. They are about four times the size of grapes but don't have any seeds. They grow in a cluster like our blackberries do back home. They have a delicious, sweet, thick skin and a thick, juicy pulp center. What did you think of them?"

"Great, Larry, it was like having something to eat and a drink all at the same time. What's in your library?"

"Things I have recorded about this planet. I wanted to share it with you. I thought Art would jump at the chance to come here. I miss being able to read or communicate verbally. Almost all communication is done here telepathically.

"I started to keep a diary of activities and daily happenings. After that I started a book on foods, animals, plants, geology, atmosphere, weather and etc. There is a book for inside, meaning in the Crystal Prism Crater, and one for the area outside the Crater."

Adrian looked at one of the leaf books. "Look, Delbert, he has facts on the different plants and pictures of them. How did you find out about things, Larry? Did the Exvascians tell you anything?"

"I found out most things by trial and error. I observed how different animals were affected when they ate different plants. I started out eating just a little of one plant at a time to see what would happen to me. As I was able to eat more, I added another. I find there are a couple combinations that seem to have a bad chemical affect on my body. Here, try a few of these. I call them Marble nuts. They are found in a large bean-like pod that grows on a tree nearby. I dry a lot of them. They are fun to eat and give you a lot of energy.

"I'm sure glad to see you guys. It's strange to be looking at Art and talking to you, Delbert. You really shook DorLetha up. She never communicates verbally! TetTrella does the most talking! She likes to help me and is outgoing."

Delbert took a turn. "It's good to see you again too. We sure were upset when we lost you in that cave. We didn't know until just today what had happened to you. All kinds of things have happened to us since you left."

"DorLetha told me she couldn't let you remember anything about her trip to breed with you. I thought that was a little unfair. What was it like Delbert?"

"It was different, I can tell you that! We just weren't made to mate with them. If I hadn't torn myself away from her, when I did, I would probably have been impotent for life. As it was, I was that way for 13 months. I remember now, that I found a sensitive spot on her side that distracted her concentrating on me. It sexually aroused her and caused her to relax. That's when she said we were going to have a son. It seems her last egg passed to another part of her body than the others had. That's the first time I've ever remembered what happened to our lost weekend, Adrian."

"I can remember now too, Delbert. I remember talking to her about how my teletransporter worked. It seems like such a simple machine now."

"Larry, these Marble nuts are great. Tell me, do you know what caused your mind to become so strong?"

"I don't know but I think it's some kind of radiation from a mineral they have here. I didn't get that power from eating anything that I know of. Do either of you feel strange?"

"Are you kidding? After all we've been through today; we couldn't help but feel strange. You'll have to ask us again tomorrow."

"Don't worry; I'll be talking to you a lot until I feel I've gotten caught up. There's so much I want to tell you and so much for you to see and experience here. I think I'll take you out for a walk in the Crater first and let you see some things. Then we can eat and sit around in my hot tub."

"Hot tub, how can you have a hot tub up here?" Delbert couldn't believe what he had heard.

"Come on, I'll show you! Go ahead and climb up that ladder I've made. It leads to my apartment above."

Delbert led. "Adrian, he does have a hot tub!"

"I don't believe it! How does it work?"

"Well, there is a slight trickle of geothermal water running from the wall of my apartment cave. I just made a tub of bamboo-type stocks from the Tube Plant and bound them together with a lot of vines. I then sealed it with pitch and lined it with a few animal skins. I have two hollow stocks from the Tube Plant as a drain at the bottom to keep it clean. I have another drain near the top so it doesn't run over.

"Because of the warm rocks in this area it makes an excellent bedroom at night, when the reflector is directed away from the prism. If you two are going to stay with me, we'll have to dig the cave out a little larger. It'll do for a few days."

"Where's your kitchen?"

"It's through that archway. I keep an oil shale fire burning in there just like I do in here. Go ahead and take a look."

"I see a table Larry but where is your sink and stove?"

"If you move that bench, you'll see my spit. I can cook my meat there over a fire and the draft carries the smoke out through that crack. Behind this woven drape, I have my icebox. The gourd catches the water as the ice melts. I'll have to show you the cave where I get the ice. I have more meat stored there too. The sink is over here where I have hot and cold running water.

"I didn't want to kill an animal larger than I could eat in a day until I found the ice cave. With the ice cave I can store the larger ones and they taste better. Everything you do here will be an example so you have to be careful. In fact, before you kill any fowl or animal, be sure to ask it if it's a Kaydra. The Directorate told all the intelligent inhabitants, Kaydras, to verbally answer me so I wouldn't kill them."

"I don't think Adrian and I understand what you mean, Larry."

"The Kaydra take the form of the animal they want to kill, by use of their transmutative power. When they are mixed in with the Fletch, they change to a form that can quickly and easily kill their prey. That way they are able to keep the population down and make sure selective breeding takes place. That isn't the case outside."

"How do you get outside, Larry?"

"I have marked a trail through a series of tunnels. Every few feet I have a bowl of oil shale. It isn't really oil shale, but it burns very easily and gives off a lot of heat and light. It is a little trouble to put out, but in the tunnels I don't want them going out quickly. I have a book of tunnel maps in the library so you can grasp where you are."

"No wonder you didn't want to come back to Earth!"

"I've been so busy doing and learning things, I haven't missed Earth at all. We'll see if my knowledge takes some of the excitement and stimulation out of your experiences here."

"If the days are 20 hours long and the nights ten hours, how often do you eat?"

"I usually eat four meals a day Adrian. Of course, you can have the tropical-type food any time. I fired some clay pots in the oil shale fire and turned them into a ceramic type material. I use them at night to heat a vegetable in. I either heat or cook fresh meat. I bake a root that is somewhat like a potato. I can get milk in the morning from the Mardi Goats and keep some in my icebox at all times. I have used the udder from killed Mardi Goats for a number of things.

"If you're ready, we can go out for a walk or a swim in the waterfall pool. When I'm in the Crater, I only wear my loincloth. I have other animal skin clothes to wear outside the Crater and when I'm exploring the tunnels.

As you can see from all the furs and hides I have around the floor and across my cave opening, I don't have to worry about material. The Exvascians don't need clothes because of their animal nature. You'll notice there are about four different forms they have. I don't know which is closest to their original form. I wondered if I should wear clothes when I first arrived but I thought that as a possible future example, or under other weather conditions, I should continue to wear clothes since I had them on when I arrived.

"Tonight we could watch mental telemetrical viewing. That's my TV up here. TetTrella seems to have itchy feet to travel. She's hoping she will become fertile soon, so she is looking at the creatures and life styles on several planets. She is a little older than DorLetha. I'm afraid she will turn out to be sterile. She prefers the ape form to the Fem-Bird form DorLetha uses. When she tunes in to a planet's wavelength, I can see everything that is happening there that she sees. It's like telepathy.

"We can see all around the planet surface and see what the inhabitants and environment are like without physically going there. I can even go there by the free soul flight method if I want to. Then I can move all around the planet surface unseen and see everything that is going on. I've even started a book on other planets, their inhabitants and what they do. I've recorded how advanced their civilizations are and what technology they have."

"What do you mean; you can go there by the soul flight method, Larry?"

"Let me see. How can I explain that? First, I go to the ice cave where there is a cool area that is about freezing. I lie down and let my soul and spirit free from my body. Then I tune into TetTrella's mental telemetrical viewing and just kind of drift to the actual place I'm viewing. When she stops viewing, I'm instantaneously returned to Exvascia. It might be that I don't leave here at all but just tune her thoughts in sharper. When I come back, I levitate my frozen body toward the front of the ice cave where it's above sixty degrees. When it's warmed, I reenter it and start it functioning again. If I don't want to use my body outside the Crater, I can do the same thing. I have left it in hibernation like that for a couple weeks at a time and it seems to be just fine, when I return. When I awaken in it, it isn't even any hungrier than if I had only been asleep one evening. It's not suspended animation, but cryogenics!"

"How long did it take you to learn to do that, Larry?"

"It took over a year. I don't know what all we can do with our minds here. You really must think that all things are possible and then just use your mind to cause whatever it is you want to happen, to actually happen. Do you want to go out and look around now?"

"Yes! I can't wait." Adrian followed Larry out of the cave and down the ladder. Delbert found it difficult to operate Art's overweight body.

"Let me help you, Delbert. Think about my commands and I'll help you control Art's body. While it's operating, think of what his subconscious level is doing to make it operate. That way you will be able to learn to operate it quite easily here. I wonder how much trouble Art is having trying to use yours, or if he even will be able to?"

"OK, left leg, lift. Now, drop it! Right leg, lift. Now, drop it! Right arm, lift. Left arm, lift. Now, let them both drop. Get the idea?"

"Let me try it on my own for a while and see how it goes."

Both Delbert and Adrian were amazed at the jungle atmosphere on most of the Crater floor. They enjoyed eating the strange tropical fruits, many of which were similar to those they had enjoyed on Earth. In order to get a higher view of the entire area, Larry led them up to various tunnel openings where they could look down on the Crater floor.

"Larry, this tunnel is so phosphorescent you don't even have any oil shale bowls lit. Does that mean that the radiation level is high?"

"I don't think its radiation. It must be something else because this planet's intelligent inhabitants live over 20 times as long as we do with greater IQs than ours."

Adrian saw what he had been looking for, a bird with the form that DorLetha had used on Earth when he had first found her. "Larry, is that a bird?"

"Ask it."

"Are you a Kaydra?"

The strange, beautiful bird just cooed and flew off. "Well, did that answer your question?"

'"Yes, but what if it wasn't a bird? Would it have talked to us?"

"Sure, they all know me. They will even take their natural form if you ask them to. Look! There's a little dwit. He's kind of a pet of mine. I call him Andre." The little monkey-like creature, without a tail, scampered through the Mellow Drop vines clinging to the side of the Crater outside the cave entrance where they stood looking down at the paradise below.

The little dwit jumped into Larry's arms and then settled down on his hip with his legs wrapped around Larry's waist. He clung to Larry by wrapping his long arms around his neck. He looked so cute there on Larry's side. He curiously looked at the two new arrivals and then at Larry. He obviously could tell more creatures like Larry had arrived. Adrian and Delbert petted it and made it even more content than it was. When they were ready to continue their tour, Larry put the friendly little dwit down and it scampered off.

Part of the Crater floor had a lush green meadow where various kinds of strange animals were feeding. They saw some of the Mardi Goats Larry had mentioned. The goats ran through the rocks near the walls and part way up the walls. The new arrivals were surprised to see how many animals the Crater could support. With the long days and warm nights and lush plants, numerous animals thrived.

"I've tried to have all the plants and animals that were either dangerous to me or the Kaydra moved out of the Crater. For that reason you must become very familiar with everything inside. Some of the plants outside look similar but they are dangerous. The Mellow Drop Vine and the Living Vine outside look similar, but the Living Vine is carnivorous. If it gets wrapped around you, you are dead."

"You had better go over that once again Larry."

"The Living Vine has smaller leaves and it doesn't have fruit. It grows on trees near the edge of the sticky quicksand-like quagmire, which traps its food for it. If you cut the Living vine, it instantly sprouts and grows another new branch about three feet long. From there it grows slower. See those large red poppy-looking flowers?

"That's a friend and a foe in here. Its pollen is dangerous to both the Kaydra and us. However, it is loved by the Poison Flies. They are like mosquitoes on Earth. The pollen from the Pollen Shooter neutralized the poison of the Poison Fly. Its bite only swells in here. Outside the Crater it will kill you because there are no Pollen Shooters out there for them to feed on."

"Why don't you get rid of the Pollen Shooters in here?"

"Because I can't get rid of the Poison Flies. See that bullfrog-looking creature over by that small pond by the stream?"

"Yes, what do they do?"

"They eat the poison flies. I've transplanted a lot of them outside to get rid of the Poison Flies so there aren't enough to eat all the Poison flies that live in here."

"It's a good thing you're guiding us Larry. How did you happen to make it until now?"

"I was very careful Delbert. That large lily pad growing in the frog pond is only about one tenth the size of the ones that grow in the quagmire. If you fall into a quagmire, they can be used like a life preserver. You have to keep an eye on the Living Vine that grows by the quagmire. When you are in the quagmire, it senses heat and knows food items are close by!

"If its limbs grab and start pulling you, you are free from the quagmire but you will soon be strangled by the Living Vine. The only way to escape it is to sprinkle some of the Pollen Shooter pollen on it. That will put it to sleep temporarily so you can escape."

"What would the Pollen Shooter do to us, Larry?"

"It will make you hallucinate. You have to be careful to stay up wind from it. If a Poison Fly bites you outside and you don't have any Pollen Shooter pollen with you, your only hope is to find an orange Blood Sucker."

"You're losing us Larry!"

"I know guys but let me go ahead and tell you a few things so you'll have something to think about. Everything is interlocking in nature here as it is on Earth. I know I may tell you more than you need to know right now but it will be a different story when we go outside and you want to stay alive.

"Outside you could be bitten by a Poison Fly. If you are, find the hole of an old Blood Sucker. Stick your arm in the Blood Sucker's hole. It will wrap its tentacle nose around your arm and try to suck blood out of you at the point where it smells blood. You naturally pull your arm from the hole as soon as it grabs you. You will see that the Blood Sucker is orange. That is because it is old, has few teeth and isn't very strong. When they turn orange, they dig a hole in the soft marshland around a quagmire or a stream bank. When an inquisitive animal crawls in the entrance of their hole, their tentacle nose is used to grab it and they have their meal. The hole will be in soft soil that will not cave in from natural causes.

"To free your arm, grasp the Blood Sucker firmly on the soft part of their body, behind their eyes, and squeeze it as tight as you can. This will make their tentacle nose unwrap and stiffen out and their mouth open. Be sure to keep a firm hold on them until you throw them away from you. If you relax your hold their tentacle nose will instantly whip around and grab your hand."

"What do they look like if they aren't old?"

"Well Delbert, let me try to explain. They look like a giant lobster without any legs, feelers or pinchers. They are about four inches wide with an 18 inch tentacle nose or trunk. They are snail slow and gray when young, but their tentacle nose is unbelievable powerful and moves with lightning speed. I don't think a man can squeeze one hard enough to phase it. After they wrap up their prey with their tentacle nose and curl it to their mouth, they kill and eat it with their many teeth. It uses its tentacle nose just as an elephant uses its trunk to bring food to its mouth. What's worse, the gray Blood Sucker's bite paralyzes its prey."

"How does the young Blood Sucker get its prey?"

"It's very smart, Delbert. It is usually found around well-used trails. It lies very still and strikes with its tentacle nose like a bullwhip at any part of its prey that passes close by. It senses the heat of the creature's body. After it has bitten its prey, the animal is paralyzed and the Blood Sucker continues to suck its blood. When other predators come to eat what looks like a free lunch, since the Blood Sucker doesn't move much, the Blood Sucker grabs it. This method of hunting almost always assures it a continual food supply."

"How can you get one of these creatures off of you since they are both biting and strangling you at the same time?"

"Now you're thinking, Adrian! You have to make the sound of a crow. That sound will bring a weasel-like creature out of its hole. This is a food signal that tells others a Blood Sucker has been spotted. They are extremely fast and have a powerful bite that they inflict behind the eyes of the blood sucker, in the soft body area. Their bite kills it and straightens it out at the same time."

"Why can't you just strike its head with a stick or rock?"

"Remember I said it was like a lobster, Delbert? Its body, from the starting of its tentacle nose to the tip of its tail, is armor plated with a very hard, thick shell-like material."

"What's that weasel-like animal called?"

"It's a Prog, Adrian. They live in a hole like a weasel. It's good to remember where you see different animals like these outside. You might need their help at any time."

"Larry, are you sure this is the wonderful place you wanted to give up Earth for?"

"Yes! I know you are probably frightened somewhat but we won't go out of the Crater until you are ready."

"Why did you call that poppy-like flower, a Pollen Shooter?"

"If you accidentally hit the stock with any force, it pops wide open and sends its pollen flying straight out. If someone was close by, and breathed that pollen, they would be unable to protect themselves for a couple days, just from a couple of good sniffs."

"Do you have a shelter built outside Larry?"

"Not a large one yet, Delbert, I've been trying to cut some boards from the giant Cotra Plant. It's like a large cactus. It's about ten inches in diameter. I'm using a flint-like wedge to split its solid stock while it's green. Then I laid the slabs out to dry and put some rocks on them so they dry straight. Later I'll coat them with pitch and lace them to larger beams with rawhide strips. The pitch comes from a Twal Plant. You can get a sticky honey-like material from it to use as glue. I milk it like they do the maple trees in Vermont to get the sap to make maple syrup. I'll show you the house I built, by the stream, for privacy. The Exvascians are always watching me."

"Is that one of them?"

"Ask, Adrian."

"Are you a Kaydra?"

"Yes! Are you another Larry?"

"I'm another man, yes! Would you change to your primary form for me?"

"Can I touch you then?"

"Is that permitted, Larry?"

"It must be one of the females like DorLetha. They think it's strange that we don't have feathers on our body. Yes, that is allowed."

"If you'll change your form you can touch me!" Adrian expected to be stimulated like DorLetha had stimulated him on Earth, when she was there during her breeding time. They watched the bird change to a large upright eagle-like bird creature with arms under the wings. She had soft feathers on her body like a one-piece body suit and a full head of beautiful feathers. She reached out her feathered arm and touched Adrian's cheek. Adrian was surprised to find her touch was only warm, soft and pleasant.

"Larry, she didn't stimulate me!"

"Are they supposed to?"

"DorLetha did, when she was on Earth to breed. I just thought they would all be that same way."

"I don't know, Adrian. None of them that have touched me have been that way. Of course, I've never been touched by one that was fertile and ready to breed. In fact, DorLetha is the only one that has become that way since I've been here. Somehow she could sense Delbert's aura out there and, well, you know the rest."

"Not really Larry. Why don't you tell us about it?"

"OK Delbert. When I first arrived here, DorLetha wanted to know where Dell Bert was. I couldn't figure out what she was talking about. She had to show me a mental telemetrical view of you there on Mt. Baker and pointed you out to me. I told her we were all friends and told her as much as I could about you. It was strange to see that bright blue aura around you."

"Is that your house up ahead in the trees?"

"Yes, Adrian, I used those four trees as corner poles to lash cross beams to in order to build the second story. I think I'll sleep out here tonight and let you two have the cave. You'll probably want to sleep in longer than I do in the morning."

"Could be, I can't believe this mountain's Crater covers 75 acres. Do you think they used some kind of power beam to dig it out some before they tried to send their women here?"

"I think so, Delbert. It's amazing to see it from outside. It looks like a volcano with a prism in the top. I think they probably beamed some soil ahead, but you heard DorLetha's explanation. They've done an excellent job of controlling the atmosphere in here for me. If it gets too hot, the solar reflector satellite can be changed a little so it doesn't get unbearable.

"TetTrella is learning fast but I think she sees it as a way to get praise and power and that bothers me. What do you think of your bird friend, Adrian? It looks like she is fascinated by you. It takes some of them longer to get used to us than others. Sometimes I feel like I'm in a glass cage but they are really good to me and help me any way they can."

"How do I get rid of her, Larry?"

"You'll just have to talk to her and tell her you'll be around for a while and that she can see you again tomorrow."

Adrian turned to the Fem-Bird who was still stroking his cheek. "What do they call you?"

"Esdra, do you have a name?"

"I'm Adrian. We're very tired. Why don't you leave us now and come see us tomorrow?"

"Would that make you happy, Adrian?"

"Yes Esdra. Why don't you change back to your bird form now and you can sit on my shoulder for a while as we walk back to Larry's cave?"

"I'll do anything I can to please you, my pretty Adrian!" With that she changed instantly and flew onto Adrian's shoulder.

"I feel more comfortable with Esdra as a bird, Larry, but what did she mean when she said, 'My pretty Adrian'."

"I'm not sure, Adrian. In the first place, they generally like to communicate telepathically. If they verbalize, as she did, it usually means they are trying to please you. I know you have always liked birds but I'm not sure you should pet her as much as you are."

"I didn't notice I was doing anything wrong Larry."

"I didn't mean it that way Adrian. I just have this feeling that even in their animal form they judge and experience everything just as they would in their primary form. If what Delbert said about touching DorLetha's side during mating applies to others, no telling what she is experiencing and no way to tell if she will be sterile or not. She appears to be younger than some of the others."

"I'll have to be careful of that then I guess. What else did you notice about her?"

"TetTrella is the only other inhabitant of Exvascia that I've heard use a phrase indicating something belonged to them. Everything is always shared here. That "my" in her statement surprised me, especially when it's combined with the word pretty."

"Keep talking, Larry. We have a lot to learn about this place!"

"I understand that pretty means that your aura is visible to a female, Delbert."

"Is that bad?"

"Unless a female is fertile she will never see your aura Adrian. If this one already sees your aura, it must mean that she will be fertile. If you were to become her choice as a mate, it would mean that over the next six months, to a year, your aura would become brighter to her than all others in the universe. During that time she would start to slowly change physically for her breeding period. Since I haven't viewed that, we would have to ask DorLetha or the Matriarchal Directorate about that."

"I'm not too excited about mating at my age."

"Don't think it isn't possible here, Adrian. The Exvascians have fantastic mental capacities."

"If you don't mind, Larry, could we go back to your cave. I've tired out Art's body and I would like to soak in your hot tub for a while."

"OK Delbert. We're almost back to the waterfall as you can see. We'll be back to my place in a few minutes."

As the trio continued toward the cave, Delbert mentioned he thought the temperature and humidity had both risen. Larry told him that was because it was getting close to the end of the light period for the day. "Each evening TetTrella comes back to the surface from the solar reflector station to feed and recuperate. She's been spending more time up there than usual because DorLetha is just about ready to turn complete control of it over to her. Every evening she checks with me to see if she has kept everything about right for me! It is important to her to please me. One reason for that is the lack of things for the intelligent inhabitants, Kaydra, to do here.

"All the Kaydra find it enjoyable to do things for me. Once in awhile I can use their help with something. Other than caring for the younger ones and teaching them, there isn't much for them to do. They don't compete for anything or at anything. They have a lot of knowledge about tools and equipment but they haven't found any reason to develop them further or use them.

"The equipment, they keep in a special cave, is too advanced for me to understand. I've made a few stone tools and a few crude weapons from plants. I've fashioned a club; a blow-dart gun, from the Tube Plant, which looks like bamboo; an old fashioned sling, from a piece of the tough lily pad of the quagmire and a vine from the Mellow Drop plant; a bow and arrow; a bone knife and bone needles.

"DorLetha blasted a hole in a couple round rocks for me so I could use them for wheels on my cart. I've made my own bowls and pots. If I could find some iron ore, I think DorLetha or TetTrella could turn it into its molten form for me to pour some knives and spear heads in sand molds. An iron anvil and hammer would give me a greater ability to make things."

"How could they turn iron ore into molten material?"

"There are a few surfaces of the prism that allow a very powerful light beam into the Crater. I would just have to place the ore in the proper place for exposure. Or, the way I understand it, they would just have to stare at the ore and laser beams would be emitted from their eyes and melt the ore. I've never seen that though."

"You say they enjoy keeping this place right for you. What all does that entail?"

"The main thing is the temperature. Then the water supply has to be controlled so that there is enough for the atmosphere and the plants. The oxygen supply must be kept constant. I'll show you a special plant from my second level cave entrance. It looks like a six inch Bluebell flower that is completely closed. They produce and store pure oxygen. If too many of these get ripe and pop, the oxygen supply gets too rich for me. The Kaydra open and close the tunnel entrance that leads to the outside. This increases the oxygen supply outside. They have transplanted a lot of the Bluebell flowers outside to increase the oxygen supply. When a large transplantation has taken place, they have to make sure that not too many of the ripe, giant, closed Daffodil like flowers pop because they store carbon dioxide. Sometimes they have to pick some of these in a hurry and take them out of the Crater."

"How do they know how you're feeling?"

"Once in awhile one of the Kaydra will approach me and ask. I've used a udder from the Mardi Goat to make an air sack for use outside. I put a few of the Bluebells in the bag, lace it closed and seal it with pitch. I then take it outside, strapped to my chest with the nipple up. If I get short of breath, I put my mouth over the nipple and pop one of the flowers inside. By doing that, I can get extra oxygen to use for a while. Just don't fall on your face and pop all the flowers at one time. If you do, you have to keep a clamp on the nipple so all the air doesn't escape."

"Sounds a little risky, Larry."

"Not if you're careful. The air is thin outside but you can get by if you move slowly."

"What happened to DorLetha's eggs?"

"They are kept under continual care in the hot cave. It's hot like an incubator for hatching chicken eggs. It's kept warm by the geothermal steam vents that open into that particular cave."

Larry used his developing mental powers to lift the three of them up to his apartment cave several feet above the Crater floor. Delbert and Adrian climbed into the hot tub while Larry fixed a big, hot meal. Larry was quite hungry because he had missed his third meal of the day. He had observed his friends eating the tropical fruit, which he would have had for his third meal, but he had been too excited to eat and too busy talking.

The transition from night to day only took about 15 minutes. Larry told them that he had asked that the transition period be extended to that long so he would have time to make it back to his cave or have time to find something to make a torch from. He said he always carried a pouch with spark stones in it around his neck.

Larry told them he hadn't adjusted to the sudden change from day to night but he could tell it was going to happen soon when he got tired or when he saw the animals started to bed down for the night about an hour ahead of time.

Delbert and Adrian enjoyed the meal. The meat, vegetables and milk all had a different taste than they had ever experienced. After dinner, as they sat and talked, they enjoyed more Marble nuts and some aged Mellow Drop juice from a Mardi Goat udder.

The Crater was totally black once the reflected rays of a distant sun were no longer directed at the Crystal Prism. The night was silent except for the pleasant sound of the nearby waterfall. They could see why Larry had enjoyed his cave. The gentle breeze was still warm. Larry had decided to spend the night in the second story of his crude wooden house on the Crater floor. He told Delbert and Adrian to pull the skin drape over the cave entrance before they were ready to go to sleep.

Larry even had a bench potty built in a small cave off the main cave. It was just a bench with a ceramic bowl beneath the hole but it served its purpose. At the end of the bench were semidry Mellow Drop leaves to use as paper. If they had to use the unit at night, it would be emptied in the morning.

Before they were ready for bed, TetTrella suddenly appeared from a million tiny sparkling particles that had entered the room. After taking the form she preferred, somewhat like an ape, she began to question Larry about his day and whether she had pleased him with the temperature. He assured her she had done well and then introduced her to his two friends.

She was eager to talk to them and look them over in the light of Larry's oil shale lamps. It was obvious to them she was glad they were males and said she wished they would be able to stay, even though it was against the Matriarchal Directorate's rules. It was quite obvious that she was proud of her new position. She seemed quite aggressive, possessive and competitive. She even mentioned looking forward to her breeding period so she could go looking for a powerful male to help her have a male offspring or two. She offered to let them sit in on her evening's mental telemetrical viewing. Since they were tired and ready to sleep, she and Larry excused themselves and disappeared before their eyes. TetTrella's particles sparkled as they left the cave through the solid rock overhead.

Adrian and Delbert went to sleep on the soft animal skins and furs that Larry had provided. It had been a very tiring day packed full of adventure. They had started the day on Mt. Baker on the planet Earth and then been transported through space in a subatomic particle state on a light beam to Exvascia. Delbert had even taken the body of his friend, Art, after unbelievably leaving his own body on Earth for Art to use. They had talked with the Exvascians and taken a tour of the planet.

CHAPTER 5

LIFE ON EXVASCIA

When Adrian awoke, he didn't know where he was. The cave was only semilight because of the animal skins stretched across the entrance. He sat up with a start. What he had thought was a dream of being whisked off to another planet apparently wasn't a dream at all. He got up quietly and slipped on his shoes. According to his watch it was two o'clock but that didn't mean anything where he was. Delbert appeared to still be sleeping. It shook him up a little to see Art lying there, but he remembered Delbert was using Art's body. This certainly had to be a different world.

Adrian left the cave and climbed down the ladder to the floor of the Crater. As he did, he saw Larry waving to him from the pool by the waterfall. He walked over to his friend who had lived on this strange planet for over a year and a half. “Good morning Larry. Do you have an outhouse around here somewhere?”

“Good morning Adrian. It's down the trail in the opposite direction. How did you sleep?”

“Great! I was really tired by the time I got to bed last night. I'll be back in a few minutes.” Larry had utilized a light pole framework covered by animal skins to provide him some privacy. Mellow Drop leaves strung on a vine were again available for use. After a few minutes he rejoined Larry.

“You'll find that you will only do that about once a day after you've been here awhile. The food and atmosphere will have a different affect on your body and you'll feel stronger. I think the pull of gravity is less here and the food is more nourishing.”

“You mean my old body is going to last even longer here than on Earth?”

As they talked, one of the strange but pretty birds flew up to Adrian.

“Hello Aden.”

“Hello. It's Adrian but I can't remember your name. It seems like a dream, seeing you again this morning.”

"My name is Esdra. What is a dream?"

"It's like a mental telemetrical viewing of something that has happened to you in the past. We do it when we sleep without trying to do so. When we wake, we remember that we had a review of the past in our mind or a dream."

"We don't do that. Why do you?"

"I don't know! Do you want to change to your other form?"

"That isn't necessary."

"No, but I'd like to see you in your form that's more like mine."

"OK, my pretty Adrian, if it pleases you."

"Larry am I getting into something here?"

"I can't say, because others are coming to see you and to listen to us talk."

"Esdra, would you sit here until we get our friend?"

"Will you be back soon?"

"I think so. We'll come back as soon as we can." Larry and Adrian left before any other Kaydra joined them. On the way back to the cave, Andre, Larry's pet dwit, caught up with them and jumped up on Larry's hip, which was where he liked to ride.

"I'll have to show you how smart Andre is. He can do lots of tricks. He seems to get a lot of satisfaction out of praise for learning something new."

Larry let Adrian climb up the ladder to the cave opening. He preferred to levitate himself to the level of the opening, which he did in a normal standing position.

Once they were in the cave, Larry could tell Delbert wasn't able to operate Art's body. "Let me get you started talking and walking, Delbert. As I help your body function, think how it feels to operate it and then you'll be able to take over by yourself in a few minutes." Larry levitated Art's body and got it moving for Delbert. Sure enough, in a few minutes, Delbert was able to move about by himself and talk.

'Thanks, Larry. I sure needed your help to get Art's body working. I don't think he has anyone like you on Earth helping him get my body working."

"You're probably right, Delbert. I'm sorry I let him take your body. I just didn't have the power to send his body out of the "Adralack Crack". I thought he would like to join us for a while. I couldn't believe how scared he was. I always thought he was an opportunist."

"I don't know why he was so afraid Larry. I've got to use your outhouse."

"It's down the trail to your right. I'll fix you some hashbowns, eggs, steak and potla while you're gone."

"What's potla?"

"It's my substitute for coffee. I grind up some seeds and soak them in hot water. It makes a great hot drink."

"Whatever you say, you've been right so far."

Larry started breakfast by lighting an oil shale fire in his barbecue pit. He then took a large flat stone off of a geothermal steam vent and placed it on two rocks on either side of the fire pit above the fire. By starting with a stone that was 200 degrees already, it didn't take him long to get it hot enough to fry eggs. By using a bellows he had made, he was able to make the oil shale quickly burn extremely hot.

The three men ate and talked about the strange new planet they were on. "Larry, I can't believe this meal. You seem to have more than you need to take care of yourself. What do you do with your garbage?"

"I feed it to some hog-like animals that live here Delbert. You notice I don't call anything wild. None of the animals here are afraid of me. They don't consider the killing of each other for food as anything unusual. I have several Kaydra that hunt for me. You'll probably meet some of them with Esdra later. Providing me food has made some of them feel needed and kept the animals from fearing me. I do spear fish myself, but that is all. I gather eggs very early in the morning and put extras in my icebox area. Eggs that are not watched are soon eaten by other predators. Otherwise, they are set on in a nest. So, if you find eggs early in the morning, that aren't in a nest, they're fresh."

"It all seems very secure and organized but what happens if something goes wrong with the transmitter station, the hyperatmospheric force field, the solar power stations or the deflector/reflector satellite that keeps the heat regulated in the Crater?"

"I don't know Delbert. I haven't seen their equipment, tool or weapons storage areas. I imagine they have such items but I can't prove it. I know they have a vast amount of knowledge in their time-exempt historical telepathic storage banks but they seem to lack motivation. Without males, and with their great transmutative powers, they seem to have been content to live in this paradise without changing it.

"Since there isn't much for them to do, I imagine they would enjoy an emergency where they would all be needed to save their planet. Since I can now function in free soul flight, I know a couple weeks without light wouldn't kill me. I'm not sure how the plants and animals would take to the change in temperature and lack of light. Maybe most of the animals would be brought inside. Some may die outside but a majority would survive. If they didn't, they could easily appropriate new animals from other planets, if the transmitter station continued to function."

"Great meal Larry. Can we help you with the dishes?"

"No Adrian, I wash them in a little geothermal stream of water and steam further back in the cave and then set them out in the sunshine to dry. Why don't you two go out and talk with the Kaydra? They won't be in the form you expect and other animals may be there with them. Let me know if Esdra kept her form for you Adrian.'

"Why?"

"Well, as a general rule, they don't do that. If she does, something is going on."

"OK see you later." Delbert followed Adrian the best he could in Art's body. His being in another person's body fascinated the Exvascians. They communicated at length with him telepathically about his experience, his world and their world.

Adrian, on the other hand, preferred to speak out loud. He enjoyed the beautiful voices the Exvascians had and how they were able to talk his language by reading his thoughts and speech patterns. In an attempt to make himself better understood, Adrian put his hand on Esdra's feathered shoulder. Unthinkingly he stroked her feathered back as he removed his hand. In response, Esdra cooed and ruffled her feathers. This immediately interrupted his communication. The other Kaydra wanted to know what was wrong with her. Esdra tried to tell them nothing was wrong but they wouldn't believe her. Why did she make that sound and ruffled her feathers? Each wanted Adrian to touch them to see if he had the same affect on them.

Larry tried to calm the group down but it didn't help. Soon the full Matriarchal Directorate, including DorLetha, was present.

"DorLetha what's going on? Please speak so we can hear what you're talking about."

"We'll try, Delbert, but everyone is pretty excited. You see, Esdra cooed and ruffled her feathers?"

"What does that mean?"

"We're not sure, since we supposedly can't do that when we are in that form. According to the Matriarchal Directorate, the time-exempt historical telepathic storage banks spoke of mating taking place among the inhabitants of our former planet a long time ago. Some males of our species caused the females to lay fertile eggs at will, not just during the one breading time that only a few of us now enjoy. Adrian seems to have awakened that instinct in Esdra!"

"Ha! Ha! Ha!" Larry couldn't control himself. "You old cock!"

DorLetha did her best but she couldn't answer all the Directorate's questions. "Adrian, would you mind touching each of us like you did Esdra?"

"But DorLetha, I don't know the Kaydra from the animals."

The Directorate talked telepathically for a while, at an incredible speed. Adrian and Delbert were not able to follow much of what was talked about. Fortunately, Larry's superior mind was able to pick up the drift of what was about to happen. "Adrian, they are going to have all the Kaydra take their primary form. They then want you to go around and touch each of them, with the form Esdra has, the same way you did her."

"How many of them are there?"

"I don't know Adrian, but were about to find out. The Directorate has asked all of the Kaydra with Esdra's form to come closer. We each have to stroke their shoulder and back as you did Esdra."

It was only a moment later before they were surrounded by several Kaydra. The nine member Matriarchal Directorate members passed by them first. DorLetha followed them and TetTrella followed her. There was the same response in DorLetha, to Delbert that she had the day before. She had no response to the other two men even though all three stroked her the same way.

Only Delbert affected DorLetha, which was what should have happened, since he was her mate. Esdra was the last of the Kaydra that used her form to be touched. Once again, Adrian's touch caused her to coo and ruffle her feathers. Although she had the Fem-Bird form, similar to DorLetha, she was not quite the same.

"The Directorate has decided you can stay until we find out why Esdra has apparently revived an ancient characteristic. Although she's too young to be fertile and hasn't shown any signs of becoming so in the near future, she responds as I do to Delbert and we know our male offspring will hatch soon. What can you tell us about your special ability, Adrian?"

"I didn't know that I had any special ability, DorLetha. I just love birds. You've seen Larry play with the little dwit he calls Andre. We call that a pet. It's an animal we give special attention and love to."

"What's love?"

"OK, fellas. How do I answer that one?"

"I don't have any idea Adrian. How about you, Delbert?"

"I can try. It's caring for someone else, as much as you care for yourself."

"Why would you do that?"

"It's a philosophical attitude we have on our planet because we don't control it as you seem to yours. We're like the animals here on your planet. We don't control the atmosphere, the length of the days or the path our planet travels."

"We can't understand that but go ahead and try to explain your ability to us Adrian."

"Madam Directorate, my favorite pets have always been birds. I give them special food and shelter them when the atmosphere is not favorable for them. I do it so they can live. In return, they come and see me and sing me their pretty songs." Adrian amazed the Kadra by whistling some of his favorite bird songs. They enjoyed his whistling.

"You can see the aura of our songs?"

"No, Esdra, why do you ask that?"

"I can see and like the aura that surrounds you. That is why I call you pretty."

"Pretty, means not harsh or unpleasant to hear in our language. It has nothing to do with an aura."

DorLetha spoke up. "Esdra, do you see an aura about Dell Bert?"

"Yes but it isn't very bright."

"Does anyone else see an aura about any of the men?" No response was offered. DorLetha continued, "Adrian, do you think your love for pet birds was transferred to Esdra because you don't have any other outlet for love here?"

"I guess! I know, as a bird or in her present form of a combined human and bird, Fem-Bird, I would try to take care of her needs for food, shelter and protect her from danger."

"Then that is part of what you call love?"

"Yes, DorLetha, that's part of it."

"How do you feel about Adrian, Esdra?"

"I feel complete and don't worry even though I don't have a worthwhile job to do or any real responsibility. I feel warm all over, when he touches me or talks to me. I don't have any desire to change to my bird form again and I like to talk verbally with him. His words are like bird calls to me. I understand what he says without consciously reading his mind."

"TetTrella, you're almost the age to become fertile, do you have anything to say about this?"

"Nothing, Madam Directorate, I just wish my time would come. I've been doing a lot of mental telemetrical viewing but I haven't yet seen an aura around any male creatures!"

The Directorate's questions had put TetTrella on the spot and she didn't like it. Why should this young female be given the privilege of being fertile long before her time and perhaps not even have to leave the planet to breed?

The Directorate leader spoke again. "You may all go about your own pursuits." With that directive, all but a few of the 350 inhabitants left. Most assumed their animal form before leaving. DorLetha told Delbert she would talk to him later about the situation, after she had attended the Matriarchal Directorate meeting to follow.

"Larry, why didn't you tell me to keep my hands off the merchandise?"

"I didn't know your love for birds would cause her to react that way! Look, it didn't affect any of the others. Besides, we don't really know how they function except for what they say. Maybe she isn't going to act like a hen around a new rooster!"

"Wake me when this is over, would you, Delbert."

"Take it easy, Adrian. I don't think she could be that different from DorLetha. If your aura is slightly visible to her now, it might be she will become fertile sometime in the future. In order for her to pick up an aura from a distant planet, it would have to be many times brighter than yours. If she becomes fertile and does any mental telemetrical viewing, she will start seeing a lot of males on different planets with bright auras."

"You two are probably right. Shall we go swimming in the waterfall pool?"

"Sounds like a good idea, Adrian, how about you Delbert?"

"I don't think so. I wouldn't want Art's body to shrink on me or anything." Delbert watched as Adrian walked away a little more proudly and a little less stooped.

The waterfalls pool was cool and refreshing. Adrian swam in his shorts while Larry enjoyed himself in his loincloth. After swimming for a while, they got out of the pool to lie on the grassy bank. The light coming through the prism tanned the men and made the plants grow rapidly.

"Larry, could you make us some sandals like yours and a loincloth too? You look comfortable."

"I can do that in a few minutes. I'll tell TetTrella it's too hot for us and she can take care of that tomorrow."

"On second thought, Adrian said, "Why don't you forget the loincloths or perhaps not?" He grinned as Esdra materialized.

"Pretty, Adrian, what were you doing in the water?"

"It's called swimming. On land we walk, run and jump. You can sit in water and bathe to clean your body or feathers or you can play in the water. As you saw, we held our breath to swim underwater, swam with our head above the water or just floated. There are several strokes we can do with our arms and legs or we can just move our arms and legs up and down, or tread water, to keep our head above the water without going anywhere."

"Can you show Shida and me how to do it?"

"Well, Shida has the primary animal form we call an ape on our planet.

I'll show her how to dog paddle and then several other strokes. You'll have to change to her form to learn to swim. In your current form you would just float."

"We should be able to learn quickly if we use our levitation ability to hold ourselves near the surface of the water."

"That shouldn't be necessary Esdra. OK Esdra and Shida walk out into the water with me and lie on your backs and relax. Keep your head back and don't breathe if you go under the water." They did as Adrian directed and were soon able to swim. Shida decided she had enough of swimming. It was interesting, but very primitive. She would rather take the form of a dolphin or such and just swim off.

Esdra decided she would try it again when Adrian did, so she could get to know this inferior human ability better. Adrian wasn't offended to think he was inferior because he knew it was true. The powers they had were amazing! His scientific mind was gathering information about the Exvascians all the time, just as they were gathering information about him.

While his friends were swimming, Delbert worked on making Art's body do what he wanted it to. He started to feel as though he could make it work at least satisfactorily.

For their second meal of the day, Larry showed them where to find other exotic plants, seeds and nuts to eat. They realized how much they had to learn and were glad Larry had been there ahead of them.

DorLetha returned later and talked with Delbert about Esdra. The full Matriarchal Directorate had decided to watch Esdra's development closely. After explaining to the Directorate how human males breed, they accepted her explanation that Adrian couldn't have done anything wrong. She spent time showing Delbert around her planet using the disintegration method to transport the two of them outside. Delbert was surprised to see how much water was on the planet outside the Crater. The reflected sunlight outside the Crater caused the jungle to grow rapidly and helped absorb some of the water. There was such a stark contrast between the barren land, the sea and the jungle. There were valleys, plains and mountains.

After and aerial view of the planet outside, they returned to the safety of the Crater. It was almost dark before DorLetha was ready to leave Delbert. She was glad he was on her planet but she wished she could locate his own body back on Earth so they could see what had happened to it. She left after promising to let him know when she found out anything.

On the sixth day on Exvascia, DorLetha called the three men and had them sit in on her mental telemetrical viewing session. For some reason the aura of Delbert's body had grown strong enough for her to locate it. When the men saw her vision, they realized his bright aura was caused by Carol and Myrna being at Art's bedside. Art was really having a problem trying to operate Delbert's body. In desperation Delbert let his soul and spirit drift to Earth and reenter his body. He told Carol to take care of him, meaning Art. He even reached his hand over and touched her shoulder. Realizing what he had done instantly brought him back to Exvascia.

Good for Carol, she was still willing to help her friend Delbert. He hoped she would still remain sensitive to Art and his telepathic messages. That might help Delbert get his body back in the future.

"DorLetha, that is incredible. How could I actually go there?"

"It's just a matter of exercising your mind to realize its potential, Delbert. It looks like Art is going to make it. That must be the hospital you told me about. If his aura stays bright, I should be able to view him more often now that I've found him. That will enable me to keep track of his progress."

"Do you have a plan for getting me back into my body yet?"

"Yes, Dell Bert. In a few days we'll try to send a strong enough beam down there for you to travel on and trade him bodies. We'll have to disintegrate the two of you while holding on to each other, then regenerate both of you back into your own bodies. We'll then bring you back here. We're just waiting for our power to build up now."

"OK, you let me know when you're ready."

The Matriarchal Directorate was happy with DorLetha's discovery and was anxious to get Delbert put back together with his body as soon as possible.

When TetTrella checked with the three men about their comfort that evening, Larry asked her to see if she could drop the temperature a little. She stayed and listened to their conversation for awhile before leaving.

"Larry, what would you think about enlarging your cave so all three of us could live in it?"

"We could try, but the rock seemed to be getting harder to chip away the further I got from the surface. We could try to work on it in the morning unless your appointment calendar is full."

"I'll check with my secretary!" In the morning the men started trying to enlarge the cave. When they worked, they tired quickly because of the heat.

"Larry, how about making a running trail around the inside of the Crater? I have to get Art's body back in shape. Between that and swimming we should be able to stay fit."

"That sounds like a good idea Delbert but do you think you can get Larry's body to run?"

"I'm getting better at operating it every day." For the next couple days the men worked on the cave expansion and then on the development of their running trail. TetTrella was able to bring the temperature down to the high 70's. That made the cave about 70 degrees without a shale oil fire going or the entrance drapes pulled open.

Esdra had joined the men in their swim. Others including Shida, were content to watch. Larry was surprised to see Esdra petting Andre the way she had seen him and Adrian do it. It was obviously she wasn't used to the emotional feeling she was getting from that or being around Adrian.

TetTrella arrived one evening after dinner when the men were sitting and talking about the small amount of progress they had made on the cave expansion. She seemed extremely happy and talked aloud. “Larry can I help you expand your cave?”

“Are you kidding? Of course you can! What do you have in mind?”

“I remembered a historical fact from the time-exempt telepathic historical data storage banks. It told how our people first traveled in space in machines and had to mine their fuel from caves. They had used a form of metaphysical intake and dispersion of laser power through controlled thought transference.

“I've stored in my body and mind a little of the power not transmitted down here during the last few days. Can I see if I can do what I learned, to help you enlarge your cave?”

“Yes, go ahead! We'll stand back” TetTrella concentrated and started to take on a whitish glow. Her eyes turned red and then two powerful laser blasts shot from her eyes. It was a good thing they had stood back because her one blast cleared a 12 foot by 12 foot area. The dust flew and TetTrella disintegrated.

“Are you all right TetTrella?” She tried to telepathically say she was OK but her thoughts were weak. She sparkled like a million particles almost ready to take shape, but couldn't. That naturally brought DorLetha and the full Matriarchal Directorate.

“What happened to your cave?”

“TetTrella was trying to enlarge it for us DorLetha, through some ancient process she learned about from the storage banks. She doesn't seem to be able to take her form again though. Can you help her?”

“I'll try Dell Bert!” By concentrating and combining her mental power with TetTrella's she was able to help TetTrella take her form again. “TetTrella, how did you learn to do that? None of us have ever personally sent forth that much power before?”

“The men asked me not to heat the Crater as hot as it had been over the past few days. I stored the excess power in my mind and body, like I read in the historical data storage banks. I think I either stored too much power or let too much power loose at one time. Because of how hard I was concentrating. I almost permanently disintegrated myself. Thank you for saving me!"

"You're welcome. I know you want to do everything you can for the men but be careful you don't overdo it. Remember, we need to save all the excess power we can to send a beam down to earth so Dell Bert can get back into his own body."

All the Kaydra gathered around TetTrella to communicate with her about the ability she had displayed. To Larry's surprise, most of the Kaydra appeared in their primary form. Before his friends had arrived, he had only seen them that way when he arrived. Now he had seen it three times in less than two weeks. They seemed to be taking more of an interest in being a society again and not just living as animals.

They were becoming more aware of the men staying together, cooking food and eating together and improving their shelter to better care for themselves. Although they were using primitive fire and elementary tools, they seemed to have a structured life. They had things to do to occupy their time. They wrote, read, worked and played. Had the Exvascians forgotten what had gone on in the past for a good reason, or had the lack of the inquisitive male mind made a real difference?

For the next two days the men spent time trying to split the Cotra plant into slabs to dry in the form of straight boards so they could make another shelter. When TetTrella arrived that evening, many Kaydra gathered in their primary form to see what she might do for the men. They were hoping she would perform for them again. They weren't disappointed!

"How has the temperature been, Larry?"

"Great, TetTrella, you're doing a good job."

"What are you trying to do?"

"We're trying to make boards. I know that doesn't make any sense to you. Do you know what my outside shelter looks like?"

"Yes."

"I'm trying to make some more of those flat pieces like that. On our planet we use equipment to cut trees off at the ground, remove the limbs and then cut slabs off the trunk. They call the pieces boards and they are strong when dried. We used them to build very nice shelters."

"Would you like me to make some boards for you?"

"Could you?"

"Yes, you find a tree you want boards made from and I'll see if I can make you some."

"Let's find a tree, fellas. Find one with leaves like an English walnut. When I tried to break some of the fallen limbs, they seemed to be very strong."

"Isn't there one by the outhouse?"

"That's right, Adrian. This way everyone!" This time the Kaydra walked along with the men rather than disintegrating and appearing instantly where the men were going. When they reached the tree, TetTrella concentrated on the limbs first. As she did, her eyes turned red but she hardly had a glow at all. Then she sent darting laser beams from her eyes that stripped all the limbs from the tree. Adrian and Delbert were amazed.

"Now what do I do?"

Larry took a second to mentally gather the limbs and levitate them to one side, out of the way. "Now cut the tree off at the ground. Be careful it doesn't fall on anyone. Everyone step back. I want you to see how we fall trees on our planet. Remember, we don't have any more power on our planet than your animals do here so we have to use equipment."

As the tree fell, Delbert yelled, "Timber!" The three men cheered TetTrella and clapped their hands.

"Did I do something wrong? Why are you yelling and pounding your hands together? Are you unhappy with me?"

"No! That's what we do on our planet when we are happy and pleased with someone. The louder we yell and the harder we clap, or pound our hands together, the more pleased we are. Now see if you can slice the log into slabs. If you go from left to right, the laser beams from your eyes will cut through pretty evenly."

TetTrella did as Larry suggested and the first slab was sliced. Adrian and Delbert lifted it and set it aside. When she finished cutting up the tree, Larry gave her a big hug and a kiss on the cheek. "Why did you put your mouth on my cheek? Did you want to bite me?"

"No, TetTrella! I just pressed my lips on your check like this. It's called a kiss. It's kind of a reward and 'Thank You' for helping us."

"Shouldn't I help if I can?"

"Yes, but on our planet people don't always help others even when they can or are asked to."

"Why don't they?"

"I don't know! Our people, or Kaydra, don't always do what is expected of them. We'll need more boards TetTrella. Do you think you could cut up a few more trees for us?"

"I'll try. Do you have any others picked out?"

"We should try to take them from the area that has the densest growth." As the group went through the tree area, they located several more of the desired trees. TetTrella cut all the boards they needed before her special power reserve was gone. The more she used her special laser power, the better she was able to control it. The other Kaydra levitated the boards and the limbs to where Larry had piled the first ones. "Let's all give TetTrella a hand for all the help she has given us." All the Kaydra joined the men in their applause. By then, the Matriarchal Directorate had arrived along with DorLetha.

Many of the Kaydra wanted to see what a kiss was like. Each man had to pucker up and kiss over one hundred each. TetTrella was quite pleased and was followed by many of her primary form Exvascians. She had become their champion.

The Matriarchal Directorate approached with DorLetha as the others left. "We're not sure your ways are best for our Kaydra. If too many of your expressions enter our society, it might start to change. That may be good or bad."

"We didn't mean to do anything wrong. We always express our feelings and emotions. Your Kaydra don't seem to understand emotions. We are trying to be very careful to pass on only the best things from our culture. As far as our using only one form, we don't have the mental capacity to take another form. I'm just learning to disintegrate and regenerate and I've been here for some time." Larry's comments seemed to appease the fears of the full Directorate.

Delbert wanted to make sure the Exvascians understood human emotions better. "DorLetha, remember how you felt about me before your last egg passed into place?" As he said that, she walked over to him and held him close. Her 6 foot 6 inch frame hovered over Larry's 5 foot 10 inch body.

"Dell Bert, I wish you were in your own body. Yes, I remember! I'll try to tell them." By telepathic communication DorLetha tried to tell the Directorate about her fear of dying before being calmed by Delbert's love and concern for her even though he was changing her mating pattern in order to try to give her a male offspring. Since none of the Directorate had ever allowed a male to change their mating habits, they had difficulty understanding what she meant or how she had felt.

"I tried Dell Bert but I don't know how much they understood or just had to accept."

"Thanks DorLetha. We just don't want to make any mistakes here on your planet but we probably will."

"I know you wouldn't do anything wrong intentionally."

During the next few days the men kept busy drying the boards in the light and heat of the Crater. "I have an idea. If I build a sand mold of a hammer head, do you think TetTrella could turn some ore into a molten form for us? I thought we might get her to make a drill for us and a handle to turn it. Maybe we could get her to make us some spear heads and knives too."

"She does seem to have her laser power under control. She could easily make all the items for us except the drill. How do you figure she could do that, Adrian?"

"I thought I would get her to make a long knife like piece of metal with a large square head on it. We could sharpen the edge against some of the harder stones here. We could then heat it up over an oil shale pot and twist it several times. I'd put a handle with a square hole on it to twist the drill. That would enable us to bore holes. We could apply pitch from the Twall plant to the hardwood pegs and hammer them into the holes to hold the house together. That would make it fairly stable."

"I'll talk to her about it, when you get your molds made."

Several days later Adrian had his molds made and Larry asked TetTrella for help. She was happy to help again because of the attention she got when she turned Adrian's ore into a molten form and filled his molds.

The boards continued to dry and Adrian started sharpening one edge of his metal to be used for a drill. The handle TetTrella had helped him make fit perfectly. Adrian used an oil shale lamp to quickly heat the drill at the exact point where he needed to. Each time he heated and twisted it, he dipped it in water to cool and heat treat it to make the drill bit very hard

"Larry, I'm ready to try out my drill bit."

"OK, the lumber is drying nicely. We'll have to start thinking about what we want to build before long. Are you and Delbert ready to go outside the Crater and take a look around?"

"Sure Larry. Adrian was just waiting for me to be able to operate Art's body well enough to feel comfortable in it."

Before TetTrella arrived that evening, Esdra, Shida and DorLetha joined the men for dinner. "You men won't laugh at us, if we eat with you will you?"

"No, Shida. You three are our friends. We care for you and we wouldn't want to make you unhappy. The three Exvascians enjoyed watching what the men prepared and how they cooked it.

As they ate, they made observations. Esdra spoke first. "The Mardi Goat tastes different when I eat it, after it has been burned by the fire."

"We call that cooked, Esdra."

"In my primary form, like yours Adrian, it takes so long to get the food inside me."

"Chewing takes time and it is tiring but we get more energy from it if we eat it slowly."

Shida was a vegetarian, since her primary form was that of an ape. However, she was fascinated at the process of cooking. She wanted to know why everything was done the way it was. The men tried to explain everything as clearly as they could. She obviously understood what they did, but not why it was done.

Adrian took his new drill outside and demonstrated how it worked but the Kaydra weren't impressed. Since they couldn't laugh, they didn't, but they showed their superiority by burning three holes through the end of each board with laser beams from their eyes, a simple job they could all do now.

TetTrella didn't get any praise from the Kaydra that evening and quickly left. Adrian sent Esdra and Shida away, leaving DorLetha alone to converse with the men.

"Did you see the afterglow TetTrella left when she disintegrated, Delbert?"

"Yes, DorLetha, what does that mean?"

"I think it means she is sterile. That is the first sign."

"Does she know it?"

"She can't see what we see. I'm more perceptive than the other Kaydra. Until they notice it and tell her, she won't know it unless she starts having trouble with her mental telemetrical viewing."

"You seem concerned, DorLetha. What's really bothering you?" Larry's increased mental powers told him she wanted to discuss something with the men rather than with the Matriarchal Directorate.

"Does the Crater seem cooler than usual to you lately?"

"Yes, but we asked TetTrella not to heat it as much. We've been busy working with our boards which heats our bodies so we hadn't noticed."

"But Larry, you never covered your legs with skins before. Why do you do it now?"

"My loincloth hasn't been enough to keep me warm lately. The temperature must have dropped about ten degrees in the last two or three weeks."

"I don't understand it!"

"You mean the temperature drop, DorLetha?"

"No Delbert. You haven't been using much power through TetTrella lately have you?"

"No, you said we needed it to get me back to Earth to get my body back."

"That's right but the power storage in the transmitter station hasn't increased very much and it should have. I think TetTrella has been improperly using her position as keeper of the solar reflector station. I think TetTrella would like to be the Queen rather than me. She didn't get all the power she used, to cut down the trees and make your boards from her physical and mental storage. She drew it from the Kaydra around her or she got it from some other source. She impressed them with her ability. We haven't had anybody do that for a long, long time. That isn't good."

"What do you think she has in mind?"

"I don't know, Larry. The Directorate has me so busy learning telepathically from our historical data storage banks that I haven't had time to check on her."

"Can we help you some way?"

"Yes, try not to ask her for any use of power to help you and ask her to increase the heat in the Crater for you. I'll keep a check on the power build up, or lack of it, in the power transmitter station. I'll check back with you later. Have a good night's sleep."

"Good night, DorLetha." Delbert kissed her and she was gone. The men went to sleep a little concerned for their own safety. Before they went to sleep they decided they would try to be more observant of the conditions and events that went on around them.

In the morning, they decided to venture out of the Crater. Larry picked a few Bluebells, which were full of oxygen, and put them in his Mardi Goat air sack, sealed it up and they were ready to go out. They took a few extra furs because it took-time to walk through the cool tunnel to the outside and they didn't know what it would be like out there. They wanted to be able to keep warm, if they stayed out over night.

Larry packed a Mardi Goat bag full of Mellow Drop juice with ice in it. Delbert carried a pack of food and Adrian carried a supply of oil shale and everyone carried a spark stone pouch with a few oil shale stones in it and a lamp.

Adrian told Esdra where they were going. Larry handed her Andre who had been following them around and asked her to take care of him. It surprised him how Esdra and Andre got along. None of the other Kaydra even touched a dwit. It didn't make any sense to them.

Adrian and Delbert were amazed by the phosphorescent glow of one of the tunnels leading to the outside. As they went along, Larry would ignite the oil shale pots he had placed along the way on earlier trips. The extra lights made them feel more secure even though each carried his own oil shale lamp that would easily burn for a full day.

"Fellas, doesn't this tunnel seem warmer than our cave as we get closer to the entrance?"

"Yes, Larry. I thought you said it would be cooler."

"I don't understand it. I guess we'll find out why, when we get outside. According to my marks on the wall, the entrance should be visible when we round the next bend."

Delbert was leading so they expected him to call out that the entrance was visible when he went around the bend in the tunnel. "What do you see, Delbert?"

"Nothing!"

"You're kidding! I can't be wrong! It's always been there before!"

"Well, it isn't there now!" The entrance was where Larry had said it was, but very little light was coming through it because jungle vines had overgrown it. Larry and Adrian used their knives to clear the entrance.

The men finally cut their way out of the cave. "What has TetTrella been up to fellas? She must have kept the solar reflector trained on this jungle all the time since she has controlled the system. She must be trying to develop her own empire out here. She must have converted more of the water to oxygen and hydrogen."

"Remember my telling you the atmosphere out here was dry and the oxygen about as thin as it is at 10,000 feet on Earth? That isn't what I sense now. The temperature must be 20 degrees hotter than it used to be. I'll bet the ground cover has spread another mile since I was out here last. This is a case of the barren land being slowly covered by plants and animals. As the animals eat the tender plants at the edge of the growth, they leave more fertilizer for the plants to expand into.

"The Kaydra wanted to develop the area outside the crater first and then work their way around the mountain. I told you about the work I did to change it out here. Let's go to our left. There was a grassy slope over there that we started with a zoysia-type grass plug. All you have to do is get it started and it crowds everything else out."

Larry was right. TetTrella had caused things to expand rapidly over the past month. The increased oxygen and temperature was good for the plants and animals. The plants themselves added to the oxygen supply.

"Keep your eyes open for the things I've taught you and remember what you've read. I brought my sling in case I have to scare anything away. What we have to be careful of is the unknown."

"It all seems unknown to us Larry! Why don't we sit down under this tree and rest? We can watch all the weird animals and birds for a while." In just a few minutes Delbert was asleep.

"Delbert sure gets tired in Art's body. I wonder how hard it has been for Art trying to live in Delbert's body on Earth."

"I don't imagine Art is doing much more than standing by himself yet. Even with my help, Delbert hasn't done that well. How do you feel Adrian?"

"I'm about to go to sleep too. It must be the thinner air. That light mist falling from this tree is sure refreshing."

"Oh, no!"

"What is it?"

"Get up. We've got to get Delbert out from under this tree. It's the dreaded Mist Tree. Its cooling mist is a sedative. I said get up, Adrian!"

"I'm not sure I can, Larry."

"Here Adrian, take a gulp of air from the Mardi Goat air bag. Now, can you get up?"

"I think so. See what you can do for Delbert and I'll get myself out into the open."

Larry levitated Delbert from beneath the tree. "I forgot to tell you two about that tree. Anything that stays under it very long dies. That's why there weren't any birds resting in it."

"Why didn't we see anything dead under it?"

"Scavengers use it as a priority hunting ground, especially the old or crippled ones."

"How long will Delbert be out, Larry?"

"I can't say. This is the first time I've actually seen the Mist tree. DorLetha told me about it once as we sat under a tree in the Crater."

"Exvascia is a strange new land, Larry."

Delbert was out for hours. When he awoke, he convinced his friends not to go back before dark but to stay in the tunnel that evening. They ate some food and started preparing the tunnel for the evening when it was time for the reflector satellite to be redirected to the transmitter station for the evening. They started a fire for more light in the tunnel so they could save their lamps for the trip back.

"Larry, do you see what I see?"

"What's that, Delbert?"

"It's not getting darker outside?"

Larry jumped up and ran outside the tunnel. Delbert was right. TetTrella was keeping the sunlight reflected on the outside all night too. Now on the outside there was no night and no power was being stored. "No wonder the vegetation had grown so profusely! "

They decided they had better go back and tell DorLetha what was happening outside. First, they had to sleep whether it was dark or not. The 20 hour day and the hotter temperature were too much for the men physically. Adrian took the first watch while his friends slept. When he couldn't stay awake any longer, he called Larry who kept watch until morning.

After eating food from their backpacks for breakfast, they put out their fire, picked up their backpacks and started back toward the Crater. Each time they passed an oil shale pot, they put it out. They put the excess shale they had brought in the first few pots they came to. In the future, they would have to make a trip back to replenish the oil shale supply in the other pots.

Before they reached the tunnel entrance into the Crater, they heard what sounded like a trumpet call. “What's that Larry?”

“I don't know! I haven't heard it before.”

When the men entered the Crater, they saw a golden horn being blown. One long blast followed by three short blasts. The horn was being blown from the hatchery cave. “I wonder what's happened up there. You don't suppose I'm a father do you?”

“Let's go find out, Delbert!” Larry led the way and they soon reached the cave entrance where they found Esdra and Shida taking turns blowing the horn. Esdra would blow the long blast first and then Shida would blow the three short blasts.

DorLetha met Delbert at the entrance. “We have a male offspring and three females!”

“You mean I have a son?”

“Is that what you call a male?”

“That's the name of the relationship between the male offspring and his parents. What does he look like?”

“I don't know.”

“Are you ready to find out, Delbert?”

“Yes I am. Where are our offspring, DorLetha?”

“The four of them are over there in the nest.” The men looked down at what looked like three tiny owls and a cardinal chick. The cute little birds had hatched from one pound eggs. As they watched, they realized the horn wasn't being blown any longer.

“What was the horn for DorLetha?”

“That is the sound we are to make when a young male has arrived. It is suppose to call the parents. The long blast signals the birth of a male and the short blasts are for the females.”

“What if the male parent doesn't come?”

"The young would not be cared for! The horn has to be sounded until both parents are present when there is a male offspring."

"Does the female parent always come forth when they have female offspring?"

"Not always Delbert. If they have died, they can't."

"No wonder your populating is dwindling. Even the female chicks should be cared for. What if I wasn't here?"

"I guess we would continue to blow the long blast until we couldn't stand it any longer or until we changed the rule. Since we haven't had a male offspring before, we have never had that problem."

"How did you choose Esdra and Shida to blow the horn?"

"All the Kaydra tried to blow the horn. Only those that will become fertile soon can blow it. Esdra was the only one that could blow the long blast and Shida was the only one that could blow the three short blasts."

"I guess they are honored."

"Definitely! Since Esdra could blow the long blasts, she is supposed to have a male offspring too. She and Shida get to care for the new arrivals until they are able to transform themselves into their primary form. They just have the bird form now because that is the form I had when I became fertile. In six of your months, they will be able to change their form. Then we will see what their primary form will be."

"Hasn't Esdra kept her primary form since Adrian arrived?"

"Yes, Dell Bert. If she chooses Adrian, I wonder what changes will start taking place in her body soon and what her offspring will look like."

"Are some born and some hatched?"

"That's right Adrian, depending on their primary form. Would you be willing to help Esdra mate when her time comes, if she chooses you?"

"I don't know. Besides, I understand she will have plenty of males to choose from."

DorLetha changed the subject and made the announcement that they had named their son, Dell Britt, which meant 'Cheerful Way'. If he turned out to be fertile, he would be made king. They would have to name their daughters in the next few days. DorLetha would now be crowned Queen, because she has a son.

TetTrella was so angry she couldn't blow the horn that she left a greater afterglow than ever, when she made her disintegrative departure. DorLetha knew others would soon start telling TetTrella she was going to be sterile.

When DorLetha was crowned Queen, TetTrella immediately started making trouble. She urged her followers to have DorLetha show them more of what the people of Earth did. Since DorLetha couldn't locate Delbert's aura on Earth, she couldn't show them a mental telemetrical viewing of Earth and its male and female creature's activities.

The Kaydra following TetTrella outside the Crater insisted everyone start using their primary form so it was easy to see things they did. Even though the Matriarchal Directorate and the Queen told the Kaydra it wouldn't be good to use only their primary forms, since they hadn't done so for such a long time, they didn't listen to them. Some of the Kaydra really weren't prepared to hunt for food in their primary form. The 55 with the ape form that followed TetTrella definitely had the advantage over the others since they were vegetarians.

The Fem-Bird form, which Delbert called it, would need to hunt the scarce small game or find seeds to eat. If they didn't use their transmutative powers to change their form and feed themselves, they would die of starvation.

Hate, fear and dominance, which had been absent in all Kaydra, except TetTrella, was suddenly unleashed on the area outside the pleasant Crystal Prism Crater.

During the excitement of the early days of DorLetha's reign, the men had completely forgotten to tell her what TetTrella had been up to on the outside. They were busy trying to figure out what could be done to feed the 250 Kaydra remaining in the Crater. If they decided to keep their primary forms, they would consume much more food.

As a bird, Esdra ate a little every day. As a Fem-Bird she had to eat twice a day and eat much more. In fact, it appeared she would soon have to eat four times a day while she was caring for Delbert and DorLetha's offspring.

What had happened to Exvascia? It now had many of the problems that Earth had. Everyone had less space. The Kaydra started getting possessive. Outside the Crater there were fights over food. In their primary form, the Fem-Birds now disintegrated and disappeared for ever when they got too weak to regenerate.

As things grew worse, Delbert felt he had to have his own body back to help the other men handle the situation. One day, when his body on Earth had a strong aura, DorLetha was able to locate it and show Delbert a mental telemetrical viewing of Art and his activities. With Larry's help, Delbert became a part of the scene, via the soul flight method. Unfortunately, DorLetha's concentration was broken by a loud commotion in the Crater and Delbert was instantly retracted to Exvascia.

CHAPTER 6

ART IS REVEALED

Being in Delbert's body gave Art a good opportunity to look at his wife, Myrna. Their relationship had been severely strained before he had walked into the "Adralack Crack". Months earlier Myrna become upset when he said he wanted to walk into the shallow cave on Mt. Baker that was energized by an alien force. She thought he would be committing suicide. He had stomped out of the house and gone to see Carol who was just too beautiful and available to resist.

Nurse Liz was a lifesaver for Art in the early days of his return to Delbert's apartment. His speech was returning a little each day. Each time Myrna came Art would say he was tired and had to rest. Nurse Liz would help him into the bedroom so he could rest. Myrna knew Delbert was putting her off, but she didn't know why. Maybe his old problem had returned and he couldn't perform as a man again. If she could just get him away from his nurse for a short time, she could find out. She had to think of a way.

After Art's first week back in Delbert's apartment, Myrna stopped by to see him. "Hey Liz, would you mind if I took Delbert to visit my kids? They have been asking about him?"

"Sounds like a good idea. What do you say Delbert?" Art nodded. Liz and Myrna helped Art into the car

As they drove off, Myrna casually put her hand on his thigh and stroked it softly. He ignored her. Embarrassed, she assumed his old problem had returned. Instead, Art was thinking about seeing his son and daughter. He didn't care why they wanted to see their Uncle Delbert, as long as he got to see Lisa and Todd. The visit seemed way too short.

After taking Art home, Myrna decided not to see him for a few days. Delbert didn't seem himself around Todd and Lisa. He was too anxious to see them and wanted to love them too much. Sure, they enjoyed all the attention because they missed their dad, but what was he up to? Was Delbert just trying to impress her because he had often said he would be first in line to take care of her and the kids, if anything ever happened to Art? He didn't have to marry her if he didn't want to! It seemed strange that his previously strong affection for her never showed through. Was he injured more seriously than she believed? Couldn't he remember what they had shared before? She thought to herself, *Perhaps time will straighten things out.* That was the only hope she had. It was evident that Delbert wasn't going to be himself for some time to come, if ever.

When Art got back home after seeing his kids, he was both physically and psychologically tired. He asked Nurse Liz to help him into the tub for a bath before he went to bed. He started to bathe himself, but after a few minutes in the warm water he lost some of his ability to use his hands and arms.

"Nurse Liz, can you come help me? I can't use my hands and arms very well!" It was strange for Art to watch Nurse Liz bathing Delbert's body. How could Delbert's nude body not be responsive to this lovely nurse's touch? If it was his body, and a sweet person like her was handling it, he would be excited.

That was all Delbert's subconscious mind needed to know, that something was happening to it that he should be interested in and it responded.

"Delbert, you're certainly responding to me today. Don't blush! I know you can't help it and the bath was necessary;" She had to dry all of him, which didn't help to calm him down.

Art's looking at Delbert's excited body in the mirror didn't help either. Art wished he could function better in Delbert's body. When he got excited, he lost both mobility and control. As Nurse Liz put him in bed, he could tell she was enjoying her job and his embarrassment. Or else, why would she have given him an extra pat where she did before she pulled the covers over him and turned out the light?

As he lay there in the dark, he calmed down and started to get control of his hands and arms again. That was good for now, but he would have trouble getting them working again in the morning after sleeping all night.

Art didn't want to be helpless. When he awoke in the morning, he tried to imagine himself typing. After a few minutes he was able to get his hands and arms working. That was encouraging to him. The therapy session, which Nurse Liz directed him through, were more satisfying than he had expected. That meant his abilities were gradually increasing.

His speech was still slurred and jerky. Nurse Liz tried to keep him talking as much as she could. Since she was new to his country, it was easier to get him to talk about things than it would have been in a structured speech therapy session.

He really wanted to be Michael's best man. All he had to do was walk out with Michael, hand him the ring and then walk down the aisle with Myrna. That didn't seem like it should be impossible.

"Delbert would you like to go to the store with me before lunch?"

"Sure, Liz, I'd like to and I'd enjoy the ride." With his slow, slurred speech, it took him awhile to say that much. It was a normal, warm, wet day in Oregon. It would be another two months before winter arrived. Most years, snow only fell once or twice during the winter in small amounts and never stayed very long.

They arrived at the grocery store between showers. As Art shopped with Nurse Liz, he pushed the cart. It gave him something to lean on. Nurse Liz would leave him now and then to get things and bring them back to the cart. That allowed Art to participate in the shopping without walking a lot.

He was surprised by the foods his hands would reach out and grab every once in awhile. All he knew was that Delbert's body seemed to like the things he and Nurse Liz were picking out.

They were almost finished going through the checkout stand when Trudy walked in. "Hi, Delbert. Will you be home this afternoon? I thought I might stop by about three o'clock and go on your walk with you. Would that be OK?"

"Sure, I'd enjoy that. I'll see you later."

After lunch, Art took a nap. His afternoon walk was important for his recovery. He could walk a mile now, but it took him quite a while to walk that distance. Maybe with Trudy's company he could force himself to speed up.

Trudy showed up at 3:00 p.m. and Nurse Liz helped Art into his coat and handed his umbrella to Trudy. "If it starts to rain, you'll have to hold the umbrella for the two of you. It's best if you interlock your arm with his to help stabilize him when you walk. He'll let you know if he wants to go any faster than a slow walk. Don't try to go too far, Delbert! I'll expect you back in half an hour or so."

"OK, Nurse Liz. I'll hurry!" With that remark Art opened the door for Trudy and they were gone. He thought this would be a good time to try and get some information out of Trudy about her and Delbert's past. He thought to himself. *If I can get her thinking about us, maybe I can read her mind.*

"Trudy, I'm having some problem remembering our relationship prior to my stroke. Can you fill me in on some of the details?"

It was obvious to Art that he had caught her off guard. He immediately tuned in on her thoughts. There they were, as clear as day, the full details of their past. She had just used Delbert to make Dick, her sometime lover, jealous. She had forced herself on Delbert and he had behaved just as she had wanted him to. He had dated her a lot for several months, but she had never been able to get him to sleep with her.

Dick had dropped her for good and she was trying to get Delbert interested in her again. Now that he knew what she was thinking he wondered what she would say? "Well, we were dating regularly before you were hurt. You seemed interested in me and I wanted to see if you had changed your mind about us. I know you're going to get better, but I couldn't wait that long to be around you again. I really like you." She gave his arm an extra squeeze against her breast as she said it. He appreciated that and the fact that her arm wrapped around his bicep gave him stability.

"I hope I get better soon. I sure don't talk very good."

"I don't care, Delbert. You go ahead and talk and don't be embarrassed. I understand. You're lucky to be alive! You're doing pretty well with your walking though."

"Thanks. I need all the encouragement I can get." Art could tell she was lonely and needed someone. He wasn't sure it should be him, but he'd love her until someone else came along to replace him. Back at his front door, he held her in his arms and gave her a kiss before he opened the door and they entered his apartment.

"How did he do, Trudy?"

"Not bad, Liz, he seemed much more stable on his feet today."

"If you're going to stay for a while, Trudy, I could go pay some bills for Delbert." She knew when three was a crowd! Besides it was 3:40 p.m. what trouble could they get into? It wasn't any of her business what Delbert and his lady friends did.

"Fine, I'll be here until five o'clock."

"OK. I'll see you at five, Delbert."

Trudy helped him take off his coat and they walked over to the sofa and sat down close together. Art got the urge to put his arm around the lovely lady, but couldn't quite make it. Rather than that he settled for turning toward her and putting his hand on hers on her knee. He leaned his head against hers as he spoke. "Thanks for coming over and going for a walk with me. That was nice of you."

"Well, I enjoyed it. I really didn't have anything to do."

Art turned more towards her and kissed her on the cheek. He could sense her excitement growing. In her mind she was urging him on. Art would have been glad to oblige her. At 33, she needed all the loving she could get. Art could tell from her thoughts that she wasn't satisfied yet. He wished he could operate Delbert's body much better. Her hand on his leg had stimulated his aroused condition. They were decent when Liz returned, having done nothing more than a little light petting.

Trudy prepared to leave as Liz arrived. “I'll call you in a couple days, Delbert. Take care of yourself.”

Art was glad Trudy had stopped by. It gave him a chance to compare her with Myrna. Why had he started looking at other women during the past year? Myrna was more intelligent than most and better looking. Besides having a beautiful body, she was downright sexy with him. He thought of the time they had spent together in Denver. She was very sexy one evening there

He now wondered about the relationship between his wife and Delbert. Had it always been as innocent as he had thought? How long had it been since he had given her the attention he had just given Trudy? Would she respond any differently? Maybe he should try it as Delbert and see what happened.

On the Sunday afternoon before Gail and Michael's wedding, Art called Myrna and asked if she would like to go out for dinner.

“Do you think you're up to it? Why don't I pick you up around 6:00 p.m. and we can have dinner at my place. We can just sit in front of the fireplace and talk and relax. If we go out, we might run into someone we know. You know how difficult that is yet.”

“OK, Myrna.”

“Would you mind if the kids aren't there?”

“That's fine with me. I would really like to talk with you alone.”

“Good, I'll see you later.”

Art thought to himself. *If I'm Delbert, and look at Myrna as my special friend, perhaps I'll see her differently.* Could he use Delbert's subconscious level of thinking? He must try.

When Myrna picked him up, Nurse Liz reminded her, “be sure you bring him home before he gets too tired.”

“Thanks, Liz, we shouldn't be too late.” It seemed strange for Art to approach his own home as Delbert. He just had to be Delbert, think like Delbert and say the things Delbert would. He made his way slowly to the front door, determined to relax and let Delbert be Delbert. As he turned his conscious thinking over to observing the operation of Delbert's subconscious level, he felt as though he was outside Delbert's body and observing all it did.

Myrna opened the door for him. As they entered the house, he could feel the excitement surge in Delbert's chest. He turned and looked at Myrna, his very special friend. “How's my favorite girl?” that was an old familiar line Art had heard many times before. The kiss on the cheek was necessary because it was always there when they greeted. When they embraces, her beautiful figure pressed against him and sent a wonderful feeling through Delbert's body. Art thought to himself. *That kiss was more than just, hello. Look at her!* Through Delbert's eyes she was beautiful. Her light brown eyes and beautiful brown hair were lovely to look at. *Besides that, she loves me*"

Art watched and enjoyed again the love he thought only he had known, but now he was enjoying it as someone else. When he was alive, Delbert had been their best friend, but she was still his wife. *I got back out of the crack because I didn't want to lose her. Now I have lost her, but how can I lose to myself? The feeling this body feels are Delbert's feelings, but they are mine too. I've got to tell her that I'm in Delbert's body! But, but, how can I tell her? She'll think I'm crazy.*

Delbert was talking, saying the very things he would tell a beautiful lady, "Myrna, you're beautiful! I love you. I've missed you!"

Her only response was moist eyes and a strong embrace. Art could read her thoughts even though she didn't speak. *Delbert, I need you! My Art is gone. I loved him so! Why did he have to leave me? Oh, Delbert, I'm sorry you got hurt risking your life for me. Is there some way I can return all the love you've shown for me?*

It seemed normal to Myrna for Delbert's hug to become more firm as they stood locked in each other's embrace. As she shed a tear, somehow Art could tell there had been tears shed between them before. Myrna didn't know that Art's love for her had made Delbert's arms hold her tighter, or that the tears he shed were because he couldn't tell her who he was. "Myrna, Myrna, I love you." Another kiss and then another.

"Well Delbert, come on in and eat. I've made your favorite dish." Art could finally appreciate the fine cook his wife was and flourish her with the adjectives Delbert had always used. He knew now he would never again make love with either Trudy or Carol.

Art returned to Delbert's apartment that evening, determined to learn how to operate Delbert's body perfectly and to conquer the speech problem he had. His first big test would be that week. There was the wedding rehearsal and then the wedding itself. He was sure he could make it through his part in the wedding.

Gail made a lovely bride and Art (as Delbert), did his part perfectly. Carol noticed one thing as Delbert turned to walk down the aisle with Myrna, after Gail and Michael were pronounced man and wife; he lurched on his first step. He then straightened himself, unusually straight, and walked perfectly down the aisle.

After the wedding pictures were taken, Michael pulled Carol off to one side. “Carol I've left you a copy of the 12 pictures from Gail's camera that Adrian pulled back out of the Crack with his teletransporter. I think the pictures will tell you a little about where Larry has been the last two years. I left them by your purse in the room where the ladies changed their clothes. I'll see you later. Let me know what you think of the pictures.”

Dr. Darrell Lyons had accompanied Carol to Gail and Michael's wedding to see how Art would do as Delbert. Carol took Darrell's hand and pulled him into the room that Michael had mentioned. As Carol laid the pictures on the table she got the familiar, strange feeling she usually got when she was to receive a telepathic message. Darrell recognized the expression on Carol's face and felt her strong grasp of his hand.

“What's wrong Carol?”

“I feel like I'm going to get a message from Delbert, he's just about to enter the room!” As she spoke, the door opened. Before she could turn around, Delbert's body entered the room.

“Hi, Art, how are you feeling?”

“Darrell, that isn't Art, its Delbert.” Carol spun around and threw her arms around Delbert. “Delbert it's you! How can that be? Where's Art?”

“Carol I see you got a copy of the pictures Larry took inside the Crystal Prism Crater on Exvascia. I'm only here for a few seconds, so listen carefully. When I leave, Art will still be in my body. I don't have the power yet to switch us back into our bodies, but I need my own body back!

“You've got to get Art to go back up to the Crack in late June. We've really got some problems on Exvascia. I need you and Dr. Lyons to enter the Crack with Art. I'll trade him bodies and let him out so he and Myrna can be together again. I want you and Dr. Lyons to come to Exvascia with me for a while. Be sure he packs his bag with the most practical surgical items he can think of. Will you do it?”

“Delbert are you talking or communicating telepathically?”

“Sorry, Carol. It's telepathic. I may be jerked back to Exvascia at any second. Do you have any other questions?”

“Can you get us back to Earth safely?”

“I think so!”

“I'll find a way to get him there.” Carol said out loud, “Any special words for Art?” She stepped back from Delbert and looked at him.

“Yes, tell him not to lose Myrna!”

“Is Exvascia as pretty as the pictures?”

“Sometimes but things are so different. I've got a son and three daughters now. You'll get to see them when you get there.”

That was all Delbert got to say to Carol before DorLetha's concentration was broken and he was snatched back to Exvascia.

Carol asked a very startled Darrell. "Are you all right? Darrell! Come out of it!"

"I, I'm OK, Carol. Look at Art, I mean Delbert's body. It's all stooped over again. Did I ever have a strange feeling! Did I really hear all that Delbert said, in my head?"

"That's right, Darrell, except for that last statement."

"Carol you're going to have to tell me about your whole experience, not just what happened on Mt. Baker last time. Let's see if Art, I mean, Delbert, is OK."

"I'm ok, Doc. I'm just scared to death. I'm afraid when Delbert takes over his body like that he will just keep it. What does he want or need?"

"He wants you to return to the 'Adralack Crack' in late June so he can exchange bodies with you. He wants you to be whole again."

"What are you going to tell Myrna?"

"I don't know. Art. Oh, it's so hard not to call you Art. I must remember to call you Delbert or we'll have a lot of explaining to do. I can just see the trouble Myrna and you will have with your insurance company if your body shows up well and alive next summer."

"Help me to a chair! I don't need any extra trouble. How can I convince Myrna I'm not Delbert. When she looks at me, that's who she sees and when I speak that's who she hears."

"I don't know, Art. While I'm still living in Chicago, I can't help unless it's something I can accomplish on the phone. If you don't get anywhere when you try to tell her, you can always have her call me."

"OK, we had better get back to the action before someone notices we're gone."

Nurse Liz took Delbert home after the wedding reception. Even though it was early evening, he was very tired. Whenever Delbert took over his body, it totally wiped Art out. The fear and loss of control, besides being in limbo for a few minutes, was almost too much for him to handle.

Myrna had meant to get together with Carol while she was in town but it never happened. Carol and Dr. Lyons wanted to spend as much time together as possible and Myrna's son, Todd, got sick.

It wasn't until mid December that Myrna called Carol after another long evening alone with Delbert. Somehow it just wasn't her Delbert. "Hello Carol, this is Myrna! Sorry I didn't get to talk to you about Delbert while you were out."

"That's OK. I talked to him and he seems to be feeling better every day."

"I know that's what he says but he just isn't the same Delbert I loved before we went to Mt. Baker. He's different!"

"What do you mean, Myrna?"

"His mind seems to be mixed up and he can't remember his friends. Carol, you know he was my only hope after losing Art."

"Why don't you try to talk to him about it? You know a lot of strange things happened on that mountain last summer. Let me know if I can help."

"Thanks for talking with me Carol. I'll get back to you. Good-by."

The Christmas season wasn't the same for Myrna because Delbert's problems had become her problem. She didn't want to upset him until after the New Year. Perhaps he would get more of his memory back in another month.

Being Delbert was getting to be almost too much for Art. He didn't know all of Delbert's old friends. It helped, when he talked with people that both he and Delbert had known. To those people, he seemed to be doing very well.

His relationship with Myrna became more strained because she saw him with Trudy a couple more times. Art tried to get across to Trudy that he was really more interested in Myrna than her, but since Myrna never seemed to be around; she pressed Delbert for his attention. Being lovely and realizing his relationship with her would seem normal to his old friends, Art/Delbert couldn't turn her down. Besides, every time he tried to talk to Myrna about his condition, she turned everything he said around and he didn't get anywhere. Art finally spent enough time with Myrna, in late January, that Trudy stopped calling on him. That helped the situation but he still had to convince Myrna he was Art.

In early February the subject came up. "Myrna, I've got to talk to you. Do you notice anything different about me?"

"Like what, Delbert?"

"Like being different than I was before we went up to Mt. Baker the last time?"

"Yes, your memory seems to be gone."

"Do you know why?"

"Yes, you had a stroke."

"No I didn't"

"Oh, what happened to your speech and what about your paralysis?"

"It's all because of Larry."

"What does Larry have to do with it?"

"He wouldn't let my body back out of the Crack!"

"Delbert you never went into the Crack. Art did."

"No, I'm Art! Remember when Delbert fell down? I took his body."

"Delbert, you fell down when you had your stroke. Art walked into the 'Adralack Crack' of his own free will. You don't have to blame yourself for his death! You're Delbert Tinsley, just like you've always been. You don't have to pretend you're Art! I was there, I know what happened. I saw it all."

"But you didn't see my soul and spirit enter Delbert's body!"

"Delbert, I want you to cut this nonsense out! It's not good for you to blame yourself."

"I'm not blaming myself! I am Art!"

"Please, Delbert. If you're going to continue talking like this, I'll have to take you home. I can't take talking about Art and seeing you in this confused state at the same time."

"But I can prove I'm Art. Ask me anything!"

"Delbert, I know you and Art could read each other's minds. You probably know a lot of things about us that you shouldn't! Now stop talking about it or get your coat!"

"What difference does it make whether I'm your husband or lover?"

"Well, you're supposed to be my lover and I expect you to start acting like it. Now come over here, hold me and kiss me!"

Art did as she asked and he didn't regret it. She was a great lover and Delbert's body got excited from her touch. Art loved her, but he wished he could convince her who he was. Maybe he could get Dr. Lyons or Carol to talk to her for him.

The next day Art got a telephone call. "Hello Art, this is Dr. Lyons. I got your message to call. What can I do for you?"

"Thanks for calling, Dr. Lyons. I'm OK. I just needed to talk to you. You know what Delbert told you and Carol at the wedding awhile back. Well, I need someone to tell Myrna who I am. She thinks I'm crazy. If Delbert can pull off our body exchange in June so I'm Art again, do you know what a problem I'm going to have! I'll have to deal with the insurance company, social security and all kinds of reporters. Can you imagine the story they would make of someone coming back from the dead.

"Even my identification will be a problem. I can get by as Delbert now, because I look like him. In a year, though, I'll be out of money and not able to support myself. If I become Art again, I could use my real identity, if Myrna doesn't destroy all my personal identification.

"I won't be able to stay in Oregon no matter what happens. I've been thinking of going to Colorado and see if I can locate a mineral deposit. If I could, we could start a new life there. Since the Army kept how I died a secret that will help."

"Why do you think you could find a mineral deposit?"

"As a geologist, I know what to look for and where to look for it. Now I seem to have a special power to detect metal underground. It's as though my body is sending out a sonic wave. I can tell you where every water, sewer and gas line is in the city just by walking over the area. I seem to get a vibration and a strong feeling in my body. The stronger the feeling, the deeper the line is. The slower the vibration, the larger the line is."

"Art, I can't believe all that has happened to you four men as well as Carol and Myrna! I've just got to go to Exvascia. Let me see, I think I've got it! I'll call Myrna and tell her I've sensed some problems in your personality and that I need all the personal identification she has of yours. Everything from social security cards, driver's license, credit cards or anything else she has. I'll tell her I need them to convince you that you aren't Delbert."

"That's great! I can keep my old identity but I can't tell her who I am! I may have to get Delbert to explain things to her himself."

"I thought you said that when Delbert takes over your body you don't know what he says or does?"

"That's right! I just feel like I'm in limbo, whatever that is. It's all dark and silent for a time. I can't even tell how long he has been in control."

"You two sure make what us doctors know, about the body and mind, to be a joke. I'm sure not going to tell anybody about you! Everyone would think I'm crazier than you are. How can you get Delbert to contact Myrna?"

"Dr. Lyons, the first time he reentered his body was in the hospital when both Carol and Myrna were with me. This last time it was the same, except he talked to Carol when Myrna wasn't there. That must mean the aura of his body is stronger when Carol is around.

"I was thinking of going to Denver next month to see my old friend, Stewart Donovan. I may be able to convince him I'm Art. That might be one way to get Myrna to believe me."

"I'll talk to Myrna for you, but let me know if you come up with any other ideas; By the way, how are you feeling?"

"I'm able to talk better and do more with Delbert's body but I seem to get tired so easily. It's hard for me to wake up too. Do you have any idea how I could overcome that?"

"Are you kidding? I don't know what you're going through or what to do for you!"

"Thanks for calling, Doc. I'll see you later."

"Good-by Art."

Art tried to talk to Myrna about his double identity, but she wouldn't give his statements any serious consideration. It made Art so mad and frustrated that she thought he was losing his mind. To make it worse, Dr. Lyons called and confirmed her suspicions by asking for all Art's old identification. She was glad to give him everything he thought would help. Dr. Lyons asked her to go along with any wild ideas that Delbert had to convince her he was Art. He told her it might backfire and bring Delbert back to reality. Myrna agreed even though she didn't like to have Delbert pretending he was Art. She still loved Art very much even though he had been gone for six months and Delbert hadn't been in any shape to take care of himself or her.

When Art asked Myrna to go to Denver, she figured it was just another one of his schemes to play his mental game. *Well*, she thought to herself. *Two can play that game as well as one. He wants to stay in the same hotel where Art and I stayed last June, when we were there for the geologist convention. That's where Delbert had his vision of me nude; wondering if he would love me, if anything ever happen to Art. He knows all about that room, but he doesn't know that Art and I made love there. If he's going to play Art, then he is going to have to do everything Art did. If he makes love like Art does, with all his kinky demands, I'll know its Art, as if that could be possible. On the other hand, if he makes love with me like Delbert did twice before; I'll know he's Delbert!*

I think I'll see if I can pull a surprise on him. I'll see if Carol can come to Denver for a day or two. I'll get her the room next to ours. Maybe we can snap him out of his make-believe world.

Myrna contacted Carol and told her how schizophrenic Delbert was getting. When she asked Carol if she could make it to Denver for the weekend, she said she'd be happy to do anything to help.

"Hello Delbert, its Myrna. I'll go to Denver with you if you must go. I'm sorry it took me so long to make up my mind."

"That's OK. I'm glad you'll go with me. Are you sure you won't mind spending a few nights with me?"

"I think I'm ready if you are."

"Well, I can't promise you much in certain areas, but I still love you. Would you like to go to a concert in Portland Saturday evening?"

"Sure. I'll pick you up about 5:30 p.m. Love you!"

"Love you too! Bye Myrna."

Art enjoyed the concert and Myrna's company. It reminded him of the evening they had enjoyed at the concert in Denver the previous June, when he had attended a geologist conference as Dr. Arthur Noack, University

Geology Professor.

He remembered that trip, especially the results of Delbert and his long distance telepathic communication experiment. Delbert's ability to receive their thoughts had been greatly enhanced by the alien force he was exposed to at the "Adralack Crack."

He remembered how beautiful his wife, Myrna, had looked when they had gone dancing at a private social club in Denver. Would June ever get here so he could be reunited with his own body? Being Art in his own body would have its problems but they couldn't be any worse than what he was now facing. There would be no returning to his wife as Art unless Delbert could make the exchange happen.

Art planned his Denver trip carefully. He couldn't call Stewart because he wouldn't recognize Delbert's voice as Art. He wrote and told Stewart that he suffered a stroke and needed to talk with him about some things from the past to get his mind straightened out.

Clara Donovan answered Art's letter and said they would be glad to see him again and would help him any way they could. Art was happy to know that his friends were willing to help him. He didn't know how he could convince them that the stranger they would see before them was their old friend. He would obviously have to draw on the past for some experience that would hold up to their scrutiny. He didn't have any idea what that past experience would be but he would have to think of something profound in the next couple weeks. Their arrival at the end of March was already set. He couldn't back out; he needed to be Art again. He needed his wife Myrna's encouragement to walk back into the "Crack" and become whole again.

A week before their trip, while visiting Delbert, Myrna could sense the panic Art was experiencing. He was frantically searching for some past experience he could relate to Stewart. It would have to be something that had happened as much as ten years earlier, when they lived in the same city, to convince Stewart he was Art, no matter who he looked like.

"Relax Delbert, I mean Art. You'll think of something. Now you've got me calling you Art. I'll admit your personality lately has been more like Art's than Delbert's. He never did goof up like you could. I'd have thought when you took over a new body you'd lose some of your defects."

"Thanks a lot. Wait till you have to go through something like this! You'd probably pick up some defects too."

"You mean I don't have any defects?" It surprised her to hear Delbert say that. *How would he know whether I had any bad habits Art didn't like, he didn't know me that well. It was more like a statement Art would make.*

"In our marriage you've been perfect!"

"That's enough, Delbert! We've never been married. Art and I have, but not you and me! Now just stop talking foolish! I can't take any more of that today." Myrna stomped out of the apartment and slammed the door. There, he'd done it again, gone too far. If he wasn't careful, she wouldn't go to Denver with him.

With only a week to go before they left, he had to try to be more careful what he said. When Nurse Liz got back, she could see that Delbert was very upset. "Why don't you let me give you a good massage? Go strip down, wrap a towel around yourself and lie down on your therapy table. I'll be right in"

Liz's strong hands worked over his tense body, allowing it to relax. Art was able to temporarily forget his anxiety and fears. That was important because every time he got upset, he lost some ability to make Delbert's body function properly.

The massage relaxed his tense back and neck. "You should soon be able to do whatever you want to physically, Delbert." When she finished massaging his thighs, he had to agree with her. When she finished, he was totally relaxed. *I wonder if I will be able to function sexually in the future.*

The flight to Denver was uneventful. For the first time in his life, Art was glad to tip someone to take their luggage to their rental car and again from their rental car to their motel room.

After dinner, Art wanted to soak in the tub for awhile. Myrna used the time to go next door and talk with Carol who had already checked in. "I'm glad you could make it Carol. Delbert is possessed with the idea that he is Art! He's even starting to act like Art. After we get back from the Donovans, I'd like you to join us. If he can't convince Stewart he is his old friend, Art, I don't know what state of mind he'll be in!"

"Myrna, does Delbert seem to be his old self? Let me put it another way. Do the thoughts and action of the man with you act more like Delbert or Art?"

"He looks, sounds and functions like Delbert. How could he be anything else but Delbert?"

"I don't mean outwardly! Who is the inner man? Think about it with your eyes closed. Does he have the characteristics of the person we've been calling Delbert?" Carol could tell by the length of time it took Myrna to answer, that she wasn't sure who he was. The possibility that Art existed in Delbert's body appeared to be something she couldn't accept. "Wait until tomorrow when you, I and Delbert are all in the same area. Don't be surprised if something very strange happens, Myrna."

Myrna returned to her room and thought to herself. *Is Delbert really*

Delbert or is he Art? What did Carol mean when she said don't be surprised if something strange happens when the three of us are together? Myrna was quiet that evening and Art could understand why. He was upset himself. It even felt strange to be going to bed with his wife and/or lover that evening. He kissed her good night and went to sleep without making any sexual advances. Art fell asleep quickly. He had a big day ahead of him and needed rest for his tired body.

Myrna wasn't tired and couldn't go to sleep. She lie awake thinking of Delbert beside her and listening to his deep, peaceful breathing. He was sound asleep. When she was about to fall asleep around 2:00 a.m., Delbert's breathing changed and he became very restless. He rolled over toward her and whispered, "Myrna, its Delbert, are you awake?"

"Yes! Why don't you make love with me?"

"That's not why I'm here!"

"That doesn't make any difference! Make love with me and then we'll talk." After awhile she spoke again. "Oh, Delbert, I've never had it feel like that twice before without a rest period between. How can you do that when you are still so weak?"

"Oh, I'm not weak, Art is! That's what I wanted to talk to you about"

Myrna sat up startled and turned on the light. Delbert smiled as he viewed her beautiful naked form bathed in the light of the bedside lamp.

"Delbert, it's you!"

"Yes, Myrna. It's great to see you again. How have you been the last six months? I enjoyed the last few minutes. Are you OK?"

"You, you're here! You made love with me! How could you?"

"You told me to!"

"I know I did, but I didn't mean it."

"Well, why didn't you tell me to stop a half hour ago then?"

"I didn't know it was you, I thought it was the other Delbert."

"You mean you thought it was Art?"

"You aren't going to tell me you've been letting Art use your body are you?"

"Yes! He asked to borrow it when his disintegrated in the 'Adralack Crack' and he couldn't get it back. I couldn't leave you without anyone!"

"Delbert, what are you doing back now? How did you get back? How long are you going to stay?"

"I'm just back for a few minutes. DorLetha was able to locate the aura of my body which was made brighter because you and Carol are near Art. I wanted to tell you about Art being in my body. Also I want you to get him up to the 'Adralack Crack' in late June. If you can get him to walk into the 'Crack' a second time, I can trade him bodies and he'll be whole again. He'll be Art in Art's body. DorLetha makes it possible for my soul and spirit to reenter my body, when she can locate it from Exvascia."

"Prove to me you're Delbert!"

"That's a strange request but I guess you have the right to demand that. Get dressed quickly and I'll prove it to you. You don't need all your clothes, just your sweater, slacks, shoes and coat. I just need to take you outside for a few minutes and find a cat."

Outside, by the first garbage can, Delbert found a cat. He picked it up and held it up in front of his face with its head aimed down the alley. "Watch this!" Delbert's ears lobes glowed for a second and then his hands glowed.

Myrna stood looking at him holding the cat. The cat suddenly looked like a cat in a cartoon that had been scared to death by a dog. Its tail stuck straight back toward Delbert. Its feet stuck straight out in front of it and its fur stood on end. For a period of about five seconds a bright light shown from the Cat's eyes. The light was like two flashlights shining down the alley. When the light went out, the cat disintegrated into a million sparkling particles and was gone.

Delbert walked Myrna back to her hotel room. "Art won't know anything about this in the morning. He doesn't know anything that happens when I'm in my body. So, our secret is still our secret. You'll have to get him up to the 'Adralack Crack' for me in June. I'm counting on you. It's the only way I can give you your husband back."

"What about us, Delbert? I thought I wanted you?"

"I can't stay. I have a family now on Exvascia, by the alien, DorLetha. Don't worry. Art will be a one-woman man from now on."

"Delbert, you know I can't believe this dream." They got back into bed.

"It's too real to believe. Can you make love with me again before you go?"

"Yes, but then I've got to go. I'm sorry. I love you though." When Myrna was satisfied, she asked for a sign that she could see in the morning to know that the events of that night had happened.

"You know that mole by the scar on your lower stomach?"

"Yes!"

"It won't be there in the morning." With that Delbert kissed the mole, turned off the light, laid back down and went to sleep so that Art could have the use of his body again.

Delbert's kiss put Myrna to sleep instantly. When she awoke in the morning, she was upset because of the dream she thought she had. For some reason, she decided to check her mole. To her surprise, it was gone! There wasn't any doubt in her mind about what had happened during the night. The only question was who had taken advantage of whom?

She was too embarrassed to discuss what she thought had happened during the night with Art/Delbert.

After breakfast Delbert and Myrna headed for the Donovan's home. “Have you thought about what you are going to tell Stewart?”

“Not yet! I sure hope I can think of something, when I see him.”

“So do I Art.”

“Thanks for calling me that Myrna. I'm sorry I seem all confused to you. Carol says that Delbert can make me whole again, if I will walk back into the Crack in late June.”

Myrna couldn't believe her ears. *Was this the same Delbert, who had talked to her last night?* She would have to talk with Carol about Delbert's conversation when they got back to the hotel that afternoon or evening.

Both Myrna and Delbert were nervous when they reached the Donovan's home. Myrna would have to introduce Art, who was in Delbert's body because there wasn't any way the Donovans could recognize him.

When the doorbell rang, Clara answered. “Good morning, Myrna. Where's Art?”

“Clara, is that Art and Myrna?”

“It's Myrna and a friend, dear.”

“Good morning Clara.” Myrna walked toward the living room where Stewart was. Good morning, Stewart. I don't know how to say this but this is my husband Art.”

It would be an understatement to say the Donovans were flabbergasted. Stewart managed to speak first. “Myrna, you don't expect us to understand your little joke, do you?”

“May we sit down?”

“Forgive me, please do.” Stewart motioned for them to sit down. He was still too stunned to even offer to shake Art's hand. Art didn't help at all. He was too excited to even speak. He wanted to throw his arms around his dear, old friends, but he couldn't since neither of them recognized him.

“I'll try to fill you in on what happened. Art and this person, Delbert, and another friend climbed Mt. Baker last August. I was one of three women who accompanied them. On the mountain Art stepped into a shallow cave. When he did, his body disintegrated. This person walked up to the front of the same shallow cave but he fell down instead of stepping into it. A doctor who was along said he had no pulse. A few seconds later, this person got up and stated to walk into the shallow cave again. Another woman and I pulled him back. He fell down again and appeared to have had a massive stroke. He was in the hospital for two and a half months

"Now, Art tells me that his soul, spirit and conscious mind entered Delbert's body, when Delbert fell down. Art says that Delbert's soul, spirit and conscious mind entered the cave and took over his body."

Stewart just sat there in disbelief. Clara stood up and asked "Would anyone like a cup of coffee?"

Myrna answered, while Art just nodded. When Clara returned with a tray with four cups of coffee, sugar, cream and coffee cake, Stewart spoke. "Why don't you go on Myrna?"

"I can't say I believe Delbert here is Art, but he keeps insisting he is. I do notice that this Delbert can't remember things and people he should and his character has changed slightly. When he gets excited, he can't speak or walk very well or use his arms as he should.

"He thinks he can convince you that he is Art, if he can think of something that only the two of you would remember."

"Well, uh, Art, this has got to be the weirdest thing you've ever done. What do you have to say for yourself? Can you think of anything that happened to the two of us, say ten years ago?"

"I, I ca can't th think of of any anything yet. I'm, I'm too excited to even make Delbert's body talk. You'll give me a chance though won't you, Stewart? Please!"

"Calm down, Art. I said I'd help you and I will. Just relax. You should be able to think of something that was exceptional. You were always catching me at making mistakes or saying profound statements. Just think back to all the things we did while we were prospecting. How long has he been walking and talking, Myrna?"

"Just since mid November and then he needs constant company of a nurse because sometimes he can't function properly. He gets tired very easily, too."

Stewart couldn't believe what he had heard but he would do anything for his friend Art. He walked over to Art and put his hand on Art's shoulder. "Why don't you stand up Art, if you can, and look at some of the old photographs I have around the room?"

Art needed Stewarts help to get up and get started walking. Stewart guided him around the room from picture to picture. Back at his seat, Art used a shaky hand to take hold of his coffee cup for a big drink. He slowly began to speak. "I think I have something, Stewart. Ten years ago three men stood on the snowy banks of the ice laden Colorado River and talked. There was Aaron Day, you and me. You said, 'So the tailor must sew, so the reaper must reap. Whatever happens to you on this Earth, never forget who you are.' That's exactly what I'm trying to do, Stewart, remember who I am."

The startled look on Stewart's face caused the hair to rise on Clara's arms and cold chills to go up and down her back. "What's wrong, Stewart?"

Stewart didn't seem to hear Clara. He was staring at Art who had stood up. He then startled Myrna with his question. "Art, is that you, really you?"

"Yeah, Dirt Ball, it's really me!"

Stewart gave him a big hug and Clara got a big smile on her face. "Dirt Ball" was what Art had always called Stewart when they had gone prospecting, because he always managed to get dirty from head to toe. She hadn't heard that name for a long time.

"But, but, Delbert, I mean Art, I er, uh, read about what happened to you in the newspaper! How can this be?"

"We were doing an experiment with a revolutionary new teletransporter device a scientist friend of mine had made for the Army and they wouldn't let us tell anything that happened."

"I would guess not! Are you stuck in that body forever?"

"No, if you can believe it! Delbert will trade me bodies in June in that same cave on Mt. Baker. He has been taken to another planet, Exvascia, by an alien force for a visit. The visit to Exvascia is necessary for him to see his offspring after mating with one of their life forms. It seems they don't have any males on their planet and have to look elsewhere for them. She just happened to choose him. Their power source activated the shallow cave or 'Crack' as we call it.

"Inside the 'Crack' I got scared and wanted out. At the time all Delbert and I could think of was to change bodies so we did. Now he can come back at times and take over his body. When he does, I don't know what happens. He has to tell someone else what he wants me to do. It's scary.

"If we can make the exchange in June, I'd be the happiest man in the world. Have you noticed how my speech has improved since I got started talking? I'll be able to get around fine now that I am not as excited.

"What I wanted to talk to you about was making a living once I get my body back. We'll have to move from where we live. There are other problems like the life insurance payment that has already been paid, social security death benefits and other things to deal with. Also, millions of people would like to know what it's like to come back from the dead but I haven't been dead."

"What do you have in mind?"

“If I could find more silver than you ever dreamed of, could you use a third partner in your firm?”

“Of course, there isn't any way the two of us could run a larger operation. If you could do that, it would be like finding the pot of gold at the end of the rainbow.”

“Since the exposure to the Alien power beam in the cave, I can feel metal under my feet. I kind of feel a vibration in my body.” Art spoke as he moved around the room. “For instance, there is a pipe below me now. It feels like it is deep. Since there is a slower vibration, it must be the sewer line. The gas line is probably located over here. This pipe over here must be the water line.”

“You're right on all three, Art. I'll tell you what. My partner is out of town for a week and I have to be out at the mine tomorrow. Would you like to go there and do a little prospecting? If you can find ore of any quality or quantity I could make you a partner and you wouldn't have to meet my partner until you get back to being yourself. That way we wouldn't have to explain all these unbelievable things to him.”

“That sounds great, Stewart.”

“What do you think about all this Myrna?”

“I don't know. It's all difficult to accept or believe. I was just starting to get used to dealing with Art being dead. Now, Delbert, I mean, Art, says he is coming back. It means that, if he does get back to being himself, we have to sell our home and forget our past and friends. That would be very stressful!”

Clara walked over to Myrna and comforted her. “We'll be here to help you! If Art can locate ore, there would never be any worry about money. He could stake several claims in case his gift disappears, when he is his old self again!”

“Thanks, Clara. I'll need all the friends I can make as soon as possible. I can't wait until Art is his old self again. I just can't handle his being two people at the same time!”

“Myrna, if Art and I go prospecting for a few days, would you like to stay here?”

“I have a friend in town now but when she leaves tomorrow night, I'd be alone. I could bring all our things over the day after she is gone.”

“That sounds good to me.” Clara remarked.

“Who's your friend in town?”

“It's Carol, Art. I didn't believe it was you. I still thought it was just Delbert being schizophrenic because of guilt and stress over your death. What else could I think?”

“I think it's unbelievable, Myrna.”

"You're both right Clara. I couldn't believe what had happened myself, when I got out of that alien powered cave the way I did. I love you, Myrna, I couldn't leave you." Art took Myrna by the hand and helped her from the sofa and held her close while she put her head on his shoulder and wept.

"Carol was contacted by Delbert, through me, at Gail's wedding. Dr. Lyons was there also. That's how I know I can get my body back in late June, if I can make it back to the 'Adralack Crack'."

Myrna didn't say anything about Delbert's conversation with her the previous evening but she thought about it. *Now Delbert and I have another secret to share and it shows that he's still looking out for me.* Myrna and Art went back to the hotel and spent the rest of the evening with Carol.

The next morning Stewart and Art headed for the mine to see if Art could demonstrate his newly discovered power.

Chapter 7

The Comet

While Art struggled in Delbert's body and tried to get a new life started, Exvascia was in turmoil. TetTrella was trying to snatch power from the hands of both, the newly crowned Queen, DorLetha, and the old Matriarchal Directorate. She had convinced 100 of the Kaydra, 45 of the Fem-Bird form and 55 of the ape form, to leave the safety of the Crater and coexist outside in her kingdom, in their primary form.

Her goal was to kill off the entire population of Fem-Birds outside the Crater. Without using their transmutative power to change their form for hunting, the Fem-Birds would have to suddenly become vegetarians. Their lack of experience as vegetarians would cause them to become weak from not eating enough of the proper food. Because of their strong will she knew they would try to exist as long as they could without using their transmutative powers. If they took on a transmutative form to kill game and were too weak to change back to their primary form, they would be gone forever when they tried to regenerate.

Adrian and Delbert had quickly figured out what TetTrella's plan was. If it hadn't been for them, probably more of the population would have gone outside with TetTrella. It wasn't fair for the Fem-Bird form Kaydra to compete with the vegetarian ape form Kaydra. However, TetTrella goaded them into it.

The Kaydra that stayed in the Crater were mostly of the Fem-Bird primary form. When they decided to stay inside, they also agreed to stay in a smaller transmutative form to conserve food. Only with special permission could they continue in their primary form, for any length of time. Those who stayed were older and understood better what TetTrella was trying to do.

The Kaydra, that went outside could come back in whenever they were willing to use a smaller transmutative form. DorLetha was concerned about the slow power build up in the transmitter station, so she kept an eye on what TetTrella was doing. She found out TetTrella was no longer satisfied with mental telemetrical viewing. She had started using the power supply to make physical visits to planets in her primary form.

On TetTrella's return from her second such adventure; she was confronted by DorLetha and the Matriarchal Directorate. “TetTrella, I have called you before our leaders to have you explain your unauthorized use of power to make forbidden trips to other planets.”

“I've been looking for suitable males to bring back for the female apes on the outside. We need males to stimulate the activities of our society and to bring about an increase in our population.”

The oldest of the Matriarchal Directorate, who had been the chairperson, spoke. “TetTrella you have grossly misused your position as controller of the solar reflectors. Our first trip to another planet was to have been to Earth to get the Queen's mate back into his own body. Because of your use of reserve power, we cannot do that now for some time. We may have to convert more of our water into hydrogen and oxygen for enough power for him to make the trip. If we run into a comet in our trip through space and can't disintegrate it first, our hyperatmospheric force field may be penetrated and our planet bombarded with meteors. Our entire existence on this planet could be threatened and our population wiped out forever. We can't waste our power reserves.

“You are sterile. You know it and we know it so you don't need a mate. You also know that other females cannot mate unless they are fertile and until their time comes. Therefore, males are of no use to us here. They would only consume our valuable resources of food and oxygen. Do you deny the charges I have stated?”

“No, why should I? If we don't get males up here and find some way for more of us to mate, we'll all soon be dead. Why should DorLetha have her mate here and his two friends?”

“We haven't decided they can stay. They are here temporarily until we can get her mate reunited with his body. We cannot allow him to remain in this forbidden state whether it was our fault or his. He doesn't desire it and we don't either. It was, and we will admit it, a mistake on our part to underestimate the Earth creature Larry. No one before has ever wanted to stay on our planet, much less, return with others.”

“Well, you aren't doing anything to increase our population!”

“That brings up another matter. You have turned to your own design, the use of the solar reflector so that the vegetation outside is increasing rapidly.”

“We need more food to live in our primary form outside!”

“We didn't make a decision to have any of our population live outside where it is unsafe. They could be hit by lightning or meteorites, killed by wild animals or carnivorous plants."

"That's the chances you take if you want to live outside in your primary form."

"That decision is not the right of one Kaydra to make, TetTrella."

"Well, I made it so what are you going to do about it?"

"Because of your impertinent, impetuous acts and flagrant lack of consideration of the entire population, we are taking away your duties and banning you from ever entering the Crystal Prism Crater again. No action will be taken at this time against those who joined you. As far as we know, none of them knew anything of your plans and only followed you because of your belligerent use of power against those of us in authority.

"We are hereby appointing, with the consent of the Queen, DaKeta as controller of the solar reflector station."

"You can't control my actions outside the Crater. I'll find a way to get back at all of you and the Kaydra that live in the Crater."

As Larry stood listening to the hostile exchange between the Matriarchal Directorate and TetTrella, he couldn't help but comment, "Fellas, I think they just made their first big mistake since they have been on this planet."

"Why is that, Larry?"

"TetTrella is both jealous and zealous. If anyone can find a way to grab power it'll be TetTrella. We'll have to wait and see what happens."

"Since 100 of the Kaydra were going to try living outside, it was decided that the solar reflector should continue to be aimed on the vegetation outside the Crater as long as possible each day. The temperature inside the Crater was again increased to about 78 degrees during the day.

In late December, about three weeks after TetTrella was replaced as solar reflector controller by DaKeta, DorLetha was talking to the three men. "The power supplies are almost ready to power the transmitter beam to reactivate the 'Crack'. Is there any possibility that Art could get to it at this time of the year?"

"No DorLetha, not for 145 more of your days." Delbert's voice was interrupted by a flash of light across the night sky. "What was that, DorLetha?"

DorLetha closed her eyes and concentrated for a few seconds. She was telepathically communicating with the controller of the transmitter power station. "It's a comet crossing our path!"

"What does that mean?"

"We'll have to use our power reserve to blast our way through the comet's tail."

"With your power reserves so marginal, can you do that?"

"We have to try. There isn't any way we can power the hyperatmospheric force field so that it would withstand hitting the comets tail full force. The force field would be short circuited and the meteorites would come right through our atmosphere!"

Adrian made an observation. "If your force field is destroyed, most of those meteorites will hit Exvascia and there isn't a dense enough atmosphere outside to burn them up."

"That's right Adrian. I've got to get the Matriarchal Directorate working on this problem on a crisis basis." DorLetha closed her eyes and concentrated. A few seconds later she was ready to talk.

"We haven't had a real test of our force field for some time. Each of the Directorates will work on her special area. One of them will direct the use of power, another will take over the transmitter power station and a third will take control of the solar reflector. They will try supplementing the transmitter power station's power supply when it tries to blast us a path through the comet's tail.

"The problem of going through a comet's tail is that it is moving. You can't just blast a hole and go through it. You have to blast several times as you go through it. If we're lucky, the last few meteorites, that we can't blast away, will be destroyed by the hyperatmospheric force field.

"Another Directorate will take control of the hyperatmospheric force field. She will turn it off for as long as possible to conserve energy. Another will start the process of separating hydrogen and oxygen from our sea. That will help some. Another Directorate will be responsible for the force field that protects the Crater's Crystal Prism. Another will make the telemetrical calculations to be used for our power blasts against the comet. We'll have to try to convince those outside to come into the Crater."

Adrian shook his head. "Sounds like it will take everyone's best efforts to get us through this. Can we help?"

"Adrian, why don't I send you to the transmitter power station? It's from there that we'll do the comet blasting. Maybe you can give them some ideas as to what to do even if you don't understand the equipment. I can tell, from the teletransporter you made on Earth, that you understand our basic principles. Dell Bert and Larry can stay with me."

In an instant Adrian was gone. The planet felt like the brakes were put on for a second. "What's that?"

"That's the first blast of power, Dell Bert. They'll have to calculate the power of the next blast by the size of the hole made in the comet's tail."

"DorLetha, is there some way we can see what's going on out there?"

"Yes Larry, I'll let you see it by mental telemetrical viewing. How's that view?"

"Great view but I have never seen a comet this close-up before."

"We have always been able to blast our way through before."

"Is Adrian seeing the same view from where he is?"

"Yes. Why?"

"Can you find out how much power we have for future blasts?"

"Yes Larry." One of the Directorates was monitoring DorLetha's thought waves and all three men were linked telepathically with her.

"Hey fellas, think quick." Adrian suggested. "See how little damage we did to that comet's tail. We only have enough power for three more blasts that size."

"Will that get us through it, Adrian?"

"According to our best calculations, Delbert, we don't have enough power to blast through but they want to try. The creative right side of my brain says there has to be another way. Larry, what do you think they should do?"

"I suggest they fire the blast at such an angle that a hole will be formed in the tail that will be directly ahead of us when we get to the spot where we would otherwise collide with it. If the hole we blast isn't quite right as we start to enter it, we can fire another blast at point blank range. Whatever power is left then would be diverted to the hyperatmospheric force field."

Adrian suggested leaving the force field off until just before the second blast. "I think we'll need more protection between the first and second blast and after we pass through the comet's tail. We also need to keep producing all the power we can as we go along."

The Directorate followed the plan of the three men. They hadn't had to deal with such a big problem with so little power for such a long time that they weren't confident with their usual solution. The men's approach to the problem seemed logical. DorLetha was amazed at the speed with which the men made their decisions.

"Move the solar reflector quickly!" Larry's timing of a big meteorites collision with the reflector satellite was correct but the response of the Directorate controlling the solar reflector was too slow.

"Half of the solar reflector's power is out, Larry. Do you think we should fire one final blast using all available power?"

Larry responded, "DorLetha, when the time is right, fire one final blast?" While the Directorate staff was making the calculations, the meteorites continued to bombard the planet.

"Activate the force field before everyone on the outside is killed!" DorLetha's command was carried out immediately. The flashes across the prism of the darkened Crater stopped.

"Adrian, be sure they take into consideration our slowed speed because of the blast."

"OK. Hang on, here goes the blast." The planet acted as if the brakes had been slammed on for a tenth of a second. Adrian's warning didn't prepare the men for the jolt they took. Picking themselves up, they continued to view the hole that lay ahead like a black hole in a steak of light. As they traveled through the hole, the Directorate responsible for hydrogen production was busy. All the fuel, that was being produced and what was available, was directed to the force field. Even though the solar reflector was half gone it could still use the brightness of the comet outside the black tunnel to produce additional power.

"Feels like a smooth ride, Larry."

"Right, Delbert but we aren't through yet."

"Adrian, any idea whether we'll be able to get through the comet's tail before our hole runs out?"

"I don't think we're going to make it!"

"Do you think the force field will hold up at the end?"

"Probably not Larry, I think we are going to have to endure another meteorite shower.

"Did everyone make it in from the outside?"

"No, Adrian. I understand TetTrella and a few others are missing."

"Any idea what happened to her, DorLetha?"

"She probably used what power she had stored to physically visit another planet. She could have left when the force field was down. That would have taken less power. Don't worry, she's resourceful. She'll be OK."

"DorLetha how long will it take to get our force field back into operation and the solar reflector repaired?"

"It will take some time, Dell Bert. We haven't had to make major repairs like this for a long time."

"Larry, any idea how to make the air supply last longer and how to keep the plants warm and alive in the Crater?"

"The Crater should stay warm for quite some time. We need to block some of the air inlets and outlets. If it gets too cold, there will be permanent damage to the plants.

"You and Adrian will have to endure some cryogenics until the operation is over. Let's get down there as soon as we get through the comet's tail and see how much damage there is."

"Why are you so concerned and planning already, Dell Bert?"

"We want to stay alive, DorLetha. What about the Kaydra? What can they do to help?"

"First we'll need our atmospheric force field activated. Once we get that into operation we can shut off the Crystal Prism force field. Then we'll have to repair the solar reflector. If the transmitter power station is operational and we have any hydrogen fuel left, we can send a burst of light at the Crystal Prism Crater every once in awhile. We can keep it from losing all its heat that way."

"Is there anything else?"

"We need the entire population to use the smallest animal or insect form they can think of. That will save food and oxygen. They can still combine their mental powers telepathically for the power we need to make repairs. We need to be careful not to let them use so much of their mental power that they can't make it back from transmutative disintegration and die. I'm afraid we lost a lot of those that were outside the Crater, but we couldn't make them come in when they refused our explanation of how desperate the situation was."

"Will Adrian and I be able to function without a body, Larry?"

"Yes, Delbert, it's just like being in transition during disintegration or being in a dream where you aren't aware of having a form, but are somewhere. We'll be able to continue our telepathic communication as we are now."

After a few minutes, they were at the end of their hole. "We're going to be on our shields alone soon. When you start seeing flashes of light through the Crystal Prism, that means the force field is gone and we're no longer shielded from the meteorite showers. Remember, the Crater will still be dark when we get out of the comet's tail.

"There's the first flash, Delbert. The force field is gone already. Look at the fireworks display. If it lasts long, there won't be anything left outside." Fortunately, the bumpy ride and the fireworks only lasted for a couple seconds.

"Are we through?"

"Yes Delbert," Adrian was relieved to say.

"I'll switch my viewing to the outside now." DorLetha stated. "There is a lot of damage to the plants and animals. What we can save out there will depend on the length of time it takes to repair the solar reflector satellite Adrian." The mental telemetrical viewing was gone as soon as DorLetha stopped her concentrating. She then sent them all back to the Crater floor. "Both of you go with Larry to the cool cave. He'll show you how to obtain soul flight."

"DorLetha, could Adrian spend time with DaKeta in soul flight on the repair of the solar reflector?"

"Yes Larry. She's our best technician next to Esdra. I'll get someone to assist Shida with the new arrivals and Esdra can go with you."

"What should I do, DorLetha?"

Larry spoke up before DorLetha could answer. "Why don't I keep my form and have Delbert go outside with me? Maybe, we can save more Kaydra lives as well as some of the animals."

"That's fine with me. I'll check with you every once in awhile to see how you are doing."

"Let's go, fellas. The sooner we get to the cool cave, the sooner we can get to work." Larry led his friends into the cool cave after first stopping to get additional furs to keep warm while he was instructing the others in cryogenics. Once they were nearly frozen, they were able to let their soul and spirit out of their bodies and travel anywhere on Exvascia they wanted.

Adrian joined Esdra and DaKeta as soon as he could. The equipment they had on Exvascia was miraculous and super efficient. The right side of Adrian's brain, the creative side, had an absolute ball seeing all the equipment and how it worked.

Delbert and Larry soon reached the outside. Delbert could get there just by thinking he was there. Larry disintegrated himself to go through the side of the Crater. He couldn't take the time to lumber through the tunnels on foot. He didn't feel that would be the best use of his time and energy. "Delbert see that fletch, or herd of Mardi goats?"

"Yes, I can see them. Wait, how can I see them? I'm not in my body."

"You're really in telepathic communication with them. If you can find the leader, you can mentally steer it back through the tunnels and the others will follow."

To Delbert's surprise, he could do everything Larry said he could. In a few minutes he was back with Larry. By calling out to the Kaydra, Larry was able to locate a few more and convince them to forget the use of just their primary form and return to the safety of the Crater.

Some may have taken the form of animals in terror or an effort to get to the Crater or other possible shelter during the meteorite shower and been killed. There wasn't any way for them to tell if a dead animal was really an animal or a Kaydra.

Larry didn't know exactly what the Exvascians could or would do during an emergency. For that reason, he took all the injured animals that he could find back to the Crater with him.

The air outside the Crater was polluted from the meteorite showers. Larry was glad he had brought his Mardi goat air bag. By the time he and Delbert got all the animals in the Crater tunnel, his extra air supply was gone. Larry used his spark stones to light the oil shale lamps.

When Larry emerged from the phosphorescent tunnel, the Crater was totally dark. DorLetha met them at the crater entrance. "Larry, why have you brought all these animals in here? Don't you know they will use up some of the oxygen and food supply?"

"Yes, but we'll need them to keep the animal population stable. Is there some way you can get their injuries to heal faster?"

"Yes, we know how to stimulate skin and bone tissue so that it regenerates itself. I'll have a Kaydra, who is interested in that type of thing, attend them."

Larry lit one of the bowls of oil shale so there was light in the area. A Kaydra changed to her primary Fem-Bird form and approached. "What can I do for you?"

"Can you heal the injuries these animals have? Some have cuts, loss of blood and broken bones?"

"I'll work with them to regenerate their bodies." The Kaydra held the animal's head that she was trying to help and looked into its eyes. Telepathically she talked to the animal and told it where it needed to apply its recuperative powers. In just a few minutes, each was cured.

"We should tell Adrian about her. I think he has a few physical problems he would like to have corrected."

"Could you help heal the problems of one of my friend's body, even if they are old injuries?"

"If he wants them renewed we can make that happen. Have him ask for me when he is ready to be whole again and I'll come."

"What's your name?"

"I'm called I'La."

"Thanks for your help, I'La. When Exvascia is back to normal, he'll ask for your help."

"Larry, how long do you think the Crater will hold its heat?"

"It will hold it much longer if we can use animal skins to block off some of the crater's entrances. You know those branches we piled up a while back, when TetTrella cut down trees and made boards for us?"

"Yes."

"Why don't you get them and meet me here. I'll get the animal skins."

"How do I do that?"

"It's all in your mind Delbert. Think yourself there, and then talk to the pile of branches with your mind. Tell it to rise. If you think it can be done, it will happen. Then tell it to move. All you have to do then is think it along with your mind to wherever you want it to be."

"OK!" Without a body, Delbert was able to get from one place to another instantly. He found what Larry had said was true. There didn't seem to be any limitation to the loads he could move. The more he concentrated on a problem, the greater the amount of energy his mind could emit.

Several of the Crater openings were semi sealed off before Larry ran out of skins. When they finished their projects, Larry returned to the cave to sleep. Since Delbert didn't need to sleep he decided to join Adrian.

"How are the repairs going Adrian?"

"It's going to take several days, Delbert, to get the transmitter power station operational. While we're working on it, they are storing the hydrogen fuel they are making from the sea water. As soon as it is ready, they can use it for power to activate the atmospheric force field. If we run into anything big out here in space, before its ready, we'll have to take our lumps. When the force field is activated, the planet will have more protection.

"If we have any reason to use a blast of power, we'll have to shut off the force field. Of course, we can't blast anything until we get the transmitter power station back into operation."

"Why can't we use the solar reflector to heat the Crater?"

"They are using the solar power it reflects to keep the force field over the Crystal Prism active. It is also keeping the water pumping to the Crater's waterfall. If the inhabitants and creatures didn't have its comforting sound in the Crater they would become unsettled."

"How is Esdra doing on the repairs?"

"She is doing a great job. Of course that's just the opinion of a human. She sure knows how to make difficult things simple. Their technology is so far advanced that I can see why they don't have anything to do. They have reached the point where the robots that replaced the Kaydra have themselves been replaced. Esdra uses the combined mental energy of the Kaydra at times to form the strange metals they have here. Circuits and programs are inspected by Esdra in her disintegrated subatomic particle state. You can't imagine how much information one of their memory units hold! Their circuits seem small even when she is only subatomic particle size."

"Well, enjoy yourself. I'll see you later." As Delbert left Adrian, he thought about his children. When he arrived at the geothermal cave where they were being cared for by Shida, he was relieved to find they were OK. They were three months old now. By the time Esdra finished repairing all the damage done to the equipment, during their passing through the comet's tail, it would be time to start watching for them to change forms. He realized he was starting to look forward to the time when they reached six months old and were able to use their transmutative powers if they had any, to assume their primary form. *Would their primary form in anyway resemble the human form?* For now, he could only wonder.

Each day Larry would get up and make sure the many large oil shale fires spaced evenly around the Crater were still burning. Since it wasn't oil shale but a higher grade, cleaner burning ore, the fires didn't smoke up the Crystal Prism, but provided light for the animals to eat by and some heat to help keep the Crater warm. The first few days the Crater wasn't too cool, but the longer the solar reflector was out, the cooler it got. As the Crater cooled, Larry made sure he kept the fires burning around the clock. Every other day, DorLetha would come down and blast a little more oil shale loose and bring it to him to use.

After a week Larry was forced to wear animal furs to keep warm He could tell the plants weren't going to make it unless they could get heat and light soon. They were tropical plants and must have tropical conditions to live. Larry decided to discuss the situation with DorLetha. "Is there some way you can send a few bursts of power through the prism to warm the Crater?"

"We could give you a few burst of rays from the transmitter power station. Stay in your cave because that ray will provide a lot of instant heat as it comes through the prism."

"Give me a few minutes to get back to my cave and then go ahead." After a tremendous flash of light, which frightened the animals, the result was an immediate warming of the Crater. There wasn't enough power available to do it very often. A couple days later, Larry could tell that all the plants and their fruit would still be OK since it hadn't gotten too cold for them.

"Larry, its Adrian. Where are you?"

"I'm over here in the tunnel that leads to the outside. Got any news for me?"

"Yes, they think they can operate the hyperatmospheric force field now and the power beam transmitter power station is working again."

Larry responded, "That means they can cut the power to the Crystal Prism force field and start directing sunlight into the Crater. Even if its half power it will help. I'm going to release all the oxygen from the Bluebells and we'll be short on food until the trees have their next crop."

"We almost have a second, more powerful, solar reflector ready. We'll use it to heat the Crater and part of the outside. Things are a lot worse out there than they were because it got so much colder than it did inside the Crater. The partially working solar reflector will be continually aimed on the outside and not repaired."

Larry offered a suggestion. "If we heat the Crater up to 100 degrees, we can use it as a greenhouse to get additional plants started for both inside and outside. The outside is going to be even hotter now and more of the fertile sea bed will become land because of the production of hydrogen. So, we should be able to get more plants growing outside without too much work. There should also be more oxygen than before. The dust and ash from the meteorite showers will also have fertilized everything that is alive."

"Can the Exvascians cause the plants to accelerate their growth like they got the animals to regenerate their damaged parts?"

"Let's check. DorLetha, can I'La cause the plants to multiply more quickly?"

"I'll check the telepathic storage banks and see if we have any history of such activity."

"One thing the Kaydra could do as birds is spread seeds all over outside. They could get a large area seeded in no time."

"That's right, Adrian. If all the Kaydra keep their transmutative forms for a month or so, it would help the food supply a lot. Another thing would be to keep continuous days, or very long days, outside for a month or two. That would cause a dramatic increase in the plant growth."

"Larry, the telepathic historical data banks have information on increasing the growth of plants. I'll have I'La go over them and see what she can do about the situation.

Dorletha continued. "Dell Bert and I were talking about the necessary delay of his trip to Earth until we get our reserve power supply built up again. Even though he's in a hurry to get his body back, I don't think that will be a problem."

"Are we going to be able to use our bodies again now, Larry?"

"Sure. Let's go down and get started thawing them out. I see the reflected sunlight has just started coming through the prism. By the time your bodies thaw out, it should be warm enough for you."

"Good. I want I'La to try to rejuvenate some of the worn out parts of my body. She said she would help me as soon as I was ready didn't she? Just imagine Delbert, you having a time keeping up with me?"

"That's what she said, Adrian. Besides, in Art's body, I already have trouble keeping up with you."

The lighter conversation was indicative of the men's mood after the crisis appeared to be over. The restoration of the planet's life support system was a real relief. Now they had to start getting the animal population redistributed in a fresh lush environment.

The damage to the plants inside the Crystal Prism Crater was minimal.

Outside the plants and animals had suffered extensive damage. I'La worked with Larry in her primary form. Adrian and Delbert directed the seed dropping activities of the Kaydra who changed into birds.

Once the initial work outside the Crater was completed, the men took clippings and starts from plants inside the Crater and got them started like a nursery project. With the new solar reflector keeping the temperature near 100 degrees, the plants grew quickly. The men all ran around in loincloths. Only their cave home gave them relief from the heat.

After three weeks had passed, all the extra animals, that had been brought in and a few extra from inside the Crater were taken outside. With the new solar reflector and the remaining half of the old one being directed almost continually on the plants outside, they had made a dramatic recovery. Once the animals were taken out, the days were extended to 22 hours and the nights cut to eight hours. This schedule was maintained for over a month. At that time, any Kaydra that wanted to continually use their primary form were allowed to go outside the Crater to live.

Of the 100 that had initially gone out, only 75 survived the meteorite shower before they gave up and came into the Crater. For the first month, the group of Kaydra 35 Fem-Birds and the 40 apes got along satisfactorily outside. Unfortunately, six were later killed by wild animals or poisonous plants outside. After they got used to living outside again, they started fighting over the fruits and nuts that were available. The apes, being vegetarians, had the advantage over the Fem-Birds. The Fem-Birds had a difficult time killing fish or game without changing to a transmutative form, which they again refused to do.

After about three months, the days outside were changed back to the regular 20 hours of light and ten hours of darkness. The temperature inside the Crater was dropped to 90 degrees. The temperature reduction enabled the men to increase their activities.

The three men were enjoying watching Delbert's children fly around. They were very active little birds at six months old and almost fully grown. They would soon start trying to take their primary form.

The men talked about building Delbert and DorLetha a home. If they were going to be allowed to stay on Exvascia, Delbert wanted to develop a family and thought his children might need more care and training, when they took their primary form. He wondered. *Would his half-breeds be able to communicate both verbally and telepathically or have full or limited transmutative powers? What would their physical characteristics be?* He and his three friends would have to wait and see.

The hostility between the two groups outside was growing. There would be about another month before the first new fruit crop was ready since the storm hit. The transplanted nursery plants the men had planted from the Crater were growing quickly. The seeds the birds had dropped were starting to grow even in the newly planted areas. I'La's assistance had caused the plants to grow and mature faster.

While the men were outside they found the Fem-Bird population was down to about 33 and the ape population was at 36. Many of the Fem-Birds were so close to starvation they didn't have the power to take on an animal form to try and kill game for food. They had to have enough energy left after disintegrating to retake their primary form or they would be gone forever.

The three men were bothered by the fact that somehow TetTrella was back. Also the men saw one instance where a Kaydra with the primary ape form, took the form of a wild animal and killed a weak Kaydra of the Fem-Bird form. That confirmed their suspicions that TetTrella intended to kill all the Fem-Bird Kaydra she could lure from the Crater. She knew the Fem-Bird Kaydra would try to maintain their primary form as long as the Kaydra with the ape primary form. Even in their weakened condition, the Fem-Bird Kaydra refused the safety and comfort of the Crater.

Chapter 8

Let's Go Look at Mines

While conditions on Exvascia were getting tenser, Art was finally getting away from the pressure he had been under for the last eight months. Stewart Donovan had accepted the fact that Art didn't look or sound like himself, but that he was still Art.

On Friday afternoon Art and Myrna returned to the hotel after spending several hours with the Donovans. They stopped by Carol's room and invited her to dinner.

"Things must have gone well at the Donovans, Myrna."

"They sure did, Carol. Art was able to convince me that he was who he said he was. The Donovans also accepted him as Art, even though they can't understand Art being in another person's body."

"I've known since the time in the hospital, when Art said he could feel our touch that he wasn't Delbert. At that time, Delbert reentered his body and told me telepathically I should take care of Art who was in his body. That was confirmed the Saturday after Thanksgiving when Delbert entered his body at Gail's wedding and told Dr. Lyons and me he wanted to trade Art bodies at the 'Adralack Crack' in late June.

"I tried to tell you again last night, but I couldn't. You've had such a closed mind on the subject it hasn't been possible for any of us to tell you."

"I know. It was such a traumatic experience for me, losing Art and then having Delbert affected the way he was. I was starting to think that Delbert should be committed for the way he was behaving. I never once thought Art could possibly be in Delbert's body."

"Do you know when Delbert reenters his body; Art doesn't know anything that happens? The way I understand it, DorLetha can locate the aura of Delbert's body, when we are around him, because it gets brighter. He could show up at any time."

"I know that now. Let's go eat. Carol, would you like to spend some time sightseeing with me while you're here? Art will be with Stewart trying to find mineral deposits. If he can, we'll be moving here after he is back to his old self again. "

"That sounds great Myrna but what are you talking about, finding mineral deposits?"

Art explained, "I can feel a vibration from metal pipes underground. I thought I may be able to find mineral deposits from those vibrations. As long as I have Delbert's body, I may be able to locate ore deposits to mine when I'm myself again. Stewart is going to give me a chance at it anyway."

The next morning, Myrna drove Art to a rendezvous point with Stewart. As soon as he arrived and they headed for his mine, Myrna returned to the hotel to pick Carol up so they could spend the day shopping and sightseeing.

As they drove to the mine, Stewart started the conversation. "Art, I've been thinking about your possible ability. I was too excited to sleep much last night. I think I'll start you out in tunnels where we think we have mined most of the worthwhile ore. From there we can move into the areas where we are now mining. After that, there are two areas I'd like to have you check. We think one area has a lot of promise but we have given up on the other."

"That's fine with me Stewart. By working that way, I'll have a chance to see whether or not I can find ore. It'll give me a chance to see what the vibrations feel like from silver."

"I have a small crew working this weekend. I thought they could help us check out any areas you get strong vibrations from. I can carry a pick. I've got helmets with lights for us and a complete set of maps of the tunnel system. The different pages of the map are for the different levels of tunnels."

"Are there any mines for sale around here?"

"Sure. In fact I'm supposed to look at a couple old mines Monday. Maybe with your help I can decide whether or not to buy them."

"Let's see if I can find anything here first. Then we can go from there."

Stewart didn't tell the men on duty at the mine what was going on except that they may be needed for some exploratory work. "This is the area we worked last year. Here is a little speck of silver that we missed. Does that give you any feeling for the ore?"

"Yes, it's what I would call a rapid vibration with not too much strength. "There seems to be a larger deposit in this area. It's either larger or deeper I haven't figured out what the different feelings mean yet. Why don't you try your pick here in this area?"

"That's quite a ways from where we found the main vein. Of course, there were a few fingers branching out from it. Maybe we missed ore." Stewart swung the pick several times. The tunnel was fairly high so he could swing the pick hard. The rock particles flew as the pick dug in. Stewart pried the material loose each time the pick dug in. "I don't see anything yet."

"Let me check it out. It's still there. It's a fairly fast vibration with not too much of a feeling to it. If we can find what is giving me this feeling, it'll help me in our search. Try right here, Stewart."

"OK here goes!" The pick dug deep into the tunnel's rock wall. On the third try, Stewart's helmet light picked up sparkling material. "It's a small pure vein of silver all right. It isn't much of a find, but it's worth digging out later. Let's get back to the area we are working now and see what kind of a feeling you get."

When the men reached the area where the mine was presently being worked, Art walked over to the wall of the tunnel and inspected the rock. His geological training told him this was a high quality ore with a large quantity of silver present.

"What's the feeling you get from this area, Art?" Stewart asked.

"It's a slower vibration with not too much strength to it. I think the speed of the vibration indicates the size of the vein. The larger the vein is, the slower the vibration. The stronger the feeling, the deeper the vein is. Can we check out another area where you are working?"

"Sure. Let's go down another level. We have one tunnel that looks promising." They walked along the tunnel where Stewart said the area looked promising. "Do you feel anything, Art?"

"Yes, it's a slow vibration and the feeling is fairly strong."

"I'll signal Jake and have him come down here." As they waited for Jake, Art looked at the maps. As he ran his finger along the drawing where they were, he felt the vibrations just as he did when he walked along the tunnel originally. Stewart was looking at Art. His helmet light lit up Art's face."Art, why did your expression change, as your ran your finger over the map?"

"I may be able to get all the readings I need just by running my fingers over the map. After you explain to Jake that we want him to dig six to eight feet back at this spot, let's go check out another area."

When Jake arrived, Stewart explained what to expect and about how far back he would have to go. Jake said he would get the crew on it and contact him when they had either gone eight feet or found something.

"I'm ready to go, Art. Do you have any special area you want to look at?"

"Yes, the lower level, northeast tunnel. We'll probably have to go all the way to the back."

"We've never found anything in this area, Art. What makes you think there might be something here?"

"It's a great shaking feeling that's real strong. If I'm right, you haven't taken anything out of this mine yet!"

"You've got to be kidding, Art! I've taken a lot of silver out of here!"

"That doesn't matter. If I'm right, you aren't going to believe what you'll see."

"Art, I own 60 percent of this mine. I'll give you half of my share, which would be 30 percent of what you find in this area. I'll see what my partner is willing to give you when he gets back."

"Thanks for the offer, Stewart, but we haven't found anything yet."

"Let me lead the way, Art. If this tunnel gets much smaller, we'll have to crawl. Watch your head!"

"How far back does it go?"

"Looks like another 50 feet or so. We'll have to crawl from here on, Art. Watch your knees; you can cut them easily on the sharp rocks. I've got to rest. There isn't much air in this area. How are you doing?"

"I'm tired, but I want to keep going. Give me five minutes and we can go on." A little further on, Art made a mark on the wall.

"What's that for, Art?"

"I can't do this anymore today. I'm too tired to make a sound judgment. When we come back Monday, we should start from this point where this tunnel branches off from the main one and work our way to here."

"Let's go see how Jake and the men did on those six to eight feet of material they were to work their way through, Art."

When they got back to Jake, they found that he and the men had only been able to move three feet of the material.

"Thanks Jake. Why don't you see if you feel any difference in this area now that you can stand three feet closer to your find than before, Art?"

"I'll try, Stewart, but I think I'll be able to tell better Monday when I'm fresh."

"You're probably right. No use pushing it. Are you ready to go back to your hotel?"

"Yes, I'm tired. After dinner I'm going to soak in a warm bath for half an hour and then go to bed. Thanks for believing in me and giving me a chance, Stewart."

"Think nothing of it. Besides, I want to thank you for making me look like a dirt ball again. It's been a long time since I've been in on any real action. I can't wait to see what we can discover next week."

Stewart drove Art back to his hotel where Myrna and Carol were waiting for him. "Hi, Sweetie, hi, Carol. Did you have a good time today?"

"We sure did! How did your prospecting go?"

"I didn't find anything they could get to in a hurry. They blasted about three feet deeper into one tunnel, but I feel they have three to six feet more to go. They'll start blasting again on Monday. There is another tunnel on the lower level that I feel may hold valuable ore but I got too tired to concentrate on how I felt about it. We'll start from the spot I marked on Monday and see if I can get a stronger feeling where there may be ore. It's in an area where they have never found any silver. I'll shower and be ready to go in a few minutes."

"We'll be next door at Carol's, Art. Stop by when you're ready."

At dinner that evening the three friends discussed Art's efforts to find silver ore and Delbert's future return. Art was glad to see Carol.

"How's your job working out, Carol?"

"I really enjoyed it, but I don't like Chicago."

"What do you mean enjoyed the job?"

"Dr. Lyons had found me a job in Portland, Art. I'll live about 85 miles from you two in another week."

"Did he have anything else in mind when he found you that job, Carol?"

"Well, his phone bill has been a little high lately and he sends me a lot of text messages and emails, if that's what you mean, Myrna."

"I think he's the right man for you, Carol."

"Thanks, Myrna. I know I love him!"

"I wonder if that will make it easier for Delbert to contact us. It seems like the closer all of us are the more likely we are to hear from him. I'm surprised he hasn't contacted one of you this weekend. He hasn't contacted you has he, Carol?"

"No, Art. This morning, when I awoke, I felt he may have tried, but I didn't wake up at all last night."

Maybe if I had known you were here, Carol, my aura would have been brighter."

"That's entirely possible, Art. It seems that he needs the aura of your body to guide him to you. Of course, you are quite a distance from where they would expect to find you."

"Maybe, if you and Dr. Lyons come to visit us, he'll be able to contact one of you. If not, we'll just have to wait until June to see him and find out how things are going for him. I hope he will know when we're actually to be on Mt. Baker. It would be devastating if he didn't make our rendezvous after months of anticipation."

"You'll be so hyper about getting your body back, Art, and starting a new life in Denver, I don't think there is any way you could keep him from locating you!"

"I hadn't thought of that, Carol. That takes a load off my mind."

"What about you and me, Art? Do we have to wait until June to start our lives over?"

"Probably, Myrna. I'm going to have to make plans for my make-believe move from the city in June. I'll also have to resign from my job and pull Delbert's retirement funds out in a lump sum. I think Delbert would want you to have those funds, Carol. If I'm able to find silver in Stewart's mine, we wouldn't need them. You'll be busy trying to sell your house, Myrna, and finding a new one in Denver. You only have about 60 days left before we'll be moving."

"We can spend more time together though can't we?"

"We can spend as much time together as we can manage. If I'm here looking for extra deposits, I won't be as available as I have been."

"I'm glad all I have to do is move from my apartment in Chicago to one in Portland. I don't know if I'd like leaving my friends like you two will be doing. Of course, my life could get more complicated if Darrell and I get married and then go to Exvascia."

"Go where?"

"Exvascia, the planet Delbert is on. He said they have some problems there and could use our help. If he can arrange a visit the same time Art gets his body back, we'd like to go. He wants Darrell to bring his little black bag full of equipment."

"Myrna, do you remember Gail's camera that had been lost in the 'Adralack Crack' for a year, before Adrian retrieved it? Well, Michael developed the film. It looks like we've got pictures of Larry's new planet."

"Why didn't you tell me about them?"

"I got them from Michael after the photographer finished taking pictures of their wedding, Myrna. Just after that, Delbert came and visited Darrell and me, in the room where everyone changed clothes. He told us we had to get Art back up to the 'Adralack Crack' in late June. We told Art, but we couldn't think of any way to tell you. Delbert told us the pictures were of Exvascia."

"Then that's why Dr. Lyons made up that phony story about Delbert's memory and wanting Art's identification."

"That's right, Myrna. Art wanted to make sure he had all his identification in case he gets his body back. That would make it easy for him to get back into circulation without any hassle."

"Here are the pictures. Art hasn't seen them either. Delbert called that area there, the Crystal Prism Crater. Isn't it pretty?"

"It sure is, but I think I'll just stay here with Myrna."

"I'll be so glad to have you back as my husband; I won't know what to do. I know the kids are going to be so happy. They still think you're on Mt. Baker. I'm not going to tell them anything about our trip until you return whole. You can say good-bye to them as Delbert and tell them you're moving. I know they'll understand that."

"I need to get Delbert's body working well enough to get him off his disability insurance claim too. That will make one less detail to carry over after he's gone."

"Are we going to take Carol sightseeing tomorrow until it's time to catch her flight?"

"I'd enjoy that. Myrna and I looked around a little today, but there were a lot of things we didn't get to see. I have to be to the airport by 3:00 p.m."

Art was tired from all the exercise and excitement of the day and went to his room to soak in a hot bath before going to bed. Myrna and Carol went next door to talk.

Carol enjoyed the time with Myrna and was surprised to learn that while she was home caring for her kids she had become an expert on Tiffany lamps and jewelry.

The next day they spent time in a coffee shop in the afternoon before they took Carol to the airport. "I want to thank you two for the weekend. I'm glad I could come. I'm sure looking forward to getting back to Oregon."

"Thank you for coming, Carol. I really hadn't expected things to turn out the way they have."

"I had to come, Myrna, so I could tell you what I knew about Art. I hope you two can work out all the complications that will develop from bringing Art back and Delbert leaving. Let me know if I can help."

"We'll do that. We'll be looking for a visit from both you and Darrell." Myrna and Art gave her a hug and she was off.

That evening Art fell asleep watching TV in bed a couple hours before Myrna shut it off. She looked at his peaceful form. He was dead to the world. What a combination, her lover's body and her husband's personality" She thought to herself, *I can love either one or the other, but the combination is something else. I wonder if Delbert is right about Art being a one-woman man after he gets his body back. Carol is such a lovely person, I can see why he fell for her, but I can't see why he walked into that alien powered Crack. I thought I meant more to him than that.*

The next morning after dropping Art off at his rendezvous point with

Stewart, she packed up their things, checked out of the motel and drove to the Donovan's home.

Meanwhile, Art and Stewart had reached the area in the tunnel where he had left his mark the previous Saturday. “Stewart, I'm getting a strong slow vibration all along this area, but I think it is stronger between this point and where this tunnel branches off from the main one.”

“That's where you said it was strongest. Why don't you feel the wall both high and low and see if that make any difference, Art?”

“Yes it does, it's very strong here. Move back a few yards, but keep your eye on this spot and the one I mentioned earlier. I think this is the strongest spot. It seems as though the ore vein would be about chest high and about ten to 15 feet beyond this point.”

“Go ahead and spray a big yellow X on that spot. How do you feel about your ability to judge the distance?”

“I'm not sure. Let's go see how Jake made out with our first spot. If he's through another three feet of rock, I may be able to judge better in the future by what we find there.”

“Art, let's go back to the main tunnel, then go to our right and stop about 20 feet from the dead end. If you get a stronger feeling there, it means we could reach the vein about 40 percent faster by drilling and blasting from there. Since that tunnel is larger, it would be a lot easier to remove the ore from there.”

“Let's walk down to where it dead ends and see what I experience. The tunnel dropped between here and the entrance. That accounts for the feeling being stronger here above my head than at chest level. I think you're right.”

“I can't believe you can feel a vein of ore that far away, it would have to be enormous.” Stewart was an astute, savvy business man and realized what Art was doing for all involved.

“Let's go see what Jake has found.”

Back at the first spot where Art had started Jake digging, the dust was just settling when they arrived. They put on their dust masks and approached. “Find anything yet, Jake?”

“We just reached the eight feet you wanted. As soon as the dust clears, we'll see if there's anything there.”

“Shine your light in there, Art. What do you see?”

“Just dust! I don't have a strong feeling, so we must be close if we're not there”

“While the dust is settling, I'll send Jake down to the next level and have him start a tunnel toward the area where you felt we might find something.”

"Jake, how are you doing on our production goal this month?"

"Not too good. The volume of ore is up, but the amount of silver is down."

"I know we owe all of you back wages but I think we'll find that vein again and be able to get caught up. Anyway, would you make a small test tunnel where I've marked this map? Start right here and try to end the tunnel at head level at this point."

"But, we didn't find anything where we dug this other tunnel and it's just 20 feet from there!"

"I know, but I think we'll find something if we dig this one right."

"That's going to take more time than I have!"

"Come on, Jake. See if you can at least start."

"OK. I'll work at it all day, but that's it. We'll have to come back to where we can get ore out of our regular dig."

"Stewart and Jake, would this help solve your problem? Aim your lights there!"

"Art, you did it. Jake, isn't that beautiful?"

"I'll say! That's the largest vein we've found in this mine. Hey, Stewart, why don't I get the crew to switch to this area today? I'm sure that will give us enough high quality ore to catch up on all your back bills and our pay. That way I can work full time on that other tunnel you want. Boy, I want to thank you, Art. Stewart's been good to us, but things have been lean these past three months. I'll dig you a tunnel anywhere you want."

"Glad I could help."

"I'll get the crew down here immediately. Wait till they see this! Wow!"

"Thanks, Stewart, for believing in me!"

"I had to, Art. I didn't think anyone else would listen to your crazy story. I gambled you'd be able to do what you said you could do. If the other vein you've found is larger than this, then we'll be able to mechanize a lot more. We'd need another partner then. What do you want to do now?"

"Let me check this map again. Hum? There are two or three other areas that seem to be possibilities. Let's check them out."

As the two men made their way along the tunnel, Stewart spoke. "Did you see the look on Jake's face when he saw the vein he had exposed? I haven't seen a smile on his face like that for years."

"You've got a pretty big smile on your own face, Stewart!"

"You don't know how relieved I was to see that silver, Art. Things have been bad this year. We needed to find something or close down. I've been taking money out of my savings to keep things going. That's the first time

I've had to do that in years."

"Let's go up to the next level and see what I can find."

"We started a test tunnel near that area once. We can work from that point and see what you feel. Do you want to check the other area on this level before we go up?"

"Might as well. Boy, your ventilation isn't very good in here. I certainly wouldn't want to be a miner for a living."

"It's all tied to the economics of the mine, Art. You just can't have everything. We generally get what we need most to get by. Watch your head here, Art, its a little low. Here's your spot. Have you felt anything along here?"

"Yes, it's not much, but I'll give you something you can get to easy. It's not very deep in the rock. I feel as though my energy is being drained each time I find another possible ore area."

"I hope it doesn't wear off too soon. I've got a couple other small mines I want you to check out. Why don't we quit for the day after you check out that other spot in the tunnel above."

When they reached the test tunnel they wanted to explore, Stewart let Art lead and commented, "It looks like I'm going to be dirt from head to toe again, Art. We'll have to crawl most of the way. Feel anything yet?"

"Maybe, wait there while I check the next few feet. He used his rock hammer to do some digging. He apparently had found the other end of the vein Stewart was working on. The vein must have curved just the opposite direction of the tunnel he was in. He sprayed the area after actually digging out some silver ore then slowly crawled backward to where Stewart was still working.

"Did you find anything?"

"I think I found the other end of the vein you are working on. Have you got to the silver ore yet?"

"Yes, it looks good, but I'm getting too old for this pick work."

Art was tired, so he carefully and slowly crawled out. He noticed he lost more energy each time he found ore deposits. *I wonder how long my special powers will last.*

"That gives us three finds and one spot to check out. That's great! How are you feeling? You look really tired!"

"I am, Stewart. It's two o'clock already, no wonder I'm hungry."

"I'll call Clara and have her fix us a meal. I'll tell Jake about the other areas tomorrow. Would you like to visit one of the other mines that are for sale tomorrow?"

"I had better before I lose my touch!"

Stewart called his wife and told her he had some good news for her. She said she would have their meal ready for them when they got home.

When they reached the Donovans, Clara and Myrna met them at the door. “Well there's my ‘Dirt Ball’. Look what you've done to him again, Art!”

“He does look a mess doesn't he, especially with that mud still on his forehead and the end of his nose.”

“Thanks, Art. Why didn't you say something?”

“I was too dirty myself to give it a second thought. You must have wiped the sweat from your forehead when you were digging in that last spot.”

“It was worth it! You should see the vein Art found today, Clara. Jake is going to work on it for a few days. Besides that one big find, he found two other veins and a third spot that's a good possibility. We're going to be able to catch up on all our back payroll, pay bills, buy equipment and have a lot of money left over, thanks to Art.”

“Oh, that's wonderful. I know Royal will be thrilled. He's worked so hard in that mine all these years. Having it apparently run out didn't seem fair.”

“Let's get cleaned up, Art! That steak smells great Clara. We'll take a quick shower and be right back.”

They discussed several things regarding Art and Myrna's future as they ate. “If you don't need me, Art, I could go home and put our house up for sale. We'll probably need all the time we can get to sell it by late June. How long do you think you'll be here?”

“I'll probably be another four or five days. You go ahead, that's fine with me. Stewart and I want to look at two or three more mines that are for sale.”

“OK, I'll fly out then in the morning after you two leave.”

“Well, how does it feel to be sleeping with your lover rather than your husband?” Stewart had meant to be funny, but it caught Myrna by surprise. Her face turned a bright red and she hesitated for a moment. Everyone could tell she was very embarrassed. Clara didn't know what she could say to put her at ease.

Myrna finally spoke. “This is the first weekend we've done this. It's not what I usually do but, he promised me he isn't who he looks like. You know how lovers are, promises, promises!”

Stewart chuckled. He was glad she had taken his comment as a joke. “I'll tell you, Myrna, when you first told me this fellow was Art, it would have been easier to believe he was your pet dog.”

“You can't imagine how I feel when I look into a mirror. I still feel like saying ‘Hello Delbert’, but that is supposed to be me. I can't wait till June gets here. That reminds me, I'll need a forwarding address for Delbert when he supposedly leaves town. Can I have his mail sent here?"

"That's right! If you get your body back, and Delbert wants to stay on Exvascia, he will be gone. How are you going to cover that?"

"I'm on sabbatical now. I'll just resign his position, draw out his retirement, give notice on his apartment and he'll be gone, except for his forwarding address. I'll also have to remember to close his checking and savings accounts. I hope I don't miss anything. If I do, there won't be any way for me to resolve it except by correspondence."

"You'll have to start making a check list, Art."

"That sounds like a good idea Clara. I'll do that!"

The next day, in another mine, Stewart asked Art, "Do you get any impressions from this map?"

"No, Stewart, we'll have to go through all the tunnels and see what happens."

As they opened the long abandoned mine, Stewart suggested they start at the upper level and work their way down because of the lack of shoring, "It has probably been 50 years since it was last mined. To get from one level to the next, they just blasted a ramp. We'll have to be careful not to fall when we go up or down it. I've brought a couple extra lanterns for us to carry. I understand all the tunnels are high enough to walk in. The air is bad in here but let's go as long as we can. The three mines we'll be looking at are for sale cheap."

"This one sure isn't much of a mine. Be careful of that loose rock there. Love the cob webs at the entrance too. I can tell you they haven't mined out all the silver that is here. I feel they went mainly for the larger veins. Yes, I'm getting some good feelings as I walk through here. I hope you're keeping track of where we are. I get to concentrating on locating ore and forget to notice all the turns we've made."

"You just keep looking and paying attention to your feelings, Art. Tell me when you think I should mark a spot on my map. I'm not going to make a mark on the walls for someone to find."

"Mark this spot on your map. It feels like there is something good on the right side of the tunnel and not too deep."

About halfway down the next tunnel, Art stopped. "Do you want me to mark this spot?"

"Yes, but I'm not sure whether it would be closer from this tunnel or the next. There seems to be a deposit located somewhere between them. Let's check the next one and see if the deposit seems closer to it. I like the feeling I get here. It should be a good deposit."

The two men surveyed the other tunnels and found other possibilities, and decided it would be a good buy. The steep grade of the ramp from one level to the other made it difficult to get back out of the mine. When they got out of the mine, it was past noon. They rested and enjoyed the lunch Clara had packed for them.

"Let's drive over and see how Jake is doing and then call it a day."

"Fine, I'm already tired. My energy for finding deposits isn't going to last too much longer."

"That's OK; we only have two more mines to look at." When they checked with Jake at the mine, they found he would need four or five days to complete the test tunnel, but the crew had taken a lot of silver from the new find.

"It looks good so far Jake. I may not be back this week, so keep the men working so we can surprise Royal when he returns."

"That's no problem! When the crew saw what the ore looked like, they started working with renewed energy. Those two men alone will produce more than the three of us usually do. That should enable me to get to the new vein before Royal gets back."

"OK Jake, I'll be looking at other mines for the rest of the week. I'll see you later or call and find out what you've found."

"See you later Stewart. Thanks again, Art."

"You're welcome, Jake. I'll see you later."

The next morning Art and Stewart drove to a mine that had been mined more recently, would cost more and was larger. The mine they were to inspect the following day was even larger.

After arriving at the mine, they unlocked the entrance and blocked the doors open so that fresh air could blow in. Before entering, they went over the map of the three levels very carefully. To get from one level to another, they would have to climb down an old elevator shaft. The ladders were made of heavy timbers so there wasn't any fear of them breaking.

"Are you ready to light your lantern and go in?"

"Sure, Stewart, lead the way. Let's start from the bottom and work our way back up."

Stewart guided them to the shaft leading to the lower levels. When he reached the bottom he stopped so they could both rest. As they sat there on the ground, with their lanterns lighting the area, Art got a strange look on his face.

"That's a different expression than I've seen you have, Art. What's the problem?"

"Is this supposed to be an old silver mine?"

"I guess, I told my friend I was interested in getting another mine. He knew I already owned part of a silver mine."

"My geological training says this isn't the right type of material to hold silver."

"Let me look closer. Yes, you're right. It looks more like gold. Will that make any difference to you?"

"I'll have to identify the feeling I get from gold first before I can tell what is going on inside me."

"What do you suggest we do?"

"Bring your pick and follow me, Stewart. Let's see if we can find some gold! I'll see if I can get a reading on some gold flecks close to the surface. I just need a few grains to identify the feeling I'm supposed to tune in on. Go ahead and use your pick right there."

"Stand back, I'll hit it about three times. Did I get anything?"

"What does this look like to you?"

"That's gold all right. Will that give you enough to go on or do you want to try for a larger sample, Art?"

"Let's try for a larger sample. I want to be sure of the feeling and vibrations I feel. Here's a spot that will probably take about six good licks, but it should give us a good size sample."

Stewart swung the pick as hard as he could in the limited space he had. After about four swings, he stopped. "Why don't you check to see how I'm coming?"

"Well look here. Looks like a popcorn kernel size chunks. OK. I know what I'm after now. Mark this spot on the map." The men went through every inch of the lower levels before they climbed back out and sat in Stewart's truck to eat their lunch.

Now and then Stewart would talk to a friend on his CB. "Come in Candlestick, this is Jack Be Nimble."

"I'm here Jack Be Nimble. Where are you and what are you doing?"

"I'm looking at the Cougar Creek mine with a friend."

"Hope it turns out to be a good one. Talk with you later. Over and out."

The men took two hours to eat and rest before they went back in to check out the entrance level tunnels. Art thought to himself. *I hope nothing happens to us, because nobody knows where we are. I don't even think Stewart's truck would be seen by anybody out here. A search plane could probably spot it during the day but Clara certainly wouldn't worry about us until late this evening. I just won't think about it. The cave-in that caught me on Mt. Baker was all I care to experience!*

"I'm ready if you are, Art. Do you want to work from the back toward the front?"

"Yes, when I'm really tired, I don't want to have very far to walk back to the truck."

"OK, let's go find ourselves a pot of gold!" At the far end of the tunnel Art got a strong, slow vibration with a strong feeling that ore was present. That meant the ore would be several feet back in the rock but it should be a good size vein.

"Mark that spot on your map Stewart."

"How about getting another sample?"

"I'll see what I can do. Let's try the next tunnel. Here's a good place, right where this crack is. Three or four good licks and we should have a good size sample."

Stewart swung the pick and hit right in the crack. Joy turned to horror in an instant as the ceiling of the tunnel began to fall around them. The dust flew as the rock hit them and then the tunnel floor. First one lantern was smashed and then the second. Although they tried to jump out of the way of the falling rock, they were neither quick enough nor strong enough to jump to safety. The tunnel was too narrow where the mishap occurred for them to escape it. After the lanterns were destroyed, the lights on their miner helmets were next. Now they were without light and the dust was thick. They choked and coughed as they tried to breathe. Both had cried out when the rock started falling but their initial scream was all they were able to utter. The small sample now amounted to half a ton of rock. It crashed down on their helmets and covered most of their bodies as it violently knocked them off their feet.

It wasn't until the dust had settled that Art regained consciousness. He looked at his watch which was still working. It was six o'clock, which meant he had been out cold for several hours. This cave-in really meant to claim his life. He felt a strong throbbing in his left calf. He knew he either had a bad cut or a broken leg, maybe both.

Besides hurting everywhere, their lanterns were destroyed. His head and left arm were somehow not covered by the falling rock. He started to uncover his upper body. As he did so, he called out to Stewart. "Stewart, can you hear me? Stewart, Stewart, answer me, Stewart!"

Stewart didn't answer Art. Without any light for Art to see Stewart, he had two choices. He could believe he had escaped or he hadn't. If he hadn't, he was probably just as seriously injured as he was, maybe worse. He could tell from the little progress he was making uncovering himself, that he was under a lot of rock. For some reason he was very weak. He must have lost a lot of blood from his leg wound.

Art stopped to rest for a minute. It was then he realized there wasn't a very good air supply where they were trapped. His hopes rose as he heard Stewart moan. “Stewart, can you hear me? Stewart, answer me!”

Stewart still didn't answer. Art was all alone. The air supply was limited, he was weak from loss of blood and nobody knew where they were. *I wonder if the friend Stewart talked to on his CB knows where we are from what he said. That is our only hope but it would be a long time before he had any reason to look for us. I feel like I'm going to lose consciousness again and there isn't any way I can get to Stewart's truck. I'm afraid I'm going to die here.*

The anguish, the pain and the anxiety caused Art to call out for Delbert. Art knew he would have a difficult time getting free even in his own body, but being in Delbert's made the situation humanly impossible. “Delbert! Delbert! Delbert! Your body is going to die! Delbert, you've got to hear me! I heard you on Mt. Baker when you needed help. DorLetha! DorLetha, can you find me? DorLetha, if I don't get help from you and Delbert in a few minutes, Delbert will never be able to get his body back.”

Art didn't know if there was any way DorLetha, the powerful alien who had taken Delbert from Earth, could hear him. Could Delbert see what was happening to him on Earth? Would his desperate, urgent plea for help make his aura bright enough for DorLetha to see it? Art spit dirt from his mouth as he listened to Stewart moan again and again. “Delbert, come save me!”

Chapter 9

Delbert Help, Save Your Body!

While Art was in dire straits on Earth, things weren't much better on Exvascia. "Larry, are we going to have DaKeta drop the Crater temperature to the low 80's?"

"Yes, Adrian, I talked to her a couple nights ago. It shouldn't get any hotter than that today. Have you talked to I'La about rejuvenating parts of your body?"

"Yes, she's going to start working with me today. I'd like to get rid of the arthritis in my hands and back. Also, I'm tired of having stooped shoulders. I do notice that my breathing is better since I haven't smoked for eight months. If my kidneys and heart worked better along with the other things I mentioned, I'd feel 55 rather than 65."

"How about getting your eyes back to normal? I'd hate to have you break your glasses up here. Here comes I'La now."

"Is it cooler out there today, Delbert?"

"Yes. Why don't we talk to I'La out there?"

"Might as well! Good morning, I'La. How are you today?"

"I'm the same as always. Why do you ask?"

"Well, our human bodies deteriorate much faster than yours. Whereas you live 1,000 to 1,500 years, depending on whether you're sterile or fertile, we only live about 85 years. So, we often ask each other how we are feeling to see if old age is starting to catch up with us or just to see if our bodies are malfunctioning."

"Is your body malfunctioning?"

"It certainly doesn't work like it used to years ago. I have to wear these things, glasses, on my eyes so that I can see. If I don't wear them, everything in front of me is blurry."

"Would you like to be able to see like you used to?"

"Yes, plus I would like my kidneys and heart to work better too."

"Is that all?"

"No, I'd like my shoulders to be straighter and my joints in my hands and back not to hurt and be stiff all the time."

"I'll take you for a walk and show you Telaw. You'll be the same as you were previously."

"What is Telaw, Larry?"

"I don't know! Remember, I'm still learning like you are. I'La, what is Telaw?"

"It is proper food for your body. Don't you know what to eat here?"

"No. I never asked and no one ever bothered to show me." Larry thought to himself. *How stupid of me not to ask the Kaydra what I should and shouldn't eat.*

"Eating is such a primary thing; we just thought you would know what to eat. Don't you have these plants and animals on your planet?"

"We don't have any of them on our planet."

"How can that be? I don't understand!"

"We don't know how either. Would you like to take us for a walk so we can all learn at the same time?"

"Yes, I'd like to help you." As they walked along, I'La would stop and show them different plants. "This plant will make you spin when you fly."

"But, we don't fly yet. Maybe it would still make us dizzy."

She showed them one that looked like an asparagus plant and said that it would make their joints flexible. One that looked like spinach leaves were said to be good for the heart. One that looked like a yellow beet was to be eaten to straighten their eyes.

"Comparing these plants to ones we have on Earth will make it easy for us to remember which plants do what until we get use to eating them. You mean to tell me, I'La, that just a proper diet or Telaw will take care of all my problems?"

"That's right. You don't have a short leg or one eye that can't see, so you are easy to heal. Those other types of problems I can fix too but they are much harder to correct."

"Thanks, I'La. Can you tell us about other plants and fruits that we can eat?"

"Yes, just show me what ones you want to know about and I can tell you whether or not they are good to eat and what they will do for you." Delbert wished Dr. Lyons could be with them for the tour. He'd have to be sure the two of them met when and if he visited.

Before I'La could finish answering the men's questions, DorLetha arrived. “Dell Bert, I think there's a problem with your body!”

“No, I'm getting better at using it every day. With the information I'La is giving us on plants we can eat, I should be in great shape in a couple weeks.”

“I don't mean the one you're using here. I mean your own body on Earth!”

“What makes you say that?”

“Because I got a strange feeling it was trying to contact us. When I went into mental telemetrical viewing, I could see your aura shinning very brightly but it is far from where it usually is. Can you take a look and see if it's OK?”

“Sure, go ahead and give us a view of what's happening.”

“Let me see if I can find it again. There it is!” As DorLetha concentrated, she got a fix on Delbert's aura. She could see it distinctly in her mind. The men were able to tune in to her thoughts by telepathic communication and see what she saw.

“I don't understand what I'm seeing, DorLetha. I just see a blue glow in a totally black area. What does it mean?”

“DorLetha can you go back in time and let us see what happened?”

“Can she do that, Larry?”

“I think she can, Adrian. It seems like they can see events as a continuum on a time line. Everything that has and is happening is all there at the same time.”

DorLetha's thoughts went back in time and picked up Art and Stewart eating lunch in Stewart's truck. They saw Stewart talk to a friend every once in awhile on his CB. The two men then went into a mine where Art started trying to get a fix on some kind of ore. “It looks like Art is up to his adventurous ways again. The experience at the ‘Crack’ apparently has given him some ability to sense minerals. He's using it to find himself a gold mine or something.”

As they viewed her mental thoughts, they found Larry was 100% correct. “That makes sense. If he gets his old body back, he's going to have to leave town and find some other way of making a living. How long do you think he will have that type of ability Larry?”

“I don't know, Dell Bert, but I would think it will wear off unless he gets another charge of power some way.”

In a couple minutes the three men saw what had happened to Art and knew why he was calling for help. “DorLetha, do we have enough power to beam me down there to help him?”

“I'm sorry Dell Bert but we don't have that much power stored up yet.”

“There must be some way we can help him! If we don't DorLetha, I'll never get my body back!”

“We don't have enough power to send you down, Dell Bert!”

"There has to be some way I can help him!"

"Let me try Delbert. I'll link my mind to the telepathic picture. That will allow me to go down there in soul flight."

"But that won't do any good, Larry. You can't operate my body and there's too much rock for Art to move before the air runs out even if he wasn't hurt."

"That's right, Delbert, but I can levitate the rock out of the way and move his body and Stewart's out to the truck."

"What good will that do them?"

"Remember what Art was thinking when he heard Stewart talked with his friend on the CB?"

"Yes!"

"I'll get him out and then I'll return so you can go down and enter your body and use the CB to get help."

"Then move it!

Larry lay down on the ground and mentally entered the scene they were viewing. Delbert couldn't see Larry, but he could see the rock being moved and then Stewart's and Art's bodies floating out of the mine to a spot beside the truck.

Larry sat up. "I'm back, Delbert, get going!"

"How, Larry?"

"Just think you're there and you will be. Lie down and relax and keep your thoughts on the telepathic picture you're seeing."

Delbert lay down on the ground beside Larry. In a few seconds he was back and sat up. "Art's too broken up for me to stand my old body up to use the CB. What else can we do?"

"Could I'La repair his body?"

"Not while he's unconscious."

"Larry, what if Delbert went down, then his body wouldn't be unconscious and he and I'La could fix what needs healing in order for him to get to the CB and try to get help to get him to a hospital." Adrian had a good idea.

"I can't keep the telemetrical viewing strong enough for two minds to travel on at the same time."

"Can we help, DorLetha?

"Maybe, if I draw on both Larry's and your mind, Adrian, I could let them have a few seconds together down there."

"I'm willing, how about you Larry?"

"What could happen to us, DorLetha?"

"If I over use your minds, you'll die! When that happens, I'La will instantly be back here. Dell Bert will have to do what he can on his own then. Adrian, your mind has the greatest chance of injury or death. Larry's is stronger since he has been here longer."

"I don't care! I can't let both Art and Delbert be messed up all their lives."

"I'La, have you ever been to Earth or any other place yet?"

"No, DorLetha."

"You must not get any desire to stay and look around or Adrian will die and so will Dell Bert's Earthly body. You'll be tempted!"

"I'll try to remember. Will it be hard once I'm there?"

"Yes I'La, very hard. Do you think you can control yourself when you're there?"

"I'll try!"

"I'm still willing to help, DorLetha." As Adrian finished speaking, Esdra arrived.

"I don't want to lose my pretty Adrian, I'La, please hurry."

"If everyone is ready, let's get started." Everyone lay on the ground and concentrated while Esdra looked on. She had never been anywhere or looked in on a mental telemetrical viewing where this type of activity was involved.

Delbert and I'La made it to Earth in an instant. Once inside his old body, Delbert told I'La that he needed his leg healed. It was broken, as Art had suspected, and he had lost a lot of blood. He also had a couple broken ribs and internal bleeding. "Think of your leg, Dell Bert. Tell it to stop bleeding. Now, straighten it out. Think back to how it felt when you used it and it will be healed. Try it."

"I think I'm OK. It feels like the cut has stopped bleeding. Now I'll straighten it out. Oh! That hurts, I'La. What can I do? I'La, where are you? DorLetha, she's gone!"

At that instant Delbert was back in Art's body on Exvascia. "I've got to get I'La back before she strays too far!" DorLetha said.

"Ah!" Adrian's cry meant he was almost ready to die.

"DorLetha let my pretty Adrian's mind go and use mine." DorLetha did as Esdra suggested. In an instant I'La was back on Exvascia.

"I'La, what happened to you?"

"I'm sorry, Dell Bert. Your planet is too tempting. I can't keep from wanting to see it. I can't go back down with you! You'll have to do the best you can with the repairs I made. I'll help you think about your leg again when you get down there. I think it'll be OK."

"As soon as my leg is OK, I'La, take a look at Adrian. He looks very bad." Delbert returned to Earth and concentrated on his leg while I'La, Larry and Esdra did the same. In a few seconds he was able to straighten his leg and it felt normal again. All the pain was gone.

Larry continued to watch. DorLetha didn't need his mental help any longer but he wanted to see what was happening. Delbert took the keys for the truck from Stewart's pocket and opened the door. He turned on the CB with his left arm. He could tell his right arm was broken and that he had some broken ribs. The internal bleeding seemed to have been stopped by I'La, but he was having trouble breathing on his right side. Perhaps he had a punctured lung.

"Candlestick, this is Jack Be Nimble, can you hear me?"

"Go ahead, Jack Be Nimble. I just turned my CB back on. How long have you been trying to get a hold of me? Did you find anything in the mine?"

"Cave-in, Candlestick! Help!"

"What mine are you at?"

"Cougar Creek. Look for the truck lights."

"Are you badly hurt? Can you hear me OK? Stewart you sound awful, come in. I can't hear your answer. If you can hear me, Stewart, I'm going to get the air rescue helicopter out there as fast as possible. I'll call Clara and let her know you have been hurt and help is on the way."

Delbert had pulled the truck lights on after letting go of the CB mike. He was so dizzy he had to sit back down on the ground before he fell and hurt himself more. He was glad to hear Candlestick's last statement even if he didn't know who he was. Now he had to leave his old body before he blacked out or he would be alive and well but Art would no longer exist and Art's body would die on Exvascia.

Delbert had done all he could for Art. Now, all they could do was hope Stewart's friend could get help to them in time. As Delbert finished, he was instantly back on Exvascia.

"How's Adrian doing, Larry?"

"Both I'La and Esdra are working on him."

"Your aura is gone Delbert, I think Art will make it now."

"DorLetha, help, It's Esdra."

When DorLetha turned to see what I'La's concern for Esdra was, she didn't see her and realized Esdra had used too much mental energy trying to save her pretty Adrian. She must have disintegrated and wasn't able to regenerate herself. DorLetha quickly disintegrated herself so she could find Esdra and bring her back before she was gone forever. DorLetha returned to her form with Esdra in a few seconds. "Is she going to be OK, DorLetha?"

"I don't know Larry. It took me awhile to find her. I'La, take a look at her. How is Adrian?"

"I think Esdra's mental power helped me save him. Maybe Larry and Delbert can take a look at him while I work on Esdra."

"Sure I'La. Adrian, wake up! Can you hear us Adrian? Adrian, open your eyes."

"Is that you Art? Are you OK?"

"You're not on Earth, Adrian; you're still on Exvascia with Larry and me."

"Oh, I thought I was with Art."

"Are you OK?"

"I'm awful weak, Delbert. Can you sit me up?"

"Sure Adrian."

"Thanks! What's wrong with Esdra?"

"She disintegrated and couldn't regenerate after trying to bring I'La back from Earth and trying to save your life."

"She shouldn't have done that! Can you help me over to her please?"

"Sure! There you are."

Adrian cradled the unconscious body of Esdra in his arms. He stoked her beautiful feathered head and kissed her forehead. "Esdra, its Adrian, can you hear me? Esdra wake up. Oh, Esdra, what have you done to yourself? You shouldn't have risked your life for me." Adrian's warm tears fell silently on Esdra's cheek. Larry and Delbert hated to see his sorrow.

"DorLetha is she going to be OK?"

"I don't know, Dell Bert. I think she must have experienced your emotion, called love, to have done what she did for Adrian. She hasn't been developing the way our fertile females usually do. I'm afraid this experience may affect her forever."

"Can we do anything for her?"

"No, we'll just have to wait and see how she is when she wakes up. That should be any minute now."

"Uh, uh, what happened?"

"How do you feel Esdra:"

"My Pretty Adrian, is that you?" You're all fuzzy. I'm dizzy."

"How does she look to you, I'La?"

"Not too good, Adrian, I'm sorry. I just couldn't make myself return from your planet. I just had to look around."

"I don't blame you, I'La. How long do you think her vision will be blurry?"

"I don't know. We'll just have to wait and see. I'm surprised DorLetha could even bring her back in one piece."

"Do you want to go back to the cave? We could take Esdra with us."

"OK, but tell me how Art is, first."

"We don't know, Adrian. I had to come back in a hurry and shortly after I returned DorLetha lost her fix on Art. All we know is that help is on the way."

"OK, take Esdra and me back to the cave. I'm really tired. Why don't we try some of those special plants I'La talked about? Maybe they will make me feel better and help Esdra to see better sooner."

Larry spoke up. "I'll make them a part of the meal tonight. If they don't taste good raw, I'll cook them for you. It'll be interesting trying something new. We'll have I'La complete her tour for us another day.

"I'll help Adrian, Delbert. Why don't you see if you can help Esdra?"

"Can you walk Esdra?"

"I think so, if you hold me, Dell Bert."

"Of course you could just think yourself there if you prefer and have enough energy."

"I'd prefer to go that way. Dell Bert, wait."

Delbert walked back to DorLetha, I'La and Esdra. "What's the problem?"

"She can't change her form anymore or levitate her body."

"Was that caused by her extended period of disintegration, DorLetha?"

"I don't know, Dell Bert. I'll have to check the time-exempt telepathic historical data banks to see if there is any information on this type of situation. I'll let you know tomorrow"

"Well, Esdra, let's try it the human way, one foot at a time."

Back at the cave, Larry and Adrian were waiting. "Delbert, what took you so long?"

"Esdra was going to transport herself here without walking but she couldn't. It may be a problem from her experience earlier. DorLetha will let us know in the morning if she can find out anything about this condition."

"Larry, are you there?"

"That sounds like Shida. Hi, Shida, is something wrong?"

"It's Andre, he wants me to follow him somewhere. Since Esdra isn't around, I can't leave DorLetha's little ones to find out what he is excited about."

"Come on, Andre; show me what you're excited about. I'll be back after awhile Delbert."

Andre jumped up on Larry's hip and pointed to the Crater exit. Larry started out not knowing where he was going or what to expect. Andre was like a dog. There was no telling what he wanted to show his master.

Larry's interest increased as he neared the entrance to the tunnel that led to the outside. He put Andre down so he could show him where he wanted to go. Andre scampered from the Crater entrance as Larry followed him. Once outside, Larry could tell that Andre had to find what it was that he wanted him to see.

Andre climbed a tree, looked around, sniffed the air and listened for some particular sound. He climbed down from the tree and led Larry off through the fast growing vegetation. After a few minutes Andre found what he was looking for. It was TetTrella and a small, strange-looking creature sitting along the bank of a stream. Andre was careful not to be seen as he crept through the brush downwind from TetTrella and the strange looking creature. Larry followed Andres lead and kept low.

"I've never seen one of those creatures around here Andre. I wonder where TetTrella got it and what she has in mind for it to do. I'll talk to TetTrella and see if we can find out what she is up to."

"Hi, TetTrella, who's your new friend? I don't think I've seen him around here before."

"This is Twillie. He's a durl from Contrar. Remember the planetary games we saw him in, when we were telemetrically viewing? He's the gymnast you enjoyed watching, because he was so good on the parallel bars. I told him I wanted him to represent us here when we hold games like that."

Larry thought for a while. *Exvascia didn't have any way of sending images of games to other planets or receiving space shuttles. Besides that, they didn't have any population. How could they put on such an event? He knew TetTrella was up to something but he didn't know what it was.* Finally he spoke. "I don't think we'll hold any games like that for a long time. I've got to get back."

As Larry walked back toward the Crater entrance, a thunder and lightning storm struck. He was glad to get inside the tunnel. He had never seen a lightning storm on Exvascia before. The lightning flashed in sheets across the sky and the rain beat down.

Since the new solar reflector had been installed it was awfully hot and humid on the outside. The oxygen level was building because of the amount of oxygen that had been released during the separation of the hydrogen and oxygen from the water during their energy crisis. Also, the foliage was getting thicker and producing more oxygen. It appeared to him that the meteoroid storm had stirred up a lot of dust which had acted as a fertilizer to the plants and made them grow even faster.

"TetTrella, what was that funny-looking creature that was just here?"

"That was an alien from the planet Earth, Twillie. They are called men. He and others like him control the area in the Crater. They and the Fem-Bird animals are keeping us out here. They don't want to let us have the games on our planet. They don't like sports. If we could find some way to get some really strong help, we could take over the planet and do anything we wanted to. I'd let you run the 'Galaxy Games.' You'd be responsible for all the invitations to the other planets. Wouldn't you like that?"

"I sure would. Can I see the facilities they won't let you use?"

"Sure! Just concentrate and I'll give you a mental telemetrical view of what they look like."

As Larry sat inside the tunnel to the Crater to catch his breath and recuperate, he got the feeling TetTrella was involved in mental telemetrical viewing. He closed his eyes and joined in on her thoughts and what she was seeing.

He thought to himself. *I wonder why she is looking at a previous Olympics site on Earth. Is she showing Twillie that site as if it was on Exvascia? She has never been interested in sports before except for a casual interest when viewing various planetary events by accident. I'd better tell DorLetha that she has brought someone here. I know she isn't supposed to. I wonder where she got the power to do it. I'll have to have DaKeta check and see if the power surplus is still building up. Delbert will need a lot of power in less than two months. I hope TetTrella hasn't found some way to tap the power source again.*

"That's some system you have for looking at things, TetTrella. Can you teach me how to do that?"

"Sure, Twillie, it's easy once you've been on our planet for a while. You'll also find we age very slowly here, so you won't get as old as the athletes you've been competing with. We can also help older athletes rejuvenate injured parts of their bodies."

"If you can do that, we could have a great training camp here. With the facilities you have here, we could put on a great combination of games!"

"You help me find someone who is big and strong who can get rid of those Fem-Bird animals and those alien men and we can take over this whole planet. You'll be the most powerful person in my control group. I think if someone could just hurt the Fem-Bird creatures they would back us and turn on the planet's rulers and the alien men."

"I think I can find someone to help us. My friend, GarGweth is a durk. You know how strong those gentle giants are. He throws the 50 stone suto but he isn't doing very well any more. He is getting too old and he has some injuries that plague him."

"What's a 50 stone suto?"

"It's a heavy circular piece of metal about one arm's length across. It has two handles on it. They hold the handles that come out of one edge while they spin around and then let go of it to see how far they can throw it. He can still throw it from here to the water."

"He must be really strong. If he came here, we could correct his old injuries and he wouldn't get any older. He'd be our champion and could compete again in other places."

"Let's go back to the planet, Lidy. We are in a big event there and I can talk to him."

"OK. Are you ready? Hold onto me tight so I can disintegrate us both to a subatomic particle state and transmit us there."

"You'll have to tell me how you do that and how you could stand to have those lightning bolts hit you without getting hurt. I've never seen anyone as powerful as you are."

Using the power she had gathered from the electrical storm, TetTrella beamed herself and Twillie back to Lidy and the athletic field where he and his friend were competing. Because of the amount of power she had stored in her body, from the lightning storm, she was able to send a strong enough beam to Lidy for the three of them to use to return to Exvascia.

She would use her mental powers to activate the beam when necessary. If she didn't have enough power to return the three of them, she could return herself and store up more power in her body or find a power source on the planet she was on to provide the energy she needed.

"It seems like the last time I viewed Lidy, there was a lot of fighting going on."

"That's quite possible. The intelligent inhabitants here, who have the strong form you have, are always fighting. They'll also go other places to fight if they are given something valuable."

That started TetTrella thinking. *Is that so? If GarGweth can't get rid of the Fem-Birds for me, I'll pay some of the Lidyans to come fight for me. I wonder what we have on Exvascia that might be of interest to them.*

"I'll see you in a couple days after you've had time to talk with your friend GarGweth."

"That's fine. I'll see you then."

While TetTrella was there, she took a look at the planet Lidy. Twillie went to find his friend, GarGweth. "GarGweth, when do you throw the suto?"

"Hi, Twillie how's my little friend?" GarGweth picked him up and sat him on his shoulders. "I'm in the finals tonight. Are you going to watch me?"

"Sure, how's your form?

"Here, let me set you down and you can watch me. GarGweth grabbed the two handles of the three foot wide brass discus and walked to the throwing area. He set himself for the throw, lifted the 125 pound disk (50 stone suto) and started it swinging in a large ark. When he had it going pretty well, he whirled just as the momentum from his initial swing brought it to the top of its arc. The second complete spin gave the disk enough centrifugal force to almost pull him off his feet. All the way through the second complete turn he strained to keep his footing. As he faced forward again, during the spin, he let it fly. As heavy as it was, it still flew 50 feet.

"That was good Gar, but you shouldn't look up until you are ready to let go of it. That will give you more distance."

"Oh! I forgot again. I'm glad you reminded me! I don't know what I'd do without your help or how I'd get into all these games. I don't know how to do anything else! I'd have a hard time feeding myself if I didn't have my game winnings. I'm getting too old to do very good anymore and my old injuries are stopping me from getting as much practice as I should."

"I'll be there to cheer you on tonight. How would you like to be able to compete in bigger events? What would you think if I said I knew a place where you could get proper treatment to make you feel ten years younger?"

"I'd go in a minute! Where is that place?"

"It's called Exvascia. They are going to hold the next 'Galaxy Games' there, if they can get a few problems worked out."

"Let me know if I can do anything to help you. I'll see you tonight."

"OK, you had better rest until your event. You don't want to be too tired."

TetTrella found a few Lidyans who were willing to go to her planet and give her assistance with her problem. "What might I have of value that I could give you for your help?"

"Do you have any gold or uranium?"

"Not any that I know of."

"How about that type of rock you have around your neck on that cord?"

"Is it valuable?"

"It is to us. We would gladly offer our services for some of it. Does it spark when it's struck against another piece?"

"Yes."

"Do you have a lot of it?"

"We have a whole mountain of it. We call it 'Spark Stone'."

"You couldn't have that much, nobody does!"

"We do!"

"You've got yourself a deal. Just come get us whenever you need help."

With the deal closed, TetTrella continued her tour of the planet. She was sure she would never be fertile now but she had learned how to travel to other planets on her own power and she felt that was even better. *If I only knew more about making war, I could take care of the problem on Exvascia myself.*

To increase her knowledge of warfare, she visited several battle fields on Lidy that evening and the next day. She knew that Twillie wouldn't be able to convince his friend, GarGweth, to leave with them until the games were over. Although TetTrella saw what was happening during battles, she didn't have any emotional reaction to it. It all seemed rather dull to her. Besides, she didn't know why the fighting was going on.

Twillie returned that evening to see GarGweth compete. The suto throw was getting harder and harder for him to place in. In the past he had always been first in it and the bulk throw. The bulk throw was where each contestant tried to throw a large log further than the other. GarGweth was having a problem even placing in this event now because of the strain on his knees when he initially picked up the log.

"Twillie, these creatures are all so young, big and strong. I don't know if I can beat any of them."

"It's your turn Gar. Go out there and find out how good you can do against them. Give it all you have on your first try! Remember you have five throws."

"OK. I'll try."

"There, I knew you could do it. You're tenth on your first throw out of twenty contestants. If you can do a little better on your next throw, you'll move up."

"I'll have to! Only the top five earn anything. Oh no look at how far everyone is throwing on their second throw."

"How did you feel about your last throw?"

"I didn't think it was very good! I know I can do better, but I don't know how much better or if it will be good enough to win me anything."

"Let's walk around until your next throw, Gar. Don't even watch the competition."

"I'm going to do better this time, you just watch and see!"

"Great throw, Gar, you moved up to eighth. Just don't try to fight the weight, let it work for you."

"OK, I don't think all the contestants are going to use all five of their throws. No wonder they did so well on their second throw."

"I told you, you could do it. Just go out there and make this third throw a good one. Maybe you can move up to fifth."

GarGweth put all his weight and skill into his throw and moved up to fifth. The weight of the125 lb disc was taking its toll on everyone.

Twillie noticed GarGweth bent over too much to get the greatest distance out of his throw so he mentioned it to him. “Lean back a little more and remember to get the suto swinging more like a pendulum before you start your turn and anticipate it reaching its peak when you start your spin. I think you can win this event if you'll listen to me. Do I ever tell you wrong?”

“No, Twillie, you always help me. I appreciate it.”

“Just concentrate on this throw and consider it your last. Give it all the concentration and energy you have left. You want that top prize don't you?”

“Yes, but I have to at least get second to be invited to the next big games, wherever they may be held.”

“You'll make it. Just get out there and give it your all.” GarGweth did everything his little friend told him to, and he took second place.

“They're too young and too good for me, Twillie. I can't compete much longer. I can hardly feed myself on one second place prize money. I'm not 90 lbs and 4feet 6 inches like you. I'm 440 lbs. and 7 feet 6 inches. That means I have to buy five times the food as you with less winnings.”

“That's OK! I'll help pay your way if you run short.”

“I wish I could win more so you wouldn't have to help me all the time!”

“Don't worry about it. What are friends for?”

The next evening, before GarGweth was to compete in the bulk throw, TetTrella arrived. She couldn't see how or why anyone would want to try to physically throw a huge log. The telekinesis method was so much more efficient and practical. Or, they could just levitate it. She decided GarGweth had an even less practical body than the humans. It didn't matter, as long as GarGweth could get rid of the Fem-Birds and the humans.

“Twillie, how did you do in your gymnastics completion?”

“I placed second twice Gar. The competition was very good today. Are you ready for the bulk throw?”

“Not really, my knee hurts. I may not get more than one throw in. I'll just have to see what happens.”

“You had better give it your all on your first throw and hope for the best.”

“Here I go.” GarGweth lifted the log from the blocks it rested on and quickly brought it into position for the throw. With a loud cry he thrust both giant arms up and away from his body. The 300 pound log thumped on the landing area and sent up a large white cloud of marking material.

“Great throw, Gar. You're first and there are only ten more competitors. I think it was smart to pass up those first two rounds. It let you know what you had to beat. Do you think you could have thrown again?"

"No! Look at the way my knee is swelling. I'm sure several of these creatures can do better than I have." GarGweth was right; he placed sixth and didn't get any prize money.

"I'll probably have to go to work on a star freighter. At least I'd know where my next meal was coming from."

"Hello, Twillie. How did you and your friend do?"

"Who is this lovely creature, Twillie?"

"This is TetTrella, GarGweth, she's from Exvascia. She's the one from the planet I was talking about. If she can get a few problems worked out on her planet, they will host the next 'Galaxy Games'."

"I've never heard of them."

"They're big on her planet. Besides, they can heal your knees with a special diet they have there. Shall we go and see what she has to offer?"

"I'm ready anytime you are. Let get our things together and join her."

"OK. Where do you want to meet us, TetTrella? The same place where we landed?"

"That's fine!"

"We'll see you in the morning then, TetTrella."

"Nice to meet you GarGweth, I know you'll do great on our planet. I saw you tonight. If you weren't injured, you would have done fine."

"Nice to meet you, I would do my best."

Chapter 10

Off To Exvascia

The next morning Twillie and GarGweth walked onto the athletic field with their bags in hand. “Twillie, this isn't a space port! How can we get to any place from here?”

“You'll see! This is really advanced state-of-the-art travel. You've never even heard of this kind of travel before.”

“Hello Twillie and GarGweth. Are you two ready to go?”

“Where did she come from, Twillie? She just suddenly appeared!”

“That's the way she travels. We're ready, TetTrella” With that statement TetTrella stepped between the two and put an arm around each. In an instant they disintegrated into a million pieces each and traveled on TetTrella's power beam to Exvascia.

As their bodies regenerated, GarGweth gasped, “Where are we?”

“We're on the planet Exvascia, outside the underground city. Isn't this a beautiful jungle?”

“Yes, I guess. What can we eat here?”

“We can eat anything that doesn't have a yellow or red leaf. If you eat a lot of this stalk that pulls apart, like this, your knees will heal as good as new. This one will make you strong.

“Twillie I'd like to have my knees working like the old days. TetTrella, was Twillie right about our not getting older very fast here?”

“That's right. Our time is over ten times slower than it is on other planet. If you stay here ten years you will only appear one year older to your friends, but they will be ten years older.”

“Can I see your facilities?”

“Sure, close your eyes and I'll give you a mental viewing of the last games and all the facilities. There you are! How does that look to you?”

“That's beautiful. Why can't you use the facilities?”

“See that creature over there? We call it a Fem-Bird. They and some other intelligent creatures, called men, won't let me back in the underground city. Its entrance is through that tunnel. What I need you to do is to grab them and give them a big squeeze. They will give up and let us through then."

"Why don't you do it yourself?"

"Because they are very strong and I can't squeeze them hard enough."

"They don't look strong!"

"Don't let them fool you. They can pop right out of your grasp without your knowing it. When you look around, you'll see them standing somewhere else close by. Don't forget that!"

"I won't, but couldn't we just talk to them?"

"They don't talk like you and I do. There isn't any way to communicate with them." Since the Fem-Birds had never seen Twillie or GarGweth before, they naturally wouldn't talk to them verbally. Since Twillie and GarGweth weren't very intelligent, she knew the Fem-Birds wouldn't be able to communicate with them telepathically.

TetTrella knew if GarGweth could catch and squeeze a Fem-Bird hard enough, they would be terminated. The pain would make them disintegrate and the fear of great pain would cause them to delay regeneration until it was too late. Of course, GarGweth would just think the Fem-Bird had slipped from his grasp because of what TetTrella had told him. When he looked around, he would really be seeing another Fem-Bird. She knew they would all look alike to him.

"Why don't you two just relax and enjoy the sunlight and fresh fruits? Take a little time and look around"

"OK, we'll be back after awhile."

While TetTrella was busy bringing her two new guests to Exvascia, Larry was busy inside the Crater helping Delbert and Adrian improve the house he had built in the Crater. As soon as Delbert got his body back, he and DorLetha would be living in the house with their offspring.

"What did Andre want to show you the other day, Larry?"

"Is DorLetha around?"

"I'll call her." Delbert sent a telepathic message to her and she appeared before them in an instant.

"What do you want Dell Bert?"

"Larry has something to tell us."

"DorLetha, Andre took me outside and showed me that TetTrella has brought an alien to Exvascia. He has about the same form as she prefers. I remember seeing him in a mental telemetrical viewing session I observed with TetTrella. He is an athlete, a gymnast from another planet. He is very small."

"That's forbidden. She can't bring aliens here without permission. What does she want with him and how did she get him here?"

"I'm not sure how she got him here. I don't understand why she was trying to convince him we have a whole city underground here. She showed him a view of a previous Olympic site on Earth and told him it was on Exvascia."

"What are you talking about, Larry?"

"The Olympics are sporting events that one country on Earth will host and athletes will come from all across the world to participate in. The one she showed him was in a city on Earth about 1600 miles from Mt. Baker where you picked me up. The Olympics are a type of planetary games for our world."

"I don't really understand any of that and I don't see the relationship between that and what TetTrella has done. I'll check with DaKeta and see if the power supply is still building up."

"While DorLetha's checking with DaKeta, can you tell me if anything else unusual is happening outside?"

"Yes, Delbert, there was a very strange and very strong electrical storm over the jungle area. I was glad to be in the tunnel leading to the Crater."

"Any idea what TetTrella is up to?"

"I don't know but I don't like the idea that she can bring aliens here somehow."

"I'm back. TetTrella isn't getting the power from us, unless she has built some kind of interceptor system. I'm not even sure she knows what one is."

"How do you think she brought the alien here, Larry?"

"I don't know Delbert. Let's go outside and see if we can find her and talk to her about it."

Although they searched all over the area outside the Crater, there wasn't any trace of TetTrella or the alien. "Do you think she is hiding from us?"

"No, Delbert, I don't think she is here. I'll post a couple guards at the entrance to the Crater and have them tell us when she returns. Let's go back inside."

"Why is Adrian swinging his arm like that?"

"That means he wants us to come to where he is right away, DorLetha."

"I wonder what has him so excited."

"We'll soon find out, Larry." With Delbert's approval DorLetha instantly delivered them next to Adrian.

"What's the excitement, Adrian?"

"The kids were flying around their favorite tree and landing on the limbs when Dell Britt changed to his primary form for the first time. He's just sitting there as naked as a jaybird. You can tell he is a little boy, other than having red feathers instead of hair he looks like you Delbert."

"Del Bert, he's like a little you. Did you look like your parent?"

"Yes, but I wasn't as grown up looking as he is. He would appear to be about two years old. I had better get him down before he falls. Can you tell if he will be able to change his form if he wants to?"

"Not for a while, Dell Bert."

Delbert climbed up the tree and took Dell Britt from the tree. "He seems frightened!"

Adrian chuckled. "I would imagine he is. He now has to learn how to function as a human being. He'll have to learn everything we had to by himself."

"Isn't he able to take care of himself? All our offspring are able to care for themselves at his age.

"No DorLetha. He is just a little child. He will need constant care for several years. I'm not sure how fast he will mature here. That's why we have been working on a house for us to live in. That way, he won't be in as much danger as he would be in the open."

All the Kaydra had joined the group now and were enjoying looking at the new little child.

"May I hold him, Dell Bert?"

"Sure DorLetha. Be careful, though, he may start trying to stand on his legs or start kicking." Delbert showed her what he meant. Dell Britt, meaning "Cheerful Way" had finally arrived, the planets first male offspring.

Shida was excited about learning how to care for the little boy. If Delbert wasn't there to show either Shida or Esdra what to do, "Uncle" Larry or "Grandpa" Adrian would provide the instruction. Larry and Adrian thought it would be fun to be called uncle and grandpa.

Esdra wasn't feeling strong enough to join the group. "We'll have to show Esdra when she awakens, Delbert."

"Sure Adrian. Shida, keep a close eye on the others. They may change at any time. Get them down to the ground as soon as possible and call one of us."

As Delbert finished talking, Dell Britt started to cry. DorLetha was so startled she almost dropped him. Delbert took him and held him close to his chest. Dell Britt put his head on his Dad's shoulder and the tears rolled down his cheeks.

"What's the matter with him? Why is water running from his face?"

"He's upset because he doesn't understand his new circumstances. He will find that he gets tired more easily, now that he can't feed himself and can't get around at all for a while."

"How will he learn these things?"

"We have to show him how to do everything. Let me show you what I mean." Delbert took Dell Britt by his two hands and walked him across the ground. On his first try he walked on his tip toes. "He has to strengthen his legs before he can walk. Then he will have to learn to keep his balance. This is just like his having to learn how to fly for the first time. He will have to learn how to use all parts of his body."

Delbert took his son with him to the cave that evening for dinner. He didn't eat much, but he ate a little. Everything he did was a learning experience he could build on. Delbert talked to him so he would get used to his voice. "It's sure nice to start with a baby that's two years old. You'll occupy enough of my time even at that."

Dell Britt crawled around on an animal skin while his dad made him some clothes. Larry had gathered a lot of animal furs and skins after they had gone through the comet's tail. He knew if more people came to Exvascia, they would need more pelts.

"That's quite a picture, Delbert, you sewing baby things. I wonder what the girls will look like."

"I guess they will either look like their mother or Dell Britt, Larry. I think Dell Britt likes Andre. I can't believe how patient Andre is with him. He seems to like the petting even though it's being done in an unusual way."

"You're right, Delbert. He seems to sense there is something special about this new arrival."

Delbert spent most of the next day with his son who he packed around in a sling across his chest. They spent the night in the house because Dell Britt had kept everyone up with his crying the night before. During the day, Delbert gathered extra fruits for his son to eat. During the day he tried to teach him how to drink Mellow Drop juice from a cup but he couldn't yet. He did better eating them one at a time.

Delbert had to be careful not to let his son get sunburned from the bright light that came through the crystal that covered the volcano-like opening in the top of the Crater.

Esdra was very excited about little "Britt", as she called him. "Adrian, will our little ones look like that?"

"What are you talking about?"

"I'm not going to another planet to look for a mate. I want you to be my mate."

"I guess what you've done for me shows how you feel. If you're sure you want it that way, we'll see what I can do for you when the time comes."

"Can you hold me, Adrian?"

"Yes, but why?"

"I just like the way it makes me feel."

"How's that?"

"I don't know? it's different now than it was the other day before I couldn't regenerate. It doesn't excite me the same way."

DorLetha heard her comments and asked Esdra some questions. "Can you use your transmutative powers or levitate yourself?"

"I haven't tried lately."

"What did you find out about her condition from the time-exempt telepathic storage banks, DorLetha?"

"Adrian, in our past, some Fem-Birds lost a lot of their powers when they became fertile. It depended on the abilities their mate had. They didn't care to have any greater abilities than their mate. Also, they tried to look as much like their mate as possible. Be sure to tell me if she starts gleesing."

"What's that?"

"Losing her feathers."

"Oh, you mean molting. What happens then?"

"I guess you'll have to make her clothes like you wear. She'll never get her feathers back because you don't have any."

In the afternoon two of the owl-like baby birds took their primary form. They looked exactly like their mother. After a couple hours they retook their bird form. That meant they could feed themselves and get acquainted with their Fem-Bird bodies at their leisure. Delbert was thankful for that. It meant he, Shida and Esdra only had to watch one child-like creature. That would give Delbert a little more freedom than he thought he would have.

The two little Fem-Birds would take their primary form now and then and try things Delbert was teaching their brother. Delbert could tell they had more of the powers of their mother because of the speed at which they learned. Their ability to learn things quickly helped to speed Dell Britt's learning process too.

The next day the final little owl took its primary form. It was different in that this little girl-like child had human hair but a feathery covering on her body like a one piece swimming suit like her mothers. With clothes on, she would look human. Delbert called her Letha. She wasn't able to change back from her primary form either. That meant her and Britt, as everyone was now calling him, would both have to be given special assistance and training.

DorLetha was as happy as she could be. Unfortunately Larry interrupted her enjoyment of her children late one afternoon. “DorLetha, we had better have a look around outside. TetTrella must be back. I've seen her mental telemetrical viewing of an old Olympic site again. She's back with Twillie and another male.”

DorLetha transported Andre, Larry and herself in a subatomic particle state to the outside of the Crater. “Andre, see if you can find TetTrella.” Andre obeyed Larry's command and after a few minutes he was able to locate TetTrella. He took them to where she and her two new associates were.

DorLetha took the form of the animals in the area and openly observed what was happening. Larry and Andre had to be careful not to be discovered. Unfortunately, neither Larry nor DorLetha were able to find out why the two aliens were there. Before dark they returned to the Crater.

“Larry, we had better go out again tomorrow and find out what they are up to. I still need to find out where TetTrella gets enough power to transport herself and others back here to Exvascia.”

“I'll be ready early. Let me know when you're free. What will you have to do about TetTrella bringing aliens here?”

“I'll check with the Matriarchal Directorate. The only punishment we have left is to spot her.”

“Spot her, what does that mean?

“We have to inflict pain someway until she can't stand it. She will disintegrate herself and be too afraid to regenerate herself. She'll just become a spot on the ground. It's such a cruel thing to do but we can't have everyone bringing anybody here they want to. Our males use to administer the pain. It's something the females could never do. We haven't had to do it to any of our own kind since we have been here. We may have to have your help. I know we would never to able to protect ourselves against aliens trying to kill us.”

“We don't intend to let any of you be killed. We'll do everything we can to protect you.”

“Thanks, Larry. I'll see you in the morning. I'll stop by the shelter and see Dell Bert, little Britt and Letha. Good Night.”

“Good night, DorLetha.” Larry went back to his cave and ate his evening meal.

The next morning Larry and DorLetha located GarGweth, Twillie and TetTrella just as they had finished a discussion. TetTrella went one way and the two aliens went the other. DorLetha followed TetTrella while Larry followed the aliens. With Andre's help, Larry was able to keep downwind of the two creatures and still keep them in view. They were up to something but he wasn't sure what.

The little 4 feet 6 inch creature started chasing a Fem-Bird. Every once in awhile he would do a tremendous tumbling run and cut the Fem-Bird off, directing it back toward where the Sasquatch-looking 7 feet 6 inch creature was waiting. Since the new fruit crop was just starting to come on good again, the Fem-Birds hadn't yet gotten their full strength back. Since they had been using their legs continually over the past three months, they were able to maneuver quite cleverly. They were tricking Twillie by switching off. While he thought he was only chasing one, he was actually chasing three. The Fem-Birds obviously thought it was a game the strange new arrival wanted to play.

Finally Twillie got tired and had to rest. When he took up his pursuit the last time, he managed to flush one of the Fem-Birds past GarGweth. GarGweth reached out with one giant hand, grabbed the Fem-Bird and strangled it as he lifted it off its feet. The pain and fear was too much for the Fem-Bird and it became a very small spot on the ground. The giant creature acted as if he had let the Fem-Bird slip through his grasp as the other two Fem-Birds darted around. He appeared to think they were the one he had held earlier. It was apparent he didn't know he had killed an intelligent being. The small creature appeared to be just as ignorant of the killing he had been a party to.

"So that's it. TetTrella plans on using these two and possibly others to rid herself of the Fem-Birds on the outside. Quick, Andre, find DorLetha!" Because of DorLetha's changing forms, Andre finally gave up trying to find her and found TetTrella instead. He knew DorLetha would be close by. DorLetha came and joined Larry in his hiding place behind some bushes. "I know what she's up to. Shall we get out of here?"

"You go ahead, Larry. I want to find out where she gets her power."

"I'll see you back in the Crater." Larry disintegrated himself and Andre and transported both of them back into the Crater. *I wondered what would have happened to Andre if I had let go of him in my mind when we were being transported in the subatomic particle state. I'll have to ask DorLetha.*

"Hi, Larry, what did you find out?"

"TetTrella has brought in a second creature which looks like a Sasquatch, Delbert. She has tricked him into killing the Fem-Birds. The little gymnast creature chases them into the Sasquatch's grasp. It squeezes the throat while holding it off the ground. The fear and pain causes them to disintegrate one final time. They just become a spot of subatomic particles on the ground. DorLetha calls this type of death being spotted."

"What are we going to do about it?"

"The first thing we have to do is tell the Fem-Birds what TetTrella is up to and warn them about the aliens. They just thought the little one, Twillie, was playing hide-and-seek or something with them. Twillie thought he was just chasing one when there were actually three of them giving him the run-around.

"They had his tongue hanging out for a while. They weren't even watching the Sasquatch. The Sasquatch seemed to think the Fem-Bird just slipped out of his grasp after he had squeezed it and made it become a spot of particles, because when he looked up there was another one close by watching him. It went after the other one, but it will never catch one of them itself. It seems TetTrella didn't tell them they were killing the Fem-Birds. I think they thought the Fem-Birds used some magic or something and slipped away from them."

"What will happen if they get tired trying to catch the elusive Fem-Birds?"

"I don't know but the new fruit crop will give them back their strength. I still don't know what it will take to get them to use their transmutative powers again or to believe that TetTrella would do anything to hurt them. If they will change to the ape or small bird form, they can escape almost anything."

"Is DorLetha coming here, Larry?"

"No, she wants to find out where TetTrella gets her power. "We may be able to get rid of one or two aliens, but if she continues to bring more it will be harder. These two aren't very intelligent, but others could be and have advanced weapons."

"I hope she finds out soon where TetTrella gets her power! I thought you said this was such a pleasant place?"

"It was until you arrived. I hope we can get things calmed down before you bring Carol and Darrell up here."

"So do I."

"How are little Britt and Letha doing?"

"Come see! Esdra is watching them. They are just starting to take a few steps on their own. They are also making some sounds and deciding what foods they like and don't like. I can tell they wish they could still fly. They enjoy playing with Andre too."

"I saw him rush over to them as soon as he got back. He seems to like having someone his size around, especially when he can do more than they can. How is their hand-eye coordination coming?"

"They're learning fast, but they are still at about the one-year-old stage. It's fun to watch them. Esdra made their outfits. She sure is enjoying them."

"Any sign of her molting yet?"

"Not that I can see."

When DorLetha went out the next day, it appeared that Twillie, the smaller of the two aliens, and the Sasquatch called, GarGweth, had decided they couldn't catch the Fem-Birds. TetTrella was angry but let them go off to enjoy themselves. She could see that GarGweth was eating a lot of the plant needed to heal his knees. That would only make him more dangerous.

TetTrella was trying to get them to catch the two Fem-Birds by the Crater entrance. Since they were guards of DorLetha, she didn't know whether or not they would keep their primary form. She assumed they wouldn't but there was only one way to find out, send the aliens after them.

Twillie and GarGweth finally gave it a try. When they did, the guards changed forms to animals more vicious than they cared to fight with. TetTrella was satisfied on that point, but she still wanted to get rid of the Fem-Birds in the Crater.

DorLetha watched TetTrella's activities for two more days without taking any action. The two aliens ate almost everything without red or yellow leaves. Before DorLetha returned to the Crater, she noticed that GarGweth was eating plants close to a path with yellow leaves. Suddenly their leaves turned green. *What is TetTrella's doing? I wonder why she wants that big creature to eat the yellow leaf plants. I'll check back tomorrow and find out what happens to him.*

When the morning arrived, Twillie got up and went searching for something to eat for breakfast. He didn't think anything of his big friend sleeping late since there wasn't anything for him to do but train anyway. After eating, Twillie worked at his gymnastics for some time before he even thought about GarGweth. When he thought of him, he went back to the cave TetTrella told them they could stay in temporarily.

"Hey, Gar, are you going to sleep all day? Oh, hi, TetTrella. What's the matter with GarGweth?"

"He's not feeling well. I gave him something to make him sleep. He'll be OK in a couple days."

"OK, I'll be back after awhile."

TetTrella muttered under her breath. *Don't hurry on my account. As many of those yellow leaf plants GarGweth ate, he won't wake up for a couple days. When he does, he'll be weak and feel dopey. Then I'll make him go without eating for several days. I'll have to move him where Twillie can't find and help him.*

She thought to herself. *When he gets so hungry he'll eat anything, I'll give him the roots of the red leaf plants. They'll make him wild and crazy. He'll hallucinate and have nightmares. He'll become addicted to them quickly.*

Since I'm the only one who knows what I've given him, he'll have to do what I say before he gets any more.

DorLetha won't be in control for long. I'll rule Exvascia. If there's another electrical storm soon, I'll be able to bring some Lidyans here and wipe those Fem-Birds out even quicker. I don't have to pay them! When I'm through with them, they can either do as I say or I'll disintegrate them. Once I get my hands on that solar reflector and the power beam transmitter station, I'll be more powerful than anyone.

TetTrella used her mental powers to move GarGweth to another cave. When she regenerated him, he was in a large cave with a very small opening. He could never get out, but he could get air. There was a small trickle of water in one corner where he could get a drink. The temperature during the day was about right but it got cold at night. TetTrella hid him from Twillie for two days. When Twillie finally found her, he was frantic.

"Where's GarGweth and where have you been? I've been looking for you for two days?"

"GarGweth got worse so I took him to Lidy. He'll join us again when he's feeling better. Do you have any ideas how to get rid of the Fem-Birds?"

"No, they're too tricky for us!"

"Well, there won't be any games unless we can make some changes. You heard the human yourself!"

"You'll have to bring some Lidyan warriors here to get rid of them."

"We'll see! Go out and enjoy the warm weather and all the free food that's there. GarGweth will be back in a few days."

"OK." Twillie went out into the jungle area and ate tropical-like fruits. He watched the Fem-Birds and accidentally talked to one. To his surprise it responded.

"What are you?"

"We're Kaydra, one of the intelligent species on this planet. Why are you here?"

"For the games!"

"What are games?"

"You know the different physical events your inhabitants hold in the underground city!"

"What underground city? What inhabitants? What games?"

"You know, the 'Galaxy Games'. TetTrella has been telling me about your inhabitants and the alien men who won't let her hold the games here."

"All we know is TetTrella isn't telling you the truth. We have no such things on this planet."

Twillie got mad and threw a rock at the Kaydra. The Fem-Bird instantly changed form and flew away before the rock could arrive. Twillie's small brain couldn't understand what he saw. He decided he would lie down in the grass along the stream and think about what he had been told. It wasn't very long before he was asleep.

DorLetha could only find Twillie when she looked for the three of them again. It worried her that GarGweth and TetTrella were nowhere to be found. At least she didn't see any more Kaydra spots. While she was looking for TetTrella she suddenly had a mental picture of Delbert's aura coming to her strongly from Earth. She transported herself back to the Crater.

"Dell Bert, Larry, Adrian come quickly." Delbert brought little Britt and Shida carried Letha. Adrian came with Esdra and Larry from the cave.

"Why did you call us?"

"Art's better. Look at this!" Everyone closed their eyes and concentrated on DorLetha's thoughts so they could join in on her mental telemetrical viewing.

"That's Art and Stewart in the hospital. It looks like Art is ready to leave with Myrna."

"Hurray, it looks like Art will be able to meet us in June on Mt. Baker and I can have my body back!"

"Let's listen, Dell Bert!"

"Thanks Art for getting me out of that cave-in. All the gold and silver in the world wouldn't be worth anything if I wasn't alive."

"You can say that again Stewart! I want to thank you too, Art."

"It's not right to thank me Clara. I knew Delbert needed his body back so I asked him out loud to get us out of there. They say there isn't any limit to how far a telepathic message can travel. Now I know it's true. On some star out there in the universe, he or DorLetha heard me and somehow managed to get us out. I'll have to ask him in June how they did it."

Stewart spoke up. "Please thank Delbert for me too. I would like to know what he tells you. Royal and Jake have uncovered the vein of silver you had Jake dig 35 feet for. Royal says it's the biggest silver vein and best quality he's ever seen. He says he'll give you half his share too."

"Oh, Art isn't that wonderful!" Myrna gave Delbert's body a big hug.

"Oh! Easy does it. Remember I've got broken ribs besides this broken arm. I couldn't tell the doctor how Delbert's body got the scar tissue on his lung or how he got the recently healed broken leg. The doctor said that there was blood in my stomach, as if there had been some internal injuries, but he couldn't find any. He says all the injuries appeared to have been very recent."

"Don't tell me Delbert and his alien friends had to patch you up before they brought you out!"

"They must have done something!"

"Don't you remember anything, Art?"

"Not after I passed out. You were awake before I was."

"But Candlestick says someone, who didn't sound like me, but using my handle, said I was hurt bad and to get right over to Cougar Creek Mine and look for truck lights. He called the rescue helicopter and it was there in ten minutes. They parked by the truck and had us to the Denver hospital in another ten minutes."

"Do you realize that Delbert and his alien friends made that call within ten minutes of when I last looked at my watch?"

"That's incredible, Art! Your leg must have healed before the blood dried on your pants. No wonder you can do a little thing like finding minerals. I sure hope you will forgive me if I claim ignorance about the whole incident. If I told anyone about this they would think too many rocks fell on my head for my own good."

"Don't think I'm telling anyone either, Stewart. When you get out of here, arrange for all three of us to buy both of those mines."

"I'll do that, Art. Next time I see you perhaps I'll recognize you. Bye."

"Take good care of him, Clara!"

"Don't worry, I will. It looks like you might as well have brought your nurse with you. I'll bet she has a fit when she sees what you did to yourself on your vacation."

"I'm glad I found him a nurse to take care of him. He's getting to be more than a hand full in many ways."

Stewart chuckled. "I agree, Myrna. If he keeps this up he'll have to hand Delbert his body back in a sack!"

When Delbert/Art returned home, he called out. "Nurse Liz, I'm home!"

"How was your vacation? Oh no, what did you do to yourself?"

"I got rocked to sleep."

"You got what?"

"I got caught in a gold mine cave-in. I broke my arm and a couple ribs on my right side plus the black eye. Being right handed, I naturally had to break my right arm."

"Well, I'm leaving at the end of May whether or not you're well. That gives you about six weeks to get well enough to take care of yourself."

"I'm trying to get well, but I don't seem to be having much luck. This will give you a chance to earn your money."

"I don't mind that, but I hate to see you all busted up. Are you going to stay for dinner, Myrna?"

"No, I have to pick up my kids. I'll call you Delbert when I hear from Carol."

"OK, good-by." Art kissed his wife before she went home. He thought to himself. *I can't wait to be my old self and be back with her.*

Back in the Crystal Prism Crater, Delbert laughed as DorLetha's viewing came to a close. "Thanks a lot, Art! Here I give you back a suntanned, physically fit, trim body and you give me back an I'La's mechanic's special!"

"Ha, ha, what are friends for?"

"Sure Adrian, go ahead and laugh. Old men who keep getting younger and stronger every day can say anything they want. If you don't watch out, you'll overdo it and end up too young for Esdra."

"Ha, ha, ha, look at our hosts' faces. They look like Americans watching a Chinese movie and trying to figure out what's going on!"

"I don't think that explanation helped them understand our little personal joke Adrian."

"You humans are strange creatures!"

The three men were so relieved to know that Art was OK; they laughed and joked for some time. Larry thought to himself. *How strange it is that only humans can laugh.* To his amazement, little Britt and Letha were laughing, but the other little Fem-Bird girls, Dora and Cara couldn't.

"Delbert, what are the two kids doing? Is there something wrong with them?"

"Ha, ha, ha, no, DorLetha, they're just happy. We humans probably use our laughing like you do your cooing."

DorLetha tried to "laugh" but it sounded more like a human cough. "I'll be glad when you get your body back Dell Bert, so you, I and the kids can all live together. I'll have to learn about these two and you'll have to learn about those two." With that, Dora and Cara who DorLetha was holding, changed back to their owl form and sat on each of her shoulders. They liked her to turn her head and rub her feathered head against their breast and wings. The two children Delbert held, Britt and Letha, acted like two happy, contented two year olds being held on their daddy's knees.

Meanwhile back on Earth, Myrna called Art Sunday evening right after Carol phoned her. "Art, Carol called a few minutes ago. She has taken a furnished apartment in Portland for about six weeks. She and Darrel are going to get married on June first."

"That's great. What else did she have to say?"

"Darrell wants to give Gail power of attorney over his affairs while they're on Exvascia. He is telling everyone that he is taking a trip around the world for his honeymoon. He said Gail and Michael could pretend to be in touch with them and then handle any problems the way they think is best.

"He has lined up another young doctor to take over his practiced until he returns. Carol suggested you sell Delbert's things that we don't want."

"That makes sense. If she was going to stay single for a while, a lot of Delbert's things would have been useful to her."

"She says Darrell owns a nice home that has recently been furnished by an interior decorator. She says the place looks beautiful."

"That will help me know what to do with Delbert's things."

"Gail's house sold this past weekend and she gave me their new address. They are doing great. Michael really likes his job and is doing very well. I'll have to give Carol their phone number so she can contact Michael about filming our next trip to Mt. Baker. I had a couple through the house today who are interested in buying it. They want to move in by June 1. I told them that is fine with me."

"Maybe we should go to Denver and look for a home there just in case ours sells, Myrna?"

"Let's see if they actually buy it first. There are a lot of homes on the market right now. If we have the money, it'll be easy to find a house."

"Let me know what happens. I'll see you later. Love you!"

"Love you too. Good night."

Chapter 11

TetTrella's Revenge

While things were OK with Art on Earth, and with the three men in the Crater, it was another story for GarGweth. He was unconscious for three days. When he awoke, he was dizzy and confused. Twillie was nowhere in sight and his bones ached from sleeping on the ground. His joints were stiff and his knees were swollen. He couldn't understand how he got into a semi dark cave with an entrance too small for him to crawl out of. He was hungry and the cave smelled awful for his relieving himself.

There wasn't any food in the cave and GarGweth was starving. He'd do anything for a meal. "GarGweth, I brought you some food and drink."

"Where did you come from? How did you get in here? Where is Twillie?"

"I just transported myself in here but I can't get you out of here until I get enough power stored up. The Fem-Birds used their power to put you in here to keep you captive. I took Twillie back to Lidy. He's trying to get some Lidyan warriors to come back here and kill the Fem-Birds and free you. How did you like the roots I brought you?"

"They're delicious. Can you get me more? I'm starving!"

"I'll see what I can do but the Fem-Birds are watching me."

"Will you tell Twillie where I am when he gets back?"

"Sure! I've got to go and try to get you some more food."

"Can't you stay? I can't stand it in here by myself. I'll go crazy. There isn't any light in here, it smells and the cold is causing me great pain in my knees."

"Try to hold on GarGweth, I'll be back just before dark!" TetTrella called out as she disappeared and transported herself to the outside once again. *That dumb animal, the way he gobbled up those red leaf plants he'll be climbing the walls with rage before morning. If he drinks any of that plant juice I left him he'll hallucinate every time he goes to sleep. I'll bring him more roots and red leaf plants tonight.*

TetTrella kept her word and returned that evening with more of the red leaf vegetables for him. She only brought half enough for him to have as a normal meal. Since he was starving, it only whetted his appetite. “Have some more to drink! It'll help to fill your stomach.”

“OK, I'm still hungry and I have to relieve myself, but I can't while you're here.”

“Oh, please wait till I leave. It's starting to smell worse in here. If I was you, I wouldn't let those Fem-Birds keep me in here like this. I'd kill all of them! They aren't intelligent beings. They just do what those men tell them to. When you get out of here, you'll have to kill all those Fem-Birds and the men to.”

“I'll kill all of them. I don't even know what men are! Why do they hate me?”

“Because they think you're important to games wherever you go. They don't want you to help hold the ‘Galaxy Games’ here! You'll have to kill all those Fem-Birds that are keeping you here!”

“I'm so hungry! I've got to have some more food! Can you bring me some more food please? I can't get out of here! You'll have to leave so I can relieve myself. I have to go so bad.”

“I can't get you more food until it gets light. Even then, the Fem-Birds watch me all the time. I have to pretend to eat everything I pick or pull up for you.”

“You'll have to leave. I've got to relieve myself.

“I can't leave; the Fem-Birds won't let me. I bet you'd get them good for this if you could get out of here, wouldn't you?”

“Yes, I'll kill all of them! I'll strangle them and stomp them into the ground. I'll smash them like this.” GarGweth smashed his fist into the sharp rock wall. TetTrella could smell the blood pouring out. GarGweth clawed, at the small opening trying to make it larger. His claws broke and the ends of his paw-like hands bled.

“Please leave I've got to relieve myself I can't stand the pain!”

“The Fem-Birds said I had to stay a long time after dark. They may kill me if I leave! OK, I'll risk my life for you.”

“I won't forget it, TetTrella. When I get out of here, I'll kill all of those Fem-Birds for you so we can hold the games. Please, please leave.”

“OK, I'll see you in the morning.” As TetTrella left she almost laughed out loud, not that she could.

“Aaahhh, oh, aaah, oh, the pain!” Thump, thump, thump! TetTrella could hear GarGweth pounding the wall. She knew what to expect. She had gotten him to drink an awful lot of juice. She knew that unless he drank water with it, his urine would burn when it came out. The longer he tried to hold it, the more his bladder would hurt.

From sheer exhaustion, GarGweth finally went to sleep. He had the worst nightmares imaginable. Often he was awakened by the pain in his bladder. He went through even greater pain when he urinated, but it couldn't be helped.

Very early in the morning TetTrella transported GarGweth out of the cave to the outside. She put him by the entrance to the Crystal Prism Crater where she knew the Fem-Birds would be waiting. When he awoke, the first thing GarGweth saw was the Fem-Birds. He let out a crazed yell and raced for them. They turned into giant wild cat-like creatures and fought with him. They were no match for a crazed Sasquatch. Both were killed in a short time.

After that GarGweth found and killed another Fem-Bird. When he could not see any others, he began to eat. As time went by, he found water to drink. It tasted good to him and even though it made his bladder hurt more for a while, it helped his body return to normal and he felt much better.

GarGweth slept through the afternoon. Twillie didn't look for GarGweth because he thought he was safe on Lidy and getting proper treatment. At the same time, GarGweth thought Twillie was on Lidy, trying to get some Lidyans to return to Exvascia with him and didn't bother trying to locate him.

Before he went to sleep, GarGweth soaked his hands in the cool stream. He couldn't understand how his hands had become so beat up. He figured the Fem-Birds had done it and that their cruel treatment must have been the reason for his nightmares. He wished he could find TetTrella because he had a strong urge for the plants or vegetables she had brought him before. Maybe he would see her in the morning.

DorLetha and Larry found the bodies of their two Fem-Bird guards outside the cave entrance the next morning. They were not spotted, but had been killed in the form of a strong wild animal. Only something more powerful could have killed them. It must have been TetTrella's giant alien associate.

"Let's see if we can find that giant creature she has brought up here. We've got to find some way to stop what he's doing."

"Larry, here's another spot of one of the Fem-Birds from outside. It looks like he's been busy." DorLetha and Larry looked for the Sasquatch for two more days without finding him. They decided to search for him every day until he was found.

After GarGweth went to sleep in the warm afternoon sun, TetTrella found him. That night she transported him back into the tiny cave by holding onto him and disintegrating both of them into a subatomic particle state. Once inside the cave they regenerated.

When GarGweth awoke, he thought the Fem-Birds had again grabbed him when he was asleep. Since he was inside the cave, he started looking for the good tasting vegetables TetTrella had brought him before. He took a couple bites and felt strong again. After a short time he started hallucinating and he liked it. After finishing all the vegetables that had their red tops removed, he ate the other vegetable. Soon he was in a rage, dizzy and still hungry. The same old juice was there but he wasn't about to go through that kidney and bladder pain again.

GarGweth searched the cave when he was lucid and found the small trickle of water. It didn't satisfy his thirst, but it helped. He didn't have enough sense to dig out a little pocket in the rock for the water to gather in. Instead he filled the juice container and drank from it. Before he did, he relieved his bladder. That made him feel better but it added to the stench from his feces.

When TetTrella brought GarGweth more food, she found him asleep. She didn't even bother to wake him. She could tell by the way he writhed in his sleep that he was either hallucinating or having nightmares. She was happy with his three kills, but not satisfied with the time it took her to get him into an adequate rage to catch and kill the Fem-Birds.

TetTrella decided she would have to bring some Lidyans to Exvascia as soon as she could. Back outside the cave she was soon seen by Twillie.

"TetTrella, I'm getting tired of being here all alone. Where have you been?"

"I've been trying to figure out some way to kill the Fem-Birds."

As TetTrella and Twillie talked, Larry and DorLetha came across them and listened in on their conversation.

"Let's go get some Lidyan warriors and bring them up here."

"It looks like it's going to storm, Twillie. If it does, we'll be able to."

"DorLetha, talk softly, so they don't hear us. What does a storm have to do with her bringing aliens here?"

"I don't know. We'll just have to wait and see." It wasn't long afterwards that the rain started to fall and then came the thunder and lightning. As Larry and DorLetha watched, TetTrella walked to the center of a meadow, stretched her hands toward the sky and waited for the lightning to strike her. In a few minutes it did. She lit up like a flash bulb. Then just as quickly she sent a bolt of power from her eyes out into space.

"What's happening to her, DorLetha?"

"I think she just used the power from the lightning bolt to activate an old power beam path to another planet. It's like the one I have to Mt. Baker. It looks like she plans on using it."

"Why hasn't she taken shelter yet?"

"She needs more power to bring the aliens back to Exvascia!" DorLetha was correct. TetTrella stood in the field until she had absorbed several more direct hits by lightning bolts. When she was satisfied, she beckoned for Twillie. With Twillie clutched tightly in her arms she disintegrated them both and disappeared on the power beam.

On Lidy, TetTrella contacted those who had agreed to fight for her. To her surprise, they demanded partial payment before they would go with her. That meant she would have to return to Exvascia for some Spark Stone. TetTrella hated to return to Exvascia empty handed. Besides that, she had to use power to gather the spark stone and later transport it to Lidy.

Back on Exvascia, TetTrella went to see GarGweth and took him more vegetables to make him crazy. "TetTrella I wondered what the Fem-Birds did to you. Did you bring me some more of those good tasting vegetables?"

"These?" she said, as she clutched them tightly to tease him. To her surprise, GarGweth laughed at her. His powerful swollen paws clutched her throat and he picked her off the floor and bellowed in her face.

"Give them to me! Give them to me! I've got to have them." In order to keep from being spotted, or killed, TetTrella had to unleash a powerful energy charge at him through her eyes. The two strong electrical charges that flashed from her eyes threw him against the opposite wall. His hand sprung open wide in a violent spasm as the bolts of electricity hit him. He lay unconscious on the floor of the cave in his own feces from days past.

TetTrella was wild with anger herself as she left the cave. *The next time I unleashed my wild, crazy giant on the Fem-Birds, they had better beware or GarGweth will kill a lot of them.*

TetTrella returned to Lidy to get her help. Because of the power she had used to zap GarGweth and to mine and transport the Spark Stone, she would only be able to bring back a few Lidyans.

Meanwhile, Twillie was thinking about what the fem-birds had told him. *Is it true TetTrella is using me?* He'd find out for sure by checking with GarGweth. Although everyone knew GarGweth on Lidy, Twillie couldn't find anyone who had seen him since they had left the day after the games. That must mean that TetTrella had him captive somewhere on Exvascia. He would have to play along with TetTrella in order to save his friend.

"I'm back. Are you Lidyans ready to go?"

"Where's the Spark Stone?"

"Here it is. Is that enough?"

"Yes, that will pay half of what is due for about 25 of us. Let's go."

"I'll show them where we take off from, TetTrella."

"OK, Twillie. I've got to rest for a while. I'll meet you all there."

By the time the Lidyans and Twillie got to the spot on the athletic filed, from where TetTrella would take them up to Exvascia, she was ready to give it a try. TetTrella was worried about a lack of power to take that many bodies back with her to Exvascia at one time. "Everyone take hold of the person next to you and hold on tight. Get as close together as you can."

"Quipla! This doesn't make any sense! We aren't going to go anywhere like this!"

Twillie spoke up. "She has a lot of power. We don't need the conventional space vehicle to get there. Give her a chance."

"We're not going anywhere. Forget the whole thing."

"Wait, I've given you more than enough Spark Stone to pay the entire amount for at least a dozen of you. Who wants to go with full pay?" Twelve decided to give her another chance. "Hold on tight to one another. The rest of you stand back. You too, Twillie, I'll come back for you."

Twillie knew TetTrella wouldn't have enough power to return for him, until she had gone through another storm. He couldn't leave his friend, GarGweth, in her clutches that long. She may have killed him already. "Wait TetTrella, I've got to go back with you. I've got a plan that can help the Lidyans kill the Fem-Birds quicker."

"All right, hold on and let's see if I can get all of us to Exvascia." TetTrella used all her power and borrowed energy from the minds of her army of 12 to get them to Exvascia. Her use of their mind power made all her army tired. They had to rest before they could do anything on Exvascia. TetTrella set GarGweth loose, hoping his hatred and anger would enable him to find and spot a few more Fem-Birds.

GarGweth woke up outside the cave again. He still had the same pain accompanied by greater hallucinations and worse nightmares. Unfortunately for Larry he was outside the Crater looking for TetTrella, Twillie, Fem-Birds and aliens. He was just crossing a stream at the top of a waterfall when GarGweth came charging from the undergrowth. DorLetha was downstream, below the waterfall. When GarGweth bellowed, she looked up.

"Ooooahhhaw!"

"What the hell is that?" Larry answered his own question by turning around. *Oh hell, it's that giant Sasquatch. I have to get away from him, I can't fight him. Look at how fast he's coming. I won't even make the other side of the stream. I'll have to dive over the falls far enough out so I'll be able to hit the pool below it.* As he dove, he wondered if he would hit the bottom of the pool. Swoosh! He made a perfect entry. The Sasquatch hit the water and rocks below in an awkward position. Larry thought it might die from the fall, but he didn't wait around to find out. He quickly swam and climbed out of the water onto the bank where DorLetha was.

"Are you all right? How could you do that? Look, there goes the Sasquatch lumbering off dragging his left leg as he goes."

"Let him go! I can't stop him without some kind of weapon."

"Weapon, what's a weapon?"

"Just let me rest, DorLetha, I'll explain to you later. Please take us back into the Crater." DorLetha did it instantly.

Adrian, Esdra, Shida, Delbert and I'La rushed over to meet them. "What happened to Larry?"

"Check him over I'La and I'll explain. We were looking for the giant creature that TetTrella brought here. I was downstream below a waterfall, when I heard an awful noise. I looked up and saw the Sasquatch chasing Larry toward the waterfall. Larry jumped over the falls and the Sasquatch fell over trying to grab and kill him. I couldn't react in time to disintegrate Larry and bring him down to where I was. I was afraid he would get hurt when he hit the water below the falls, but he didn't."

"How could you do that and not be hurt, Larry?"

"We call it diving, I'La. I've done a lot of it before. It was either dive or be killed."

"Larry, I don't understand why you only see TetTrella and her alien friends once in a while?"

"I don't know either, Delbert. That Sasquatch acted like he had rabies or was crazy."

"Do you think TetTrella has him drugged? She may be controlling his mind with a plant that makes him dizzy or causes him to have weird dreams or thoughts when he's awake."

"Anything is possible with TetTrella. We saw she gets her power by absorbing the full force of lightning bolts."

"If she can withstand that kind of power surge, why doesn't she just kill all the Fem-Birds herself?"

"I don't think she has a killer instinct. She is just insanely jealous because she is sterile and DorLetha has always beaten her at everything they've done. She is trying to get even and take over control of Exvascia at the same time. Who knows what she is doing out there now? She just got back from somewhere this morning."

"Are you two going out again tomorrow?"

"We have to Delbert!"

"Who is the visitor you've brought with you?"

"She's part of the navigation team Delbert."

Larry sensed there was a problem. "What's wrong DorLetha?"

"There is a small moon from another planet ahead that is on an elliptical orbit. It may be in our orbit about the time Dell Bert is supposed to be sent back to Earth to get his own body."

"All we need is to have another energy crisis just when we need power. What options are there in a situation like this, DorLetha?"

"We can try to speed up our planet or change the orbit of the other body. Our sophisticated navigation system will make the decision as to what is the best solution. It will also determine how close our two paths will come."

"Don't you make any decisions?"

"Yes, we'll decide to go with the navigation system suggestion or decide for ourselves what to do. We generally prefer to take less risk than the navigation system says we can."

"Does that mean you'll be tied up with that problem for a while?"

"Yes, Larry. We've never asked for outside help, but could you see what you can do to stop TetTrella and whomever she brings here from killing the Kaydra?"

"I'll do everything I can."

"I'll help you, Larry."

"Thanks, Delbert. I'll explain what is happening out there this afternoon and then we'll go out in the morning."

"Should I leave my body in the cool cave and use free soul flight?"

"Good idea. I can disintegrate and transport myself, but I haven't tried to transport another human being. DorLetha, what happens if I let go of the person I'm transporting before we regenerate?"

"They will be gone forever, spotted, killed."

"OK, OK, I get the picture. Better travel on your own Delbert."

CHAPTER 12

LIDYAN WARRIORS

While Art and Myrna were preparing to close a chapter in their lives, Larry and Delbert were getting ready to face a new challenge. "Are you ready to go down to the cool cave, Delbert?"

"Yes, Larry." Delbert walked to the cool cave and lay down on his back with his hands folded over his chest. Larry kept in constant touch with Delbert until his body was close to freezing. As Delbert's body functions slowed almost to a stop, he set his soul and spirit free to roam. He accompanied Larry back to his cave. Larry used his increased mental capacity to disintegrate and regenerate himself in the cave he called home.

Delbert communicated telepathically with Larry. On the outside, he would be able to go everywhere and see everything without being detected. He and Larry were sure to find out what was going on outside in the morning.

GarGweth was hurt in the fall from the waterfall, but TetTrella didn't care. While he was sleeping late in the afternoon, TetTrella transported him to the cave for further confinement and feeding of hallucinogenic plants.

Twillie searched all day for GarGweth but couldn't find him. He was starting to get desperate. Tomorrow he had to find him. He hoped TetTrella would be busy in the morning with the Lidyans so he would have a chance to slip away.

The next morning, Larry and Delbert went outside the Crater and found TetTrella. They were very concerned when they saw the dozen new recruits she had brought to Exvascia to form her army. Obviously she wasn't satisfied with the job of killing the Fem-Bird Kaydra that Twillie and GarGweth were doing. They listened in as she gave them orders.

"You are all very skilled warriors. There are only a little over twice as many Fem-Birds as there are of you. They aren't armed in any way. I want you to kill all of them. At the entrance to the Crater and the underground city you will find two clever Fem-Bird guards. Be careful of them. They are the Queen's guards. They can change to other creature's forms. The other Fem-Birds can change forms, but they are trying to prove they can make it out here without doing so.

"There are also three humans to look out for. I don't know that they have any weapons, but they may be able to make themselves some. They walk upright and are about this tall." TetTrella raised her hand to her head height of about 6 feet. "They have a light skin and no fur or hair covering their bodies. They have slender builds and don't appear to be very strong.

"You've all received your payment and I expect results. If I don't see results, you'll have a hard time convincing me to take you home. Are there any questions?"

"What can we eat?"

"Anything but the Crinum, you'll recognize them by their yellow leaves. Don't eat the red leaf plants either. Are there any other questions? OK, let's go to Spark Stone Mountain. There is a bonus for you if you get the job done soon."

"What kind of bonus?"

"When you return home, I'll take the weight of anyone who gets killed back in spark stone to be divided up between those left."

"That's more than fair. Show us what we're after and we'll get the job done for you. What an easy way to get rich."

"I'll show you a Fem-Bird on the way to Spark Stone Mountain." The Lidyans had to walk to Spark Stone Mountain to become familiar with the area where they were to search for the Fem-Birds.

"Is it always hot and humid like this?"

"Yes, the days are twice as long as the nights too, so it doesn't cool off much at night."

"Are there any natural dangers out here, like in the jungle areas?"

"There are a few. I'll tell you about them as we go along. This is Spark Stone Mountain."

"It can't be! No planet has a whole mountain of Spark Stone." The Lidyans took stones and struck them together to see if sparks flew when they did so. Sure enough all the stones were real whether they could believe it or not.

"Delbert, it looks like we'll have nature on our side out here. That will help. Also, if there isn't another thunder and lightning storm, TetTrella won't be able to build up her powers to bring others."

"You're right, Larry. I just wonder what their weapons do. When they split up, we're not going to be able to keep track of all of them. Look! Twillie is trying to slip away from the group unnoticed. I'll follow him and find out what he's up to."

"OK. Remember, you'll have to find me, Delbert. I won't be able to find you when it's time to go back into the Crater tonight."

Twillie did slip away from the group to look for GarGweth but he didn't have any idea where to look. He didn't dare call out for him because TetTrella may hear him and do to him what she may have done to GarGweth.

Twillie searched for GarGweth until midday without finding him. He finally decided to try and talk with a Fem-Bird, if he could find one. After several hours he was able to find a Fem-Bird. "Can you tell me what happened to my giant friend?"

"TetTrella keeps him in a small cave with an entrance too small for him to get out of. Every three days she lets him out for a few hours to hunt us."

"Why would she do that?"

"She is giving him yellow and red leaf plants to eat. She has taken the leaves off so he can't tell she is giving him something he shouldn't eat."

"She said you creatures would lie! What kind of animals are you anyway?"

"We aren't animals. We're one of the two larger groups of intelligent beings on this planet. TetTrella is from the other main group. She wants to take over the planet."

"You just don't want her to hold the games so your inhabitants can enjoy them."

"There are less than 300 inhabitants on this planet. About 250 live inside the Crater and the rest of us are out here!"

"What about the underground city?"

"There isn't any city like that on this planet."

"I can't believe you! Prove to me you are telling the truth!"

OK, I'll take you to your friend!" Twillie followed in disbelief.

"Your friend is in there."

"This had better not be a trick." When he was almost in the cave, TetTrella appeared in the cave.

"GarGweth, you have to get out there and get rid of those Fem-Birds."

"I can't, I'm too dizzy, my bladder hurts all the time, my knees are so swollen I can't walk and my hands are all cut up."

"When I tell you to kill, you'll kill or I won't bring you any more vegetables."

"I need some of those good tasting vegetable to stop the pain!"

"You're letting those Fem-Birds ruin my plans. It's either the Fem-Birds or the apes. There isn't room for both groups of us."

"You'll have to leave! I've got to relieve my bladder. If I don't, it'll burst. It hurts so badly when I urinate, that I can only stand to do a little at a time. Please leave, I can't hold it any longer.

"You'll hold it till I'm ready for you to relieve yourself."

"I don't think it's the Fem-Birds that are holding me here, it's you." As GarGweth started to get up, he let off a little of the pressure on his bladder. "Aahh, aahh, it hurts so badly." TetTrella didn't waste a second. She sent two short blasts of power, in the form of bolts of electricity, from her eyes into the tine puddle GarGweth was making.

The power she emitted almost electrocuted him. "Aahhh, oh the pain, the pain! Please don't kill me!" GarGweth was too weak to get up. "No! Please no more! Aahhh, help! Help! Don't kill me!" Zap! Zap! 'Aahhh, oh." TetTrella was starting to enjoy torture. She left him unconscious on the ground, totally helpless.

TetTrella left the cave steaming mad. Outside the cave she saw two Lidyans sitting and eating while a Fem-Bird could be seen off in the distance. "I thought I told you to kill those Fem-Birds. Now get to it or I'll kill you." One of the Lidyans moved too slowly and two lightning-like bolts of electricity shot from her eyes and fried the Lidyan on the spot.

Zap, snap, crack! The other Lidyan was ready to fight. He had rolled over on the ground and was firing blue bolts of power from his own weapon at TetTrella. A big chunk of the mountain, next to TetTrella, crumbled and fell around her. To escape, she instantly disintegrated and transported herself to safety.

Delbert was in awe. "How much power can she have left in her body?" He saw Twillie crawl into GarGweth's cave. The alien with the powerful weapon then killed two Fem-Birds that were over 400 yards away.

Twillie raced from the cave to where he had left the Fem-Bird. Unfortunately it had been killed by the Lidyan. He looked for a long time until he found one that would talk to him. "Help me. I know that TetTrella has been using my giant friend and me to kill you. Since we didn't kill enough of you she has brought in others. They have weapons. I just saw them kill two more Fem-Birds not too far from where TetTrella keeps my giant friend.

"We didn't know we were killing you. When you disappeared, we thought you were some kind of magical creatures that had slipped away from us like TetTrella said you would. She never even told us you were intelligent beings.

Twillie continued, "She is torturing my friend with bolts of electricity and giving him red and yellow leaf vegetables. I've got to save him. I've got to tell him she lied to us."

"Don't let him eat or drink anything she brings him. Put Mellow Drop juice in the container and get him some vegetables with the broad green leaves. Then pull him some of the green shoots that grow by the quagmire. Be sure not to step in the quagmire or it'll suck you in. Watch out for that living vine that is hanging from that tree beside you. It seems to be swinging in the wind toward you. If it gets you, it'll make a meal of you. You had better not let TetTrella see you either."

"What can I do to repay you?"

"Help get rid of the new ones that have come to kill us."

"I'm awful small, but I'll try. Thanks! Tell your friends we're sorry we harmed any of you. We just didn't know."

"I'll tell them!"

"Look out! Here comes a Lidyan. I'll see if I can get rid of him. Hey, warrior, some of the Fem-Birds just went across this marshy area. If you hurry you can get close enough to blast them."

The Lidyan raced past Twillie and rapidly sunk beneath the surface of the quagmire because of his struggling. Before he went under, he took a couple shots at Twillie. Twillie hadn't wasted any time getting away from the quagmire. Unfortunately for Twillie the shots brought another Lidyan. "Was that a ray blaster I heard?"

"It sure was. One of your warriors was chasing a Fem-Bird and tried to cross the swamp. He just went right under. I've never seen anything like this stuff. Come on over here and check it out."

The Lidyan leaned down with one eye still on Twillie. "It sure is a sticky mess!" Twillie casually brushed the ivy-like limbs of the Living vine, growing on the tree by the quagmire, toward the crouching warrior. Instantly the limbs grasped their prey and wrapped him up like a cocoon. Once the first few limbs grabbed him, others quickly came to their assistance. The life was squeezed from the Lidyan before he could get a shot off.

In a few minutes little Twillie had taken care of two of the strong, brave Lidyans by himself. He even grabbed the weapon as it fell from the limp hands of the warrior. *Perhaps the human aliens can use this to help get rid of the other Lidyans.* He asked a Fem-Bird, "Can you take this thing to the human aliens? Tell them I got it from the Lidyan warrior who got caught by the living vine."

"I'll take it right to them."

Twillie headed for GarGweth's cave with a load of food and Mellow Drops. "Gar, Its Twillie, are you in here?"

"Oh, ah."

"Gar, I saw what she did to you. Here, eat some of these Mellow Drops. The Fem-Birds say they will correct your bladder problem. They want to help you. TetTrella has been feeding you yellow and red leaf vegetables."

GarGweth couldn't even lift his head. Twillie propped his head up on his lap and fed him a cluster of Mellow Drops. After the Mellow Drops, he feed him some of the shoots and some of the vegetables that would make his joints feel better. After a couple more clusters of Mellow Drops, GarGweth sat up.

"Twillie, where have you been?"

"TetTrella told me you were ill and that she had taken you back to Lidy. I didn't look for you because I believed her."

"She told me you had gone back to Lidy to get some help to kill the Fem-Birds. They sure are strange animals. I think I have them and then they disappear."

"They are killed when they disappear, Gar. TetTrella fooled us there also. Besides that, the Fem-Birds aren't animals; they're intelligent inhabitants of this planet. 250 live inside a Crater. There isn't any underground city and no games."

"I've never killed anyone before. I just thought we were going to scare them! TetTrella's mean. She hurt me. She says she is going to hurt me more until I kill the Fem-Birds. Can you get me out of here?"

"I don't know. I'll have to ask the Fem-Birds if there is some way to get you out. Don't eat anything unless you can tell I picked it. The Mellow Drops should make it easier for you to relieve yourself. What she had you drinking was bad for you and meant to make you hurt."

"She's very bad, Twillie. If I ever get my hands on her, I'll make her disappear!"

"The Lidyans have powerful weapons. I gave one to a Fem-Bird to take to the alien men. Maybe they can get rid of the Lidyans. TetTrella killed one today after she left you. I killed two more by the quagmire. It's sticky and so soft you can sink out of sight in a minute. The living vine, the vine growing on the tree by the quagmire, gets its food by a heat seeking method. Once one of its long droopy branches touches something it's dead. The branches all work together to completely wrap up its prey. Can you eat any more?"

"I'd like something for later. If TetTrella treats me like she has been, she'll not bother me for a couple days. She'll think I'm starved and weak."

"You should play dead when she returns. Maybe she'll forget all about you then. That would give me a chance to feed you and figure some way to get you out of here. I'll bring you more food tonight. I have to go get something to eat myself now."

"Thanks, Twillie. I don't know what I'd do without you to look after me."

Delbert had followed Twillie all day and it was almost dark when he left Twillie and GarGweth to go find Larry. As Delbert traveled through space in free soul flight, he saw a Lidyan about to fire on Larry. He sent Larry a telepathic message, "Larry look out behind you."

Larry whirled around just in time to grab the arm of the Lidyan and thrust it upward as his weapon discharged. Larry disintegrated the two of them as they grappled. Before he regenerated himself, he mentally pushed the alien from him. "I guess I'm about to find out whether DorLetha was right or not and if I know what I'm doing. Am I alone now Delbert?"

"Yes, great job. That means there are only eight of them left."

"What happened to the others?"

"Tricky little Twillie got two himself. He got one to step into the quagmire and got another with the living vine when it looked to see what happened to its friend. He also got one weapon and gave it to a Fem-Bird to deliver to us. TetTrella saw two Lidyans resting rather than hunting and she fried one of them. The other tried to kill her. His weapon sure took a chunk out of the rocks behind her."

"What do you mean she fried one of them?"

"She stared at him and let out two bolts of lightning from her eyes. She won't have much power for long if she keeps using it like that."

"I wouldn't care if she didn't have any power left. Let's get back inside the Crater."

Back in the Crater, Larry greeted Adrian. "Do you have anything I could eat?"

"Yes, I've got a couple large fish on the spit. They should be done about now."

"How did things go out there today?"

"We got four of the Lidyans. Twillie and GarGweth will be on our side now. TetTrella has been feeding GarGweth vegetables with yellow and red leaves. I think he has become addicted to the red leaf plant root already. Today TetTrella was torturing him with bolts of electricity from her eyes."

"You sure were right about her, Larry. Has she gone mad or something?"

"I think so, Adrian. She knows she is sterile and is obsessed with power. Did a Fem-Bird bring you a weapon for us to use today?"

"Yes, it's right here. It's a strange looking device. I haven't figured out how to fire it yet."

Delbert continued to communicate telepathically with Larry and Adrian.

“Their weapons unleash an unbelievable amount of power. I saw how they used it. Like Larry said the other day, Twillie and GarGweth didn't know they were killing the Kaydra. GarGweth still doesn't know the Kaydra can take other shapes. We need to get him out of that cave someway.”

“We'll have to talk to DorLetha about that one. I have an idea of how to get rid of the Lidyans.”

“How's that, Larry?”

“Remember my telling you about the bite of the poison fly, outside the Crater, being lethal?

“Yes.”

“Well, if we could catch a couple of them outside and milk the poison from them, we could put the poison on darts and use the stalk of the tube plant as a blow gun.”

“What would you make the darts out of?”

“We have a plant here that has very large thorns on it, like a Hawthorne tree. They are about 1½ inch long and over ⅛ inch thick at the base where we would break them off the stalk.”

“How are we going to catch the poison fly?”

“I'm still working on that. They're about the size of a bumble bee. We don't need to catch them alive. If we could just kill a few, we could pull their heads off and get their internal poison sack. I've never tried to kill one because I didn't want to be bitten. I suppose we could just try hitting one with a stick as its feeding or resting.

“I've got a sling that I've become fairly good with. It'll take a couple days before I'm ready to go back out. Why don't you keep an eye on what's happening outside, Delbert, and I'll work on the weapons.”

“That's OK with me, Larry, but those are Stone Age weapons against the alien's space-age weapons. There are only eight of them left. If we can get rid of them, maybe we can develop better weapons for the next group TetTrella brings up.”

“Better yet, Larry, why don't we just get rid of TetTrella. Then we'd know for sure we only have to kill eight of them.”

“I don't know how we could kill her, Adrian, I can't imagine her death coming by spotting, but I could be wrong. She has such power compared to us, there wouldn't even be a struggle to report if she came after us herself.”

“What about the area beyond the quagmire? Is there a bog there Larry?”

“Yes, it's kind of like a bog, Delbert.”

“Is there any ignitable gas there? If so, would there be some way we could get them in that area and then set it on fire?”

"I don't know. If there are gas fumes and we lured them there, the fumes alone would kill them Delbert. I think TetTrella can only store so much electrical energy. The way she has been using it, she should be weakening soon. That might give us a chance to get her, if we can find her."

"If there's another storm soon, we'll really have trouble. I'll bet she brings up more Lidyans."

"Delbert, would you explain to Adrian how the weapon was fired while I go ahead and start working on our crude weapons. Did DorLetha have any idea when she would be able to spend some time with us?"

"It sounds like the analysis of that other planet's moon might take a few days of constant monitoring. I'll tell her you need to talk with her whenever she is free."

The next day Larry worked on weapons and Delbert observed what was going on outside. "I'm back, Larry. How did your day go?"

"Fine, I got a crossbow made. I'll work on arrows tomorrow. What happened outside?"

"Twillie and GarGweth are working on enlarging the cave entrance. He is digging it out from the inside and passing the dirt and rock to Twillie to dispose of. Also, two Lidyans made the mistake of taking a nap beneath the mist three. Now the other six know about that."

"At least we now only have six to get rid. How's the weather out there?"

"There's no sign of a storm yet. The sea looks like it's starting to get a slight tide."

"I know I've seen the planet where TetTrella got her warriors. It was one night when she was mental telemetrical viewing. It would help if I could go back and take another look at that planet and what goes on there. It would give me a better idea of what these warriors are capable of. Did you see TetTrella out there today?"

"Not once. She didn't even go to torture GarGweth. Twillie and GarGweth expect her tomorrow. GarGweth is going to pretend to still be ill and hallucinating. He wants to keep from being tortured and he wants to get his strength back. I hope he fools her. If she ever finds out he's OK, I'm afraid he's done for."

"I can't feel too sorry for him. He did kill a few Kaydra even if he didn't know it. I'll need the hunting knife you brought from Earth Delbert, when I work on arrows. I've got a supply of arrow heads that I made from pieces of rock I picked up while on Spark Stone Mountain. I also have a supply of feathers for the quills. I'm going to sleep now. I'll see you tomorrow night."

"Good night, Larry." Delbert traveled to where DorLetha and the navigators were working on their problem.

"Hi, Dell Bert, how are things going outside?"

"Hi, DorLetha, we're down to six Lidyan warriors now. TetTrella hasn't been seen for several days. GarGweth and Twillie, the two athletes from Contrar, want to be on our side. Twillie got one of the warrior's weapons. Adrian is learning how to use it'

"Why don't you have DaKeta look at it also. She is good with equipment."

Twillie wants to know if there is some way we can get his friend out of the cave that TetTrella transported him to and where she is keeping and starving him. She is also feeding him Crinum and red leaf vegetable. It makes him crazy. Now she is also shocking him with jolts of electricity. I think she has gone crazy."

"Is there anything else I should know about?"

"Larry thinks he has seen those two athletes before in TetTrella's mental telemetrical viewing. If there is some way you can get his mind to recall that viewing, we may be able to learn something about our foes."

"I can do that. Give me another day or two. We are at a critical point now. If we use the right amount of energy, we can speed up our planet and the moon would then pass behind us. We have to use enough force to be sure we accomplish our goal."

"Do you have enough power to accomplish the amount of boost you need?"

"No Dell Bert. Would it hurt if I shut off the power to the outside for a couple days?"

"No, in fact, that would really help us outside. The Fem-Bird Kaydra are strong enough to last a couple days now, but I don't think the Lidyans would like it. They would be too hungry to think about fighting. It would probably give GarGweth and Twillie more time to try and dig him out of his cave without TetTrella seeing what they're doing. It would also give Larry a couple more days to work on weapons. I'll tell him in the morning."

When Larry awoke, he was glad Adrian was there to talk to. "I wish things were quiet on Exvascia like they were until you came. I don't like having to go to war every day. If DorLetha wasn't tied up, it would make things a lot easier."

"I'll agree that it's been active since I got here."

"One good thing has happened anyway. I'La's plant and vegetable diet has made you look five years younger and some of your gray hair is turning black again."

"I feel great. I think I feel Delbert approaching in his free soul flight form."

"You're right, Adrian, it's me. Larry, DorLetha says she can help you remember what you saw on Lidy when you were watching TetTrella's mental telemetrical viewing. She also said she is going to shut the light off to the outside for a couple days in order to store up enough power to boost our planet's speed. She said that was the best bet because it would take much more power to slow our speed or try diverting the oncoming moon."

"So we don't have to go outside either today or tomorrow. There's only one thing wrong with that. How are we going to know whether or not there is a lightning storm?"

"I'll go out. I don't think the Lidyans can do anything but search for food for the two days it'll be dark. Maybe they'll succumb to the forces of nature out there."

"We'll have to wait and see. You go on out and keep track of what's happening. I'll continue to work on our mighty weapons."

DorLetha stored the power from the solar reflector for two days. When all the calculations were made, a powerful burst from their power beam was unleashed. The power of the beam caused the planet to lurch forward. Would it be enough? They wouldn't be able to tell for a couple weeks.

The navigational maneuver left DorLetha free for a short period. "What can I do for you, Larry?"

"Is there any way you can get GarGweth out of the cave TetTrella has him in? Also, do you know of any way he can withstand her electrical charges she uses to torture him?

"Not until I am sure our course has been corrected so that the approaching moon will swing around us and go into orbit rather than colliding with us."

"How about getting my mind to go back to the mental telemetrical view it had of the planet Lidy, where TetTrella got her warriors?"

"Yes, I can do that."

"Keep a sharp eye out for anything that we can use against them or for any weakness they may have Delbert and Adrian."

"DorLetha, should we try to kill TetTrella?"

"That would solve the problem outside unless the split between the two different groups of Kaydra has grown too deep. Do you have any knowledge of that situation?"

"I don't think they would be fighting or refusing to use their transmutive power if TetTrella didn't keep them agitated,"

"That might be the case, Dell Bert. Then she should go! The law says the punishment for willfully bringing aliens to our planet for one's own cause is punishable by death. We just don't have any males to enforce the law. They always did it and this is the first time such a situation has come up since they have been gone.

"As far as the telemetrical viewing goes, think back to the first time you saw Twillie. What was he doing?"

"He was just breaking into the elite gymnast group. That's him you see there on the parallel bars. This was earlier than the time I was talking about. He had finished his event and had won a second place. After that he started to talk to GarGweth about his second event. Wait a minute, there's TetTrella. That isn't the viewing I had in mind. It looks like you've picked up on one of TetTrella's other trips to the planet. Let's back up and see what she was doing. There it is, fighting on Lidy. That's the same thing I saw in an earlier viewing. TetTrella appears to be trying to learn about warfare and warriors."

"Look at those weapons. Any idea how they work, Adrian? I don't see how we'd have a chance against warriors like that."

"You're right, Delbert. OK, that's enough of that! Anybody have any ideas?"

"Yes, Larry! During soul flight and disintegration, do I have telekinetic abilities?

"Sure, remember how you herded the animals into the cave after our last power outage?"

"Yes! Maybe I could use their own weapons against them if they lay them down?"

"I could join you Delbert in my disintegrated form and hurl or levitate rocks at them. We may have them yet. Let's get out there and see how many are left."

"Thanks, DorLetha. Larry and I'll see you tonight, Adrian."

Outside it was much cooler than it had been because of the solar reflector not being turned toward the outside. The first thing the men checked for was TetTrella. Again they couldn't find her. They had no way of knowing what form she may have taken.

When they got to GarGweth's cave, they entered and found that he and Twillie had been busy most of the time it was dark. It was slow going for them because they had to be sure not to make the cave opening look any larger than it had been. This meant they had to move a lot of unnecessary rock both above and beside the hole on the inside. It appeared that in a couple days GarGweth may be able to break out. How could he keep TetTrella from taking him back to the cave or any other place when she wanted to?

Outside the cave they came across the remains of two of the Lidyans.

"What do you think happened to them, Larry?"

"From what I've been told, a Kelcha beast must have found them in the dark. They are the most ferocious animals on the planet. They fight like a wolverine. I've never seen one, but the Fem-Birds have told me about them.

Larry continued. "Look what do we have here? It looks like two gray blood suckers sensed two more Lidyans warm bodies and had themselves a banquet. I told you you'd have to look out for them when you're out here. That's why I wear this pouch around my waist out here. It also looks like they dropped their weapons and now we have six against the two remaining warriors. If we can take care of those two we would be free of our problems for a while."

"Free for a while may be the case. I'm afraid there may be an electrical storm late this afternoon after it being so cool the last couple days. I hope it's small. I'd hate to see TetTrella bring another group of warriors here!"

Larry and Delbert quickly moved around the inhabited area invisible to the naked eye. Late in the afternoon they located the two remaining Lidyans in a jungle area stalking three Kaydra. "Any idea how to get rid of these two?"

"I think I'll regenerate myself, Delbert, and then give out a crow call. That will bring a couple weasel-like Progs racing to find the gray blood suckers. Of course we know there aren't any. That will distract the warriors. I'll try to grab one and disintegrate him. If the other shoots at me, think of his weapon. You should be able to raise it up. That will affect his aim and I'll be able to regenerate later. See if you can find out how he makes his weapon fire. Now that they've separated it looks like a good time to show up. Here goes!" Larry regenerated himself and called out, "Cah! Cah!" Sure enough, two progs ran to the spot where the startled Lidyan stood. Larry knocked his weapon away as the Lidyan grabbed him. Larry instantly disintegrated both of them. He separated himself from the Lidyan. As he did so, the other Lidyan opened fire, not worrying whether or not he was shooting at his own kind or not.

Larry moved a distance away from the area of the action and regenerated himself. That did away with one of the last two Lidyans forever.

While that was going on, Delbert saw how the safety worked on the weapon. The weapon had to be grasped firmly before the safety mechanism was released. To fire the ray gun, one had to apply pressure on the hand grip furthest from the trigger and pull the trigger at the same time. It would stop firing when the trigger was released and the pressure on the furthest hand grip was released. At that time, the safety could again be moved into position to keep it from firing.

Delbert found he could levitate the weapon and deliver it to Larry. He told him telepathically how to operate the safety mechanism and how to fire it. Larry took the weapon and readied it for firing. He yelled at the Lidyan. When he turned around, he fired. The blast disintegrated the Lidyan.

Larry spoke out loud to Delbert. “That's the last of them. Now we have seven of their ray blasters. That will help if TetTrella brings others.”

Twillie approached the two men. “Will you take me inside to talk to your leader? I've got to find out what I can do to get GarGweth out of that cave. If not, I need to find out how he can protect himself from TetTrella's strong bursts of power. If she can withstand a lightning bolt, the inhabitants of this planet should be able to tell us how to ward off a relative small amount of power that she may direct toward him.”

“What do you think Delbert, you're the psychologist?”

“Let's take him in and see if DorLetha can at least give him an answer to his last request.”

Twillie didn't understand who Larry was talking to and didn't hear any answer but he walked with Larry through the tunnel to the Crater. “Where did TetTrella get that vision she showed us of the fantastic games?”

“She took them from her past memories of mental telemetrical viewings of events on our home planet, Earth. She was just using you two to get rid of the population that didn't look like her. Not as many of the Fem-Birds followed her outside as her own kind. Therefore, there wasn't any reason to kill them. They were actually already on her side. I think she's crazy.”

“I have to agree with you humans. What she did to GarGweth, after he did his best for her, doesn't make any sense. She just seems to enjoy hurting him now. Why couldn't she just kill the inhabitants she didn't like herself?”

“She didn't want her own kind to turn against her. I suspect they don't know she brought the Lidyans here. The ape form Kaydra doesn't work like the Fem-Bird form ones. They are trying to see whose form is the strongest. I guess they figured that the group with the greatest number left in the end would be considered the strongest regardless of how the other group was depleted.”

"”I can understand that.” Twillie said. When we compete on Lidy, we see them fighting among themselves all the time for one reason or another.”

“I hate to admit it, but we humans do too. Here we are! This is all there is to the great underground city. The Kaydra that live in here usually use an animal form so they don't eat as much or take up as much room.”

“Where's your leader?” Twillie asked.

“I think my friend Delbert is getting her. She is busy trying to correct the planet's course so that it doesn't hit a companion body of another planet, or a moon as we humans call them."

"Can they change their planet's course?"

"They have to at times to avoid collisions. It is small so it is possible. They get their power from their solar reflector which is what looks like a sun to us."

"DorLetha, this is Twillie I've told you about. Twillie, this is DorLetha the Queen."

Twillie bowed. "I'm sorry to interrupt your work but I'm trying to find a way to save my friend GarGweth's life. TetTrella tricked us into coming here with her to your planet. We're athletes and she told us you had big athletic contests in your underground city. Since we won't kill any more Fem-Birds, now that we know they're intelligent inhabitants, she is keeping GarGweth in a little cave with a hole too small for him to get out of. She is torturing him with power beams from her eyes. She was also feeding him vegetables with red leaves and yellow leaves.

"I'm exchanging the food and drink she has been giving him for what he should have so he won't be crazy or mad. We're trying to dig him out of the cave, from the inside so TetTrella doesn't notice it. I was wondering if you could somehow get him out of the cave. Perhaps he could be transported out like we were transported here. If not, is there some way he can withstand her power charges?"

"I'm very busy, so I can't come and transport him out of the cave for a few days. If GarGweth will accept the power she sends at him, as though its warm sun rays strengthening his body, he will be able to withstand a fairly strong charge. If he doubts or has his mind distracted, he'll have absolutely no defense. Do you understand? If he can kill TetTrella, he can stay here if he wants to."

"Thank you, oh Queen. I'll go tell him at once.

"I'll walk out with you Twillie."

"Thanks for everything, Larry. I'll try to tell GarGweth everything. I hope it doesn't storm. I think TetTrella's power is being used up. If she gets another charge of electricity like I saw her take the other day, I don't think GarGweth could concentrate hard enough to withstand her power."

"I hope things work out for you two, Twillie. I'll talk to the Fem-Birds guards on my way back in. Good-bye."

"Good-bye, Larry."

TetTrella had seen Larry take Twillie into the Crater's tunnel entrance. She wished she knew what had happened inside. It was easy enough for her to find out. She followed Twillie into GarGweth's cave in her invisible form and listened to everything he told him.

When she heard what was said, she was very mad. One thing Twillie didn't tell him about was the Fem-Birds power to change their form. That gave TetTrella an idea. *When I get power again from an electrical storm, I may be able to change all the Kaydra and animals to the same form as the Lidyans. That way GarGweth can't fight against my warriors because every living creature as well as the Kaydra will look alike. That will also stop the human's effort to get rid of the Lidyans. That will make the Lidyans job a snap. Just wait till I get my power built up! I'll get even with you two, the humans and the Fem-Birds.*

Chapter 13

Meanwhile, Back On Earth

"Hello Art, this is Myrna. Remember the couple that I told you looked at the house last weekend? Well, they want to buy it and move in, in late May. Do you think we could meet their deadline?"

"Why don't you just say 'yes' and then you'll have to make it? Did you get the price we asked for?"

"Yes, and they have their own financing. That means we can buy a nice home in Denver. Since I'm selling the house before you are back as yourself, is there going to be a problem?

"I don't think so. You got it free and clear when I died because of the mortgage insurance we had. Why don't you come over in the morning and help me get started closing out my/Delbert's, bank accounts, etc."

"OK, I'll see you then."

"Good night, Myrna. Love you!"

Myrna arrived early the next morning to help Art start terminating everything related to Delbert's existence. "Here it is, the last part of April. In 60 days I'll no longer be Dr. Delbert Tinsley, professor of psychology. There'll be no more Dr. T!"

"That sounds like a mystery thriller!"

"It almost is! Listen to this and tell me how it sounds. During the past nine months, while I've been on sabbatical, I have looked forward to my return to teaching. Although my physical condition has greatly improved, I'm not psychologically ready for a teaching commitment. Therefore, I am tendering my resignation effective with the close of spring semester. I trust this early notification will assist you in your search for a replacement.

"Thanks for giving me every opportunity to return to my former position. Your consideration is appreciated. I have enjoyed my tenure at the University and my association with all the faculty and staff of the Psychology Department. Sincerely. How does that sound? I assume Delbert enjoyed his job. Even if he didn't, I think it would be nice for him to say so."

"I'm sure everyone enjoyed working with Delbert. I don't ever remember him complaining about anyone. I think that will do. Remember Art, as Delbert, you may have said it differently than he would have but that doesn't matter. What else do you have to do?"

"I think I should stop using his checking account so there'll be time for all the checks to clear before the end of May. Did you notice that Delbert's hand writes his name the same as when he was using his body? I guess that comes from the subconscious level of his mind."

"Did you expect it to be different?"

"I thought it would be sloppy like my hand writing was. Now, let me see. Oh, I need to write a letter to my landlord telling him when I'll be out of the apartment. Nurse Liz says she'll be flying out on May 25th with her daughter. If you have to be out of the house on that date I think we can work it out.

"I was thinking of selling everything since Carol won't need any of Delbert's things. I think we should keep Delbert's rare books and a few other things. Maybe Carol could ask him about that soon, if he contacts her. Or if he contacts you, you could ask him about such things, as well as, what to do with his retirement money. I think Carol should get it. If she and Darrell stay on Exvascia longer than expected, they may need the extra money.

"You know, I like both Delbert's den and library. I think we should just move them when we leave."

"Art, do you remember the artist's home about a mile from the Donovans? Clara made mention of it possibly being for sale, when we were there last June."

"You mean the one that the artist's wife gave us a tour of?"

"That's the one! We both liked it! The only problem then was money. We won't have that problem now. Why don't we call Clara and Stewart and see if it's possibly still for sale?"

"Go ahead! I have their number right here. Why don't you use my cell phone and call them. You can put it on speaker so I can hear what they have to say."

"OK."

Myrna dialed the Donovan's number and Clara answered.

"Good morning, Clara. This is Myrna and Art."

"Good morning to you two. What's new?"

"Hi, Stewart, we have a cash buyer for our home and we have to be out by May 25th. Do you two remember the 'Tour of Art Show' that you took us on last June? All the artists had opened their home studios for showings."

"Sure, I know most of them personally."

"Great, Clara. Remember the home about a mile from you that the artist said might be for sale. We said we'd like to see their home because it was so big and beautiful. I think it had two and a half baths, recreation room and four or so bedrooms. The artist's wife showed it to us.

"That's the Weston's home. I just talked to Janet yesterday. They still want to sell, but they haven't listed it with a realtor because of the high commission cost. They are looking to be cashed out. At $380,000 they aren't sure they can find a qualified buyer on their own."

"Do you two think its worth that much, Stewart?"

"I do, Art, based on what others have sold for around here. I know they would be making a big profit on it at that price. What do you think, Clara?"

"I think it would sell for that price, Stewart, but since it isn't listed they should be willing to knock off some for not having to pay a sales commission."

"That sounds within reach, Myrna. Why don't you get their number and we can call them?"

"I'll get their number, Myrna." Clara said. "Stewart, why don't you tell them the good news you have?"

"What's the good news, Stewart?"

"I figure your share of the monthly profit will be between $5,000 and $10,000, Art. Royal and I are willing to make you the majority owner in the mine. We were split fifty-fifty as partners. We were just going to draw up the papers!"

"Hey, you two don't need to do that. Wouldn't you think one third would be more fair, Myrna?"

"I agree, Art. If it hadn't been for Stewart's friendship, probably none of this mine business would have even come up."

"We were just about ready to give up on mining before you came along, Art. We really don't need the money. Besides, one third of a lot is much more than 50 percent of nothing. I'll tell you what. I'll make it 40 percent for you; 35 percent for Royal, because he works at the mine all the time and I'll keep 25 percent. Can you go for that?"

"That sounds great to me, Stewart. Thanks! Does it look like we'll be able to buy the other two mines?"

"It sure does. I'll probably have the deals closed by the time you get here in May or by early June. I think I can get them on a royalty basis, so we don't have to come up with money except for the equipment to start working them."

"That would be great!"

"Art, how did the Army cover your death without letting anything out of the bag?"

"They said I was on a special scientific mission for them and was killed. Why?"

"I was trying to think of a way you could get 'reborn' by the army. I know you'll be recognized by people from time to time. It just seems that, when you're you again, it would be nice if you didn't have to hide anything. Is Myrna receiving social security payments on you too?"

"You're right, Stewart. Maybe your idea about Michael filming our next trip to Mt. Baker is right, Myrna. We'll see what we can do about that, Stewart. I just hadn't thought about how to get my entire situation turned around."

Clara gave Myrna the Weston's phone number, they said their good-bye's and hung up. "Can we call them right now, Art, and see if they are willing to sell?"

"Sure, go ahead. It can't hurt anything."

Myrna eagerly dialed the number Clara had given her. "Hello."

"Hello. Is this Mrs. Weston?"

"Yes."

"I'm Myrna Noack. My husband and I were in your home last June for the 'Tour of Art Show'. We were with Clara and Stewart Donovan. We liked your home and when you mentioned you might be interested in selling it, we had you show us through it."

"I remember. You said you would like to move to the Denver area sometime because your husband was a geologist."

"We were talking to Clara today and she said you folks may still be interested in selling your home. Is it possibly for sale? "

"Yes, we're interested in selling but we haven't listed it yet. Where are you calling from?"

"We're still in Oregon, but we've sold our home and have to be out by May 25th."

"Let me get my husband on the line with us."

"Art, she's getting her husband on the line. I'll put it on the speaker."

"This is Earl Weston. My wife says you and your husband are interested in buying our home."

"I'm Myrna Noack and my husband Art is on the line with me. We were wondering if you had any idea what you would be willing to sell your home for."

"Not really, we were thinking about a figure of $400,000 if we went through a realtor. That means we would get about $376,000 but we would like to get just a little more. Would you be willing to pay $380,000?"

"That's in our price range. What kind of terms were you offering?"

"We hadn't worked on any financing yet. We still have a $50,000 assumable mortgage on the house. I imagine we could carry a second if we had to."

"We'd like to fly out and look at it again if we could. If we gave you until day after tomorrow, could you set a price, if we offered to cash you out?"

"You mean you could give us the difference between the selling price and the mortgage in cash?"

"That's right!"

"You get here day after tomorrow and we'll show you the house again and have a price for you!"

"OK, we'll see you then. Thanks a lot."

"You're welcome and thanks for calling!"

"What do you have in mind Art?"

"I thought we could go look at the house. I can pretend to be your brother so they'll not suspect anything if they see you around Denver with me until I get my body back. If we talk to them face-to-face, I think I can read their minds. That will tell me how much they would really be willing to sell the house for. We can take a break in the negotiations and I can let you know what price they have in mind."

"Wouldn't it be nice if people could set the price they want for something and then afford to wait until a buyer comes along who is willing to pay their price?"

"Yes, but that would take a long time. Some greedy people would never sell anything."

"Gee, I can't believe we would have our own dream house so soon. I'll only be 33 and you'll just be 37."

"Most rich people are retired by the time they're forty! Well, let's get back to my letter to the landlord. I've stopped using Delbert's credit cards and canceled his magazine subscriptions. We could close his safe deposit box today but I had better keep the savings account open if I'm not going to write any more checks."

"While we're at it, do you want to write to the retirement board?"

"Yes, I'll give them a time when they'll need to make the computations. Since I won't be available to pick up the check if it comes late, we'll have to figure out how we're going to handle that."

"Here's the address for the retirement board and this is my retirement account number. All you have to tell them is that I'm retiring at the end of May and that I would like to take a lump-sum payment. Be sure to make a second copy to send to the payroll office at the university. That way, they'll send the necessary final payroll information to the retirement board as soon as it's available."

"I bet you broke your arm so you wouldn't have to write these letters. How about a kiss, as partial payment, for my help?"

"Sounds like a bargain! Hum, that wasn't half bad. How would you like another as a bonus?"

"You're the boss!"

Myrna took the letters with them when they went to the bank. After clearing out Delbert's safe deposit box, they used their cell phone to make their airlines reservations to Denver.

"Before we go home, let's stop by the moving and storage company and get set up for our move. Let's assume we'll buy that house in Denver. It'll take all our furniture plus Delbert's and some more to fill it."

"Might as well. If we don't buy that house, we'll just have to find another. We still plan on living in Denver, so the date and destination will still be the same."

"Why don't you call Gail and Michael as well as Carol and Dr. Lyons and invite them down for the weekend. If we're going to try getting my real identity back, we have a lot of planning to do."

"Do you think Delbert will join us, when we're all together?"

"I hope so, but I can't be sure.

Myrna made the calls they had discussed that evening and arranged for everyone to be at her house Sunday afternoon. The next day was spent cleaning house and packing a few boxes. There wouldn't be much time to pack things during the next three weeks or so.

Before picking Art up on the day of their Denver flight, Myrna took the kids to her mother's. Todd would soon be five and Lisa two and a half. They were seeing a lot of their grandmother lately because of all the running around Myrna was doing.

"Good morning, Liz. Have you got Delbert all ready to go? How are his ribs mending?"

"He's doing fine and mending rapidly. He's getting his suitcase."

"Hi, sweetie, you must be ready to go!"

"I sure am." Myrna hadn't been called sweetie by her husband since he had been in Delbert's body. It was good to hear it again.

The drive to the Portland Airport took almost two hours. By the time they got to their gate, the plane was about ready to leave. They arrived in Denver early in the afternoon and picked up their rental car. Art stopped to call the Donovans who had asked if they would have dinner with them when they came to look at the Weston's home.

"While we're driving out to the Westons, I thought we could talk about how we're going to present our offer. I have been thinking of making an offer of about $365,000 Why don't you offered them $360,000 and when they decline, you can say, 'Delbert, why don't we go outside and talk about it.' I don't know that I'll be able to read their minds or that the two of them will be in agreement on a price. You should offer them what I think is the lowest they will accept, as long as it isn't over $380,000."

"I think that would be fair. If that's what they want, or will take, they should both be happy that way. If we can agree on a price, will we have Stewart's Attorney draw up the contract?"

"That's what I had in mind. We could stay over Saturday if we have to, but I'd just as soon leave tomorrow."

"There's their home, Art. Isn't it beautiful? I love the landscaping and the view. I think the view would be spectacular even if it wasn't such a grand day."

"Just be sure to introduce me as your brother."

"I'll try to remember. When I get excited I call you Art. I'll just park over here by the third garage door. You certainly have it made, a nurse to help dress and feed you and me to love and chauffeur you around."

When the Winstons came to the door, Myrna introduced herself and Art. "Hello, I'm Myrna Noack and this is my brother, Delbert Tinsley. My husband couldn't make it because of other commitments."

"Glad to meet the two of you. I'm Earl and this is my wife Janet. Come on in. I understand Janet showed you around last June during the 'Tour of Art Show'. I was so busy that day I don't remember you."

"We understand. Since my husband and I were so interested in the house, I had a good reason to remember you folks. You've done some interior decorating since I was here. It looks great!"

"Well, if you want to sell something in today's market, it has to be kept up and reasonably priced."

"I feel fortunate, Janet, that my house sold so quickly and that the buyer was able to cash us out."

After the tour of the house, the three car garage and the swimming pool area, they all went inside to talk about the purchase price.

"We have a tile roof, six-inch walls, excellent insulation, triple-pane windows and a heat pump for heating and air conditioning."

"Would either of you like something to drink?"

"Coffee would be fine, Janet."

"I like the construction, Earl, and the tile roof didn't allow them to skimp on the ruff trusses. Your heat bill must be reasonable."

"Our heat and air conditioning bills are about the same as our neighbors with smaller houses. That's part of the reason we could afford to own it."

"Here's your coffee. Would either of you like cream or sugar?"

"Cream, please!"

"There you are. Has Earl told you what price we decided on?"

"Not yet, I think he's still trying to talk construction to Delbert."

"We would like to get $380,000 for the house. How does that sound to you?"

Art spoke up. "I was thinking more like $365,000. We aren't sure what its worth since we haven't looked at any other homes."

"We didn't know how to price it. Since you are able to pay cash, maybe $380,000 is too high!"

Art was getting signals from the Westons. It seemed they were between $370,000 and $375,000. "Delbert, why don't we go outside and talk about it for a few minutes? Would that be OK with you folks? I think Delbert's offer is a little low. Of course, that's what big brothers are for. We won't be long."

"Take your time. That will give us a chance to think about it too."

"What kind of a reading did you get, Art?"

"Your last statement really changed their thinking. They're both ready to sell now. Earl has come up to his wife's first figure of $368,000, but she now wants a little more just so she can say 'I told you so.' I think they will take $370,000. Originally they were thinking of $400,000, so they've come down about the amount of a sales commission."

"I think it's a good buy at that price. They should be willing to take that offer considering we're cashing them out."

"Let's go back in Myrna and you can make our offer."

"We're back. I'm willing to offer $370,000 and cash you out."

"Earl and I talked it over and we came up with that same amount. So, if you are serious, you have bought yourself a home."

"I'm glad we didn't have to argue over the price. Here is a cashier's check for $10,000 as earnest money and a simple earnest money agreement to sign. We're going to see the Donovans and we'll ask them to have their Attorney draw up the agreement. Thank you and you'll hear from us as soon as the Attorney has the contract drawn up. I'll have the funds May 25th. So, until then, it's been a pleasure buying from you."

"We thank you two for coming all the way out here. I'm sure your husband will love the home. Sorry he couldn't come with you this time, but he has seen the house before. Good-bye!"

"Good-Bye!"

"Are you driving us over to the Donovans Myrna?"

"Yes, right after we stop at the bank and set up a checking and savings account for us. I want to have Stewart get his Attorney on the paper work as soon as possible."

When they reached the Donovan's place, Stewart called his Attorney and found out he would be available to write up a contract for them the next day if they were available.

"Let's get it done tomorrow, Art. I'll call Janet and tell her where and when to meet us as soon as the contract is ready."

From then on, things went smoothly and both parties were able to sign the contract before the Noacks headed home. They would meet with their friends on Sunday to try and solve other problem areas of their lives.

Chapter 14

The Revival Plan

On Sunday, Art had Nurse Liz drive him over to Myrna's. He could tell by the number of cars in the driveway that he was the last to arrive.

"Come on in, Delbert. We were just about ready to eat without you. I was going to ask you how you've been feeling, but that doesn't seem like such a good idea. How does the other guy look?"

"Thanks a lot, Michael! Didn't they tell you a truck hit me?"

"Really, a truck hit you!"

"No, I got caught in a mine cave-in in Denver, Gail. Why don't we talk about it after we eat?"

"Sure, Delbert, you always loved Myrna's cooking. It looks and sounds like you've made a lot of progress since our wedding."

"Dr. Lyons," Delbert put his good left arm around his shoulder, "has made sure that I got special help."

After dinner, Dr. Lyons commented on Myrna's excellent dinner. Myrna blushed, just as she used to, when Delbert made such comments. Her light brown eyes danced as she tossed her long curls with the twist of her head. She was always attractive in manner and dress which complemented her beautiful figure.

"OK Delbert, it's time to tell us what you were doing in a mine in Denver."

"Gail and Michael, I have a real surprise for you. I'm not Delbert, I'm Art. I'm a geologist and I'll always be. In less than two months I'll get my body back when we return to the 'Adralack Crack'."

Both Gail and Michael were stunned. Michael spoke first. "You've got to be kidding! There isn't any way you can be Art!"

"What about you Michael. I suppose you're going to tell me weird things like you saw people disintegrate on Mt. Baker and expect me to believe that?"

"But both Gail and I did see people disintegrate Delbert. You've got to believe us!"

"Why?"

"Because I recorded the whole thing and the Army has the recording."

"Close your eyes Michael and think back to what you saw and recorded. Tell us about it out loud."

"I'll try. First Art walked into the Adralack Crack and disappeared. Then Delbert started receiving communication between Art and Larry from inside the Crack. After awhile Adrian's machine almost brought Larry out of the Crack but then lost him back to the Crack's power when his machine blew up.

"Delbert got up and started toward the Crack. Just before he did, he said 'Good-bye' to Myrna and Carol. He said, 'I've got to go to my DorLetha.' He was almost to the Crack when Adrian raced by him. Delbert fell down and the doctor rushed up to him and checked his pulse. He said he thought Delbert was dead."

"If he was dead, how could he stand up and walk?"

"He stood up as if new life had come back into his body. Delbert stood up and walked! That's it! Isn't it?"

"Isn't it what, honey?"

"Don't you see, Gail? He stood up because new life had come into his body, Art's life. How in the hell could you change bodies with Delbert. Why, that's as impossible as men disintegrating."

"How were you able to get out of the Adralack Crack and what happened to Delbert?"

"He went to another planet, Gail, to be with his alien wife. Larry told me that, if I was afraid to stay with the two of them, I would have to get someone that was still outside the Crack to change bodies with me. Since Delbert wanted to join Larry and Adrian, he said I could use his body. I just believed and I was in his fallen body. Larry still wanted me to join them and I couldn't move Delbert's body to get away. Larry used his mental powers to raise Delbert's body and start it walking toward the Crack again. If it hadn't been for Myrna and Carol, Larry would have been able to pull Delbert's body in. As his available power was fading, he said, 'May the Cosmic Force be with you, Art' until we return."

"I'll have to admit it makes as much sense as all the rest of the situation did, Delbert, I mean Art. What were you doing in a mine in Denver?"

"I was using the 'Cosmic Force' Larry was talking about. I can feel veins of gold and silver around me in the mines. I found enough in three days to make my old friend Stewart Donovan and his partner and me rich. We just bought a $370.000 house in Denver and we'll be able to pay off the mortgage in a year or less, since our home sold."

"That's our Art! You always were an adventurer and an opportunist!"

"You're right, Gail."

"How long have the rest of you known all this?"

"I found out first, Gail. It was the first day he could have visitors after being transferred to Portland. Myrna and I were by his bedside. We were holding his hands and trying to get him to move his thumb against our hand. We asked him if he could recognize us, to squeezed Myrna's hand for yes and mine for no, and he did.

"We rushed out and got Darrell and brought him in to show him that Art could move each of his thumbs a little. That's when a tear rolled down his cheek. Myrna walked away from the bed, but I wanted to see if I could communicate with him telepathically, since we had been working at it so long and I was able to on Mt. Baker.

"The message I got wasn't from Delbert but Art! He said, 'I can feel your hand on mine. I can feel your touch'. Then a stronger feeling came to me. It was Delbert back in his body for an instant. He said, 'Take care of him.' I couldn't believe it, but Delbert reached his hand up and put it on my shoulder. When he left his body, his hand was limp and helpless again."

Darrell was sitting with his arm around Carol. He gave her a soft, gentle kiss before he spoke. "I believed her when I saw the strange look on her face and saw what an almost lifeless body could suddenly do with its hand. It was like having a corpse come to life for a second and sit up. Once you're dead, you're supposed to stay that way.

"His physical recovery came in jerks as Delbert's body reacted to involuntary reflex movements. Each time Art experienced such a movement, he learned what it felt like to operate a part of Delbert's body."

"Has Delbert ever taken over his body since then Art?"

Carol spoke next. "At your wedding, Gail, he took over his body and talked to me. It was just after Michael had given me a copy of the pictures of Exvascia. Michael had developed them from your camera that Adrian had recovered from the Crack while his teletransporter was still working" Carol handed Gail the pictures.

"I've never seen these pictures! Why didn't you show them to me, Michael?"

"I didn't know how to Gail. Just like they didn't know how to tell us Delbert is Art."

"I guess you're right, Michael. Now is probably a better time to tell me. What did Delbert want, Carol?"

"He wants Art to come to the Crack in late June so he can exchange bodies with him. He also wants Darrell and me to come and visit for a while. He thinks he can get us back to Earth OK. He wants Darrell to bring his black bag with as many important surgical instruments as possible."

"I have to confess something." Everyone looked at Myrna. "When Art and I went to Denver, Delbert contacted me. He took me outside the hotel to prove to me that Art was telling the truth." She explained how he had proved to her who he was by what he was able to do with the stray cat.

"Why didn't you tell Carol and me about his visit, when we were in Denver and I asked if he had contacted either of you?"

"You didn't ask me. You said, 'I'm surprised Delbert hasn't contacted one of you. Has he contacted you, Carol?' Since you didn't ask me, I didn't say anything. He just wanted to be sure I would help get you to Mt. Baker in June."

"Well, you could have told us that!"

"I was embarrassed."

"I don't see why his telling you about me would make you embarrassed. How were you to know! I look like Delbert and sound like him."

"That's the problem Art. If you have to know, he woke me up and said, 'Myrna it's me, Delbert, are you awake?' There I was, sleeping beside a man who hadn't even touched me since we had gotten into bed or for that matter the past seven months, and he keeps telling me he's Art. When he finally said he was Delbert, I thought he had finally snapped out of it. I told him to shut up and make love to me. I can guarantee you it was Delbert.

"Do you remember the scar and mole I have together on my lower stomach, Art?"

"Hum, do I ever!" Everyone laughed at the intimate insinuation.

"He kissed it and said it'd be gone in the morning."

"Were you dreaming or was it real?"

"The mole is gone, Carol."

Michael spoke. "OK, we know that Art is Delbert, but that Delbert can be Delbert when he wants to be, especially when Art has a lot of his close friends around him. You got us here to see if you can get him to join us, kind of like a séance?"

"That's right. We have some problems! Delbert and I had the same amount of life insurance with the same company with Myrna as the beneficiary on both policies so that shouldn't be a problem unless Art Noack reappears. They should have paid on Delbert but since he didn't disappear they couldn't. Now if he disappears they'll pay on his policy but want Art's insurance payment back. That's easy enough. The one would cover the other. The real problem is how to get a death certificate for Delbert and Art's rescinded?

"I've been thinking that we should get the Army to issue the second death certificate and cancel the first. That's why we are moving to Denver, so it'll be easier for them to do it. I'm also making it appear that Delbert is resigning his job and leaving town because of his health."

"How do you plan on getting the Army to issue Delbert a death certificate and get Art out of the mess he's in?"

"I forgot to mention, Michael that the Federal veterans insurance also paid off the mortgage on my house. Also, Myrna is receiving Social Security from me for her and the kids."

"Wow! I thought the first trip to the Crack was exciting and necessary! I still want to know how you plan on pulling this off. What could possibly make the Army willingly show up there again and do more paper shuffling?"

"The very same way we got them there in the first place, the teletransporter."

"Now I don't follow you Art!"

"What we need to do, Michael, is contact Delbert and find out if both he and Adrian can come down and spend a few hours outside the Crack. If Adrian's mental capacity has increased vastly, like Larry and Delberts has, he should be able to put his machine back together in a couple hours. We just need the Army to show up with the machine and a portable shop for metal working."

"So you want me to record this experience just like I did the first time. If the Army gets the machine repaired, they should be able to pull a few strings to get you out of your bind."

"How will that affect Darrell and me going to Exvascia to visit?"

"I thought about that Carol. When it's time for you two to go, you will just walk into the Crack. Maybe the Army will forget about you two leaving. Remember, the man that activates the Crack will also be returning to another planet.

"I seem to know that you only age about one-tenth as fast there as you do here. If you two stay there ten years you would only look one year older. I can see why Delbert wants Dr. Lyons to visit the place. Besides, if you go with him, you'll probably have a greater mental capacity and then Delbert would be able to contact you easier in the future. Maybe he'll be able to communicate telepathically with you from his planet and not have to come down here again."

"Anything is possible, I guess, Art. Maybe he can change the area that he has powered as his contact point. Say, from Mt. Baker to your new mine in Denver."

"That would be OK with me, as long as they don't let anyone remember their visit."

"I hope all of you will remember that Darrell and I are getting married on June 1st and you're all involved!"

"That's about five weeks away. Myrna and I have to move May 25th but we'll be here even if we have to stay in a motel. The trip to Mt. Baker will have to be set for a specific date. I hope Delbert's watch is still running so he knows what day it is according to our time."

"Carol, how are you and Darrell going to cover your being gone?"

"We've told everyone we're going on a round-the-world tour Myrna, as part of our honeymoon. Darrell has another doctor lined up to take over his practice while we're gone. We've got a renter for the house and Gail and Michael will watch the business. Gail can sign anything Darrell usually would because her signature is on the checking account. Also, Darrell has given her power of attorney so she can sign anything else that requires his signature. The new doctor will be doing the everyday business. Gail will only have to take care of special problems that we haven't foreseen."

"I can record the event again, if you can give me a specific date. How do we contact Delbert?"

"I think, if Myrna, Carol, Gail and I join hands and concentrate on what I say, the aura of his body will become bright enough for DorLetha to pick it up. It would help if I didn't keep showing up in different places."

"You didn't see anything wrong with my walk when I came in did you?"

"I didn't, Art, but I did notice your cast!"

"Did you notice my black eye?"

"I did, but it's almost all gone."

"How long would you say it's been since I got the black eye, Doc?"

"I would estimate two weeks."

"Would you believe a week? My body is healing almost twice the normal speed. Besides that, when the tunnel crashed down on me, I remember having a broken and bleeding left leg. The rock was piled all around and on me. My friend didn't do anything but lie there and moan. Our lanterns were smashed and the air was almost gone."

"How did you get out?"

"I called out to Delbert and told him that if he and his alien friends didn't get his body repaired and out of the mine, it wouldn't be around in June for him to claim. I didn't come to until I had been in the hospital for some time.

They say someone called for help from the pickup truck outside the mine and left the lights on so they could find it in the dark.

"They got us out of the mine quickly. Besides that, my leg was healed when they got me to the hospital. No one could understand the blood on my pants leg or the hole the bone had made when it came through the skin. The doctor wanted me to explain what he called recently healed breaks but I couldn't! At least I couldn't tell him what I guessed had happened."

"So, under stress, you can communicate with Delbert."

"That's right, Doc."

"I'm not going to say you can't. I'm not into mental telepathy, only internal medicine. However, you're the strangest patient I've ever had or read about."

"If you ladies are ready, let's try to contact Delbert."

"OK, join hands and concentrate on what I say. Delbert, Delbert can you hear me? Can you see us Delbert? Carol, Myrna, Darrell and I are here with Gail and Michael. We've got a problem we need your help with Delbert. Can you contact us someway?"

Darrell was watching Carol when her face changed expression and took on a certain look. He spoke, "Delbert will be here in a second. I've seen that look on Carol's face twice before."

Art kind of shook his head and looked up. As he did so, he let go of Myrna and Carol's hands. He then turned and kissed Myrna on the cheek and said, "Hi how's my favorite girl?"

Gail thought to herself, *"How many times have I seen Delbert do that very thing in front of me, Larry and Art."*

"Delbert, it's you. They just told me what had happened to you on Mt. Baker."

"Hi, Gail, you're looking good. Michael, Darrell, Carol how are all of you? According to my watch it's April 26. Is that right?"

"That's right, Delbert. How long do you have?"

"I only have a few minutes, Doc. We're trying to avoid a collision with another planet's moon. It looks like it's either going to become a part of Exvascia or a moon for us. If it doesn't collide with us, we'll pick you up on June 26, two months from today.

"Tell Art to take better care of my body. We had to do a lot to get him out of that mine cave-in and repaired. Remember to bring a small microscope with you, Doc.!

"What's the problem, Myrna?"

"You know all the red tape we had getting a death certificate for Art and Adrian. We need the Army to issue a death certificate for you and rescind Art's so he can resume his life when you exchange bodies. Could Adrian come down with you for a couple hours and repair his teletransporter? I'm sure the Army would help us with the paper work then."

"We can locate the aura of my body when all of you are together. I think both Adrian and I can come down for that short of a period. It all depends on the accuracy of an orbit correction we made. Let's say 'yes' for now. On June 22 let's get together again and see what it looks like. If I can't come down and use my body for a while, I'll have to give you the message, Carol."

"That's OK, Delbert. Myrna and Art are moving to Denver, but they can come out on June 22nd I'm sure. We'll all meet at our place in Portland. Can you find us there?"

"If you're all holding hands with Art and do like you just did. Doc, is that a new watch? If it is, I'd like to have it. I'm not sure how long my batteries will last and I need to know what the date is here." Delbert's old watch suddenly appeared in his hand.

"Here Delbert, it's only a month or so old so it should work fine for some time."

"OK, I'll see all of you on June 22nd about 7:00 p.m. at your house Doc and on Mt. Baker June 26th at about 10:00 a.m." When Delbert held the new watch, it disappeared.

"We'll see you on the 22nd."

"OK, Carol. Tell Art what he is doing with my things and my affairs are OK with me. Glad to see you got yourself that nice young man."

"Thanks, Delbert. We're anxious to join you on Exvascia. Good-bye."

"Good-bye everyone." With that Art's head dropped for a few seconds before he appeared to wake up.

"What happened?"

"Delbert conned me out of my new watch Art and gave me his old one."

"You didn't think you were going to get a free trip to another planet did you, Doc?" Michael's sense of humor helped relax the group. Delbert's presence, as well as his ability to come and go, astounded all of them. For some reason, Darrell was open and receptive to the idea of Delbert being on another planet and was able to talk freely with him, even when they exchanged watches, he had no fear of touching him. He also had an incredible ability to read what was happening to Carol as far as Delbert's presence was concerned.

"I've got to sit in a straight backed chair, Myrna. Sorry, but my ribs are hurting."

"Here, Art, let me help you up. I wish I could just touch your ribs and make them well." To Art's surprise, that is just what Darrel's touch did.

Myrna and Carol saw a strange look on Art's face and knew that something happened but they didn't know what. Michael joked, "Well, Art did that touch heal your ribs? Art, are you OK?"

"Yes, Michael, it's..., it's..."

"Yes Art, it's what?"

"When Darrell touched me, I felt a shock like static electricity. It seemed to jump from Darrell's hand to my side. Now the pain is gone from my ribs." Art used his left hand to pound on his ribs on his right side to prove to the group that he didn't have any more pain.

"Darrell, did Delbert touch you?"

"No, we just exchanged watches and I put it on my left wrist as usual. It did happen to be the hand I touched your side with though. I didn't mean to. It was just as though my hand was saying, 'your wish is my command'!"

"Doc, don't think I'm crazy but I think you have received the Cosmic Force either from being close to Delbert or from wearing his watch. It's just like Delbert to try to help you do well as a doctor."

"Hey, Art, you're not under too much strain are you?"

"You've got the problem Doc not me. Be sincere and wish my eye was completely healed. Then touch it with your left hand and see what happens."

"I couldn't do that! You've got to be slipping off the deep end again!"

"Just do it! You heard me, do it!"

"OK, I'm sorry, Art. I didn't mean to upset you. Here, let me fix that eye for you." It was almost as though Dr. Lyons was using his bedside manner to calm a crazy person. Darrell was the one that was startled when his touch made the yellow disappear from around Art's eye.

"Wow! I didn't know a personal effect of Delbert's could be so powerful."

"It's probably become an energy receiver since Delbert's been wearing it so long up there. Darrell take the watch into the closet and shut the door."

"What for?"

"Just do it, would you?"

"OK, OK. There! Are you happy? I don't believe it! The whole watch glows a light pale green! I wonder if it's contaminated with radiation. I've got to have it checked out as soon as possible! Can I get a large piece of aluminum foil to wrap it in?"

"Will that do any good?"

"I don't know, Art. I'm not use to dealing with Martian objects. If you don't need Carol or me any longer I'd like to get this watch to Portland and have it analyzed."

"Go ahead. Michael and I need to talk a little is all; thanks for coming down and for healing my body!"

"I wouldn't have missed this for the world. Come over as soon as you can Gail and we'll have you sign a couple papers. Good-bye, everyone."

"Michael, do you have the names of the Army personnel that were present at the filming?"

"Sure! I've been trying to get a copy of the recording, but they won't even tell me whether they have it or not."

"If you can set up a meeting with them, I'd like to see what they would think of our proposal."

"I don't know why they wouldn't go for it. I'll let you know when we can meet with them."

After more conversation about Michael's job and Art's efforts to find silver ore, Michael and Gail were about to leave when the phone rang. "Hello Carol, what's wrong, you sound upset? Were you involved in an accident? He what? You're kidding! Oh, Carol, I don't know if I can handle much more of this. I'll see you, bye."

"Don't pass out on us Myrna. Were Darrell and Carol involved in an accident?"

"No Art. She said as they were about to pull onto the freeway from the on ramp, the car ahead of them pulled into the slow lane without yielding. The driver had his arm out signaling because his turn signal wasn't working. He was sideswiped by the car that was already in the slow lane. It sheared the driver's left arm off. The driver hit the guard rail and the car stopped. Darrell ran to the scene hoping to put a tourniquet on the stump to stop the bleeding. He was going to take the driver's pulse so he put Delbert's watch back on. Just as he did, a couple came up with a blanket and helped Darrell lay the bleeding driver on a blanket.

"Then another witness ran up with the arm. The sleeve had slipped over the bloody stump before it hit the asphalt so it was still clean and it hadn't been run over. The witness laid the arm beside the man's body. Darrel said, 'Oh, God! I wish this hadn't happened. I can't save him here with what I have in my bag.'

He was at the man's head. Carol said he grabbed the man's left arm in a frenzy and put it back on the stump and then pressed on it hard as it he were putting it on a mannequin."

"Go ahead, what happened then?"

"Carol said the arm reattached itself. The sight of all the blood was too much for most people to watch, but when it regenerated itself as he pressed it into place, a couple people fainted.

"When people saw what he had done, they called a TV station and wanted to give them his name. They took Darrell's picture because he wouldn't tell them who he was. He told them that nothing had actually happened to the man's arm, that they had just been hysterical and imagined it. However, the witnesses wouldn't buy it because a couple of them had seen what had happened.

"Because of the prayer-like statement Darrell had earnestly uttered, before the miraculous healing, the people think he's a miracle worker. The police are escorting them home and putting a patrol car in front of their house so a crowd doesn't gather. Those poor kids! If that happens, they'll need to get to Exvascia as soon as possible!

"Carol also said that the watch got such a bright green, just before the arm reattached itself, Darrell almost had to shield his eyes from it. As soon as the arm was reattached the watch returned to having only a slight pale green glow. He took the watch off immediately and put it in his pocket. No one seemed to remember seeing it glow."

Art couldn't believe it. "All we need is one more complication. Delbert, did you hear what happened? You've got to find some way to make all those people forget what they saw. Remember our lost weekend, Delbert? Can you make them all forget?"

When Delbert returned to Exvascia from Earth, a violent storm was in progress. The inevitable had happened, thunder, lightning and torrential rains.

"Looks like TetTrella will be able to gather all the power she wants, Larry."

"You're right Delbert! Talking about taking power, what did you leave on Earth that is drawing power from us?"

"The only thing I left was my watch. I wanted one that was new so I could tell when to meet Art at the Crack. I sent Dr. Lyon's watch back ahead of me, why?"

"It seems Dr. Lyons can use it to do good. Anything he wishes for happens. DorLetha said Art asked for help with one more problem. Do you know what it was?"

"No."

"Art said that leaving your watch caused a problem."

DorLetha spoke. "That's right. Art wants me to erase a lot of memories but that would require a lot of energy from here. I don't think we can afford to do that."

"Can you use a mental telemetrical viewing to see the incident that he wants erased?"

"Yes, why?"

"I was wondering if you could then block out the minds of everyone who is in the scene."

"Yes, but that won't take care of any future events he does with it."

"Let's just take care of this one event. I think Dr. Lyons is smart enough not to let it happen again."

"OK, here is the view. Those transporters touched and a human's arm fell off. Dr. Lyons wanted to put it back on, so we sent him regenerative powers though the time device."

"You mean there was a car wreck and he replaced a severed arm and it was as good as new?"

"That's right! We thought that's what you would want us to do. I'll erase the memory of this one experience but any others will be his to deal with."

"We're just not used to that much power or control of our lives. Thanks for helping us. Has Adrian been able to help any with the calculations of the possible collision with that other planet's moon?"

"Yes he has. He has a good grasp for scientific things."

"Can we talk to him or is he busy?"

"I think he could spare some time."

"DorLetha said you wanted to see me."

"Yes. Will I still be able to go back to Earth and exchange Art's body for mine?"

"Yes, if you pick a date late in June."

"Would the 26th of June be late enough?"

"That should be OK. By then we should have a better idea, when that moon will be reaching our planet. We should know three or four days before it gets here. We'll know then whether we'll have excess power for your trip."

"Adrian, I hate to keep bothering you but Art is wondering if you could come down for a couple hours at the same time and fix your teletransporter for the Army."

"Why does he need that?"

"He is trying to get the Army to explain to the insurance company why it was OK for them to pay off on a life Insurance claim for a person who is alive again. There are also other situations he has run into related to our exchanging bodies."

"That's quite a ways off, Delbert. I'll have to decide after we find out if there will be any place to bring them back to."

Chapter 15

The Miracle Worker

"Darrell this is Art. You're finally home. Is Carol there with you?"

"Yes, we're here. The police car just escorted us home. I think Carol is going to stay here tonight she's pretty upset."

"Can you switch your phone to the speaker so Carol can hear?"

"Yes, hold on."

"Carol its Art.

"Hi Art", sob, sob, "What do you want?"

"Do you remember Larry, Delbert and me having a 'lost weekend'?"

"Yes!"

"Good! Darrell do you have a paper and pencil handy? Delbert is going to have DorLetha try and erase all memories of the accident."

"OK!"

"Write, 'Call Art' and put the note somewhere so that you have to see it in the morning. Now take a sedative and get into bed as fast as you can. Please, don't sleep together."

"We'll do it, Art!"

"Good night to both of you."

"Good night, Art."

"Art, do you think Delbert and DorLetha can pull off blanking out the minds of everyone that saw the accident?"

"There weren't that many people involved, Gail. We'll know in the morning, when we read the newspaper. If Delbert and DorLetha can deliver for us, we still have to make sure that Darrell fully understands the power he has at his command, when he has that watch on. Any wish will be taken as a command by the Exvascians who are responding to it as a request for their superior mental and metaphysical assistance."

"That's enough excitement for one day, Gail. Are you ready to go home?"

"Yes, Michael. Thanks Myrna for having us down. I hope everything works out for you two. I'm looking forward to seeing the real Art again. Good night."

"Good night, it was nice to see you two again."

"Are you ready to take me home, Myrna?"

"I guess I have to. If Darrell is going to call you in the morning, you will need a good night's rest."

Myrna took Art home and didn't worry about her kids at their grandmother's. She was glad she had arranged for them to stay overnight.

Art got up in the morning and looked at his eye in the mirror and felt his ribs. They were completely healed. Darrell had transmitted some strange healing power through his body from the planet Exvascia. *"Now, for the million dollar question, did Delbert and DorLetha work their magic on a group of people gathered around an accident and police who had taken Darrell and Carol home? Had anybody been missed, when they erased the memory of the previous evening?"*

Art hurried to his front door to get the morning paper. He quickly walked to the kitchen, made a cup of coffee, sat down at the table and spread the newspaper out before him. There weren't any banner headlines about an accident where a doctor reattached a victim's arm. He didn't find anything. *Whew! DorLetha did it again, a lost evening. Darrell should be calling me shortly. I wonder how much he'll remember.*

Ring, ring. "Good morning this is Art."

"Hi Art. I saw a note on my bathroom mirror for me to call you first thing this morning. What's up?"

"What's the last thing you remember about our visit last night?"

"That's a silly question to ask! You're the one that has problems remembering."

"Please, Darrell, answer my question and then you can decide how stupid it is."

"OK, we were at Myrna's place and I traded watches with Delbert. Supposedly I healed your eye and ribs. How long did your healing job last, Art?"

"They're still well. Go ahead."

"OK. Then I said that I wanted to hurry home so I could have a scientist friend check the watch for radiation."

"That's right, then what?"

"Carol and I left for home. And now I'm talking to you. Why?"

"Darrell, what happened between your leaving Myrna's place and when you woke up?"

"Well, I, I, uh, I don't remember, Art."

"Do you still have the watch?"

"I guess so; do you want me to go find it or something?"

"Would you please?"

"Sure, if you don't mind holding on."

"I'll hold."

"I'm back. It took awhile but I found it in the bathroom. I have a bathtub full of bloody clothes: jacket, shirt, t-shirt and pants. It looks like I must have operated on someone with a pocket knife and a band aid."

"Now do you remember what happened last night?"

"Art, I don't remember anything after we left Myrna's place. I suppose you're going to tell me you do!"

"Not until you get Carol on the line with us. Is she up yet?"

"What are you talking about?"

"Carol! She's got to be there! Go look around."

"Darrell, who are you talking to?"

"Carol! What are you doing here?"

"I was sleeping until you got excited on the phone. Who are you yelling at?"

"Art! I'll put him on the speaker. Art, Carol is with us."

"I'm glad you're there. Darrell didn't seem to think you'd be there. I was about to tell him about last night. Can you enlighten him?"

"No, Art, I remember leaving Myrna's place and I don't remember anything else until I woke up in Darrell's guest room. If he hadn't been yelling so loud at you, I'd probably still be asleep. What's this all about?"

"Do you remember the 'lost weekend' Delbert, Adrian and I told you about, the one where we couldn't remember anything that happened?"

"Yes, what has that got to do with last night?"

"Do you remember the watch Delbert traded Darrell?"

"Yes, when he had it on he was able to heal your eye and your ribs by wishing he could while touching you."

"Well, after you left Myrna's place last night, you two were behind another car that attempted to get on the freeway." Art relayed all the information about the accident. "You do remember wrapping the watch up in aluminum foil don't you?"

"Yes I do, but there wasn't any foil on it when I found it a few minutes ago."

Carol asked, "If what you said is true, Art, why can't we remember it?"

"Because I asked Delbert to have DorLetha erase the memory of the accident from all involved so you wouldn't be hounded by the press and others."

"She did an excellent job of it! I don't remember a thing!"

"Neither do I, Art, but that isn't why you called us, is it?"

"No it isn't, Darrell. You must realize the power there is in that watch. Anything you wish, when working with patients, will be so. Be very careful you don't wish anything spectacular, when you have the watch on, because it will probably happen. You wouldn't want anybody to see that and start calling you a miracle worker."

"So you're telling me that anything I want to happen will happen and I have to conceal how I made it happened?"

"That's right. For example, say you are operating on someone and you reach a critical point and fail to accomplish what you want to do with the instruments you are using, you can just wish it to be done, touch the spot with your left hand, if you're wearing the watch on your left wrist, and it will be as you wish."

"If I'm able to get power from another world some way, I want to keep it an absolute secret."

"OK, the first thing is to be sure you don't have the watch analyzed. You may not even want to wear it. Just keep it in a pocket where you can get to it, if and when you need special help."

"I understand! I know I'm going to enjoy it on Exvascia. I bet they have a whole different way of taking care of physical problems than we do. How could the minds of everyone involved be wiped clean, Art?"

"You'll have to get that answer from Delbert when you see him. If there is any way a reporter can tie a miracle cure to your presence anywhere, or to a patient's room, Darrell, you'll have problems. Be very careful!"

"I'll be very careful, Art. Thanks for calling us."

After Art hung up, Darrell and Carol talked about his call. "How can we know what Art said happened?"

"Go look in the bathtub, Carol. I've got most of the things I was wearing last night, soaking in cold water. There's so much blood in the water it looks like I butchered a deer single handed. If you stayed here last night, why didn't I know it and why didn't you sleep with me? I believe him!"

"I guess we were lucky that Delbert, with DorLetha's help, could take care of the problem. I'd hate to have thousands of people following you or us around all the time."

"I might be able to do some good with the watch Carol, if I'm very careful. On my late evening rounds I could check over some of the other doctor's patients that I have consulted with them on. Cancer patients or heart patients could easily be checked on and cured. It would be easiest to cure a patient that I knew the other doctor or I would be doing additional tests on later."

"Just be careful that nobody thinks you worked a miracle. I had better get going if I'm going to work today."

Darrell had a new enthusiasm for his work from then on. His positive attitude helped him do a better job than he had in the past and he resisted the use of the watch as an easy way out.

Chapter 16

Trouble Outside

"Adrian, there is another electrical storm outside. Can you find out how to recharge the Lidyan ray blasters we have, so we'll be able to use then to kill the new warriors TetTrella is sure to bring up here?"

"I'll work on that first chance I get, Delbert. Is there anything else?"

"No, that's it. Thanks."

"Delbert, now that we're alone, have you noticed Adrian is changing?"

"Yes, I have Larry. He's making it look like we're a couple of dummies and he's a brain. I certainly didn't expect that from him."

"His looking and feeling younger has certainly revitalized him. He acts like he's starting a new career and needs every minute to get ahead. Do you think he's having a last bright burn before he goes out?"

"That could be. He shouldn't be taking in as much knowledge as he is. It could overload his brain. Maybe we can talk to Esdra and explain to her the possible damage he may suffer."

"It's worth a try. Let's go outside and see what's happening. Why don't you come on out in your body and see if you can disintegrate. I can hold on to you and you can try it. If you don't quite make it, I can help you. We can't keep freezing your body every time we need to do something outside."

"OK, let's go." Once outside the men found a tremendous storm occurring. "Larry, let's see if we can find TetTrella. If she isn't here, maybe we can find Twillie and GarGweth."

"Where should we start looking?"

"Spark Stone Mountain, she may be gathering spark stone to take with her to pay warriors to return with her. There she is! Look at that pile of stone she has. That could be good news or bad news."

"What do you mean by that?"

"It'll take more of her power to transport it to Lidy but then it might allow her to bring back twice as many warriors."

"Let's watch and see where she takes off from, Larry. Maybe we can be waiting for them when she returns. If we could blast half a dozen before she can disintegrate and then regenerate them somewhere else, then we'll be a little ahead of them."

"Good idea. That will also cause her to use more of her power. We still have to get rid of her as a final solution. She's getting ready to leave. It looks like she is going into that clearing to get a final charge."

"Hey, the lightning is over. That means she won't have much of a reserve when she gets back. I think she was planning on a lot more power. I'll bet she can't resist taking all that stone with her."

"She's disintegrating, Delbert, and now she's disintegrating the stone. Go ahead, TetTrella, be greedy and take all of it. Don't leave any of it. Think of all the extra warriors you can bring back with that extra spark stone. She is going to take it all. That will use more of her power."

"I wondered why you were urging her on, Larry. Do you think you could do some mental telemetrical viewing of her trip if you get close to her take-off point?"

"I can try. Let's lie down so we can put all our thought power into our efforts to follow her."

"Lying in the wet grass with the rain falling on my face is making concentration difficult."

"Delbert just think of it as a warm shower. It could be cold and dark too. I'm getting the picture in my mind of where she is. Try to help me by concentrating telepathically on my thoughts. You've also seen Lidy before."

"OK, that seems to be helping. I can see TetTrella now."

"Concentrate on TetTrella, Delbert and let's see if we can hear her conversation with that warrior."

"What do you mean all the others died? You said there wouldn't be any resistance at all."

"I didn't think they would fight back. Besides they didn't have any weapons until nature took some of the warriors. Then they used your own warrior's weapons against those remaining. In our jungles there are dangerous marsh lands that you can't get out of when you step into them. They are sticky sand-like material that doesn't seem to have any bottom. Also, the area around the marshes has trees with vines hanging on them that feed on animals that their limbs contact and hold onto."

"Wait a minute. You didn't tell us we would have to fight nature too. What other hazards are there?"

"There are blood suckers to look out for. I'll explain what they look like later. Also there are Kelcha beasts, which usually only attack intelligent beings at night. Someone has to stand guard at night so they know you're ready for them. Then they won't attack."

"It's definitely going to cost you more for some of us to join you. We'll decide how many of us and who should go with you this time. We'll meet you here in the morning."

"But I can't wait!"

"You can wait or forget it! We're not your slaves. No amount of Spark Stone is going to do us any good if we're dead. You'll need the best and most experienced warriors we have."

"But I brought enough Spark Stone for 50 of you!"

"That's what you think! If you don't like our price, you can go somewhere else!"

"What is she going to do now, Larry? I don't like the way her eyes look. They're like two burning coals."

"That's good! Remember how her eyes looked when she made the boards for us? I think she's going to use some of her power. The only thing around her in that sports complex is the large building and the smaller equipment building she's looking at now. Scratch one equipment building. She's blasted it away."

That's good; it means she won't have as much power to bring Lidyans back. Also with the higher price being asked, her number will be limited."

"That's just what we wanted her to do. We might as well go back and return in the morning when they are going to give her their answer. Hey, there's Twillie. We're over here, Twillie, come talk to us. TetTrella is on Lidy."

"Is she going to get more warriors?"

"That's right and she has told them some of the natural dangers. Because of that, they are going to change the price they are charging her. She took a lot of Spark Stone but she won't be able to bring back the number she wanted."

"Any she brings back will be too many."

"Once we got rid of them and her, we know there wouldn't be any more come. We're going to be waiting for them when they first appear, if she returns to the same place she left from. Maybe we can use their ray blasters on a few of them before she can disintegrate them. How are you and GarGweth doing on the cave wall?"

"We should be able to get him out in a couple days, Delbert."

"Larry, could you help them for a while? You could levitate the rock out of the cave for them. TetTrella isn't here to see you do it."

"Sure, I could do that. Don't forget to remind GarGweth what DorLetha told you about him defending himself against her bolts of electricity. Keep feeding him a lot of good food in case TetTrella visits him tomorrow. She won't have as good a supply of power this time when she gets back."

"OK, I'll remember. GarGweth is feeling much better even though he can't stretch much in that cave. The plants Kadra told me about are healing his old injuries. The work at digging out the cave is making his muscles strong again."

After Larry levitated the rock that had been dug out of the cave, they told Twillie that they would be back in the morning to try listening in on TetTrella's conversation with the warriors and find out when she would be back. After Twillie told them that he and GarGweth may be able to join them in the morning, because of their help on the cave, they returned to the Crater.

The next morning it looked like it was going to be a beautiful day. Larry and Delbert were outside the Crater and by TetTrella's landing site early in the morning. By lying on the ground and concentrating on Lidy they were able to get Larry's mental telemetrical viewing of the planet tuned in much quicker than before.

TetTrella was waiting for the Lidyan warriors in the athletic field. After a few hours waiting, they showed up. "We've picked 20 of our best warriors to go with you."

"20! I've brought enough Spark Stone for 50 of your warriors at your original price." TetTrella thought to herself. *They have me cornered. If I blasted a few of them, then none of them will return to Exvascia with me.*

"That isn't our price anymore!"

"OK, gather around and hold onto each other." Larry could tell by the slow disintegration of the group that TetTrella didn't have any excess power.

"Delbert, let's get behind those rocks to ambush them. Remember to keep firing as long as you can see any part of a Lidyan. If we're quick, we should be able to get about half of them before TetTrella can disintegrate them again, because of her reduced power reserve. I'll disintegrate as soon as they're gone so that I can search for them quicker. Do you want to try disintegrating?"

"I'll try it now that we have time."

"Just think of yourself as being subatomic particles and let go of your body as if you were in soul flight. I'll hold your wrist so I can either help you disintegrate or regenerate to your human form if you have trouble. Go ahead and give it a try. That's good, just keep thinking of yourself as particles and release your mind from your body.

The two men continued conversing telepathically as they disintegrated. Delbert was able to regenerate his body quickly. Larry had him try disintegrating again. This time he said, "Try to do it quickly without my help." Delbert was able to quickly disintegrate and regenerate his body. He now knew he had another form of protection.

"Let's get ready for their appearance. Let's wait until most of them are regenerated then start blasting. If we give them any more time than that, they'll probably get us first. Be sure to stay hidden behind the rocks. That will give us something stable to rest our weapons on and it will also make it harder for them to see or hit us. When I drop my hand, start firing. Get ready here they come. Take your safety off."

Delbert watched out of the corner of his eye for Larry's signal. The group started regenerating. When a dozen were visible, Larry's hand fell.

Ssss, Ssss, Ssss. The powerful ray seemed to hiss through the air. Delbert and Larry both fired five times before TetTrella started disintegrating the group that was left. "Disintegrate, Delbert and start looking for them!"

Delbert located the Lidyans not far from GarGweth's cave. Communicating telepathically, he passed the information on to Larry. Delbert picked a spot not too far from the cave to regenerate. He knew Larry would be doing the same thing shortly.

TetTrella was furious. The humans had wiped out several of her 20 warriors before they knew where they were. Even now, she knew they must be waiting for them to be regenerated.

"I'll send GarGweth after the humans and if he won't kill them, I'll kill him!"

TetTrella entered the cave and demanded GarGweth go kill the two humans.

GarGweth refused. "GarGweth no kill for you. You are the bad one!"

"Twillie, what are you doing here? You've been feeding GarGweth haven't you?" GarGweth started toward TetTrella.

"Stay away from me, GarGweth!" Zap, Zap, Zap went the electricity from TetTrella's eyes, but GarGweth kept coming. "Twillie, you've talked with DorLetha or else my electrical power would have dropped GarGweth in his tracks. I told you not to interfere, you little durl" Zap!

"Ah," Twillie gasped and fell to the ground. GarGweth took his mind off TetTrella for an instant when Twillie fell. Zap, Zap, Zap.

"Ah, ah, uh!" GarGweth crashed to the ground. TetTrella thought the big durk was dead. She left the cave and started talking with the Lidyans.

"Out in the grassy area there is a big mist tree. It is cool under it, but the mist is dangerous. It will knock you out first and then you will die from it. Two of the last group made that mistake one hot afternoon."

As TetTrella continued to talk and give directions to the Crater, Delbert heard GarGweth groan and groan again. Then there was a period of silence. Then GarGweth let out a loud roar and smashed through what was left of the cave wall.

"What's that?" the Lydian warrior asked.

"It's a giant durk. Grab it! Don't let it get me." GarGweth cracked two Lidyans heads together killing them. In the commotion, Delbert shot two more.

GarGweth was still roaring. "Twillie, you killed my Twillie. I'll get you for that! I'll get you, TetTrella."

"Get him you Lidyans! Stun him with your weapons and bring him with you. I'll show you what the living vine can do."

Delbert had to watch from a disintegrated state, as his shooting at the Lidyans had been returned. Two Lidyans searched for Delbert and the other six carried GarGweth to the edge of the quagmire and touched a couple branches of the living vine to his hot body. The branches started to entwine around his body.

Delbert had followed the Lidyans when they took GarGweth to the quagmire. Behind him he heard the ray blaster fire two more times. Maybe Larry had surprised the two that had been after him.

GarGweth threw himself into the quagmire. The living vine branches tried their best to pull him free. "You're not getting away, GarGweth!" TetTrella sent a laser beam toward GarGweth's writhing body. She missed him and severed the branches of the living vine that had pulled him from the quagmire, setting him free.

GarGweth rushed for TetTrella as she sent bolts of electricity toward him. GarGweth was ready for her this time. The power didn't affect him. TetTrella disintegrated and soon all the creatures around him took on the shape of the Lidyans.

As Larry arrived, Delbert commented, "Now how are we going to find out which are the Lidyans and which aren't?"

"It's going to be hard. I killed the two that had been left behind. That means there are only six left, but which is which? She really fixed us this time."

"If you say there are six left we must have killed eight when they arrived."

"That's right!"

"TetTrella, I'm going to get you! You killed my friend Twillie!" GarGweth was still furious.

Suddenly TetTrella appeared on a giant lily pad in the quagmire. "I'm going to get rid of you forever GarGweth!"

GarGweth leaped at TetTrella and landed with one foot on her lily pad and his other foot on another. He had TetTrella by the throat and her feet were in the water. Weakened bolts of electricity shot from TetTrella's eyes as she tried to electrocute him. His giant hairy hands crushed her entire neck, bones and all. The excruciating pain caused TetTrella to stop her electrical bombardment of GarGweth. She didn't stop soon enough however, and she disintegrated and was gone forever. The particles that had previously been her body were now a spot on the lily pad.

If TetTrella hadn't changed everything in her kingdom into the shape of the Lidyans, she may have overcome GarGweth's strength, even though he had DorLetha's secret of how to withstand her power charges.

"Larry, how are we going to get GarGweth to the cave?"

"You mean, how are we going to get him off those giant rubber-like lily pads in the quagmire? If we regenerate the Lidyans will see us. We have to change to our human form to be able to communicate with GarGweth."

"Let's both change at the same time. You'll have to tell him what we're going to do to get him out of there while I cover you. You had better change instantly, if there is any problem, Larry."

"I've got some of the pollen shooter's pollen in my pouch. All I have to do is get a limb of the living vine from the tree to him and it will pull him to the bank. I'll then use the pollen on the living vine to stun it and he can get free."

"The only reason those Lidyans are letting him live is to get at us. You had better tell him to keep concentrating in case they start shooting at him."

"Are you ready, Delbert?"

"Yes, go!"

They both appeared. "GarGweth, we'll get you out of there if you trust us."

"Duck!" Larry instantly disintegrated and Delbert killed another warrior and disintegrated. "Now we've got them in a bind. If they fire, we can tell which of the look-alikes are Lidyans."

"I'll regenerate and talk with GarGweth. You stay in your invisible form. If one shoots at me, I'll instantly disintegrate and you can regenerate and zap him. OK?"

"Let's give it a try. Go!" Larry changed and threw GarGweth a vine. There was no shooting and he disintegrated and watched as the vine pulled GarGweth free. Larry regenerated and sprinkled the pollen shooter pollen on the vine and stunned it. As the pollen landed on the living vine it relaxed and GarGweth was free. "Run for the Crater entrance GarGweth! Keep concentrating on accepting a ray blast as a ray of sunlight warming you. We'll try to stop any Lidyans that follow you."

"Thanks." GarGweth hurried on his way, tearing a big hole through the jungle as he bulled his way through it heading for the Crater tunnel entrance. In the open areas he made good speed lumbering along on two legs, upright, like a giant hairy man.

Larry disintegrated again as he and Delbert, in their invisible form, followed GarGweth hurrying for the safety of the Crater tunnel entrance. "I don't see any Lidyans following him, where do you think they are?"

"They're probably waiting for him up ahead, Larry. Why don't you go ahead and see if you can spot one of them. We'll be to the Crater tunnel entrance soon."

Everywhere Delbert looked now, he saw Lidyan forms. By turning all creatures into the Lidyan form, TetTrella had turned the tables on them. GarGweth finally reached the Crater entrance. "Larry, are those Fem-Birds or not?"

"They should be, Delbert. I'll disintegrate them and see if they can regenerate to their primary form."

"Thanks, Larry. What happened to all of us?"

"TetTrella changed you Crater guards and every other living creature into the Lidyan creature form so we would have trouble finding and destroying them. Guards this is GarGweth. He killed TetTrella in a fight. She won't be bringing any more aliens to Exvascia. He is the giant durk DorLetha said she would give sanctuary to if he could kill TetTrella on his own."

"Where are we going, Larry?" GarGweth asked.

"Inside the mountain to a big beautiful Crater with a crystal prism enclosing the hole at the top and letting the sunlight in from the solar reflector."

"GarGweth can't go into tunnel!"

"It's OK, GarGweth. Nothing is going to hurt you in this short tunnel. It's not like the cave TetTrella kept you in."

"GarGweth can't go in, too afraid."

"OK, let's find a safe place for you out here. We'll watch for Lidyans for you while you eat. Then you are going to have to concentrate on receiving power beams as they come at you so you won't be killed. One of those five remaining Lidyans may still fire at you!"

"Larry, when it gets dark, let's put a blindfold on him and led him into the Crater. That way we won't have to spend all our time protecting him."

"Why not keep him out here and use him as a shield. He can concentrate on receiving the power beams while we turn all the Kaydra back into their primary form and send them back into the Crater now that TetTrella is gone. I assume no animals will follow them here tonight. I could be wrong of course."

"You're right. What's your plan for getting the Kaydra inside?"

"We'll call them telepathically and tell them we can change them back to their primary form and that TetTrella is gone forever. We'll have them come to the Crater. We'll know the Kaydra aren't animals when we hold them and disintegrate and regenerate a few of them to their primary form. They can then help us contact others."

"Should we have GarGweth stand by in case we get a hold of a strong wild animal by mistake?"

"Let's ask him Delbert. GarGweth we need your help. Come over to the cave entrance guards and I'll explain to all three of you at the same time what we have in mind.

"You Kaydra know how we turned you back into your primary form. Well, we want to do that to all Kaydra and get them inside the Crater so we can find the five remaining Lidyans. We'll call all the Kaydra by mental telepathy. There may be a few confused animals that follow them, but that's ok. We need your help to turn all the animals back into their real form too.

"To change the animals back to their form, we have to hold them all the way through disintegration and back to regeneration or they will be gone forever. GarGweth, the Kaydra can take care of themselves in their disintegrated form. Also, they can talk no matter what form they are in but the animals can't. Right now, every creature looks the same and we need to get as many changed back to their natural form as possible before morning."

"What can GarGweth do to help?"

"If I get hold of a Lidyan form that turns out to be a wild animal, please don't let it hurt me. Just grab it and throw it a little ways away. Now, GarGweth, I want the two guards to turn themselves into Kelcha beasts so that they can scare away any wild beasts. They could even hurt you in the Kelcha beast form.

Larry called the Kaydra and they all agreed it was foolish for them to have gone outside in the first place and they would be glad to return to the safety of the Crater.

The Kaydra helped each other retake their primary form. If one of them came across a Lidyan form creature that couldn't talk, they knew it was an animal. As far as all the Kaydra knew, all of them that had remained outside were now back in their primary form. They all took their most enjoyable transmutative form before they returned to the Crater.

Larry and Delbert worked for several hours turning animals they found back into their natural form before they went to sleep that night. The guards were replaced before GarGweth, Larry and Delbert retired for the night.

"Won't those Lidyans be surprised in the morning, Larry?"

"I hope so. I'll see you in the morning."

In the morning GarGweth had to feed for some time before he could concentrate on anything else. While GarGweth ate, Larry and Delbert went off looking for Lidyan form creatures. After they saw they didn't have any weapons, they would regenerate them to their animal form. Larry would grab the Lidyan form creatures and disintegrate. When he regenerated, he had to let go of the animal quickly so that he wouldn't get bit or scratched by them. If the animal turned out to be large or wild, Delbert would stun it.

"Larry, I've got news for you."

"What's that?"

"The animals are doing just fine out here. I don't think we'll have to worry about them any more now that the new fruit crops are coming on regularly."

"You're right but I would still like to get another planting crew out to seed more of the area. I'd like to get more trees growing out here and more grassland. Let's be sure to leave a fairly wide barren strip between the grassy area and trees in case of a grass fire."

"That sounds great to me, Larry. Does DorLetha care what we do?"

"We should probably check with her. I wonder if they are going to let us stay after you get your body back."

"I hope so. I don't want to go back to Earth to live. As long as only a few Kaydra are fertile, they shouldn't have to worry about over population for a long time."

"Delbert, let's go see if GarGweth is ready to be our shield. If we just stun the Lidyan form creatures when we see them, getting them back to their natural form would go a lot faster."

"OK, anything that will speed up the process. There's GarGweth now."

"Are you ready to go looking for those five bad Lidyans, GarGweth?"

"Sure, Larry, let's go. I thought about their ray beams and I feel strong enough to withstand a good jolt."

"I'm glad to hear that after what TetTrella did to you. There are two or three ahead, Delbert. I'll take the two on the right. You can have the one on your side."

Methodically and systematically Larry and Delbert covered the area. Time after time they changed Lidyan form creatures back into their natural animal form. They had become great hunters since the animals weren't afraid of them.

"It's late afternoon, Delbert? How are you holding out?"

"I'm OK. How are you GarGweth?"

"I'm hungry."

"We'll watch while you eat. Delbert, tomorrow we should get the Kaydra out here with us in their disintegrated state. We could sweep the outside from one end to the other. Each time we came across an alien form creature, we would check it out. I don't want to go on for days out here looking for those five Lidyans, and none of the Kaydra will get hurt that way."

"Now you're thinking. The more we can change today, the easier tomorrow will be. I'm going to help GarGweth gather food. I should be able to cut his eating time in half."

"Go ahead, Delbert, I'll keep watch. Disintegrate if anything looks suspicious."

As Delbert was gathering vegetables for GarGweth, he thought he heard something in a large clump of trees. He disintegrated and saw a Lidyan burying his weapon. "Larry, are you getting my telepathic message?"

"I can hear you inside my head, yes."

"At about two o'clock from your position, using GarGweth's position at twelve o'clock, there's a Lidyan burying his weapon."

"GarGweth hasn't moved has he?"

"No. He's in the same place. How far away from me is he?"

"He's about 100 yards away. Head toward four o'clock and I'll flush him into the clearing in front of you."

"Go ahead."

"Get him! Fire! There he goes." Delbert's fake calls had to be taken seriously by the Lidyan. He didn't have time to uncover his weapon. He just ran away from Delbert out into the clearing where Larry blasted him to pieces. Delbert went back and got the ray blaster. They now had six weapons and four opponents.

"What was he trying to do?"

"I think he was going to pretend he wasn't a Lidyan. Maybe he got separated or was just afraid. Let's send GarGweth back to the Crater tunnel entrance and see what we can see from the sky in our disintegrated form."

"Good Idea. GarGweth, here is some more food Delbert got for you. When you're finished eating, go back to the Crater tunnel entrance and wait for us."

"Sure, I'll see you there."

With that, Larry and Delbert went racing around, stunning and changing Lidyan form creatures into animals again. "The way it looks, Larry, we'll have this job done today by ourselves. Hey, that sounds like GarGweth. He must be in a big fight."

Delbert and Larry transported themselves to the Crater tunnel entrance and found the two guards dead and the bodies of two crumpled Lidyans. There were two ray blasters on the ground. "I'll change and pick them up, and then I'll go through the tunnel to the inside. You had better rush ahead and prevent them from getting into the Crater. It sounds like GarGweth is hot on their trail.

"See you inside, Delbert."

Delbert grabbed the other two ray blasters. He was now trying to carry eight of them, so he couldn't hurry as fast as he wanted to. He could hear GarGweth's roars reverberating through the tunnel. Now and again Delbert stumbled over loose rock. It had obviously been dislodged, by the power of the ray blaster's beam.

Delbert was over half way through the tunnel when he came upon another dead Lidyan. He picked up his ninth weapon and rushed after GarGweth. Just before Delbert reached the last bend in the tunnel, he heard GarGweth roar and heard two loud blasts. He was now in the Crater but the final Lidyan and Larry were nowhere in sight.

Delbert dropped all but one weapon just in time to see the last Lidyan knock Larry off his feet. The alien picked up a rock and brought it down to crush Larry's skull as Delbert stopped, aimed and fired.

The Lidyans arm was coming down when Delbert's ray blaster destroyed it but he was a little too late and the rock struck Larry a glancing blow. "I'La, I'La we need you here, Larry's been hurt."

She appeared instantly. "What happened?"

"The Lidyan I blasted away hit Larry in the head with a rock. Can you do something for him?"

"I'll try, Dell Bert. I'll try."

I'La was doing all she could for Larry. His skull had been crushed by the Lidyans final blow with a rock. Larry had suffered severe brain damage.

"Dell Bert I'm afraid there isn't anything I can do for Larry. The regenerative portion of his brain has been destroyed."

DorLetha arrived and asked, "What's wrong, Dell Bert?"

"Before I could kill the last Lidyan he killed Larry, DorLetha."

"I'm sorry, Dell Bert! I probably could have helped you two some if I knew it was that serious."

"DorLetha, all wars are serious! We were doing all we could do without your help. Even GarGweth tried his best. He's probably dying somewhere inside the Crater near the exit tunnel. He almost got the Lidyan that killed Larry but the Lidyan's final blast of power stopped him.

"Andre, you can't help Larry now. Why don't you show I'La where

GarGweth is? If he lives, he'll need a friend."

"I'll look at him, Dell Bert."

"Delbert, what's wrong with Larry?"

"He's dead, Adrian! The last Lidyan warrior killed him, before I could stop him."

"No! No! Larry can't be dead. I haven't even looked at that ray blaster for you yet!"

"No need to bother yourself with it now!"

"I should have helped you two. I might have been learning things up there, but they didn't need me!"

Adrian broke down and cried. Delbert called for Esdra. "If you want Adrian to be a man with a sound mind, you'd better spend some time with him away from the navigation system. You're burning up his mind! He let his best friend die without even taking a minute to look at the ray blaster. We needed to know more about it and how to recharge it in order to protect ourselves and all of you. None of you even came outside to help us! Only the guards that were outside were concerned and both of them were killed!"

"It's not their fault, Dell Bert. I told them what to do. I just dismissed you from my mind and worried about the course of our dwarf planet. I thought that was more important!"

"It is important; DorLetha, but a few minutes with us would have saved GarGweth from injury and Larry and the guards lives. I'm sorry, but I've got to go outside and dig a hole to bury Larry in. I don't want the animals to eat his flesh."

"Dell Bert, can I take you outside and dig the hole for Larry? I'm sorry I didn't watch out for you two! I really liked Larry. He was good for us. I tried to spend time with him and teach him things."

"I'd like your help, DorLetha. Right now I just want to sit down and cry. Larry was a very close friend. He taught me how to disintegrate the other day. Together we were even able to bring about a mental telemetrical viewing of Lidy and what TetTrella was doing.

"By the way, TetTrella is dead. GarGweth was able to inflict such pain on her that she spotted. TetTrella changed all the creatures outside to the Lidyan form. We had to change them all back to their natural form before we could look for the Lidyan warriors. We killed all the Lidyans that TetTrella brought up here."

DorLetha transported Delbert, Adrian, Esdra and herself along with Larry's body outside. She dug the size hole Delbert requested with the power of her mind in a minute. She then levitated Larry's body to the bottom of the grave and levitated the dirt in on top of him. Adrian and Delbert cried openly for some time. Burying Larry that way was so gross. Exvascia was so primitive by human standards. True, they had advanced minds and could be an advanced culture, but they were really self-centered individuals living in an advanced animal state.

When it got dark, DorLetha transported them back to Larry's cave. Delbert had taken Larry's two pouches off his body before he was buried. He now laid them beside the library of books Larry had written. Delbert knew there was one book he had to write for Larry. He'd call it, “The Lidyan Battles”.

Chapter 17

Time Outside

Delbert decided to spend a few days outside after Larry's death. He took all the material for his book, "The Lidyan Battles", he would need. It only took Delbert a couple days to write the book. Later he would store it in the cave where it would be safe.

He decided to walk on the beach by the sea. He could tell the water line had dropped several feet because of the separation of the hydrogen and oxygen from the water. The abundant amount of oxygen released during the separation period had improved the atmosphere. Of course, the abundance of plants was also increasing the air supply.

Delbert wondered how many centuries the beach he was walking on had been covered by the cold waters of the sea. He thought to himself. *I wonder what the extra heat being directed out here will do to the water temperature. I wonder what life there is in the sea.*

It was strange to see a body of water, so large that the eye couldn't see the other side, without a tide. *Will the new moon we're getting give us tides? Will we have beautiful moonlit nights to enjoy and how will the animals react to its light.*

Delbert had brought a couple of the ray blasters with him for protection. He didn't know what to expect but he figured it was better to play it safe than be caught without any protection. He didn't feel completely helpless now that he could disintegrate. He tried it from time to time to get more practice at it. *What if I think of another creature when I'm disintegrated, could I take its form?*

Delbert had to try. *I wonder what I'd look like as a hawk. I've seen enough of them in Oregon to picture myself as one. My brain is surely larger than theirs. Since I've learned how to operate Art's body, I should be able to learn to operate as a hawk.*

Delbert disintegrated himself and thought of himself being regenerated as a hawk. Sure enough, he was a hawk. *I'm a hawk! I can see my reflection in the water. Now that's a foxy looking hawk if I've ever seen one. So now what do I do. Hum, my clawed feet feel more like hands to me. I can walk on them, but I don't feel they are for running. If I think of flying what happens? That's interesting, I am flying. All I had to do was think of it and my wings flapped and I was lifted on the breeze and here I am looking down at the planet.*

My wings feel more like human legs. Flying feels like walking. If I put a little effort into it, will my speed increase? It sure does! Now let me see if I can turn and bank. Hey, everyone, look at me! No hands!

I think I'll try landing. Let's see, no flaps! I must have to tilt my wings to slow me down. Ah! Ha! That's the way it works. Well, here goes a landing. I'll do it just like I've seen ducks do it back home.

Although Delbert had a picture of his landing in his mind, he wasn't very successful at landing. He laughed at himself to think what a real hawk would think of his flying display. Delbert spent most of the day that way. It wasn't long before he got hungry. *I wonder how I'd do hunting. I guess the only way to find out is to try catching something.* He found his vision was very good from quite a height. He saw a rat size rodent and thought to himself, *Charge!* He immediately went into a steep, fast dive. At the last second he pulled up. As he did so, he scooped up the rodent. *I think I'll land on that rock and eat it."*

Being very careful Delbert was able to land on a large rock and killed his prey as a Hawk would. For some strange reason, the rodent looked like a banquet to him. He devoured it and enjoyed every bite. *That's enough of being a hawk today. Maybe I'll try it again tomorrow. For now, I need to find a place to rest. That spot by the rocks on the sand should be OK.*

I hadn't thought about it but this ability will allow me to spend time in the air with my other two children, Dora and Cara. Even though I've now changed back to a man, I'm still full from that meal I ate as a hawk.

Delbert walked back up the beach away from the water's edge. He realized that he would soon have to make himself another pair of moccasins. His were getting thin and the sand felt hot to his feet, so he walked back down to the water and got them wet. He went over and picked up his backpack he had brought for camping. One thing he didn't notice was the small amount of shell-like material his backpack uncovered as he picked it up.

The animals outside the Crater were spreading the seeds of plants far and wide. The additional reflected light and increased rain were good for the plants. Delbert wanted to camp in an area with less vegetation. He found a tree some distance from the more heavily vegetated area. He draped one large skin, made from two, over a lower limb of the tree to form a tent a little larger than a pup tent. He stretched the four corners out and put rocks on them. When it got dark, he lie under his makeshift tent and looked up at the stars. There wasn't any big or small dipper or even a north star. Because of the thin atmosphere and clear weather, the stars seemed bright and close. It was strange not to have a moon to look at, but they would have one soon.

Have animals and other beings lived on this dwarf planet in the past or star travelers been forced to land here? I think I'll spend a few days exploring. If I light my oil shale lamp I can look at Larry's book about the outside. I'll need to make maps of different areas I see, since Larry didn't get around to making any.

The next morning Delbert got up, ate some fruit from his backpack and started walking. He expected to find another river feeding the lake or whatever it was. Although he walked all that day and the next, he did not come across another stream. He often thought he should take the hawk form so he could see what was ahead quicker but he didn't. Delbert was walking a few yards from the beach where it was easier to walk. Even the terrain there was rough, rock strewn and barren of any vegetation.

Delbert had tasted the water of the enormous lake It wasn't very salty. If there was a tide, the wind would surely drive some of the water further from the shore and then plants should start growing. The lake, as he decided to call it, was placid. He'd have to come back and make himself a raft and explore it. It wouldn't take much of a raft to sail on it, as it was always so calm. Maybe it would be good therapy for Adrian to come along. He'd have to ask him when he got back to their cave.

Delbert had to start back. His food supply wouldn't even get him back to where he started. He'd have to skip eating one day before he could reach the tropical paradise that extended for some distance on either side of the silver stream which flowed from the Crystal Prism Mountain. Before he reached it, he wanted to look at the cave in Spark Stone Mountain where TetTrella had kept GarGweth captive.

Had Delbert continued along the lake, he would have noticed life starting to move from the large eggs that were completely covered by the hot, loose sand. Only four months earlier the sand had been covered by the cold waters of the lake. Before the new solar reflector was positioned, the area outside the Crater was not heated very much or very far from the Crystal Prism Mountain.

Delbert was getting Art's body in good shape for him. Skipping another meal would make it even leaner. He decided on the last day of his trip back, he would jog quite a ways. After eating all his food, his backpack was light. His body was tanned from the sun and he was only wearing a loincloth and moccasins.

Delbert enjoyed camping out. He wondered if there were fish in the lake. The river seemed to have a variety as well as the pool in the Crater although the river ones were very small. When Delbert reached Spark Stone Mountain, he stopped and looked at the cave where TetTrella had held GarGweth captive. The rock was laden with fissures. He could see how GarGweth, using his strength and patience, could pick his way out, with Twillie's help, over several days.

While he was in the cave, he thought he heard something, on the other side of the cave's back wall, doing the same thing GarGweth had done; slowly and methodically picking away at the rock, trying to dig its way out of Spark Stone Mountain.

Delbert left Spark Stone Mountain in favor of the fruit growing area of the jungle. He enjoyed eating again. He had run out of food the day before but it didn't worry him because he knew there would be plenty when he reached the jungle.

Delbert practiced being a hawk again before he went back into the Crater. By concentrating harder, he was able to change from his human form to that of the hawk more quickly. Perhaps he should have looked over the area outside in the hawk form, it would have taken him a lot less time but time didn't mean anything on Exvascia.

Adrian greeted Delbert, when he returned to the Crater. “How are you feeling Adrian?”

“OK, but I need to get out of this Crater for a few days.”

“How would you like to go sailing?”

“You've got a boat?”

“No, but I think we could build a raft that would be light weight and buoyant. There's a good breeze on the lake or whatever it is. Since there isn't any tide, it should be easy to sail on it without having to have a real rugged craft.”

“You mean we could go exploring for a few days, Delbert?”

“I don't see why not. We'll have to carve some paddles and a rudder first. With a couple animal skins for a sail we should be set. We should be able to use those ray blasters to cut down some of the larger tube plants. They're a lot like bamboo. We might look to see if there are any dry bones around that we could use for fish hooks. Of course, we could use the crossbow to fish with, if we tie a thin leather thong to the arrow.”

“I'm going to start work on the paddles. Why don't you go see your kids and DorLetha for a while?”

"OK. I'll see you later. Hi, I'La, how's GarGweth?"

"He's going to be OK. He just needs a few more days rest and plenty of the right kind of food."

"Is Shida around?"

"Yes, she and your little ones are in the house."

"Thanks." Delbert walked to the wooden building that Larry, Adrian and he had built. It was OK for the conditions inside the Crater, but it would never stand up outside. Dell Britt and Letha ran to meet their dad. They were getting good at walking and running now. They were trying to learn to talk, but that would take some more time.

"Dora, Cara, dad's got a special surprise for you. His two Fem-Birds children flew onto his shoulders. They preferred to use their owl form most of the time. "Let's go outside." Out on the balcony, Delbert put Dora and Cara on the railing. He stood by them and took his hawk form. When he did they all flew off. As they were flying around, DorLetha came home.

"Who is flying around with Dora and Cara, Shida?"

"It's Delbert."

"When did he learn to do that?"

"I don't know, DorLetha. It's the first time I've seen him do it."

When Delbert saw DorLetha, he flew back to the railing. He then hopped down on the floor and took his human form. "Dell Bert, when did you learn to do that?"

"I learned while I was outside these past few days. How did I do?"

"Great. I never thought a human could learn to do that. Did you find what you were looking for out there?"

"No, that's why Adrian and I want to go out and look around more. Have you ever looked over all the area outside?"

"No, should I have done that?"

"I don't know. I'll tell you after I get through looking at it. How are the calculations coming on the moon's path?"

"It's looking good. We will probably only have to make one more course correction."

"I want to look things over outside before the gravitational pull of the moon changes things. When we do have a moon, I want to take you down by the lake on a moonlit night, walk along the beach and listen to the breakers pounding in the surf. I hope you'll like that."

"Dell Bert, I'll be glad when the pressure is off me because of the moon and you not having your own body. When you're in your own body, I can come live in the house with you."

"That will be a real pleasure. I haven't got to relax with you since I came here and that's been too long."

"Did Adrian tell you it looks like Esdra will start gleesing soon?"

"No, he forgot to tell me. If I can teach Adrian how to take another form, levitate things and disintegrate like I can, would that convince Esdra to keep more of her powers?"

"It might but only if he tells her very soon. She has to change her attitude or she will still lose all her feathers. I'm not sure that would necessarily mean she would forget how to do other things."

"In the morning, I'll try to tell her all the things I can do. Do you know if any other creatures inhabit this planet?"

"We've never seen any but then we've never looked. I don't know why we weren't interested in the outside like Larry was."

"Dell Bert, why did you want to fly with Dora and Cara?"

"They're my children just like Dell Britt and Letha. If I love their mother, why shouldn't I love them? Regardless of the form they prefer, it's good for them to get to know me better. If I can't do anything with them, they aren't any better off knowing who their father is or what he looks like. Are you enjoying being Queen?"

"So far it's been all work and study. I've got a lot of responsibility on my shoulders. Since you men have been here and started doing things that you call normal, I can see how abnormal we've become. We use the form of animals for a superior animal life. We haven't used our bodies or minds for anything. I know I'La, Esdra, DaKeta and Shida are happier now that they have something to occupy their time.

"It's like you to want to go outside and look around. We don't seem to have any desire to be active as an intelligent society. We've completely forgotten what living is all about.

"I want you men to stay so we can learn from you what we've forgotten. I'm glad you are going to bring two of your friends here. I'm especially glad one will be a female."

"I could never go back to Earth to stay now that I can disintegrate myself and change my form. I know that your planet is quite different from ours. Somehow your mental powers have rubbed off on me and strengthened my mind. I can certainly see why Larry could never go home."

DorLetha could tell that Dell Britt and Letha needed the love, attention and handling that only their dad could give them. They were more human, while Dora and Cara were typically Exvascians, loners, self-sufficient and aloof. They tried to learn by observing, while the two offspring, with the human outlook, learned by doing.

"Dell Bert, GarGweth has asked to stay for a while. He is sorry Larry was killed. He said he almost had the Lidyan that killed Larry, but the last blast of the ray blaster was too powerful for him. He'd like to live outside. He says he feels much better physically and that he feels younger."

"Why are you willing to allow him to stay, DorLetha?"

"I said he could stay because of his actions after he found out what he was doing was wrong and realized TetTrella caused it by feeding him mind altering plants. Also, he did rid us of TetTrella."

"He might like to stay, but I wonder if he will get lonely out there?"

"I don't think so; Andre has been by his side since he saw him trying to help Larry. Sometimes I see him on GarGweth's shoulder. It reminds me of him ridding on Larry's hip most of the time. Who knows, perhaps one of the Kadra with ape form will be attracted to him"

"That's good. That way they'll both have company. GarGweth and Twillie were very close just like Larry and Andre. When I was in the cave where TetTrella held GarGweth, I thought I heard something trying to dig its way out from further back in the mountain. Perhaps I was hearing things or maybe I should go check it out."

"I don't know that anything lives in or on Spark Stone Mountain."

Chapter 18

First Island

"Adrian and I are going sailing on the lake outside. We'll be gone for several days. Do you have a navigation device we could use to get back?"

"Not that I know of, I'll see if I can find something for you to use the next time. Can you figure some way to get by until then?" DorLetha asked.

"I think so. I'll see you when we get back."

"Good-bye, Dell Bert."

Delbert kissed DorLetha on the cheek and went back to the Crater tunnel entrance where Adrian was. Esdra was still working on the navigational problem related to the moon that they may collide with.

He'd have to talk with her in the morning.

"Adrian, I understand Esdra is gleesing. She seems to be sure you are her mate. In order for her to keep from molting, she has to be reassured that you have a variety of abilities. So, in the morning, I'm going to tell her that I can bring about telemetrical viewing, disintegrate, travel in free soul flight, levitate things and change forms. While we're outside, maybe I can teach you how to do those things too. I know you won't have any problem learning how."

"I don't see any problem with her gleesing. She could wear clothes like our women do and the only thing different would be her bald head if she lost her feathers there too. But then I guess her wings would look strange.

"She's good for me! She takes good care of me and I'm getting to where I want her around. I hope she doesn't have any serious problems in her fertility development because of having chosen me."

"DorLetha doesn't know what will happen to her because of her mental attitude. We'll just have to wait and see. Did you cook the meal?"

"No, Esdra did before she went back to work with the others on the navigational team. She is becoming a good cook."

After dinner the two men worked on carving paddles. They would drill a hole in the handle of the paddles and attach a leather thong to them so they wouldn't get lost at sea. They took a couple dried giant lily pads to use as life preservers. They were taking a lot of spark stone and a few ceramic pots to burn oil shale in for light and to use for cooking. They would take Mardi Goat bags full of water and food. Marble nuts and other dried items like dried Mellow Drops, which looked and tasted like large raisins, would keep for a long time.

"We can take two or three ray blasters with us. We can use one to fall the large tube plant stocks. I thought we could make a two-foot-wide path of oil shale rock about 210 feet long starting fairly high up Spark Stone Mountain. I know where there's some loose Spark Stone nearby. We can start the fire at the lower end and it will burn up the mountain to the other end. That will give us a navigational guide. That should burn for about two weeks. Since they burn like briquettes, they should slowly start the pieces next to them on fire until they are all burned up.

"Maybe I can get GarGweth to light it after we have been gone for a day or two. If we don't get back before it goes out, he could go ahead and extend it upward. If we run across any islands, we could make a map on an animal skin with mellow drop juice."

"I think we should try to get a reading from the stars the first night out. I don't know how far we will be able to see that fire burning but it won't be very far. Do you think there is any current out in the lake, Delbert?"

"Without a moon to cause a tide, I don't think there'll be any. I think we could use some of the branches of the living vine to lash our raft together. We'll need to affix a skin canopy to shield us from the light of the solar reflector. I don't know why but I can't say 'sun'. Somehow it doesn't seem the same."

"I know what you mean. However, the artificial life support system they have in the Crater seems natural. So far, Delbert, we don't even know what the area around the mountain looks like. Isn't it highly probably that other areas have a lot of vegetation? It seems like the birds would spread seeds far and wide."

"It would depend on the amount of soil in places out there. I'd like to do some hiking when we get back from sailing. I wonder if that body of water is a lake, a gulf or an ocean. The Exvascians said most of the planet was covered with water. Maybe we're on a giant island. Adrian!"

"Are there any animals that can be ridden here?"

"Let's look at Larry's book on animals. I'll look through it and see what I can find. Hum. Here's a picture of a short necked giraffe-like animal that he says may be ridden. It's called a Kateeta. He says he's seen four or five in the meadow. Here's one he calls a Kompo. It looks like an Eland with a very wide growth of fur around its neck and a short lower jaw.

“Of course, Adrian, we could take a look at the entire area in our disintegrated form. That would give us an aerial view. Maybe we should take a look before we go sailing.”

“You're going to show me how, I hope?”

“I can try. I remember how Larry showed me. I'll just do the same with you. I'm going to turn in. I'll see you in the morning, Adrian.”

“Good Night, Delbert.”

Esdra appeared shortly after the two men had finished breakfast. “Esdra I want to tell you some of the things I can do now.”

“Why, Dell Bert?”

“Because I believe Adrian can learn to do them in a few days with my help. If you want him for your mate, you don't want to be weaker than he is. He'll need your superior skills to compensate for his weaknesses.”

“That might be true but if I don't change some there will be too much difference between what each of us can do.

“That's why I want to tell you what I can do. I can disintegrate, change forms, levitate things, travel in free soul flight and bring things up myself for mental telemetrical viewing. You see, we aren't as helpless as you had thought. I don't even think you should give up your feathers.”

“Didn't you say your females have smooth skin like yours?”

“That's right, but they have to wear clothes to keep warm.”

“I'm going to give up my feathers anyway. I'll decide whether I'll give up other powers later.”

“I'm glad to hear that! Adrian and I are going outside for several days. We want to see what more of the planet looks like.”

“I'll be busy Adrian but I'll miss you.”

“I'll be back, Esdra; I'll only be gone for a few days.”

“While you're finishing the paddles and rudder, I want to go talk to GarGweth.”

“Go ahead and take care of whatever you need to, there isn't any hurry.”

Delbert arranged for GarGweth to meet them outside three mornings later. That would give them over two full days outside to get the raft ready. He stopped and saw his kids for a while. When he returned, he found that Adrian had finished the paddles and the rudder. As they gathered supplies, Delbert was surprised at the amount of things they thought they would need.

“I had a raft of about 12 feet by 24 feet in mind. That will allow us a large sail area and a large covered deck area, Delbert. I imagine we'll need a couple feet on each side of the covered area to get around and control the sail.”

"That sounds about right. Are you ready to try levitating everything to the outside?"

"Yes! You say all I have to do is concentrate on the pile of things moving to where I want them to go? I'll try! Hey, that isn't as hard as I thought it would be," Adrian exclaimed.

"Just remember to keep your concentration on them as we walk out."

Delbert let Adrian levitate the items all the way through the tunnel to the entrance to the outside. There they decided to leave their things there until they needed them. They took the ray blaster with them as they walked to the area where the tube plants grew thick and tall.

The logging only took a few minutes with the ray blaster. They also cut up a living vine to use to lash the bamboo-like logs together. Adrian had used his ingenuity and creativity to design the raft. By late morning of the second day, they were through with the raft. They loaded it with the things they had brought and then levitated it to the sandy beach by the water's edge.

Their next project was making the strip of oil shale up Spark Stone Mountain. When they were finished, Adrian set a fire for GarGweth to light two days later. All he had to do was set the tinder afire. It hadn't been difficult to levitate the oil shale rock up the mountain, but it took quite some time to initially gather the material.

After checking over their supplies, they ate their last meal of the day. "Before it gets dark, Adrian, would you like to try disintegrating?"

"Why not, if I can, perhaps we can look around some out here! What do I have to do?"

"Just think of yourself as being particles. Now let yourself go. Just let your mind and soul float as you do in free soul flight. Think how the feeling is when we leave our bodies in the cool cave. That's right, just keep thinking it can be done.

"I'll hold your wrists so I can either help you disintegrate or regenerate your body. That's good, you're starting to disintegrate. Keep thinking of yourself as being particles. Let your body float in space. OK, now that we're both disintegrated, concentrate telepathically on my thoughts. Now think of your human form in detail and as a solid body.

"There, we're back! The way you regenerated is the same way you take another form. When I take the hawk form, I picture the hawk in my mind. Then I let my very being drift into the picture I'm seeing and what I'm thinking of. It's kind of like pretending you were an animal when you were a kid."

"Let me try disintegrating again. Why do you hold my wrists when we disintegrate? When we become particles, you surely can't still be holding me?

"My being has control of you then, unless I intentionally let go of you with my mind. If I did that, and you couldn't concentrate hard enough to regenerate yourself, you'd be gone forever. When we do it this time, hold a rock in your hand all the way through. Here we go! Now, change back!"

Adrian obeyed Delbert's telepathic commands. "Now, Adrian, try it on your own. This time, though, let go of the rock."

When Adrian returned, the rock didn't. "So that's how Larry got rid of the Lidyan!"

"That's right. Let's disintegrate and think ourselves around the area. When we've agreed on a point to go to, we'll be there automatically. If we don't agree we can end up at different places. In case we do, let's try to meet back here at the raft. We can regenerate when we want to physically inspect something."

"I'm ready, Delbert."

"Let's start by going around Crystal Prism Mountain. I'd like to see if it's an island or not. Let's go to the top of Spark Stone Mountain first." Little by little they moved around Crystal Prism Mountain in their disintegrated state. They soon found out that the area wasn't an island. They also found out that the lake was probably an ocean. Back at the raft they talked.

"That's a great way to travel Delbert but how do you keep track of where you are?"

"I'm not sure. It must be in the thought process somehow. Maybe it's like mental telemetrical viewing. You may have to picture where you want to be to get there. Then I guess it wouldn't matter whether you knew where you were or which way to go to get back to where you wanted to be."

"Let's save some of the other learning experiences for tomorrow. I want to put a couple holes in those lily pads so I can put a thong on them. I want us to be able to tie them to ourselves if we go overboard."

"Go ahead. I'm going to walk down to the ocean." As Delbert walked along the beach, he came across what looked like the majority of a very tough, hard-shelled egg. It had about a six to eight inch diameter. He picked it up from the soft sand and walked back in the dark to Adrian's fire.

"Take a look at this Adrian and tell me what you think it is."

"It looks like an ostrich egg shell. Are there any animals out here that lay eggs?"

"I don't know. Let's just leave it here until we get back. It'll be easy enough to find here by your fire pit."

GarGweth showed up in the morning before Adrian and Delbert were finished eating. Andre was happy to see them and raced ahead of GarGweth for the last 100 yards. "Hi, Andre did you come with GarGweth? Did you help him find us?"

"Hi, GarGweth came early for you."

"That's good GarGweth. When we finish eating, we'll show you where we have placed our oil shale that we want you to light. All you have to do is light the tinder by striking two spark stone together like this. It should burn for several days. You might check it after several days and see if it is still burning from one end to the other. If it looks like it's all going to burn up and we aren't back, could you spread out more oil shale to be burned?"

"I can do that for you. Andre can help me!" Andre jumped up on GarGweth's shoulder.

After breakfast, Delbert took GarGweth up to the long stretch of oil shale they had laid out. He showed him the place to light it two days later. "We think we will be able to see this for several days from out on the water. We've made this raft and put a sail on it. The wind will take us for a ride."

"Are you ready to go, Delbert?"

"Yes, let's levitate the raft to the water." In a few minutes they had set sail for parts unknown. Delbert hoisted the sail and the gentle breeze took them out to sea. "That breeze must be blowing four or five knots per hour, Adrian. If we just sail with the wind at our backs all day and the mountain in sight, we'll have made quite a distance by nightfall."

"What do you think we'll find out there Delbert?"

"I don't know. Why don't we try fishing with those sharp bone hooks we made? I'd like to see if anything lives in this ocean. There are a few birds flying around. Keep an eye on them to see if they're feeding."

"It's sure quiet out here, Delbert. It seems so strange not to have any tidal action on this ocean. Look how far we've come in four hours. We must be 15 miles out to sea already. Look at the light being reflected off the Crystal Prism in the top of the Crater. Except for that, it looks like a volcano that has blown molten lava from a small opening in its top. I wonder how far we'll be able to see the mountain."

"Ask me tomorrow! Are you feeling anything biting at your hook?"

"No, without much light being reflected out here, the water has probably been too cold to sustain life. The water is very clear. I don't have any idea how deep it is but I can see a long ways down. Obviously there isn't any plankton to form a food chain."

"Our raft seems to be quite seaworthy in this calm sea. I think I'll become a hawk and take a look around."

"Go ahead! I'll watch how you do it."

Delbert disintegrated and then regenerated as a hawk. He flew off, climbing higher and higher. It wasn't long before Delbert was out of Adrian's sight. As a hawk, Delbert could see much better and further than he could as a human. When they had sailed out to sea, they headed for what they thought was open water. In reality, they were following the coast, off to their left, and were about 20 miles away from where they started. Delbert would have to correct their course when he got back to the raft. He needed to turn it about 90 degrees to their right so they would be perpendicular to the shore they had left.

Delbert landed on the deck and changed back to his human form. "We have to change course so we don't go down the coast line. I'll reset the sail and the rudder and we can relax. "Do you want to try and change form, Adrian?"

"Yes, I think I'm ready to give it a try. How do I do it?"

"First you have to disintegrate. Then think of the form you want to become. Think of the form being a solid, existing, breathing entity. To operate the new object you become, just think the action you want to duplicate. Say you want to be a squirrel. You would think of a long gray fur coat, brown beady eyes, sharp little teeth; long, gray, curved tail and neat little paws. You'd probably think of it sitting on its haunches with its back held straight, its head upright and it looking around."

"That sounds easy enough. I think I'll try the bird form though. Let's see, I think I'll be a pigeon." Adrian disintegrated and regenerated as a pigeon. Delbert quickly changed to a hawk again. Communicating telepathically, Delbert instructed Adrian on how to take off and land. "Remember how you've seen pigeons take off. Try flapping your wings so you can see how much strength it takes to get enough lift to get your feet off the deck. Easy does it now! Remember you are a pigeon. Those wings you see out there are at your mental command. They are not arms any longer. Go ahead and give it a try. That's right! See how easy it is?"

"I'm surprised. It doesn't take any effort at all. I'm going to take off. Here I go!" Off he went with Delbert after him.

"I like the way you tucked your legs and feet up under you, Adrian. That looked like you knew what you were doing."

"It felt silly the instant I left the ground to still have them hanging down. It's an involuntary reflex action just as blinking is. I think I'll try some turns and dives. Oh, that feels great! I see what you meant about having been close to the left shoreline. It looks like your course correction will take us out to the open sea now.

"What happens when you eat in a form such as this?"

"You get full. You enjoy an excellent tasting worm or two or some seeds. When you change back to your own form, you're as full as you were in your assumed form."

"How high can we go?"

"I don't know, let's find out. You get a great view from up here, don't you?"

"That's right. It's like flying in a plane. Delbert, why don't we fly inland a ways and look around?"

"OK. We should be able to find our raft as long as it's light. We sure don't want to get caught over the water without a place to land at night. I don't know how long we can stay up."

"You're right. I wonder what's on the other side of that ridge."

"We'll find out in a few minutes. It doesn't take long to fly 20 miles as a bird, if you go straight."

After a few minutes, they reached the low mountain range that separated a valley from the coast line. "That's a good looking valley, Delbert. There is so much grass and only a few trees here and there. There are only a few birds around and very few creatures of any kind."

"That looks like a good place to have a ranch. There is a stream too. This planet sure hasn't had any development. I suppose the additional reflector light will increase its vegetation. The change in the atmosphere and the rains we are now experiencing should help both plants and animals. It will give them a broader ranging capacity. The further they range the more area they'll fertilize."

"I'm ready to go back whenever you are."

"OK, let's go."

They flew back to the raft. "Let's try a pass or two over the deck before you try to land, Adrian."

"OK. That pass felt good. I could tell I was going too fast to land, though. It felt as though I would be pressing it. I think I can land next time."

"Go ahead!"

Adrian made a perfect landing. After landing they changed back to their human form. "Let's inspect the raft before we eat. We need to make sure it's tied together securely. I'd hate to have it come apart while we're sleeping."

"That wouldn't be good. Why did you want to come outside and explore, Delbert?"

"I'm looking for any previous civilization or even space junk. Just think of the junk we humans are leaving on the surface of the moon and other planets."

"We were getting the idea on Earth that we weren't the only intelligent beings in the universe because of the flying saucer sightings that have been reported. Now that we've been on Exvascia and seen several different mental telemetrical viewings, and even encountered the Lidyans, we know there are many intelligent beings in the universe with all kinds of forms."

"The raft seems secure, let's eat."

For the next couple days the men enjoyed their new power of mental concentration and transmutative abilities. On the fourth day out to sea, Adrian got an idea.

"Delbert, what if I thought about Esdra and tried to become an Exvascian. Would I turn out to be a male of their species?"

"Anything is possible. I don't know what would happen, because you don't have any real mental picture of what males looks like. We don't even know how large they were."

"I wonder if only some of them were fertile and if they had a change in life at manhood?"

"That's another good question, Adrian. Maybe we can get DorLetha to check the time-exempt telepathic storage banks and tell us."

"There's something else I was wondering about. Do we have strong enough minds to tap into or view those storage banks? Or, maybe she could give us a mental telemetrical viewing of what she reads and sees?"

"We will have to ask her."

That night the men slept and dreamed of what Exvascians society might have been like in ages past. When they awoke in the morning, the raft wasn't moving. When they looked around to see where they were or what was new, they were pleased to find they were up against a bluff.

"It looks like we've found an island, Delbert. Shall we just levitate the raft up on top of the bluff?"

"Let's give it a try." Being excited it wasn't any problem for the two men to emit strong enough brain waves to raise the raft, with them on it, to a flat place on the top of the bluff.

"Shall we make like birds and take a look at the entire island?"

"After we eat but first let's see what the other sides of the island offers for an approach. We're lucky we didn't hit rocks or wreck the raft."

"Did you see the marks on the bluff as we came up? It looks like the water use to be ten feet or more higher. Also, I thought I saw some wear as though there had been a tide for a number of years, which eroded away part of the bluff."

"Are we going to take a ray blaster with us, Delbert?"

"No. If there's a problem, disintegrate, think yourself to another place and regenerate. I wonder what animals are on the island. Having never seen man, I doubt they'll pay any attention to us. The birds are different than what I've seen before on this planet. I'm through eating; let's take a look around as birds."

"Take off, hawk, I'm right on your tail."

"OK pigeon. Look at that reef we could have hit. There doesn't seem to be any place to land that would be safe."

"Do you think the Exvascians lowered the ocean water level ten feet over the years when separating the water into oxygen and hydrogen?"

"I would have to guess so, Adrian. You can't change even a dwarf planet's orbit without getting a lot of power from somewhere. By the way, have you even seen their Separating Plant?"

"No, I haven't. I wonder where it is and what it looks like. We'll have to go looking for it someday."

"The island appears to be five miles across. It must be of volcanic origin. The ocean spray must have caused dirt in the air to collect on it."

"It probably attracted some of these birds because of the few islands there must be. The glare of the reflected light off the water probably caused it to be warmer. That would account for the more vegetative conditions. The highest area has clouds around it right now. That would account for the fresh water lake and stream."

"Isn't that what you're looking for down there, Delbert, a wrecked spacecraft?"

"Let's go down and take a look. Let's land and change form. It's good to be in my own form again and have some solid ground under my feet."

"That's some kind of metal! It doesn't seem to be rusted. The metal has such a dull, coated look to it. It looks about the size needed to transport two pilots and about 18 cubic yards of cargo space. Perhaps it was a shuttle of some type. It looks like it crash landed, the way it's torn open. There's a part of a shell that looks like what I found on the beach just before we sailed. Let's take it back with us, Delbert, and compare the two."

"Adrian, let's see if we can find where they tried to live once they landed. I don't see any bones around here, but I guess wild animals could have carried them off. However we haven't seen any animals yet."

"There isn't any way to tell how old the wreck is, Delbert. Look at these letter or number markings on the control panel. They're strange. They didn't use any dials. Everything works on a sliding mechanism basis. There doesn't seem to be anything left lying around. In fact, it looks like it was partially stripped. They probably used everything they could strip off of it to stay alive.

Do you think we could take this wreck back with us?"

"How could we do that?"

"We could build another raft. We could use the skins that make up the canopy as a second sail. We could make another rudder."

"I doubt if we can find anything here to bind logs together with. We may not even be able to find logs here that would float. I know I don't have enough mental power to levitate the raft and that old spacecraft back to the Crystal Prism Crater.

"If the breeze isn't right, we may have to mentally power our raft along in order to get back on time."

"I guess I was dreaming, Delbert, I'd just like to get my hands on some metal on this planet. We don't have anything to make tools from."

"Well, we can see what we can rip off that spacecraft before we leave. Let's take a look around. Of course, you know that spacecraft may have been here longer than the vegetation."

"As we're walking along, I've only seen a few plants that I'm familiar with, Delbert. I suppose the birds spread them. Look at that little tree. It must be many years old. Look at the distance it has grown lately. That must have been since we put the second solar reflector into use."

"As hot as it is out here, I'm not surprised the plants are growing much faster than they did before. There aren't many animals on this island. That must mean that the planet didn't have many native animals before the Exvascians arrived."

"Delbert, let's look in those caves over there. Maybe the space travelers found them."

"You're right Adrian. There are all kinds of bones in here! I don't see any utensils of any kind in here though. It looks like they were carnivorous. Of course, they may not have intended to stay and were forced to eat anything they could get their hands on to survive. Look at us; we didn't bring a knife, fork or spoon."

"Look in this cave! It looks like two giant turtles died. Isn't that another one of those egg-like spheres in the corner?"

"It sure is, Adrian. Let's take it with us. I wonder if they were from this planet or whether they came from somewhere else. The one I found on the shore, before we left, could have drifted with the tide from here if there was a tide at one time. Maybe it was blown by the wind there as it floated. Let's go outside and see what else we can find."

"The plants are so different out here. Delbert, do you think we should eat any of them? I pulled this vegetable. It looks like the ones I'La told me I could eat to get rid of my arthritis. I think I'll take it along."

"Let's not both eat the same thing. That way, if something doesn't agree with one of us, we won't both get sick. We could take a variety of fruits with us and each try a different one each day. I'll record what we eat on an animal skin for a record of this island. By the way, what are we going to call it?"

"How about calling it 'First Island'? That way we can keep track of them easier. Later, if our new map shows there is some pattern to the islands, we can name or number them differently."

"That's OK with me, Adrian. Do you think we dare lie down in the shade of that tree over there? It looks like a Mist tree. Let's go check it out. It looks like it may have claimed two more of those giant turtles as victims."

"Shall we take that turtle shell back with us to the cave to use as an end table?"

"I wouldn't take one from under the Mist tree, but I think we've got room for one from the cave. Those things are so large I bet I could wear it if it had a hinge to open it."

For the rest of the day the men looked at different areas of First Island. They'd fly around and spot an area they wanted to look at, land, change form and give the area a thorough examination on foot.

"It's a good thing we brought our own oil shale and spark stone or else we'd be hard pressed to get a fire going. There isn't any stone on this island that will give off a spark."

"Besides that, Delbert, there is very little dead wood around. It's as if nothing has died in this area. We haven't found any sign of intelligent life ever living here other than those from that spacecraft."

Before they went to sleep that evening, Delbert said, "It sure feels good not to be on the raft. I'll see you in the morning."

The next day the men explored the remainder of the island. They took an oil shale pot to the turtle cave and found that it had some writing on the walls. Delbert tried to copy some of it down on his animal skin. Perhaps they would be able to decipher it later. Adrian was glad he could levitate the turtle shell back to the raft. He noticed when he picked it up that it wasn't the largest turtle shell, but the largest he could find that wasn't under the Mist tree.

"Is there anything else we want to see today? I'd like to leave while the weather is good."

"We can pick some fresh fruit in the morning and then leave. Shall we go to the spacecraft and see what we can pull off of it to take with us?"

"Sure." The men walked to where the spacecraft had crashed. "Why don't I pretend I'm GarGweth? I bet I could tear parts of that spacecraft then."

"Be my guest!"

Delbert changed to GarGweth's form and tried to rip pieces from the spacecraft. He finally managed to break off one support piece. With that piece as a tool, he was able to salvage a few more small pieces. Delbert changed back to his human form. "I can't believe how strong that thin metal is. It has to be some space age metal that Earth's scientists haven't thought of yet. I spent too much time and energy to come away with so few pieces."

"What do you think happened to the smashed and broken pieces, Delbert?"

"I don't know, unless they were hidden in a cave somewhere. We'd have to search a long time to cover an island this large. I guess we'll have to be satisfied with what we have. I'm ready to eat. It'll be getting dark soon."

"How do you plan on sailing during the day?"

"We'll check the stars tonight, Adrian, and put an arrow on the ground pointing the way we should go. Tomorrow we'll use the high points of the island as a reference as we start back. If we sail over the horizon, and can't see the island, we'll have to wait untill dark to get our bearings again.

"From the raft I can take the hawk form and see the island much further away than I can as a human. Going against the breeze won't be much fun. The progress will be slow. I thought we could use our mental powers to move the raft along until we get tired. With the sail down, we may be able to levitate it along like a hovercraft."

When morning came, the skies were full of clouds. The men had to decide whether to stay where they were or try to sail away, even though they may not be able to see the stars at night. "I don't think it would be wise to leave now. If we can't sail at night, we won't be making any progress even if we do set sail."

"I guess there isn't any reason to push our luck, the storms usually only last a day or two. I think I'll try some of the island's fruit for breakfast." Delbert remarked.

"I'm going to eat a couple of the vegetables I pulled yesterday. My joints are a little stiff."

"OK, Adrian, but be sure I keep track of everything you eat. I think I'd like to look around the island on foot, take a leisurely stroll through the vegetation, view the scenery and smell the fragrance of the flowers. "Even here on Exvascia we haven't learned that it's OK to take some time to relax. Larry had learned that."

"Let's take an animal skin along to put up in case it rains, Delbert. If we can find a cave to dash into, we could still relax and be dry. You know, after being in the Crater so long with the Kaydra, I expect all of the birds here to be intelligent beings. When I talk to them, I find they are just normal, happy birds. I like that. It doesn't seem normal to have to question every animal to find out whether or not it's an animal."

"I know what you mean. It leaves you with a continual uneasy feeling. Hey, this looks like a trail. That's the first one I've seen. Maybe there are more animals here than meets the eye."

"Look over there. See that Marble Nut tree? Let's go break some of the pods, shell the nuts and see if we can get those squirrel-like creatures to eat out of our hands."

They did as Adrian suggested. The furry little animals enjoyed the assistance with their food and the petting they received. The rain came and went for the next couple days. Delbert and Adrian relaxed and waited. On the morning of the third day it was clear again. After breakfast the men readied themselves and their raft for departure.

"Are you ready to levitate the raft down to the water, Adrian?"

"Ready, Delbert!"

"Concentrate! Keep concentrating! Come on raft rise! Oh, no, what have we done that we can't get it off the ground?"

"I don't know."

"Try levitating something, Adrian."

"OK. I'll try to levitate the metal you pried off. Here goes."

"Well, go ahead Adrian!"

"I'm trying but I can't do it."

"Then try disintegrating!"

"No use, I can't do either. Let's see what you can do Delbert."

"I'll try that big boulder. That wasn't any problem. Now, disintegration, no problem for me there either. How did you forget how to do those things?"

"I didn't forget! I just can't do it this morning! I know it's time to go but I can't help.

"What happened?"

"Maybe it was something I ate, Delbert. Do you have your list there?"

"Here it is."

"Hum, This one item we each ate but on different days. You ate the fruit the first day and I ate it yesterday. You didn't eat the vegetable I ate for my arthritis, Delbert. I only ate a couple of them and that was three days ago."

"Maybe it'll wear off in a couple days. I can't see pushing the raft over the bluff and losing everything on it and I can't levitate it down to the water by myself."

"Couldn't you levitate the items to it?"

"Yes, if there was anything left to the raft."

"Wait, Delbert, can you sit on the raft and disintegrate it and yourself? If you could, you could regenerate it right on the water."

"Have you really thought about that option, Adrian? Do you know what happens to the raft if I can't regenerate it?"

"You mean if you can't regenerate it, it's gone forever! That would be an awfully big risk to take wouldn't it?"

"It would be an all or nothing gamble. That's too big a gamble for me to take Adrian. We'll just have to wait until your body chemistry changes back so you regain some of your abilities."

The next day Adrian started to regain some of his abilities. "Let's go ahead and explore more of the island, Delbert. Why don't we see if we can find something else in the caves? Maybe we can find some that go further back into the mountain."

"I'll go along with that. Let's take our oil shale lamp. I remember there was one not too far from the cave where we found those large turtle-like shells. Let's head over that way."

It wasn't long before they were inside the cave. "Adrian, what do you make of this?"

"It looks like one of the marks that we found in the other cave. In fact, there's a similar mark by each of these large indentations in the cave wall. I wonder if these places were dug out to store four different types of material."

"That sounds like a possibility. This is the second cave in which we've found evidence of intelligent beings. There must be other caves they used. Let's go look in another."

"Do you think they could have used the higher level caves, Delbert?"

"Can you levitate yourself up there now?"

"I'll try. I did it! That means I'm getting better. Maybe by tomorrow afternoon I can help you get the raft back into the water. That way we could sail by starlight. We probably want to leave in the afternoon so we are away from the island before dark."

"That makes sense. Watch it, I'm coming up. We have a much better view from here. Let's look and see what we can find."

"Delbert, it looks like this cave leads into a larger one."

"This is the cave we've been looking for! There are the missing parts of the spacecraft. I don't understand the shape of those seats. They're so large and comfortable with that rounded, smooth back. They must be made for large creatures. I know its way too big for me, even if I had a space suit on."

"Didn't you think that we would find this stuff where they lived, Delbert, I don't see any sign of their having lived in here?"

"I don't understand it. Let's see if we can find anything else. This is the third cave we know they used."

"There are a lot of branch tunnels in this cave. We'll have to come back tomorrow to cover them all."

"That's OK, Adrian. I'd rather take my time so we don't miss anything. With these two little oil shale pots we have; it would be easy to miss markings on the walls."

The next day they returned to the cave and its tunnels. They didn't find anything, so they decided to leave. As they were looking through the big cave, where the spacecraft seats were, Delbert saw a small overhang close to the floor. When he looked closer, he found there was a small opening under the overhang.

"Adrian, I think we can slip through here. I'll put my light in ahead of me and crawl in. Come on in. You'll want to see this!"

"I'm in, what did you want me to see?"

"There are a whole lot of these egg-like balls in here. They are all piled in the corner. I'm going to break one open. Maybe they held food or fuel."

"Do you think you should, Delbert?"

"Why not?"

"Go ahead; we'll know one way or the other then."

Crack! "It's about one fourth full of dust. There's no way of knowing what they held from opening them. It must have been a storage room for something. Maybe they thought it would be cooler or safer in here, Adrian."

"I guess it doesn't matter. Are you ready to go? I think we can levitate the raft to the water now?"

"Sure, let's go."

The men walked back to the raft. "I think we have enough food and water. Why don't you give me a demonstration of your ability to levitate the raft, Adrian?"

"I'll see what I can do. That's all the concentration I have."

"That's not bad. You got one end off the ground. We won't have any trouble now. Climb aboard, let's go."

"OK, I'm thinking up and out over the water, Delbert."

"That's good. Let's just keep it up at this level and move it out to sea. Just keep going, that's good. Now, let's let it down slowly. Before we let it all the way into the water, let's think of it just skimming over the water headed in that direction. That's good. Let's keep it up as long as we can. When we get tired, we'll let it down. We can raise the sail, when we can't keep it skimming over the water. Once the sail is up, one of us will have to tack as long as the wind is from the direction it's blowing now."

"I can't concentrate too long, Delbert."

"That's OK; just do the best you can. I may be able to carry us quite a ways with your mental help. I'll go back and check our course when we finally touch down."

During the next two hours they covered between 20 and 30 miles against the wind before the raft touched the water. "I'll raise the sail, Adrian, and then I'll go back and see how our course looks so far."

"I'll continue to sail while you're gone. It'll give me something to do."

Delbert changed to the hawk form and flew off to check their course. When he returned, he made a slight course correction. "From here on, Adrian, we're on our own during the day. All course corrections will have to come from our reading of the stars."

"I'll sail while you sleep, Delbert. You'll probably do a better job navigating at night than I would. I'll wake you when it gets dark. Maybe in the dark I can concentrate better and help you levitate the raft across the water for a while."

"That's fine with me I'm glad you could join me. Maybe later we'll try some mental telemetrical viewing. You've learned everything else very well."

"That would be great. Maybe I could see Esdra. Maybe with their help we could get this raft home sooner."

"It's worth a try, Adrian."

After Delbert had a few hours rest, Adrian woke him. "You mean it's time to decide where we are already? Here goes, hum, uh huh. Let's think this raft up and a few degrees to the right. In fact, let's disintegrate and think ourselves toward that red looking star over there. Maybe with our weight off the raft we can levitate it longer and faster."

"I'm with you, let's go."

In two hours, Adrian was tired. Delbert liked the course correction and the distance they had covered so they reentered their bodies and sailed straight ahead.

"Are you ready to try to master mental telemetrical viewing?" Adrian was ready. "Let's start thinking of Esdra, DorLetha and the Crystal Prism Crater. If we can bring up a mental image of them, we should be able to see what is happening there at this time. You can go there by free soul flight if you lie on the deck and let your mind and spirit go right into the view we're seeing. When you get there, ask them to see if they can help me levitate the raft and draw it toward our destination. Maybe we can cut our time by a couple days and they won't have to use their power supply to do it."

"I understand. Let's start thinking of them."

"OK, Adrian, I have a lock on DorLetha's thought patterns. Can you see her and Esdra in the Crater?"

"Yes, they're talking."

"Go to them, Adrian. Lie relaxed on the deck and let your mind and spirit go to them. Tell them telepathically what we have in mind. I'll see you later."

In a few minutes, Delbert received Adrian's telepathic conversation with DorLetha and Esdra in the Crater. Adrian had accomplished both free soul flight and telemetrical viewing. Delbert thought very strongly about the raft lifting from the water and it did. His mind was locked on the view he could see in his mind. After a couple hours Adrian's spirit returned to his body.

"I'm back, Delbert. We could see you here on the raft. I hope the ladies were able to draw us closer."

"Now that you're back, I don't feel a wind on my face. They must have moved us fifty miles or better. Who knows, we may only be 100 miles from our destination."

"I'm going to hit the sack. You can put the sail up now. I hope it's all right I told them to expect me again tomorrow night."

"Good thinking, Adrian. I never even thought about tomorrow. I'll see you in the morning."

A couple days later, just before it got light and before Adrian woke up, Delbert thought he saw the fire on Spark Stone Mountain off to their right. It was getting too light for him to tell for sure, but he would change to the hawk form later and check it out. If it was the fire, he should soon be able to see light shining off the Crater's Crystal Prism.

The first thing Adrian asked when he awoke was, "How are we doing?"

"I'm not sure. After we eat breakfast, I'll go up for a look around. I might have seen the fire just before it got light. By the way, remind me to tell DaKeta I like her lighting up the planet and darkening it much slower a whole lot better than the sharp contrast we were getting when TetTrella was in control."

"Now that you've finished eating, why don't you become a hawk and go take a look around. Let me know what you see."

In a couple minutes Delbert was out of sight. Adrian tried to see the mountain in the direction Delbert headed when he flew off but he couldn't. *I guess I'll just have to wait for Delbert's return to find out how far we are from land.*

Flap, Flap, Flap, "I'm Back."

"Oh, I didn't notice!"

"Oh no, nothing like that! Your eyes lit up like a kid's whose mother was bringing him candy."

"So, how far are we away from shore?"

"If you are real anxious, levitate the raft and think hard about reaching the Crater. We should be able to make it in three or four hours."

"Let's see if we can't get there sooner than that!"

Chapter 19

Welcome Home

When they reached shore, the Exvascians acted more human for a change. Esdra, DorLetha, Shida, the four little ones, GarGweth, Andre and other Kaydra welcomed them back. The feelings of love, passion, emotion and anger were all once again being awakened in their hosts. The men's presence on their dwarf planet had been good for all of them.

"Dell Bert, Dell Bert!" DorLetha called out as she raced over to him as he and Adrian levitated the raft to a safe place on the beach. "I missed you!"

"Good! I missed you too." He gave her an extra long hug and a couple kisses on the cheek. While he was greeting DorLetha, Adrian was greeting Esdra. When each of them finished greeting their mate, the other Kaydra needed a hug or pet too. Even Dora and Cara changed to their primary form to welcome their dad back. Two Kaydra grabbed the metal they had brought back. Two others carried the strange eggs and GarGweth carried the turtle shell. DorLetha levitated the remainder of what was on the raft.

As the parade marched close by the cave where GarGweth had been kept captive no one noticed the green eyes peering at them from the cave's darkness.

DaKeta came down to join the celebration. Delbert thanked her for the slower transition between both the night and the day.

Esdra and DorLetha advised the two men of the situation with the moon racing toward them. "We're going to have to make one more speed correction; we're still not going fast enough. We're not sure exactly when we have to make the correction but we'll let you know in a few days."

"Thanks for the information DorLetha and thanks for the help the last few miles. We're going to get a good night's rest tonight and then move our raft to a protected area tomorrow. When that moon enters an orbit around our planet, there will be a high wall of water rushing to the shore. It won't come too far up the mountain side but some of the lower caves will probably be covered at high tide. For example, the cave where GarGweth was kept captive will probably be covered at high tide in the future."

"What do you mean when you say tide?"

"Esdra, I'll put some water in this dish. When I hold it still, it doesn't go up on the side of the dish. When I rock it, like this, it goes up on one side and down on the other. Well, that is how the moon's gravitational pull will affect the ocean, your large body of water."

"That will be interesting to see."

In the morning Delbert and Adrian went outside the Crater. "Let's move the raft over here, Delbert."

They soon had the raft in a safe place. "OK, Adrian, now that we've done that, let's go get the ray blaster we left by the living vine on the tree by the quagmire."

When they reached the spot where they had left the ray blaster, it wasn't there. "That's funny, Delbert, I know you left it right here by the path so the limbs of the living vine dangling from the tree wouldn't grab it. Do you think GarGweth picked it up?"

"I don't know. We can ask him, when we see him. He'll probably be around here somewhere eating. Let's go pick up the shell we left when we finished building the raft."

When they reached the spot where they had left the shell, it wasn't in sight. "I don't see the shell either, Delbert. Let's find GarGweth. Here he comes now. He sure can cover a lot of ground at 7 feet 6 inches tall."

"Hi, GarGweth how's Andre this morning?"

"He's happy. I showed him how to do some of Twillie's acrobatics. He's really proud of himself. Watch, I'll have him do a double backward summersault flip."

"That's great, Andre! You did a good job of teaching him. GarGweth, we left one of the ray blasters on the path, by the living vine, where we were building the raft."

"I'll get it for you!"

"No, GarGweth, I don't want you to get it for me. We looked for it but it was gone. We thought you might have picked it up for us already."

"No, I just kept the fire going and showed Andre how to do his trick."

"Remember the shell we brought home yesterday, the small, round, white one?"

"Yes."

"Did you see a piece of one of those on the beach by the fire pit Adrian dug?"

"Yes, it was by the raft before you took it to the water."

"You didn't do anything with it did you?"

"No, what would I want it for?"

"We just hoped it would be here when we got back."

"What do you think happened to the ray blaster, Delbert? Also, have you noticed GarGweth seems smarter lately?"

"Yes, but I don't know whether if it's the diet or just being on Exvascia. I have no idea what happened to the ray blaster, Adrian. I hope we really killed off all the Lidyan warriors TetTrella brought here. If we left one of them alive and he has a ray blaster now, we're in trouble. I hate to think of bringing Carol and Darrell here with problems still existing. It'll be bad enough bringing them here with a tidal wave about to hit."

"Besides that Delbert, we haven't made them a house yet."

"I think another cave like Larry's would be easiest to build, if we can find the right one to start with and then enlarge it with a ray blaster. My watch says it's May 31st Earth time already."

"Well, let's go in the Crater and look for a cave with a hot spring."

"We'll have to tell DorLetha about the ray blaster. Maybe a Kaydra was still out there and brought it in."

"I guess we'll know when we talk to her, Delbert."

Inside the Crater, Delbert had a chance to talk to DorLetha. "We left a ray blaster near where we were building the raft. We can't find it now. Also, we can't find a shell, like the small white ones we brought back. We left it up higher on the beach when we left. GarGweth said he didn't pick up either item.

"I think we need to keep two guards, armed with ray blasters, at the entrance at all times, until we find out what happened to the other weapon."

"I thought you said all the Lidyans were killed!"

"We thought they were. We just can't explain why anyone would want a ray blaster unless they were up to no good."

"I don't think any of the Kaydra have been out of the Crater lately. I'll call them together. If none of them were outside, then I'll post the guards." DorLetha called all the Kaydra together for a meeting. "Has anyone been outside the Crater lately? We were hoping someone had seen a ray blaster Dell Bert left by the quagmire." Nobody had seen it.

"We'll post two guards by the Crater entrance tunnel continually until we find out whether or not there is still a Lidyan alive outside. Those interested in guarding can see me and we'll assign your time.

"I hope this doesn't mean we have more trouble Dell Bert!"

"There will always be trouble DorLetha."

Chapter 20

Meetings with the Army

After the group meeting Myrna had at her house, Michael contacted the Army and got their attention. As soon as he mentioned the possible repair of the teletransporter that had been demonstrated at the "Adralack Crack", they agreed to a meeting.

Early in May, Michael and Art, as Delbert, met with the Army representative in Portland. "Good Morning, gentlemen, I'm General Kromp. It's been almost nine months since we met on Mt. Baker. What's this talk about repairing the teletransporter? I thought we confiscated all the information on it."

"I'm Delbert Tinsley; you might remember I was the psychologist that communicated with the geologist who first walked into the 'Crack'."

"I remember you! Go ahead."

"I've been contacted by the geologist. He wants to trade places with me."

"He couldn't contact you, he's dead!"

"No he isn't! He's visiting another planet and he's coming back June 26th."

"He can't do that! We've issued a death certificate on him. I suppose his wife has collected his life insurance and is probably getting social security payments too!"

"Precisely, General Kromp, that's why I can't change places with him without your help, we need you to rescind the first death certificate and issue one on me."

"What good would that do?"

"Well, it will make his reappearance justifiable. You can say he was on a secret mission for you and because of national security they will just have to accept it."

"Why do you want to trade him places? There must be something you aren't telling me! Why doesn't he just come back?"

"Stretch your mind, General! You know some strange things happened up there when this body fell down by the 'Crack'. The doctor said I was dead but I wasn't. I was changing bodies with Delbert Tinsley. I'm really Art Noack in Delbert's body! Aren't you sorry you asked? On June 26th I'm getting my body back."

"You're right I shouldn't have asked. Please don't tell that to anyone else! What about the confusion over your death?"

"Fortunately, we both had the same amount of life insurance with the same company and the same beneficiary. It doesn't matter which one of us is dead, they still have to pay off the same amount to the same person."

"Well, that should make that correction easy. What about the social security payments that have been made."

"You'll have to stop future payments and not allow those payments already made to be demanded back. Also, the Veteran's Administration will have to eat the cost of paying off the Noack's small home mortgage. Altogether, it will only cost the Federal Government about $50,000."

"What do we get out of it?"

"The scientist, who walked into the 'Crack', when his teletransporter blew up, will return and fix it. All you have to do is bring in a portable field machine shop. In just a couple hours he can repair the machine and give you the appropriate settings for its use."

"You've got to be kidding!"

"You've got nothing to lose. I've resigned my position and told everyone I'm moving out of town. I don't have any close relatives so the main people you will have to deal with are the ones with the insurance company. It isn't going to cost them anything different than what they have already paid out."

"What about the other dead man, is he going to want his death certificate revised too?"

"No, he isn't going to stay. He's only returning to repair the machine so you'll help me and the man who is returning."

"How do I know you can deliver?"

"If we don't deliver, you don't have to do anything!"

"I'm Michael Endicott, the photographer who recorded the incident. I'd like to record the event again. I'd also like to know what has been decided about the previous recording."

"What do you want to use it for?"

"I want to enter it as part of an amateur film festival. I'll enter it as a science fiction film. No one will suspect it is anything but some clever special effects. You can edit it and take out all the shots that show people's faces you don't want to be seen. I can set up bleachers later and get some friends to sit on them for me so I can fill in the parts you cut out. If I could get an edited copy, it would be alright with me."

"I don't know!"

"If we deliver, I don't see what harm it could do. You can edit the recording I shoot this time too. However, the pieces I get, along with what I can reshoot, will give me enough for my short film presentation. Getting that teletransporter back in one piece should be worth millions to the government!"

"I'll see what I can do. I'll have to call one of you and set up another meeting. When can we get this repair done?"

"On June 22 we'll know if it will happen on the 26th or not. You'll have to contact Michael. I've got a lot of things to do yet before I drop out of existence."

"I'll get back to you two as soon as I can. We can use that machine in a variety of ways. Thanks for calling us!"

"You're welcome. Good-bye, General."

"What do you think of our meeting, Art?"

"They have to be interested. They can't let a chance like this go by any more than they could afford not to fund it in the first place."

"Get in and we'll drive back to my place. It was a good thing Myrna could drive you up today. How long before you get that cast off?"

"I don't know it's only been on for three weeks. I thought I'd go see Darrell and let him try working his magic on it."

"Has he used the power available through the watch since that first night?"

"Not that I know of, I hope Gail and Myrna had a good talk. It would be great if the Army would let you have as much of your recording as you asked for. No one would believe it was an actual happening, Michael."

"I couldn't think of any other use of the recording once it couldn't be used for a news article. It seems like there should be some way to get a copy of it. Sometimes I think it was just special effects and not real."

"We're here Art but I can only stay a couple minutes. I took time off this morning for the meeting. I have some deadlines to meet today."

"I understand. It would be great just to have the problems of a job."

"Hi, Michael, Delbert, how did your meeting go?"

"They wouldn't commit themselves today Gail. Delbert and I will have to meet with them again later this month."

"Did they have anything to say about the other recording, Honey?"

"No! I gave them my suggestion. There isn't any reason why they shouldn't give me an edited copy. It can't hurt them in any way."

"I told Myrna what you had in mind for the recording; she thought it was a good idea."

"Myrna, were you able to contact Darrell?"

"No, but I did catch Carol, Art. She said Darrell was out of town for a week or more. She wants us to come up on May 18th."

"That sounds like an acceptable date. We have so many things to take care of before the 25th; our schedule will get tight if we're not careful. Did you and Gail have a good visit?"

"Yes we did. I'm glad I could come up. I'm ready to go, if you are, Art."

"Good. We'll see you the next time we come up, Gail. Good-bye."

"Good-bye, Art."

As Myrna and Art drove off, Myrna spoke. "Isn't it a pretty day Art? I love driving in the springtime. Do you realize we only have three weeks left until we move?"

"I've been thinking about that. I wish we could rush things along. One thing I'm going to rush along is the healing of my arm. I'm going to get Darrell to practice on it, when we go up on the 18th. I'm also going to have him give me my physical so I can get the disability insurance claim closed out before we move."

"That will help out Art. I wondered how you were going to get that taken care of before you left the area."

Art was thinking about Darrell who was busy taking advanced surgical training. He later found out that some of the operations they were performing were almost impossible. When the operations were finished, it wasn't known whether or not they were a success. If the technique was totally acceptable to Darrell, but the performance of the surgeons was a little weak, he made sure the patient did OK by wearing his special watch, when he made his rounds of those special patients. Everyone thought the patients got well because of their great talents on the operating table. Darrell played along. He was happy he could heal the problems the surgery didn't correct, without being suspected of anything.

One day Darrell thought to himself. *Why don't I make a few special house calls on some of my older patients? I know they won't want to see a new doctor. There are some that I haven't told what their problems are. Since they don't know what they are, I should be able to heal them without them telling anybody.*

I'll call Art, when I get back, and see what he thinks and tell him what I've been able to accomplish. When Darrell got home on May 16th, he called Art and told him of his recent experiences and what he had in mind for the future.

"That's great Darrell. When we come up on the 18th, I'd like you to heal my arm and get me out of this cast. I also need to have you give me a passing physical so I can get Delbert's disability payments stopped. I picked up the necessary forms when I talked to them today."

"I'd be glad to do that for you Art. I wanted to get the bank account with Gail's signature on it set up that day too."

"We're going to bring Delbert's car up that day and sign it over to Carol. I think I can make it with one arm that far. We'll see you on the 18th."

"Fine, Art, I'll see you then."

"Bye." Art called Myrna after talking with Darrell and told her he would drive Delbert's car up to Portland for Carol to use.

On the 18th, Myrna followed Art in her car to Portland, in case he had a problem but he managed to drive to Darrell's without any trouble. "Hi Carol. How are you this morning/"

"I'm fine Art. Good morning Myrna. Why don't we go into Darrell's office? Thanks for the car. It will be good to have one to use."

"Here's the title to Delbert's car. Are you two going to meet me somewhere when Darrell gets through with me?"

"We'll go over to the Motor Vehicle Department and take care of the car title and registration and be back, probably before he gets finished with you."

"OK, good-bye."

"Mr. Tinsley, Dr. Lyons will see you now. Come this way please. You may wait in here. Dr. Lyons will be with you in a few minutes."

"Thank you."

"Hi, Art. Did you bring your broken arm?"

"No, I left it home! Where's your watch?"

"Right here in my pocket. Let me put it on and we'll see what I can do. I'll start by cutting the cast off of your arm. I think I can help it heal quickly if I can actually touch the spot where it's broken. Did you feel anything when I healed your ribs?"

"I thought about that for a while afterwards and I think I was a little dizzy for a few minutes."

"That's what I suspected! I'm not healing you at all. All my touch does is increase your body's own recuperative powers dramatically. When I touch the injured spot, the mind seems to produce miraculous cures instantaneously by erasing the time when the injury occurred and thereby restoring the injured part to its original condition. Some of that has to be Exvascians magic.

"There, we have the cast off. Just lay your arm down on the table. I'm ready to see what I can do to get it to heal. Can you put your left hand on the spot where the break was?"

"Yes, it was right here."

"OK, here goes. Heal yourself arm! I wish Delbert's arm was just like it was last year. I wish it to be that way this very instant."

The watch glowed a bright green. "You sounded so sincere!"

"I was, Art. That's why I used Delbert's name. It's his brain and his body that must accept the healing. My job is to help people get well. I really wish I could eliminate all pain, injury and sickness but I can't. If there is any way I can effect a cure for a patient, I'll do it. I'll send you down to the x-ray department in a few minutes to see if I got the results we wanted."

"You can let go of my arm now."

"Sorry, I didn't realize I was still holding it. Sometimes I am afraid my wish won't come true. I guess I have to believe or it can't happen. Nurse, would you take an x-ray of Mr. Tinsley's arm? I think it's probably healed by now, but I want to be sure."

"Yes, Dr. Lyons. Come this way, Mr. Tinsley. That should do it. You may return to the room you were in. I'll forward the results to Dr. Lyons' computer."

Art returned to the room he had been in and waited for Dr. Lyons' return. "I'm back, Art. Look at this pretty picture."

"Where was it broken? Is the scar tissue where it mended?"

"On the X-ray, the healed bone appears 'thicker' rather than 'scar' tissue."

"What about the rest of the physical?"

"Do you want to go through all the tests or do you just want me to complete the paper work?"

"How about just putting the right answers in the right places?"

"Sure. I don't think Delbert had any problems with his body at all. How would you and Myrna like to go to dinner with us tonight while you're in the big city?"

"Sorry, Darrell, we've got to get back and pick up the kids. I bet they aren't going to believe it when they see their dad again. It's hard not to love them as much as I want to, when they're really mine. I miss not being able to be with Myrna all the time too."

"You are going to move in with her when you two get to Denver, aren't you?"

"Yes, while we're there. Then we'll be back here to go to Mt. Baker. I'm pretending to be her brother in Denver. I'm keeping a low profile."

"When are you meeting again with the Army?"

"We'll meet day after tomorrow. I sure hope they agree to help us."

"Don't they have to Art?"

"You'd think so but sometimes the military has its own way of doing things."

"Whatever happens, I'm going to enjoy helping as many people as I can during the next five weeks. There shouldn't be a case I can't help in some way!"

"Don't forget to take your watch off, Darrell."

"Oh, I forgot. I better not make that mistake again. Let us know how your meeting with the Army turns out. I'd better get back to seeing my other patients, or they'll be unhappy. I'll see you later."

"Good bye Darrell and thanks again."

"There you are, Art. That didn't take too long. I see you got your cast off. Is Dr. Lyons going to send in your disability insurance report?"

"Yes, I left all the paper work with him. That will take care of one more item for us. Are you ready to go?"

"Yes, we took care of the car registration and change of title and I was just waiting for you."

"You don't mind if I drive us back home do you Myrna?"

"Of course not Art. How does your arm feel?"

"It feels perfect. The x-ray didn't even show any sign of a break when Darrell got through with it. He's using the extra power he has available intelligently. He's finding ways to cure patients without bringing any attention to himself. It makes him happy to know that he won't have to let any patient down."

"He sure did wonders for you. Now you can enjoy our move."

"I was already getting tired of that cast. He said what he did was motivate my body to heal itself. It'll be easier for me to get things taken care of now that the cast is gone. It's only a week until we move."

"I still don't like having to move but I know that I'll enjoy the new house and new opportunities we'll have."

Two days later Art was on his way to Portland to meet with the Army about another trip to Mt. Baker. He and Michael met at the Army's recruiting office downtown. "Good Morning, General Kromp."

"Good morning, gentlemen. I've been authorized to go ahead with the repair of the teletransporter. We'll provide the portable machine shop, a welder, machinist and an electrician. We thought a little extra help in those areas wouldn't hurt.

"As far as the recording goes, Mr. Endicott, we would like you to record everything the same way you did last time. In fact, I brought you an edited copy of the first trip to Mt. Baker for your use. We only ask that however you use it, don't involve us in any way."

"Thank you. I appreciate this and I'm not going to divulge any real facts about it to anyone."

"General Kromp, are there any areas of our arrangement that are a problem?"

"No, but I'm not sure how long it will take us to fulfill our part of the bargain because no one believes we'll get the teletransporter back repaired. If it is, it will take some time for us to complete the necessary paper work. However, we'll eventually get it done."

"I understand. Do you have any other questions, Michael?"

"No, I'll just have to let the General know what time the meeting on Mt. Baker will be."

"If things work out like they are supposed to, General Kromp, I'll be gone on June 26th. When Art Noack shows up, someone better have answers for him, if things haven't been taken care of. He can go for a while without changes to his records but not indefinitely."

"Mr. Tinsley, I'll personally talk to the Veteran's Administration Director about the problem as well as Social Security and the insurance company. By giving them advanced notice that we've issued an incorrect death certificate, they can start thinking how they'll straighten out the problem. If they think it is just a clerical error, that took us nine months to discover, they may act quicker. I'll give them a June 26th tentative date for the correction of the problem but that doesn't give them much time to make the corrections."

"Thank you, General. I appreciate your efforts. Hopefully we'll see you on the 26th."

"Good-bye gentlemen. I'm looking forward to the 26th."

Back in their car, Art spoke. "Michael, while I'm waiting to get my body back, it will help a lot to know the General is personally trying to get everything taken care of. I'll probably have to give the observers some song and dance about my experience on Exvascia. Maybe Delbert could do that for me. At least I can tell them how it felt being in someone else's body."

"Everything will probably work out OK, Art. Gail and I'll see you May 29th a couple days before Carols wedding rehearsal."

"Thanks for setting up the meeting, Michael. I'll see you later."

On May 24th Nurse Liz returned home with her daughter. That day Art took care of closing his bank account, called the TV cable company to stop his service; scheduled the electricity, gas and newspaper service to be discontinued and put in a change of address for himself and Myrna. He paid his final bills with cash and they were ready for the movers to step in and do their job the next day.

On the 25th, the movers came in and completed the packing. Art, Myrna and the kids drove as far as Portland on moving day. Two days later they arrived in Denver. The furniture was scheduled to arrive on the 28th of May. Even though the schedule was tight, Myrna and Art were able to get partially moved into their new home in Denver and still catch a flight to Portland on the 29th, arriving in time for Carol and Darrell's wedding rehearsal on the 31st.

“Darrell, where did you find these two?”

“Michael and Gail picked them up at the airport, Carol. They thought you might want to have them around.”

“Hi, Carol. You didn't think we'd let moving into a new home 1,200 miles away keep us from being here did you?”

“I was afraid you wouldn't be able to make it.”

Art and Myrna stayed in Darrell's guest room until the wedding. The evening they arrived at Darrell's house, the entire group talked about future events.

“How is the new doctor you've taken on working out, Darrell?”

“Just fine so far, Art. By healing some of my chronic patients, I think he will be able to handle things OK. I still have three or four patients I'd like to find some way to heal more slowly. I may just start touching them without wishing anything and see if their recuperative/regenerative powers are stimulated some.

“That way, they may show some progress over the next four weeks without a drastic change overnight.”

“Have you found a renter for your house?”

“Yes we did Myrna. We found a single mom with two kids who would like to stay in the area for several years. We've set up automatic mortgage payments and the renter has agreed to pay all the utilities and such. If Delbert's retirement check gets deposited into the account with Gail's name on it, we can stay for as long as we want. Do you see any problems we haven't covered yet, Gail?”

“I don't see any problem keeping things running for you. I just hope Michael and I do the right thing!”

“It doesn't matter how you handle things, Gail. I know you'll do a good job. It will be much better than my giving it all up for an opportunity like this. I'd appreciate it if you can come to the office, for a while tomorrow and the next day. We can go over what I've told you about the business and show you my bookkeeping system again. I should also introduce you to my lawyer and banker. They can give you assistance on almost everything.

"They may occasionally ask advice on investment opportunities they come across for me. Generally, if they aren't too risky, I accept their advice and have profited from it.

"I've also left a full explanation of how everything should work. If my staff continues to function as they have, it'll be OK. If there are any replacements and they aren't trained them properly, that could create a problem."

"That doesn't sound like too bad an arrangement, Darrell."

"Art. I'm sure glad you two could make it. You're both very special to Carol."

"We've both had some interesting and strange experiences with her. I guess you're getting used to some strange things happening now yourself."

"That's right. Every since I've met her, things have been different in my life, starting with you and your strange condition, Art."

Michael and Gail excused themselves and left the meeting.

"Thanks for letting us stay here, Darrell. It makes things a lot easier."

"Glad to have you two as my guests. I'd better let you two get to sleep."

Over the next two days, Gail and Michael spent a lot of time with Darrell learning about his business and investments. He had done a good job of structuring everything so that they were trouble free and easy for his staff to take care of.

Carol and Darrell's wedding was beautiful and well attended by both her and Darrell's family and friends. They took a short honeymoon trip to the east coast. When they returned, they had a little over a week to kill before their interplanetary trip to Exvascia.

Art and Myrna returned to Denver after the wedding. They wanted to make sure they had taken care of everything necessary to cover Delbert's disappearance.

Chapter 21

Preparations for Visitors

While Art was closing out Delbert's existence on Earth, Delbert was busy preparing for the visitors he would be bringing to Exvascia. He was also looking forward to having his own body back so he would be allowed all the privileges of being Queen DorLetha's chosen mate. He looked forward to being on a sharing, caring, personal level with her once again. This time it wouldn't be for just a 48-hour period.

“Just think, Delbert, we've only got 21 of our days left until Carol and Darrell will arrive. I was thinking about the cave we were going to prepare for them. We should be able to use the ray blaster to enlarge the cave.”

“Good thinking, Adrian, Let's go look at the cave we found, not too far from here, the one with the hot spring running through it. Let's take our ladder over there for them since we can now levitate ourselves up to the entrance of our cave.”

In a few minutes they were at the other cave. “There's the hot spring. Let me take a low power shot at that back wall. Whomp! When the dust clears, we can see what we've done. It sounded like we enlarged the cave quite a bit.

“I'll just levitate all the loose material outside. That should let the dust clear in a few minutes. That's better! The spring seems to be coming out of the rock a little higher up.”

“That's good Delbert I think we could insert a tube plant stock into the spring opening and make a hot shower out of it. We can use a larger stock to transfer the water from the shower to the hot tub below to cut down on the noise and splash of the water falling from the shower. They will have to climb in and out of the hot tub to shower and leave the lower plug out when it's used as a shower.”

“That's a great idea Adrian. What other surprises do you have for me?”

“I've found a couple elements outside that we can mix with the rock you just removed to make a type of concrete. That means we can make smooth flat floors and stucco the walls, icebox area and barbeque pit."

"What are we waiting for? We could also make concrete blocks for walls. Let's blast a bigger cave, we could use the concrete blocks to make a kitchen and bedroom area. The remainder of the area will be the living area."

"Let's go dig some square holes in the ground outside. We can drive a couple large tube plant stocks flush with the ground inside the larger hole. That way there will be large holes in the blocks so they won't be as heavy."

As Delbert blasted away a few more cubic yards of rock for other areas of the living quarters, he noticed an orange light lit on the blaster and it no longer worked. "I wonder what that means, Adrian."

"I don't know. That's the way the one we left outside looked. It must mean it needed to be recharged?"

"That could be. They must have had an interesting mechanism to recharge them."

"I'll get another!"

"When you get finished, bring your rock and meet me by the quagmire. I'll take this rock with me and get the other minerals together that we'll need. I'll take a couple large pots with me too."

Delbert went to their cave and got another ray blaster to use. Once outside, Adrian deposited the rock by the quagmire. He used one of the pieces of metal they took from the spacecraft to dig the holes out in the lighted area for the blocks. He used the knife they had to cut the tube plant stock and place it in the holes he had made. Later he would pull the concrete-like blocks up over the tube plant and out of the hole before the material had completely hardened.

Adrian dug a bigger hole by the quagmire to use to mix the other two minerals with the rock to make the blocks. He used one of the bowls he had brought with him to dip wet sticky sand from the quagmire to add to the mixture. He then stirred the mixture with a piece of the spacecraft metal.

Delbert called out as he approached. "I'm here Adrian. I added my rock to yours. Do you want me to pour the mix in the holes you have ready?"

"Yes. If you're pouring gets ahead of my mixing, start making more block holes like the others."

Delbert put leaves in the bottom of the holes so the dirt wouldn't pull all the moisture out of the mixture and weaken it. "I think the blocks will dry fast enough so we can take them out in about two hours."

Adrian and Delbert traded off digging holes and mixing the concrete-like material. They used their increased mental capacities to help the piece of metal cut through the hard soil.

After two hours, Adrian was able to levitate the still moist blocks out of their holes and set them on fresh leaves on the ground. Because of the long days, they were able to make a large number of blocks in a day. Just before dark, they filled all the holes again and left them to dry overnight.

The next day, Adrian tried to break one of the blocks. They were already hard enough so they didn't break. He knew it would take several days for the blocks to become their hardest. They didn't need to be too strong at first to just be stacked up as walls.

They levitated the blocks left overnight to dry to one side and refilled the holes with more of the mixture. They then mixed more material and levitated it to the cave and used it to level the floor, stucco the ice box area and the walls. It took several trips to complete their task. They remembered to put a long hollow tube plant stalk under the floor to drain the hot tub. They also connected the ice box drain to the hot tub drain.

The hot tub and shower arrangement was crude, but functional. They also made ceramic bowls and plates for Carol and Darrell to use. The last things they made were a crude table and chairs. They used the drill and boards TetTrella helped them make for this task.

When they cooked meat over the open fire on the spit, it was held on by branches of the living vine, which gave it a slight hickory flavor.

They made a bellows to blow the glowing oil shale as it burned. Once in awhile they threw a few drops of water on the fire to make it burn hotter.

"Adrian, we could make a sink with hot and cold running water. I know there is a cold spring further back in the cave. Let's use some of the hollow tube plant stalks to pipe it to the kitchen area where we already have the hot spring water."

Adrian made a smooth sink with the concrete-like mix he used to make the blocks. They completed the cave by putting up the room-dividing walls with short boards inserted between the blocks for shelves. The shelves would hold the oil shale bowls used for light and some heat. It was nice that the oil shale burned hot and clean.

They used the concrete-like blocks to square up the entrance to the cave for a door and also provide a window area with an animal skin cover. They would later put animal furs on the smooth, level stucco floor. The finished walls and entry area made the cave enjoyable and more like a home.

The long hot days on the outside quickly dried the handmade clay items which they glazed and fired in the oil shale barbeque pit on the metal pieces from the spacecraft. The large piece of metal would be used as a frying pan. Nothing would stick to the strange coating on the metal. It was great for frying eggs and steaks. Poached eggs were made by setting a ceramic bowl full of hot water, with the egg in it, right into the fire pit.

Delbert used all the power in another ray blaster to dig a new five foot deep swimming pool built on a slope in the Crater floor. He used most of the material he dug out to make the lower retaining wall. The concrete-type mixture was used to stucco the banks. A rock was put in front of the hollow tube plant drain to keep the water from running out. A tube plant stalk trough carried fresh water from the waterfall into the pool.

The pool would be filled when the stucco dried, which would be several days after Carol and Darrell arrived. The swimming pool water would be warmer than the waterfall pool because it was not as deep, not shaded and the water would not be continually flow through it.

"Hi, Dorletha how is the situation with the wandering moon coming?"

"I think we should have Adrian work with us again. Since he thinks differently than we do, he often thinks of things we might overlook."

"He'd enjoy that. Come look at the new cave we finished for our friends."

"Hi, Dorletha did you come to see our handy work?"

"Yes Adrian and I wanted to ask you to come help us. This is a lot nicer than Larry's cave! Where did you get the materials?"

"We made them from material outside. It's like materials we have on Earth. I'm finished here, why don't I go on up, Delbert?"

"Go ahead Adrian. I want to go outside and see how the tide is coming." Outside Delbert found a tide of about one foot. He still had a couple days before he had to return to Earth, via telemetrical viewing, to tell his friends whether or not he and Adrian could keep the June 26th, 10:00 a.m. meeting on Mt. Baker.

Delbert returned and told DorLetha about the tide, which had already started. It will increase each day until the moon swings around us into orbit. I think we'll have a tidal wave the day the moon just misses us."

"Will that cause a lot of damage outside, Esdra asked?"

"I think so. It will change how things look out there. How are you feeling?"

"A little cold, Adrian says I'm molting very fast now. My time isn't too far off."

"How's her other developments coming DorLetha?"

"She isn't developing properly. She isn't going to function like I did. She's messed herself up letting go of so many of her powers. She's giving up her identity to try and look more like a human female.

"When Exvascians mate, they do strange things to their bodies, depending on what their mate looks like. I'm afraid we'll lose her when her mating time comes. You know how important everything is. If each of her eggs isn't fertilized when its time comes, she'll die."

"I know, that's why I've have a doctor coming up. Since he knows how our females bear offspring, he may be able to help her have hers differently. He also knows how our males function so I'm hoping he can help the two of them."

"I'La may be able to help him, Delbert."

"I'll keep that in mind. How is that moon's approach developing?"

"Adrian thinks it will continue to accelerate as it gets closer. The main problem we have is not knowing how fast it will start curving in toward us. Once it starts to leave its straight path and curves toward us, we'll have to burst forward so that it does curve around us."

"Do we have enough power?"

"We think so but the animals and plants outside will suffer because of the solar reflector not working. We'll have to use some power to convert them all to one small form to bring them inside until we repair our damage and are operating normally again. Your time for returning to Earth is OK but I don't know how long we can leave you there."

"I'll move the time up to 8:00 a.m. their time. That'll give us a couple extra hours. How do you feel about it, Adrian?"

"That should help. I'd prefer to come back before the final blast of power rather than after it. If DorLetha has the animals all inside, as well as us all back, we'll know how much extra power we have for maneuvers."

"That might mean you'll have to come back on a minute's notice."

"That's OK, DorLetha. We'll keep that in mind while we're there."

The next morning Delbert checked the tide before he joined DorLetha, Adrian, Esdra and the others working on the project. "Good morning. I just checked the tide. It looks like it is rising about a foot a day. We may end up with a six to nine foot tide. I'm ready to go see our friends on Earth whenever you locate my aura, DorLetha."

"Delbert what items are you having Carol and Darrell bring with them?"

"I've asked Darrell to bring his surgical bag and acupuncture needles. I'll ask Carol to bring a compass, binoculars, knife, fork, spoon, large sack needle and an awl. Is there anything else they should bring?"

"I can't think of anything we really need. I guess they'll recognize us with our beards. How about having them bring a pair of scissors? That would help with hair cutting. A large, good quality file would be useful too."

"What does the moon's approach look like to you, Adrian?"

“It looks like we will leave before it reaches us but it will curve around us about the time we get back. As soon as we're back, the navigation system will force us ahead with a large boost of power.

“By the way, the power converter unit for the hydrogen is located on the opposite side of the Crystal Prism Mountain from where we launched our boat. The power beam transmitter station will have to be positioned on the planet's surface to act as a rocket thruster.

“The positioning of the power beam transmitter is critical as is the length of the power burst. To move even a dwarf planet, it takes a lot of force. We'll actually have to increase this planets speed by pushing off from another planet.

Let me see if I can explain it. They extend a power beam to a planet or several planets at the same time. When the beam is extended, it gives us a push. The nearness of planets to push off from determines the amount of power that will be required.”

“That's OK Adrian, whatever you say is fine with me. I'll just watch and listen even if I don't understand what I'm seeing or hearing.”

Chapter 22

Delbert's Visit

Back on Earth, Myrna and Art were busy in Denver getting moved into their new home. With Art's arm healed, he was able to help considerably after the movers left. Art set up Delbert's library just the way it was in his apartment. That made it easy for him to fit things back into the places where they had always been. He didn't know how he would explain to people why he had all the books on psychology, but he'd worry about that later. It also gave Myrna a place for her antique books on Tiffany products.

After they were settled, Art went to see Stewart. "How are you doing on the purchase of the old mines?"

"The paper work is almost finished on them. We should be able to sign them by July first."

"Could we take a run out there? I want to see if I can feel any sensations of metal ore. I know I can't feel the pipes in streets anymore. I don't feel them below your floor either."

"We could go tomorrow, if you're free."

"That's fine with me."

"I'll pick you up Art, since I go right by your place on the way to the mine."

Art was no longer able to find any more ore in the mines, even where he knew he had felt ore was before. "I don't have the touch any longer, Stewart. Have you got that third mine tied up yet?"

"Not yet. Why?"

"Hold off on it until I get my body back. Maybe for the first couple days after I get it back, I'll be able to feel the presence of ore again. I'll get back here as soon as possible after I'm whole and go over all three of those mines and the one you've been working. I should be able to go through two a day.

"After my magic wears off, I'll have to find ore just like everybody else. I probably won't be any better at it than others are."

"I see what you're getting at. Let's go back home. It looks like we can't do anything further for three weeks."

For the next few days, Art worked in his yard and waited for the 22nd of June to come. That day they would fly to Portland and meet Carol and Darrel. They would try to contact Delbert to find out if he was going to be able to activate the 'Adralack Crack' on June 26th. If possible, Michael and Gail would join them.

"Myrna, do you think Delbert's retirement check will ever come?"

"I don't know. Today is June 21st, if it doesn't come today, we'll have to fly back here to get it, if it arrives before the 26th. If it doesn't come today, I'll start to worry."

"It wouldn't be good for the check to come after you've changed back to being Art. What would we do with it then?"

"I guess we could forge his name and have Gail deposit it in the joint account Darrell set up for her to take care of any unforeseen expenses that might come up while they're gone. Delbert won't be around to complain about who cashed it."

"That looks like the mail coming now. Do you want to walk down and get it?"

"Sure, I'll be right back." Art hurried to the mailbox. What a relief, Delbert's retirement check had arrived. "Myrna, it's here. That means we won't have any problem getting it to Gail so she can deposit it. We also received notice that his disability insurance claim was stopped as of June 1, because of the release signed by myself and Dr. Lyons. That clears everything I know of related to 'Dr. T'. Now there shouldn't be any more problems we can't handle when I trade Delbert bodies in five days and there's no longer a 'Dr. T'."

"That's great Art. Now, if the Army can just help us solve the other problems we have, we'll be able to live normal lives again."

The next day Art and Myrna flew to Portland. Carol met them at the airport. "Hi, Art, Myrna, I'm glad you could make it. Gail and Michael will join us this evening at six o'clock."

"How's Mrs. Lyons?"

"I'm great. That sounds so good."

"How was your honeymoon?"

"We enjoyed seeing Washington, D.C. and all the Disney attractions in Florida. Darrell stopped at a few medical facilities. I know he wore his watch a few times but I don't know what he did. He has a few special patients he is still seeing. He's trying to bring about a slow cure in their cases. He'll join us about five o'clock.

"I'm excited about talking with Delbert. I think visiting another planet is just unbelievable!"

"I don't know, Carol. When I entered that shallow cave last August, I thought I wanted to go to another planet. When I couldn't change my mind, because it was too late, I was afraid. I was so desperate that I was willing to exchange bodies with Delbert to get out. I don't know why I thought that could be done. It hasn't been easy being Art on the inside and Delbert on the outside."

"I know Art but I've got a lot of faith in Delbert. Here's my car, of course you recognize Delbert's car. It runs great."

Art relaxed while Carol and Myrna prepared dinner. Darrell joined him within an hour after he had arrived. They talked until six o'clock when Gail and Michael arrived.

"How are you doing with your special patients Darrell? Is the slow cure idea working?"

"Most of them are doing fine. I wear the watch and touch their ill or damaged parts without wishing anything. It's more like a routine check where I press on the patient's troubled spot and ask them how it feels.

"The thought it needs healing is there but I don't actually wish it. That starts the area to slowly regenerate and heal itself. When I see them once a week, their body is healed in a month. If I see them twice a week, they heal in about three weeks. I've got a couple patients that have terminal cancer,but I didn't tell them that. I have them in the hospital with what I've called a peptic ulcer. I tell them that if the medication doesn't take care of it, we may have to operate. That relieves their fears and gives them hope and strength. Their attitude is very important to self healing.

"I see these patients once or twice each day. In the past three weeks, they have made tremendous progress. If they aren't cured when they get their x-ray in the next couple days, I may do a little wishing so that I can release them before we go. I may have to doctor their records a little so no one can tell them what their true problem was."

"It sounds like you're being careful. It also sounds like you're doing a lot of patients some good."

"That's right! Of course, that's what my life is built around. If Delbert contacts us today and says he'll be able to meet us on the 26th, are you going to stay with us until we leave the 25th?"

"We need to stay somewhere. We brought everything we would need for the trip to Mt. Baker, especially my clothes. Delbert's would be too large for me."

"You should stay with us. By riding up with us you would be able to drive our car back."

"Whatever Carol and Myrna are comfortable with is fine with me. Let's ask them."

"Carol, I've asked Art, if he and Myrna would stay with us until we go to Mt. Baker, provided Delbert says the 26th is still OK."

"Good. Myrna and I were just discussing that too. Why don't you help Art get their bags, Darrell."

As Darrell and Art were getting the luggage from Carol's car, Gail and Michael drove up.

"Hi, Gail, Michael, come on in!"

"Hi, Darrell, I see we're the last to arrive."

"That's OK, you're still early."

"Hi, Michael, how is the movie idea coming?"

"I've got all the shots laid out that I need to retake to fill in the edited portions Art. I'll get some of my Bellingham friends to go up with me to the mountain site this summer so I can finish the recording. I'll edit it again this fall."

After dinner, the six friends gathered in the living room to try and reach Delbert. They joined hands and concentrated on what Art was saying. "Delbert we're here ready to talk with you, can you see me DorLetha? Can you send Delbert down to be with us? We're waiting! Anytime you want to take over your body, Delbert, come ahead."

The group sat quietly with their heads bowed, eyes closed, relaxed and concentrating on reaching Delbert.

Carol spoke, "I'm getting the feeling Delbert is coming!"

Art suddenly sat up and looked around. "I'm here everyone. Have you been keeping your watch under control Darrell? I didn't know that it would do anything like what it has, when I exchanged watches with you. I hope you haven't gotten into any more trouble since that first night."

"Hi, Delbert, I've kept the watch under control and still used it to help a lot of patients. In fact, look at the job I've done on your body."

"Hey, that's right. Art did have it pretty busted up didn't he? It seems to be just fine now. How are things coming with terminating my existence down here Myrna?"

"We think we've taken care of everything. We've bought a home in Denver and moved all your things there. We received your retirement check and gave it to Gail to put in a joint account she has with Darrell so that she can pay any unexpected expenses that come up for them while they are with you. We also gave Carol your car."

"That sounds OK. So you're ready to get Art back then?"

"Yes! This arrangement is too strange."

"I've grown him quite a beard. You may have trouble recognizing him."

"He can always shave it off."

"On Exvascia, we really rough it."

"How are Larry and Adrian doing Delbert?"

"Adrian's looking ten years younger. The vegetables up there have almost cured his arthritis Gail. As far as Larry goes, I've got some bad news for you. There was a mini revolution on Exvascia. The second most powerful female on the planet tried to grab power from DorLetha, who is now Queen because she had a son. The other female brought in alien warriors from another planet. Larry and I fought with them. We were doing great against their ray blasters until the last two. One was killed while the other attacked Larry. As they were fighting, I shot at the alien and killed it as it delivered a final fatal blow with a rock to Larry's head. I'm sorry, Gail. We did our best to survive but it's hard when you have to face aliens with unknown powers and weapons."

Michael comforted Gail who broke down and cried for Larry, her first husband. He had been taken to Exvascia by mistake and wouldn't come back to her when he had the chance.

"Carol, are you and Darrell sure you want to chance it on Exvascia?"

"We think so Delbert. Why do you ask?"

"Well, it can be very rough there at times. In fact, we are about to collide with another planet's moon."

"Are you going to be able to avoid the collision?"

"Maybe. Adrian and I'll have to meet you at 8:00 a.m. on the 26th on Mt. Baker. After we leave Exvascia, the approaching moon will curve in toward our planet. We don't know how much our gravitational pull will speed its acceleration. We may all have to be transported back to Exvascia in a hurry.

"We'll leave before the moon gets to Exvascia and return a short time before it enters the planet's orbit. As soon as we're safe back on the planet, all available power will be used to accelerate the planet's speed. That will cause the new moon to go into orbit around the planet.

"This might be the first time the planet has had a moon. I think it'll cause a tidal wave and permanently change the motion of the sea which is always placid now."

"Do you think they'll have enough power to move a planet?"

"Adrian thinks so Darrell. We think it's a dwarf planet. In fact, we don't know how big it is."

"Delbert, when Art and I talked with the Army the other day, they said they would have a welder, machinist and an electrician accompany the portable shop. Will that help Adrian speed his repair of the teletransporter?"

"It should help, Michael. If you are recording everything he says and does, they should be able to learn how to operate the machine by looking at the playback of the recording several times. I know when he starts explaining about the settings they won't understand everything they hear until they get some hands-on experience."

"Is that how Adrian learned how to operate it?"

"That's right. When he first tested it on me and almost lost me forever, I told him how to change the settings so it would work better."

"Did it work properly then?"

"Ask Carol, she was the next guinea pig. Can you bring a straight razor, scissors, large metal file, compass, fork, knife, spoon, awl, and a sack needle with you?"

"What's a sack needle?"

"The type used to sew burlap grain sacks together at the top when they are filled with wheat in a grain mill. We need them to sew leather clothes together. The eye needs to be large enough to run a leather thong through. You two should wear jeans when you come. They will last until you can get used to Tarzan and Jane clothes. It's hot up there all the time.

"Adrian and I just finished you a new cave home. You'll love it."

"This is getting to be more like a Robinson Crusoe adventure all the time."

"That's about what it's like, Darrell. The only reason it is that way is the intelligent creatures are so mentally advanced to our civilization that they have almost reverted back to animal life and need nothing to survive comfortably."

"Delbert, Stewart Donovan wanted to thank you for saving him and Art. Can you tell us how you did it?"

"Sure. First I want to remind Darrell to bring his black bag and be ready to operate if necessary. When Art got into trouble, DorLetha could see the aura of my body. She called us to where she was and showed us a telepathic-like viewing of what was happening. We could see and hear everything that was happening. By going back along a time line of events, we were able to see all that had happened.

"During these telemetrical viewings, we can telepathically travel in a free soul flight status. Larry came down and levitated the rock off of Art and Stewart and levitated them out to the truck. I'La and I came down the same way after Larry returned. I entered my body and told I'La what needed repairing. He explained to Darrell how she healed him the same way he had put the accident victim's arm back on."

"Why didn't she just finish fixing your arm while she was at it, Delbert?"

"Temptation! She had never been to another planet before. She took off before she finished the job. I was at least patched up enough to make the CB call and turn on the truck lights."

"What happened to I'La?"

Delbert explained how DorLetha, Adrian and Larry had worked together to find and return I'La to Exvascia and how it affected Adrian and Esdra.

"Esdra no longer has many of the Exvascians powers. She has chosen Adrian to be her mate. We think she'll be fertile soon. She's the one you may have to operate on, Darrell. You may have to alter her physical makeup so that Adrian can mate with her or she'll die. She hasn't developed properly."

"Do you have something we can use as an anesthetic?"

"Yes, that's easy!"

"Why can't I'La heal her?"

"She doesn't understand how we work or how their fertile females work. So, she can't correct Esdra's problems or convert her so she can mate with a human. It's all kind of complicated."

"If you say it's complicated, Delbert, I believe it!"

"How are things coming with the Army, Michael?"

"I think they can fix everything so Art can return and live a normal life. I think they're starting to take us seriously. What they're getting is worth much more than what they'll have to put out. I don't see how they can resist. I think they will actually come through quickly for Art."

"Delbert, Art was wondering if the power beam could be withdrawn and relocated to activate in one of the old mines he is trying to buy. Say, the one he got hurt in. It would be a lot more convenient than the Mt. Baker location."

"I hadn't thought about that. I'll have to check and see if it can be done. Is there anything else we need to talk about before I go?"

"No, we just wanted to find out if the 26th was still OK. The only thing you've done is move the time ahead two hours, right?"

"That's right, Michael."

"What kind of a family do you have, Delbert?"

"I have a son and three daughters, Carol. They all looked like birds when they hatched. When they were six months old, they were able to change to their primary form. Two look like their mother and the other two have a somewhat modified human form."

"What does she look like?"

"I forget you have never seen her. How do I explain her form? To start with, she stands 6 feet 6 inches tall. She has a more or less condor/human form. Picture a Condor standing upright on its two legs. She has arms that are hidden under her wings. She has a small beak like an owl. She has feathers as soft as down on her torso and head. Her arms, neck and face skin is soft and smooth. Her feather covered chest is flat and smooth. When she took on the human-like form, the feathers were unavoidable. Since she has a reproductive system like a bird, but different in some ways, she could not adopt the female breast form. I can't explain her appearance any better than that. You'll understand when you see her. Generally Kaydra, or intelligent life forms on Exvascia, do not talk. All communication is done telepathically, although they do talk to us to give us some comfort.

"Letha, the girl with the modified human form, has hair on her head and feathers on her body. Our son, Dell Britt, has feathers for hair on his head and has a modified human form. The other two look like their mother and prefer to change back to their bird form most of the time."

"What else can you tell us about your kids, Delbert?"

Delbert tried his best to explain what his offspring looked like and how they functioned. "Two haven't changed their primary form. The other two prefer to keep their bird form and try to learn by observing."

"How can you relate to the last two?"

"I take the form of a Hawk, Carol, and spend time with them, just as I spend time with the other two. The first two I really don't teach them anything. Although they are fairly young birds, they can fully take care of themselves."

"How do you feel as a bird?"

"It's strange Gail. It's like pretending you're a bird. You become what you change into." Delbert explained to them, just as he had Adrian before he tried to take on another form, what it was like.

"What special powers have you received since you've been there Delbert?"

"I can disintegrate and regenerate as well as do the same with someone I am holding on to. I can levitate almost anything. I can take the form of a Hawk and fly. I can leave my body and do free soul flight. I can do some mental telemetrical viewing and communicate very well telepathically, Michael."

"Do you live in a cave?"

"No, Myrna. I live in a house of sorts that we built from some boards we were able to make with the Exvascians help. Adrian lives in the cave Larry built.

Both caves have hot and cold running springs. The hot spring is geothermal and is used to fill the hot tubs. This last month we learned how to make something like concrete. That enabled us to make some concrete-like blocks. I think Carol and Darrell will be surprised at their cave. It even has an ice box with milk, eggs and meat stored in it. Making the icebox was a lot of fun.

"I could go on for hours, but Dorletha and Adrian probably have better things to do than watch me down here. I'll see all of you on the 26th at 8:00 a.m. Good-bye, everyone!"

"Good-bye, Delbert, we'll fill Art in on all you've told us."

The group watched as Delbert's body slumped in its seat and then straightened itself again. "Well, is he gone?"

"Yes, Art. How are you feeling?"

"I feel like I've been unconscious. It's not like being asleep. I'm OK though."

"Delbert says the 26th is fine but he had to move the time up to 8:00 a.m. Should we take a few minutes and tell you all he said? Myrna can fill you in on the details that we miss."

"I'd like you to do that, Darrell." Darrel did his best to cover all that Delbert had told them.

"I'll have to pick up the special things he wants Darrell and me to bring, in the next couple days. I wonder how I'll look as 'Jane'."

"Great Carol!" Darrell said, as he pretended to bite her on the neck.

"Careful you two, you'll have time for that later." Gail added.

"Me too, Gail?" Everyone laughed at Michael's remark, except Gail who turned a bright red

Not to be outdone, she came back with her own comment. "Behave yourself and we'll see!" which caused Michael to blush and kept everyone laughing.

"I guess I asked for that one!" Michael said as he tried to stop laughing and blushing. "That sounds like some cave you'll have to live in, Carol."

"It sounds a little scary to me, Michael. I'd hate to have a moon size object heading toward Earth."

"Delbert seems to think they can avoid it, though, Gail."

"I know, Carol, but I guess after hearing what happened to Larry, the place doesn't seem to be that glamorous."

Myrna filled Art in on what happened to Larry while the group continued to discuss various aspects of their conversation with Delbert.

"Art, I'll contact General Kromp and let him know about the earlier time on the 26th."

"Thanks Michael."

Gail and Michael left after the group had discussed the upcoming adventure for another hour or so.

The next two days were busy for Darrell and Gail as he explained things to her about his business. He also had to see his remaining patients for the last few times. Darrell found that the two he was worried most about still had some problems that he had to cure with his watch.

Gail spent time with Carol, when she wasn't busy learning things from Darrell. She and Carol deposited Delbert's retirement check in the joint account Gail had access to. They also picked up the items Delbert had asked Carol to bring with her.

Darrel and Carol's renter was due to move in on July 1st. The fact that it was being rented furnished made it easy to rent. That helped them stop worrying about their house. Gail and Michael would have a few days to remove whatever wasn't to be left in the Lyons' home, basically their personal belongings, before the renter was to move in.

CHAPTER 23

THE EXCHANGE

The group left for Bellingham, Washington, at 10:00 a.m. on June 25th. They stayed in the same motel they had before on their Mt. Baker trips and got an early start on the 26th so they could meet Delbert at 8:00 a.m.

The morning everyone had been waiting for had finally arrived. The group met at 5:30 a.m. for breakfast after checking out of the motel. Myrna had enjoyed the use of Delbert's body for the last time. If things went according to schedule, she would be sleeping with her husband, Art, in his own body for the first time in over ten months. She was almost too excited to eat.

"Art, how long will it take us to drive to Glacier and walk to the foot of the mountain where the army helicopter will pick us up?"

"It'll take about an hour. We'll be at the helicopter landing site at about 7:20 a.m. Ten minutes later they will let us off at the mountain landing site. It will be close to eight o'clock when we reach the 'Adralack Crack' itself. There is still a lot of snow on the mountain. It won't be like it was last August when we were up here."

"When did Michael leave, Gail?"

"He left about an hour ago, Darrell. He had to get his TV camera set up. He was up here a couple days ago with the Army making sure the bleachers were set up in the right place for the observers. He said the portable shop is there already and that General Kromp said he had everything corrected with the insurance company, Social Security Administration and the Veteran's Department. He just has to send the insurance company a copy of Delbert's death certificate and Art's insurance will be restored because Art has been making payments all along on Delbert's insurance for him."

"If everyone is ready, let's go."

The excited group hurried to their cars. The drive up to Glacier was enjoyable because of the beautiful sunny morning. The helicopter was waiting to take them to the mountain landing site when they arrived.

Darrell was surprised by the noise of the helicopter ride. "I thought these things only sounded loud outside. I'm glad it is just a short flight up there. Who's leading our climb, Art?"

"I'll lead, Darrell. Why don't you bring up the rear?"

Michael used his TV camera to record their arrival. He greeted them as they arrived but then went on ahead to his recording location at the "Adralack Crack".

The military observers and those from the National Science Foundation, who had joined them, watched as the group approached. They had been stunned the previous August by what they had seen. They were apprehensive about the events to follow. The events that had occurred on the previous trip were unexpected. This time, they were prepared for anything. Some doubted that the teletransporter could be repaired. Even fewer expected a dead man to suddenly appear and do the repairs on the machine.

Could people return from the dead? Would Art Noack's body return from another planet after being away for almost a year? Could Art and Delbert's being exchange bodies and be made whole again? How would Delbert explain where he had been? Could he explain what it was like to have been dead or had he been dead? The observers had a lot of question running through their minds.

It was difficult for those who had previously witnessed two men disintegrate in the rocky outcropping to believe what they had seen. It would be even harder for them to believe what they were told to expect to see this time.

General Kromp brought Art/Delbert to the microphone in front of the observers. "Gentlemen, I'd like to introduce this man to you today. There are three photographs in the folder each of you've been given. The three men are Delbert Tinsley, who looks like the person beside me. You may recall he is a psychologist. The second man is Art Noack, a geologist. The third man is the inventor of the teletransporter, scientist Adrian Adralack.

"Beside me is the previously dead body of Delbert Tinsley. It is inhabited by the spirit and personality of Art Noack."

The group grew noisy. "*How could General Kromp expect them to fall for such a line?*"

"Delbert Tinsley traded bodies with Art Noack last August. Do you remember when Delbert Tinsley approached the shallow cave over there, called the 'Adralack Crack'? Remember how he fell down and the doctor rushed up and checked his pulse and said he was dead?"

"Right!" shouted a couple of the observers.

"Then after a couple minutes he got up and started to walk. That was only because Art had traded him bodies. In a few minutes the bodies of Art Noack and Adrian Adralack will appear from that outcropping with full beards. You may then question them about their experiences. Adrian will then begin repairing the teletransporter. Four of you have been instructed to observe the repair and learn how to operate the device. We will have a TV camera record all his moves and what he says. That way you will be able to listen to the instructions over and over again later.

"While that is going on, Delbert and Art will walk into the 'Crack', disintegrate and exchange bodies. When they have done so, they will both come out of the overhang. You will then be able to question this body beside me about what has happened to him over the past ten months.

When Art Noack is in his old body, he will share his experiences and be ready to return to a new life in a new city. You will all be able to ask him how it felt to try operating someone else's body. When the person beside me leaves for the second and final time, there'll on longer be a Dr. Delbert Tinsley. He does not plan to return to Earth to live."

"General Kromp, we've heard what you said but it's all hard to believe. Can anyone verify what you have said?"

"Yes! This is Dr. Darrell Lyons of Portland, Oregon, who has attended to Delbert's body since it arrived from the Bellingham hospital where we took it. This is Carol Lyons, formerly Miss Carol Henley, Dr. Tinsley's assistant. You will recall she did the initial testing of the two men to see if they were ready to communicate telepathically before Art walked into the 'Crack'."

Carol began, "In the Portland hospital I communicated telepathically with Art, here, and Delbert who was no longer in his body. Delbert has since communicated with several of us by reentering his body for a short period of time. He is the one who asked for this trip back here to Mt. Baker so that he could exchange bodies with Art."

"Thank you, Mrs. Lyons. Dr. Lyons, would you like to say a few words before Adrian and Art's bodies return?"

"Thank you General. Ladies and Gentlemen, I have observed Art trying for months to operate the body he placed himself in. He responded as if he had a stroke." Darrell continued to explain, in some detail, the difficulties Art had in learning how to operate Delbert's body. "I know what you have been told here today is true."

"Ladies and Gentlemen, if I may have your attention, it's almost 800 hours. Let's turn our attention to the shallow overhang."

As everyone watched, two bearded men materialized in the rocky overhang. One appeared to be in his thirties and was wearing baggy clothes.

The other man was erect and appeared to be in his mid-fifties. The two men rose from the ground and immediately appeared at the microphones. “Good morning ladies and gentlemen, I'm Delbert Tinsley. I am currently using the body of Art Noack, which is 25 pounds lighter than when I left.”

“I'm Adrian Adralack. You will remember me as an arthritic 64 year-old man. The vegetables on Exvascia has cured my arthritis and made me strong and young again. You will also notice I no longer need glasses and my hair isn't as grey.”

Gail rushed up to Adrian and gave him a big hug. “You're looking great, Adrian!”

“Wait till I've shaved.” Adrian hugged Myrna and Carol who had also rushed up to him. In a few minutes the men were cleanly shaven. The crowd was still.

“There are two reasons for us coming here today. I want to trade Art bodies even though I've learned to use his fairly well, I'd like to be in my own body once again.”

“Mr. Uh, what do I call you, Delbert?”

“Wait until I change back to myself, but Delbert is fine.”

“What does it feel like being in someone else's body?”

“That's a good question. It's like wearing a gorilla suit. When you look at yourself in a mirror, you see someone else. When you try to do things, it's awkward no matter what you do. Art, are you ready to exchange bodies again?”

“Definitely, Delbert, what do we have to do?”

“We just have to enter the ‘Adralack Crack’ over there, disintegrate while we're holding on to each other and then think about being in our own bodies. I'll regenerate us and we can come back out whole.”

“I'm afraid to go into the ‘Crack’ again, Delbert!”

Carol spoke up. “Go ahead Art! Delbert isn't going to hurt you! He's kept his every promise to you!”

“OK Delbert, let's get it over with!” Delbert instantly transported them both to the center of the shallow overhang. As the crowd watched, in silence, the two men became a million separate particles and then were gone. Just as quickly they regenerated.

This time, Art, as Art, had to walk from the ‘Crack’. The crowd didn't have any problem recognizing Delbert because he instantly appeared at the microphone. “Now you can call me Dr. Tinsley, or as my former assistant Carol used to call me, Dr. ‘T’. This afternoon when I leave here, there will be no more Dr. ‘T’! What do you think about me being back in my own body ladies?”

“Delbert!” Carol and Myrna reached him first and gave him a big hug and a kiss. As Art walked up, Dr. Lyons and Michael shook his hand. Michael then went back to recording the event.

"Thanks, Delbert. My own body feels so good to me, but my clothes are a little baggy now."

Myrna hugged her husband. "Art it's so good to have you back whole again. I love you!"

"I love you too. I'm going to be a good and faithful husband to you from now on. You're too precious, to ever lose again!"

"Delbert, thanks for giving me Art back again!"

"You're welcome." He kissed Myrna on the cheek as he had always done in the past. "Adrian, you the machinist, the welder and electrician can start repairing the teletransporter now?"

"OK, Delbert."

"General Kromp, is everything taken care of for Art to return to a regular life on Earth again?"

"Yes, Dr. Tinsley. He can carry on with his old identity as if nothing had happened to him. His social security number has even been reactivated."

"That's good to hear. I'd hate to have to come back and visit you." With that, General Kromp was suddenly lifted into the air. "You do understand me, don't you?"

"Yes, Dr. Tinsley, you make yourself perfectly clear." General Kromp was returned to the ground. Delbert disappeared as several military weapons were jerked from the soldier's hands and buried, barrel first, up to their trigger guards, in the rocky soil of the mountain. There wasn't any further threat of them being used until they were cleaned. Delbert reappeared.

"I hope you soldiers realize you're not much opposition. How would you get around if you couldn't touch the ground for example?" With that Delbert levitated the bleachers and all the observers on them ten feet above the ground. Those who had been standing on the ground were now 15 feet off the ground.

"Myrna would you and Gail give Carol any small mirrors you might have in your purses, as well as your combs and brushes? You didn't bring anything like that did you, Carol?"

"No, Delbert. I just brought what I'm wearing plus what you said to bring."

"That's good. Darrell, do you have everything in your black bag that I asked for?"

"Yes Delbert. How is Esdra doing?"

"We're not sure. We'll have to see if there is some way you can look at the information in the time-exempt telepathic storage banks on the Exvascians physical structure. Maybe we can arrange that through mental telemetrical viewing. You'll need to have a lot of information on her anatomy, especially her reproductive system, if you're going to be able to help save her life. She should be fertile soon. When their time comes, they only have 48 hours to mate. Each of her eggs must be fertilized as it passes a certain staging area or she will die. That's if she had developed normally, which she hasn't. I don't know what you'll have to do."

"Will I need my watch to perform healing miracles up there, Delbert?"

"No, Darrell. Their superior mental capabilities have enabled them, for hundreds of years, to regenerate whatever deteriorates in their bodies. The only thing is her mind may not think there is anything wrong with her reproductive system because so few of the females actually become fertile. For that reason, they don't know what normal development is."

"Dr. Tinsley, sir, would you please put us back down on the ground?"

"Sorry, I forgot about you, is that better?"

"Fine, thank you."

"Delbert, could I have your old watch?"

"I don't care, Art, if Darrell doesn't mind."

"If I don't need it up there, you can have it."

"Delbert, I'll need the things I had in my pockets before we switched bodies. What do you want me to do with the rocks you had in your pockets?"

"Here is your billfold, keys and such. Give me the rocks so I can show everyone something. This rock is what we've come to call oil shale. It isn't exactly, but that is the closest thing to it that we know of on Earth. It burns very clean and hot for a long time. With these two rocks that we call spark stone, which are like flint, I'll start the oil shale burning. There! See how big a spark I got from the spark stones and how easily the oil shale started. If you'll come down here, you can put your hands over this small pile of oil shale and see how hot it is. You'll have to smother it with snow to put it out. Art, I thought you'd like to analyze those stones, so keep them."

"Thanks, I'll enjoy doing an analysis."

"Dr. Tinsley, can you tell us what planet you're on and where it is?"

"The planet Exvascia is too far away for any telescope you have to see."

"What's the atmosphere, animals and plant life like?"

"The atmosphere is just about the same as it is at this level. We've increased the amount of oxygen by separating the H_2O on the planet. There isn't any industry so there isn't air pollution. The plants are more tropical in nature and have a much greater healing power than those we have on Earth. Adrian is a good example of their healing qualities. He's only been there ten months and he is about ten years younger physically and has greater mental capability than he had when he left Earth. Have your experts been trying to repair the teletransporter all this time?"

"Yes, they have been but so far they haven't been able to, even with the records they have and the computer analysis they have done."

"We don't have much time to spend here today because there is a crisis situation on Exvascia. We may have to leave without much notice. We won't be activating this location again either, so it won't do you any good to monitor it."

"Is the planet densely populated?"

"No, just the opposite, there are fewer than 300 intelligent inhabitants on it. They all live in a Crater inside an extinct volcano with a crystal prism filling the narrow plume hole in the top of it. They supplement what little sunlight there is with large solar reflectors."

Art and Myrna sat off to one side of the group behaving like young lovers. Gail watched Michael recording the event. Some of the time she watched Adrian work feverishly on his teletransporter machine.

About 11:00 a.m. Adrian was ready to test his machine. The group had almost run out of questions for Delbert. At lunch time, the small group planned on keeping their silverware as souvenirs to take to Exvascia with them. The eight place settings, along with the two place settings Carol had brought, would give Delbert enough silverware to use to train his kids. *Who knows,* he said to himself, *maybe someday we'll come to Earth, so maybe they should be taught some things about human ways.*

When Adrian tested his machine, the first blast of power didn't disintegrate a very large boulder; it just took a couple chunks out of it. One piece flew off and hit a soldier and crushed his leg and another hit him in the head.

"I'll get that chunk off his leg, Darrell, but you'll have to try using your watch on him before the army doctor gets to him. I'll zap you over to him as soon as you get your watch back from Art." With the watch in Darrell's hand, Delbert instantly moved him to the soldier's side as he removed the chunk of the boulder off his leg. The crushed leg was bleeding profusely. The crowd looked on to see what would happen.

"He's has some bad injuries, Delbert. In fact, now, he isn't breathing. I'll have to revive him and repair his injuries as quickly as I can. I don't want him to die."

"How is he, Dr. Tinsley?"

"He should be OK soon, General Kromp. I think he just had the air knocked out of him and a bruised leg from the rock hitting him. Please keep everyone back. Darrell, why is your watch, glowing, a bright green?" Delbert asked.

"I'm drawing power from Exvascia to get his brain to regenerate his head and leg injury, Delbert. Concentrate on him being whole again, it should help."

"OK, I'm concentrating. How is he doing?"

"Not good. I've got to concentrate on one specific area at a time. Give Adrian a telepathic message to keep testing his machine. If he can get it working on little things, it'll take the observers' minds off our problem here."

"That cheer must mean Adrian is having success testing his machine."

"Is he getting any better, Darrell?"

"He's starting to respond. His leg has stopped bleeding so I can start working on his head. I hope he didn't suffer brain damage. That's better! His body is starting to quickly regenerate itself now."

"Why did it grow quiet all of a sudden, Delbert? Where is General Kromp going?"

"I'll check. I don't believe it. Look toward the 'Adralack Crack' Darrell and tell me what you see."

"Just a minute, Delbert, there, now I can look. He'll be OK for a minute. I think I see a female like creature with feathers covering her entire body. Do I really?"

"Yes, it's my mate, DorLetha! This is the first time anyone from Earth has ever been allowed to see her. No wonder everyone is quiet. The little guy with clothes is my son, Dell Britt, the little girl that looks like her mother except for the hair on her head, rather than feathers, is my daughter, Letha.

"Something must be wrong on Exvascia. I better finish up in a hurry. I'll check and see if they have the settings yet on the teletransporter. I'm surprised; DorLetha is even letting Michael record her and the kids."

"Go ahead, Delbert. I'll be finished here in about five minutes. He's coming to. That will help."

While Darrell was working on his patient, Adrian was again demonstrating his teletransporter.

"How do you feel, soldier?"

"My arm hurts and my ribs on my right side."

"How is that?" Darrell asked as he touched the areas and wished they were whole again.

"That feels good. What was wrong?"

"You were just lying on a stone. Sorry about that. Are there any other places hurting you?"

"My stomach doesn't feel very good and I'm dizzy."

"Here, hold these smelling salts under your nose while I check your stomach. Does your stomach hurt here?"

"Yes, that's the place."

Darrell's watch glowed as he held his hand on the spot that was hurting and wished it to be healed. "I think it was just a muscle cramp." Darrell thought to himself, *"It's a good thing he doesn't know he had internal bleeding."*

"Doc, why am I spitting blood:"

"Uh, maybe you bit your tongue when you fell. Does your head hurt here?"

"Yes."

"Why don't you sniff the smelling salts again while I press my hand on the place you said hurts? I don't want you to pass out."

"OK, Doc."

"Did that help?"

"Yeah, I feel OK now. I was so dizzy there for a while, I thought I had some really bad injuries."

"Is your mouth still bleeding?

"No, there isn't any more blood."

"That's good, I think you're OK now, you can get up. I want you to take it easy for a few minutes though."

"Thanks Doc, I feel alright now."

Darrell closed his bag and joined Adrian and Delbert and the others. "Darrell this is my mate, DorLetha."

"It's a pleasure to meet you, Queen DorLetha."

"So, Dell Bert has been telling you about me. I guess that's OK. I've been watching you and what you've been doing with Dell Bert's watch."

"Can you tell us how you blanked out everyone's memory of the time I put the car accident victim's arm back on?"

"Sure, I just went back in time and cleared their minds of the event happening. I could make everyone here forget they saw me, if I wanted to, but this time I think I'll let them remember me and let the TV record our being here. It might help Michael in the future. Besides, who would be foolish enough to tell others what they saw without proof. I appreciate everyone's efforts to get Dell Bert and Art back into their own bodies. Changing bodies with another person is forbidden on our planet."

"I know they're happy about the correction of their conditions. Art had a lot of trouble learning to operate Delbert's body. Are we about ready to leave, Delbert?"

"Just about, Darrell, Adrian has to leave more information on the settings for his machine and then we'll be ready."

"Delbert, can I interrupt you and Darrell?"

"Sure, Art, what's on your mind?"

"I was able to find minerals by a special feeling I got after you had entered your body the last time. Will I be able to do that again?"

"I don't know. Who knows what you'll be able to do with the watch you now have. Maybe it only worked for Darrell. Darrell, did you give Art back the watch?"

"I forgot to in all the excitement. I'm sorry, Art."

"That's OK; I had forgotten you had borrowed it."

"Adrian, are you ready to go?"

"I just finished, Delbert."

"Thank you, General Kromp. I hope we didn't disappoint you."

"You certainly didn't. I'm delighted with all the things we've seen and heard here today besides getting the teletransporter repaired. I just hope it isn't used exclusively for destructive purposes. Thank you, Dr. Lyons, for looking at our soldier. For some reason, I can't believe he just had the air knocked out of him. I'll keep what I saw to myself. I just hope you'll be able to help others in the future like you did him. If there is ever anything I can do for you, Dr. Tinsley, please feel free to contact me, however that may be."

"I'll do that, General, good-bye. Has everyone said their good-byes except me? Give me a hug Myrna, Gail. Thanks Michael for helping. Take care of that body I trimmed up for you Art. Good-bye, everyone!"

"Good-bye, good-bye!" With that, Delbert and his family walked into the Crack with Adrian, Darrell and Carol. They all disintegrated and were gone. Art immediately checked the Crack and found it was inactive. He knew it would never be active again because of what Delbert had said.

Gail and Michael followed Art and Myrna back to the Portland airport and saw them off. They then drove Darrell's car back to his home and gave the keys to his renter.

Art and Myrna slept until noon the next day. They hadn't arrived home in Denver until early in the morning. After they had eaten, they went over to the Donovans to see them and to pick up their kids.

Myrna rang the doorbell and Clara answered it. "Stewart, its Myrna and Art! Kids, your Daddy's here."

"Daddy, Daddy! Todd raced to his dad and jumped up into his waiting arms. Todd hugged his dad's neck as tight as he could.

"I missed you, daddy!"

"I missed you too, Todd. How has my big boy been?"

"I sure missed you, Daddy!"

"Daddy, Daddy!"

"Hi, Lisa" Art said as he scooped her off the floor with his left arm. The tears came to his eyes. His kids liked their uncle Delbert, but they loved their dad. There was a lot of difference between the two feelings. He hugged and kissed his kids for several minutes before they had enough and were ready to start questioning him.

"Where have you been, Daddy? Mommy said you would never come back!"

"I know, Todd. We didn't think I could ever come back but I'm here now and I'm going to stay. Why don't you run and play now so I can talk with the Donovans. We can talk a lot later and we'll all be home together again."

"Thanks, Clara, for watching the kids"

Stewart hugged Art as he spoke, "It's really great to see you pulled it off and everything turned out OK."

"Thanks, Stewart. The Army has fixed everything. I'll just have to think up something to tell our old friends if I ever see them again.

"Stewart, I need to get out to the mines today and tomorrow. Since I was around Delbert and Adrian again and now have Delbert's watch, I might be able to locate ore in the mines for a period."

"We can go right now, if you're ready."

"Would that be OK, Myrna?"

"Sure, Art. I'll see you at home. Just give me a kiss before you go."

Art gave Myrna a kiss and a big hug and told her how much he loved her. It had been a long time since he could hug her in his own body and it felt good.

"Let's go, Stewart"

"I'll drive, Art. Let's take the pickup. What mine do you want to go to first?"

"Why don't we go to the one you're presently mining?"

"That's a good idea. We could pick up Royal and have him join us. That would give him a chance to meet you."

"Are you sure this is the same mine? Look at all the activity!"

"We put on 20 new employees. We'll probably find Royal in the office."

"Hello there, Stewart. Who's your friend?"

"Royal, this is our new partner, Art Noack. Art this is Royal Haston."

"It's nice to finally meet you, Royal."

"So this is Art, the man with the magic touch, am I ever glad to meet you. How long do you think you'll have this gift?"

"I don't know, Royal, that's why I wanted to get back to the mine to see if I still have it. I may only have it a couple more days, if I have it at all. We'll just have to see what happens. It's caused by special events in my life and I had just such an experience yesterday."

"Royal, Art and I are going to go over this mine and the first one we bought after he was here. Would you like to accompany us?"

"You bet, I never heard of a geologist finding ore the way he does. It kind of reminds me of the fellas who dowse or go around water witching and actually finding water where none has previously been discovered. Figuratively speaking, you sure brought in a gusher when you went through this mine. Would you like to see the vein you found?"

"I'd rather check for new ore today and tomorrow in the other mines. Then I can come back here and see what you've uncovered."

"I've got the maps right here! Here's a helmet and a couple extra lanterns. Where do you want to start?"

"Is there any area where I indicated there was ore that you haven't checked out yet Royal?"

"No, I rushed to look at all of them."

"Stewart, is there any area I didn't get to look at last time?"

"Yes, the area where we've taken most of the silver from."

"Let's go over it again."

"OK, I'll show you where it is Art." Stewart led the way. "This is the area. Do you get any sensations here?"

"I feel a fast vibration but I don't have any strong feeling that ore is present."

"What does that mean, Stewart?"

"Fast vibrations tell him there are small quantities of ore present. Slow vibrations mean a large quantity. Strong feelings mean a deep vein. No feelings means the ore is on the surface."

"There isn't anything here. Is there any other place I should look?"

"You could check the new tunnel they made to get to the vein you discovered."

"OK, let's look at it!"

"This is all freshly dug. How does it feel?"

"What I can see matches my feelings all right. I feel very slow vibrations but no feeling. That isn't all I feel though. Let me put my hands on this wall a minute. Along here I get a strong feeling, but there is nothing here. I better go back a ways. Yes, there is another vein off in this direction, but it's going to be a long ways back in the rock. Is there another tunnel off in that direction?"

"There is one above us. When I put the map overlay of the level above over this area, you can see the relationship between where we are here and the same area in the level above. I'll mark it."

"OK, let's go on up there and see what's there."

A few minutes later, they were at their destination. "I think this is probably 30 feet closer to the ore, Royal. Mark the map here and make an arrow in that direction. OK, let's go to the next mine before it gets too late."

"This is the only way to prospect Art."

"It's not permanent though Royal. You'd better save your money so you can get into some other business when the ore I find is all gone."

"I hear you, partner! You mean to tell me you've known this guy for years, Stewart, and never took advantage of him?"

"Not until now, Royal. I guess I finally got wise."

"Oh, Stewart, you know I'm just doing this to get attention!"

"Don't worry Art, you'll get it from us."

As far as Art could tell, the next silver mine only had ore where he had found it before. The only information he could add was distance and depth of the ore.

"I don't feel anything new in this mine."

"That's OK Art. We have a good idea of how much work we'll have to do to get to the ore now. That's worth a lot in itself. I won't be able to go with you tomorrow but be very careful in the gold mine that caved in on you the last time you two were there."

"We'll remember, Royal. I think I'd like to start with the silver mine we didn't actually look at last time. I marked the places I thought we should look at, so it shouldn't take us too long."

The next day, Stewart and Art visited the mine they were still trying to close on. Art was able to confirm the places ore should be found, the depth of the ore and the probable size of the vein.

Both men hesitated before entering the gold mine that had caved in on them. "Art, before we go into the mine; did you ask Delbert how they got us out, when it caved in on us?"

Art retold the story of how Delbert and the aliens helping him had removed the rock and got them out of the cave-in. He also told Stewart about the partial healing that had enabled him to make the call for help.

"Why didn't the alien, that healed most of your wounds, heal your arm too?"

"She got interested in our world and took off. Delbert had to enter his body and use the CB to get help. By going back in time, they were able to hear the conversation you had with your friend at noon."

"It's all unbelievable. I think I'm ready to go in. Are you going to confirm your earlier feelings from going over the map before going to the spot where we were injured?"

"That's the plan, Stewart." After going back and checking all the previous spots for accuracy of his earlier estimates, Art and Stewart went to the tunnel that had caved in on them.

"I was right, Stewart. There is a good size deposit in this mine. We're only about 20 feet beyond the cave-in area. Let's mark this area on the map and get out of here!"

The next morning, when Stewart and Art went to their mine office to talk to Royal, Jake was in the office.

"Hi, Jake!"

"Good morning, Stewart.

"You remember Art being with me a couple months back. He's the one that found the silver vein."

"Oh, yes, I just didn't recognize him without his helmet, work cloths and dirty face. I'll have to admit you both look better the way you're dressed now."

"Art is now a partner in our operations. We were in yesterday and discovered another possible vein a few feet back in the rock off of the new tunnel you just completed."

"That's great! I can't tell you how happy you've made a lot of people around here. We really needed the jobs you provided."

"We stopped by to tell you we may be opening another mine or two. What would you say to that?"

"I know another dozen or so really hard-working miners who are looking for work. Just let me know where and when you want them to show up and they'll be there."

"We'll do that, as soon as we're ready, Jake."

"It's nice to have you with us, Art. I've got to get back to my area. I'll see you later."

Stewart and Art spent the day closing the deals on the three additional mines. His signature was all that was needed on the first two. The third mine required additional negotiating.

When Art got to the mine the next day to look for other possible deposits, his ability to find additional ore was gone. Nobody was disappointed though, they would all be well-off for the remainder of their lives, even if they didn't invest their forthcoming fortunes wisely.

Chapter 24

Visit to Exvascia

The group that went to Exvascia arrived shortly after they had left Earth. "That's the only way to travel, Delbert."

"I know what you mean Darrell."

The Exvascians long awaited arrival of Queen DorLetha's mate was about to come to pass. The Matriarchal Directorate was there to greet them, as well as all the Kaydra in their primary forms.

As they arrived on the Crater floor Delbert and Darrell were talking. Right away they noticed Delbert's voice was deeper, richer and fuller. He was taller. At 6 feet he was still 6 inches shorter than DorLetha. "This is my mate Dell Bert in his own body. Do you like him?" They liked the way he looked.

The other male was shorter than Delbert, but he looked tall when standing by the little 5 feet 3 inch female.

Dora and Cara flew on to their mother's shoulders as she introduced her guests. This is Dell Bert's young female friend, Carol, and her mate Darrell. He does work on Earth similar to what I'La does here." Dell Britt and Letha didn't know what to think of their new dad, but they rushed to greet him as Dora and Cara looked on.

Dell Britt wanted Carol to hold him so he could look at her hair. It was like his sisters, while he had feathers on his head like his mother.

The Kaydra were intrigued by the female from Earth. They wanted to see her body and started asking her questions immediately.

"Carol I'm so glad you could come visit us. One of the things I wasn't able to explain to the Exvascians was the female of Dell Bert's species. They wanted to know what they looked like and how they functioned."

"I should be able to help you with that, DorLetha. You have a complete human couple in Darrell and me. If we're here long enough, say 200 of your days or so, we could even have a child. We bear our children live. They generally weigh six to eight pounds."

"Can you mate all the time?"

"Yes, but we can only start a child inside us at certain times during a 28-day cycle that we go through."

"Our planet isn't quite warm enough for us to go without coverings. Its warm enough here though. I'd have to wear clothes most of the time at first until our skin looks the color of Adrian's. Then it wouldn't matter.

"It's usual for people to wear clothes. Our men get excited and like to breed when they see women without clothes. To prevent unwanted acts like that, except with our mate, we wear clothes."

"Will you wear clothes here?"

"You'll have to answer that question, Delbert."

"We only wear a loincloth most of the time. Larry didn't know if he should go nude or not so that's what he wore. It will depend on what you and Darrell are comfortable with.

"Let me introduce both of you to a few special Kaydra, or intelligent inhabitants. This is Esdra; she wants Adrian as her mate. Shida helps take care of the kids. I'La, this is Darrell. He does the only type of healing we have on our planet. I'La is the one I wanted you to meet. She's the one that set up Adrian's diet. She's the one that came down with me when Art got caught in the cave-in.

"What is the situation with the moon we're about to collide with, DorLetha?"

"Esdra, Adrian and I had better go check. If the moon is being pulled toward us faster as it gets closer, as Adrian suspects. We are probably close to time to boost our planet's speed. I'll tell you what's happening in a few minutes.

"We've already brought all the animals in from the outside. GarGweth and Andre have come in too. We moved your raft to even higher ground for you also. I don't think we can do anything else on the outside right now."

"You've thought of everything I would have. We'll just stay and talk to the Kaydra unless you can use our help in anyway."

With that, DorLetha was gone. "So that's how they get around in a hurry."

"That's right Carol, they use their mental power to instantly disintegrate. They then regenerate at the place they have been thinking of. It's like sending a telepathic message to somewhere and then riding on it."

"How is the effort to move the planet going to affect us Delbert?"

"There will be a quick jerk is all. The force field protecting the giant crystal prism, which blocks the narrow opening at the top of this old volcano, will prevent any damage to us. Of course, there is also a hyper-atmospheric force field to protect us from space debris at all times.

"The ocean outside has never had a tide. The moon we are about to acquire will provide us one in a hurry. That's why we are prepared for a tidal wave outside."

"Do you have the compass I asked for, Carol?"

"Here it is."

"Great. That tells me our main living quarters are on the north side of the Crystal Prism Crater, as we call it. The tunnel that leads to the outside is on the south side. As if directions mean anything here. After the trouble passes, we'll go outside. We should be able to enjoy moonlight strolls along a beach that will have an accompanying surf sound."

"What was it like before?"

"When the solar reflector was directed away from our area each evening, the area was totally dark and there wasn't any sound coming from the water. You couldn't walk along the beach because of the darkness."

"You mean the light coming through the crystal prism isn't from a sun but a satellite?"

"That's right Darrell, when the Exvascians were originally beamed here, the soil, plants and the crystal were all part of their planet. Their planet was blown apart in a war. The crystal that closes the opening to the Crater was the last part of the material that was beamed to this planet. It was regenerated before it came all the way through the slight atmosphere that was here at that time. They say that is how the crystal was formed. The Exvascians somehow ground it into a prism. The solar reflector which was used to generate extra energy on their original planet now became necessary for their existence. It has now become their sun. They are totally dependent on it for their lives."

"The Kaydra are what we would call people, right?"

"That's right Carol, they have all taken their primary forms to greet you. I'm afraid they will be watching everything you do. They generally communicate telepathically, but will occasionally speak verbally. The ones that are around us most of the time now talk so we can hear them."

"I guess I don't mind if they look at me. You're sure they're all females?"

"That's right, except for GarGweth. He's that Sasquatch over there. He's an alien and the one that almost saved Larry's life. The last alien we were fighting, the one that killed Larry, used the last of his ray blaster power on GarGweth and almost killed him. That's why it attacked Larry with a large rock. I wish I'd been two seconds quicker."

"We understand, Delbert, we know you wouldn't let your friend down. Why don't you tell our greeters that we'll be here for some time and that they can see and talk with us later. I'd like to see the cave you told us about."

"I don't need to tell them Darrell, they communicate telepathically most of the time so they already know what you were thinking before you could get it said. Come on, I'll show you the cave. It's beyond the waterfall over there."

Carol and Darrell asked questions as they went along. "What's that, Delbert, It looks like a swimming pool."

"That's exactly what it is. I'll start to fill it in a couple weeks. The concrete-like material may be ready sooner however, we'll have to wait and see."

"How did you dig that, Delbert?"

"I used one of the ray blasters from the aliens to blast the soil loose then I levitated it to this end of the pool to form the bank and deck area. The only place we swim now is in the waterfall pool. The cave is right over there."

"The ladder must be for us to climb."

"For now, that is the way you'll have to get up there."

"You just floated up Delbert. Can we do that?"

"I don't know. It's all mental power and believing it can be done. Just think, 'I'm going to go up, up, up.' If you can concentrate hard enough, you will go up. If you can't you won't, Carol."

"I'll try it another day. It's dark up here, Delbert."

"I'll light a lamp, Carol, how's that?"

"Oh, Darrell, look at what they've done."

"This is your living room. The bedroom is to your left. There you have the hot tub with a shower above it. This is the kitchen, complete with a barbeque pit and spit."

"Look, Darrell, the sink has hot and cold running water."

"It's all from mother nature. The hot water is geothermal isn't it, Delbert?"

"That's right, Darrell. Here's your icebox. The ice goes in this side area with the drain. It has two animal skins with a dead air space between them for a door. The udder full of milk comes from the Mardi goat. There are some of the larger bird eggs, some fresh fish, meat and vegetables."

"How did you think of all these improvements?"

"Larry had it all figured out. We just added the concrete-like floor, walls, icebox and the block walls."

"When you get all the lamps lit, Carol, it's not bad."

"Look at all the dishes. Now I see why you told us to bring silverware."

"When the Kaydra go and hunt for us, they change to an animal form, infiltrate the herd, or fletch, then change again to an animal form that can kill the animals they are with. It's fast and efficient. Because several kill for us, the animals aren't afraid of us."

"Delbert, what are these bound leaf things in the living room?"

"Light the lamp by you with these spark stones and take a look."

"How do I do that?"

"Strike the spark stones together real close to the oil shale. Be sure to take your hands away quick so you don't get burned."

"Boy, it sure starts easily."

"He told you to be careful, Carol. What's in the pouch with the string on it, Delbert?"

"That's a safety pouch. It has some oil shale and spark stone in it along with some other protective needs."

"These leaf things are books! Can we learn a lot about living here by reading them?"

"Yes, and I hope you'll do so, as soon as possible."

DorLetha appeared instantly and asked. "Delbert, do you three want to see the moon as it approaches?"

"Sure, DorLetha, come over here Carol and Darrell. She'll transport us up to the solar reflector station or the navigation station."

"That's the way Adrian's machine worked on me, Darrell. Look at that moon! Is it going to hit us? It looks four times as large as a full moon does on Earth when it starts to rise over the horizon."

"We're about to start our thrust, Carol. If our calculations are right, we should be OK."

"Adrian, what did you and Esdra decide about the force fields?"

"We're going to activate those around the important installations, such as this one and the one that protects the Crystal Prism. If the hyper-atmospheric force field goes out we'll not worry about it until the debris gets too large or there is too much of it. We'll use the solar shield for power then and leave the planet dark."

"That moon is getting larger too fast for me, Adrian!"

"Esdra, give us another surge of power. DaKeta, convert the solar reflectors to direct power. The navigational system says we're still in trouble! Shut off the hyper-atmospheric force field, Esdra. DorLetha, see if you can change our push, from straight ahead, to a ninety degree angle away; from the moon."

"There's no celestial bodies close enough to use for a three prong thrust, Adrian. I'll have to push against the moon itself. Esdra cut all force fields and give me all the power you've got in one final burst!"

"What does the navigation system say, Dell Bert?"

"Possible escape, but dangerous! Look out for all the debris, DorLetha! Can we continue without the force fields?"

"We have to until we build up some power reserve. We gave it everything we had. We aren't even pumping the cold water through the Crater. Activate the reserve hydrogen converter, Esdra! Direct its power to the force field of the Crystal Prism and the other important installations."

"It's done, DorLetha"

"DorLetha, we've got a large foreign body coming right for us!"

"Get ready to activate the hyper-atmospheric force field, Esdra. When you do, cut the power to all the others. Set it to continue until our power drops down to where it can only handle the smaller force fields."

"What happens then DorLetha?"

"Just hope our atmosphere is dense enough to burn up what the force field doesn't destroy."

"It's coming on through, DorLetha!"

"Switch to the smaller shields, Esdra."

"We've still got a large chunk coming right at us, DorLetha!"

"I see it, Esdra, let me take the controls."

"Be careful, DorLetha, don't touch those two controls at the same time! The power will go right through you!" ZZZZZ, zap, snap!

"She took it full force Dell Bert!"

"Don't go near her Esdra. I think she's going to pull a TetTrella on us. Now, DorLetha, blast it before it comes through our station's force field." Crash! Bang! Splat! Thud!

"Is everyone OK? I'La, get up here quick! I couldn't stop the debris that came through our station's force field."

"I'm here, DorLetha. The new man is OK."

"What happened to us, DorLetha?"

"I tried to run the power through me, Darrell, and blast that big chunk into smaller pieces, but there wasn't enough power left. Hold on, that moon is just going to miss us! We're in for a rough ride for a few seconds."

"Look at all the debris that is bombarding us." Darrell continued, "Lucky some of it is burning up in the atmosphere!"

"Uh, oh, moan, groan."

DorLetha directed I'La. "As soon as we stabilize, see if you can help the humans."

"What happened to Esdra?

"I didn't notice, I'La. She must have disintegrated." DorLetha disintegrated to find her."

"I'La, how's DaKeta?"

"She doesn't look good Darrell. How are the humans?"

"I don't know. I might be able to check them now, I'La."

"Darrell, DaKeta just disappeared. I'll have to find her!"

"OK, I'La. I think I can make it to the others now. At least I can hear them groaning, so I know they're alive."

"Darrell, I can't find Esdra. Help me!"

"How, DorLetha?"

"Lie on the floor and think of her here, with your entire mind, until I come back."

"I'll try, DorLetha. Esdra! Esdra! I've got to keep thinking of Esdra. Esdra! Oh, oh, the pain in my head! Come on Esdra. Find DorLetha if she can't find you! Oh, oh, aaah!"

"I'm back, Darrell. Darrell, are you OK? I'La you're back with DaKeta, great! Check Darrell! I think I drained his brain of too much energy. Oh no! He disintegrated!"

"DorLetha, what happened to Darrell?"

"He disintegrated, Carol! I think I drained his brain of too much power. I'm sorry! I had to find Esdra."

"I heard what she said, Carol. Tell Darrell, telepathically, to think of himself as whole and I think we can get him back!"

"OK, Delbert. Darrell, honey, think of your body! Think of it as it has always been! Darrell your body is whole! It's whole. Delbert is that him trying to regenerate?"

"Yes, Carol! Tell him to take my hand!"

"Darrell, grab Delbert's hand! Grab Delbert's hand, honey! DorLetha, they're both gone!"

"That's OK, Carol. Just keep telling Darrell to hold onto Dell Bert and don't let go. DorLetha joined the fray. Dell Bert, Grab my hand and I'll come help you two!"

"Now they're all gone, I'La, what do we do?"

"Just wait and see if DorLetha can regenerate all three of them with their help. If you try, you can see their mental communication in your mind."

"I see them. Come on Delbert! Come on Darrell! Think of being whole! Think of being whole!"

"Why are you yelling?"

"I'La, they're back! That's why I was yelling. When humans get emotional about something, they can try harder."

"Ah! Aaahhh! I did it! I'm back! I'm back!"

"Hurray! Hurray! Hurray!"

"What's all the yelling about, Carol?"

"Adrian, you're conscious! How are you feeling?"

"I don't know! If you'd stop yelling I could think about how I feel. Aah! I think I've got two heads. Look at my beautiful goose egg! Oh! What a headache!"

"I'La, can you fix Adrian's head!"

"Yes DorLetha. Look into my eyes, Adrian. Look at the red glow! Watch it grow! Keep your eyes on it. Now, think about your body. Think about your head and how it should look and feel. Touch the place where it hurts! Touch it! Now, think how it was and smooth the bump back down! Think how well it's feeling! There isn't any more pain! It's just as it was! Keep looking at my eyes! They're growing cooler now, cooler, cooler! Now, close your eyes and relax! I'm touching your head. There is no more pain. It is well! You can open your eyes now, Adrian. How do you feel?"

"I'm tired but I feel OK. I assume the moon missed us."

"Yes, look over that way."

"It's getting smaller again. What do we have to do to keep it, DorLetha?"

"We have to keep our hydrogen conversion plant working to make more power. Then we'll use a retractor beam to pull it into orbit around our planet."

"How long will that take?"

"It'll take two days to get the power we need. Why don't I transport all of you to your caves and you can rest for those two days. We'll be charging the force fields with the power from the solar reflectors so there won't be any light for those two days"

"That's OK, DorLetha. We'll be OK in our caves."

"Thank you all for the help and especially you Darrell for working with me to get Esdra back for Adrian. You have a strong mind."

Adrian then spoke. "I want to thank you too, Darrell! Esdra means a lot to me. We'll see all of you in a couple days. Good night."

I'll beam you all to the Crater floor. Hold on to one another. Here we go. There, how's that?"

Great, thanks.

"I'm going out to the house to be with my kids!"

"Wait for me Dell Bert. Remember, now that you have your own body back I can stay with you!"

"Great, DorLetha, I had forgotten all about having my body back. What do you think of it?"

"You'll find out!"

"I guess you and Darrell can find something to do in the cave for a couple days can't you, Carol?"

"You're asking honeymooners that question, Delbert?"

"Maybe I shouldn't have asked. You call us, we won't call you! Hope you enjoyed your first day here!"

"It's one we'll never forget. Good night."

Delbert had anticipated a long blackout period after the approaching moon passed by their planet and would soon become their moon. He had provided a large ceramic pot for Carol and Darrel's personal use so that the cave would not be misused. He'd show them where the outhouses were when it was light.

The first 12 hours were spent sleeping. Their injured bodies needed time to recover. Carol and Darrell enjoyed the cave and trying to cook. The piece of spacecraft metal, left for them to use as a frying pan, worked satisfactorily since nothing would stick to it. The icebox area, built into the cave wall, did a good job of keeping things cool.

The Mardi goat milk was rich and sweet. The word "goat" connected with milk had misled Carol into thinking it would be strong rather than mild. They discovered the Mellow Drops and the Marble nuts and enjoyed both. Their time alone, to make love and soak in the hot tub, was precious to them. There were no outside distractions and they could thoroughly enjoy each other.

Adrian drew on Delbert's experience with DorLetha, to please Esdra. The spot on her side was just as sexy as Delbert had said DorLetha's was. They couldn't mate because her time hadn't come, but they could enjoy sleeping together and being together.

When their parents got home, the kids took their primary form and enjoyed playing with some simple toys Delbert had made. Of course, they weren't toys like we have on Earth because they wouldn't have been able to relate to them, but they were toys nonetheless.

Darrell and Carol read all of Larry's books before it got light. They wanted to take a look at the outside as soon as they could. Fortunately, the moon didn't require as much energy from the retractor beam as expected to pull it into a proper orbit. Therefore, the solar reflector was available a few hours ahead of schedule. That was good, because the Crater had cooled off considerably.

Carol took her sack needle and made herself a "Jane" outfit and Darrell a "Tarzan" outfit while it was dark. They would be able to wear them as soon as the planet was back up to its normal temperature.

The group took all the outside animals from the Crater through the exit tunnel, as soon as it got light. There was a lot of damage to the fruit crop outside caused by the debris from the encounter with their new moon but it wasn't completely destroyed. The humans gathered a lot of the fruit to eat while they were outside and when they returned to the Crater.

Carol and Darrell were surprised at the long distance they had to hike down the mountain side from the entrance tunnel to reach the ocean. On their way down, they saw the raft Delbert and Adrian had sailed to First Island on. Delbert brought the compass and the binoculars with him from the Crater. He also brought the map he had marked directions on.

As they walked along the beach, Carol wanted to know what the weird marks were in the sand. "I don't know, Carol, I've never seen any animals in the oceans. That's some surf isn't it! We must have a six to eight foot tide here. Look how high it has been in the last few hours."

"Won't it stabilize now that DorLetha and her navigational crew have the moon in orbit, Delbert?"

"It should. I can't wait until I get to see a full moon."

"What did you say? I can't hear you for the surf."

"It's loud! I said I can't wait until there's a full moon, Darrell."

"I wonder how large it will appear and how much light it will cast on the planet?"

"I hope it isn't as large as it was just before it passed by us and swung around the planet, Darrell."

Delbert spoke. "I agree with you there, Carol. I knew when I brought you two up here we were going to have problems but I didn't expect the moon to pass that close. How are you two feeling now?"

"I'm OK, Delbert, but I was really worried when I couldn't seem to get back into my body. It's a good thing Carol kept encouraging me."

"I had that same problem when Adrian tried his teletransporter on me the first time. The power went out just as he was trying to regenerate me. Fortunately, he had a large generator hooked to his equipment as a standby measure. He kicked the generator power in and got my body back, but I couldn't seem to reenter it. Myrna pulled me through that time as Carol watched."

"I still remember that Delbert, just as if it was last night, even though it's been almost a year and a half ago."

"Through your experience there's one thing you've learned about Darrell, that is the power of your mind and concentration. What you experienced is called free soul flight. That's where your spirit leaves your body. When you learn how to disintegrate up here, you can draw on that experience when you try to regenerate yourself.

"Do you realize you would have been dead if you didn't regenerate? What happened to Esdra and DaKeta the other day was the same thing. They didn't have the power to regenerate themselves either. That's why DorLetha and I'La had to go looking for them. They found them by telepathic communication. They each took hold of one with their mind and regenerated both themselves and the other being. If they hadn't held on to them with their minds when they regenerated, they would have become a pile of sparkling particles on the floor. We call that spotting or dying. Pain can cause them to die that way."

"What happens if two people disintegrate and one can't regenerate himself?"

"The other person has to regenerate both of them with his or her mental power. If they can't, they have to get help as DorLetha did from you when she regenerated Esdra. The way we killed the Lidyans was to disintegrate ourselves and them, while holding them and then letting go of them with our minds before we regenerated. They were gone forever"

"Are we going back inside now?"

"We can Carol but first, what can you tell me about that inviting looking tree over there?"

"I'd suspect it's a Mist tree."

"That's right. Hi, GarGweth, what do you think of the ocean's tide?"

"It reminds me of home now. I'll walk back to the Crater with you."

Carol and Darrell enjoyed the fruit that grew in the bright hot area outside the Crater. "That's the quagmire you read about in Larry's book. That's the Living Vine that likes to grow on the trees by the quagmire."

"Oh look at the pretty flowers. I've got to have some to brighten up our cave. Aaahh! Ah!"

"It's a blood sucker, Darrell! Caw! Caw! Caw," Delbert called out. "GarGweth, can you grab that thing like this and squeeze it real hard? If you can, it will straighten out and let go of her arm!"

"Ah, get it off, please! Help me, Darrell!"

"GarGweth will try. Like this?"

"Yes, GarGweth, squeeze harder. You're getting it. Just a little harder. See, it's starting to straighten out. You did it. Now, throw it to that Prog that's running this way, GarGweth."

"It sure flicked its tentacle around quickly when it hit the ground. That Prog grabbed it just like it said in Larry's book. So when it dies it gets stiff and straightens out and the Prog can roll it over, on its armor-like shell back and eat it from its soft underside."

"That's right Darrell. GarGweth, can you bring Darrell to the Crater? I'll have to rush ahead with Carol and see if I'La knows what will counteract the poison of its bite that is starting to paralyze her."

"Go ahead, Delbert." Delbert disintegrated the two of them and they were instantly inside the Crater where I'La rushed to her side and slapped some leaves on the bite to draw the poison out.

Darrell thanked GarGweth for helping them.

"GarGweth doesn't like to see anyone hurt. This is the tunnel to the Crater, follow me."

Darrell soon joined Delbert and I'La. "Carol's sleeping in the cave. She'll be OK in a day or so, Darrell. GarGweth got the blood sucker off her in plenty of time. We could never do what he did. I didn't even think he was strong enough to do that!"

"I'm glad she's going to be OK. I'm not sure being a doctor helps me much up here! I'La, how is Esdra doing?"

"She's gleesing."

"Is that good or bad, Delbert?"

"She's molting, Darrell. She'll never have feathers again because she has chosen Adrian as her mate and he has smooth skin."

"What other problems will she have?"

"I don't know! Here comes DorLetha. Let's see what she can tell us. DorLetha, can Darrell look at the time-exempt telepathic storage banks that tell about the physical makeup of female Exvascians?"

"If he can make a telepathic link with my thoughts, such as in telemetrical viewing, he can see the information through me."

"What do I have to do?"

"Clear your mind completely and let DorLetha's thoughts become your thoughts, Darrell. DorLetha, can you pull his mind into alignment with your thoughts to get him started?"

"I'll try, Dell Bert. Can you see the body I'm looking at, Darrell?"

"Yes DorLetha."

"Now, we'll travel inside the body and see how it works. These are the changes that take place as fertility takes place. Here we have the egg developing and moving into the fertilization area. Here it shows the fertilized egg moving to the area where the egg will be laid. Will that help you, Darrell?"

"Yes, Queen DorLetha. I see how it should work. Is there some way that I'La can run her hands over Esdra and show me what Esdra looks like inside? We have a machine on Earth that does that for me. It is called an x-ray machine."

"Let's ask her. I'll summons her." When I'La appeared, DorLetha spoke to her. "I'La, can you mentally show Darrell how Esdra is developing inside?"

"I can see myself, but I don't know how I'd show him."

"Can you show us all, as if you were doing telemetrical viewing?"

"Before she does, DorLetha, could I have her show me how you look inside? I know you've shown me the visual medical record of your physiology, but it would help if I could verify those records by seeing how you have developed. I'd feel a lot more confident about what Delbert expects me to do if I could see your insides."

"I don't see why not, Darrell. I have mated with a human and we don't know that anyone before me had ever done that. Why don't I lie down on the animal skin and I'La can check me out."

Everyone concentrated on I'La's thoughts as she passed her hands over DorLetha's body, being careful not to actually touch her. With everyone concentrating on I'La's thoughts, they were able to bring about telemetrical viewing of DorLetha's internal organs. Although all could see the same thing in their minds, only Darrell understood what he saw.

When Darrell was satisfied that he knew what he was looking at, I'La called Esdra in. "Esdra would you come in and lie down on the animal skin? I want to show Darrell how you look inside. He wants to see if there is some way he can correct your development so that you and Adrian can mate."

"Is there a chance you could, Darrell?"

"I don't know, Esdra. I fix problems humans have on our planet. After I see what is wrong, I'll decide."

I'La slowly moved her hands over Esdra's body. "Can you see how she looks inside, Darrell?"

"Yes, I'La, but I need you to go over her again and much slower. That's better. I see what the problem is. Would you go over her again, I'La, that's good. Thanks! I'll have to think about it. I'll let you know, as soon as possible, if I think I can do anything."

"Let me transport us back to Adrian's cave, Darrell. He has some dinner ready for you.

"Thanks, Delbert." Delbert levitated them quickly to Adrian's cave.

"Hi, Darrell."

"Hi, Adrian. My, Esdra, you get around quick. You're going to have to come see Carol and have her make you something to wear to take the place of your feathers."

"I don't want feathers any more. I want to be smooth like she is."

"Well, you'll be that way soon enough, Esdra. Did you forget I liked you the way you were?"

"Doesn't my pretty Adrian, like me anymore?"

"Yes, of course I do, but sometimes you try too hard to please me."

"I'm not sure I understand what you mean."

"I want you to keep some of your Exvascians characteristics. Surprise me and keep a few more of your special abilities, please!"

"I'll think about it."

"Thanks for dinner, Adrian. I'm ready to hit the hay!"

"What does that mean?"

"He's tired and ready to go to sleep. Darrell, what do you think about Esdra's problem?"

"I'll work on it and let you know, Adrian. Good night, you two."

"Good night Darrell."

Darrell went back to his cave and lay down by his wife. He was too tired to think about Esdra's problem until morning. Darrell slept in later than usual and awoke about the same time Carol did. "I'll fix breakfast, dear. Do you want to soak in the hot tub?"

"That would be good. You know, we'll have to get one of these back home. They're great. What did you do while I was resting, Darrel?"

"I tried to find out how the female Exvascians function, via telemetrical viewing or telepathic viewing or something."

"Did you find out what you need to know?"

"No, I can see where she is in her development and where she should be, but I don't know how to change her to make her functional again."

"How did you go about the whole process?"

"First DorLetha showed me some technical medical information. Then I'La showed me how DorLetha looked inside. She did so by passing her hands over DorLetha's body so I could see in my mind how she is supposed to work and then I saw how Esdra has developed. There doesn't seem to be any way to make all the corrections that are needed."

"What if you don't?"

"If what they say is correct, she will die and Adrian loses his mate."

"After breakfast I'll make some drawings, Carol. You may have the answer!"

"Did you want any more to eat, Darrell?"

"No thanks, Carol. Adrian said to put the scraps in that dish and he'll feed them to a hog-like animal they are fattening. He'll levitate our toilet pot and the scrap bowl both out this morning again and dispose of their contents.

"Now, here is how Esdra should look and this is how she looks. This is how you look. What do you see?"

"It looks very complicated."

"Right! What if I just took this mechanism out completely? That part isn't compatible with Adrian."

"That takes care of one problem. Now, where do her eggs come from?"

"This is where her eggs start out. They are supposed to stop here, and then proceed to here, where they are fertilized. They then go into here before they are layed."

"This gismo must make the shell then."

"I guess."

"Could you take out that last area so they would attach themselves like mine would?"

"Yes, but she doesn't have the proper structure to give birth to them!"

"We'll stay here and you can do a cesarean section on her."

"It might work. Let's go talk to everyone."

When the group had all arrived, DorLetha spoke. "I think we're all here Darrell. Go ahead and tell us what you've decided about Esdra."

"I have seven drawings here. The first is how Esdra should look. The second is how she looks now. The third is how Carol looks. The fourth is how I'd change Esdra. The fifth is how Carol would have a live birth. The six shows how I could help Carol have her child if she had a problem. Since we know Esdra can't perform like number six shows, I'd have to help her by performing picture number seven."

Darrell explained each picture in detail and then started asking questions. "Esdra, do you want to chance this?"

"I don't have a choice. All the others, who have had my problem, have died. I don't want that. Besides, we are only fertile once in our lifetime."

"Do all of you agree with her?"

"Yes!" Nobody wanted their friend Esdra to die.

"OK, if I remove this area and this area, I'La can you get them to heal quickly?"

"Yes, I could do that but I couldn't remove part of her."

"I'll do that part. When do you want to do this?"

"Could you do it soon?"

"Yes, but she can't eat anything the day before the operation. Hand me my bag, Carol. Esdra let me try something on you. Lie down here please. Now, I'm going to put some acupuncture needles in you to keep you from feeling certain parts of your body. There, can you feel me press on your arm?"

"No!"

"OK, what about your stomach?"

"Nothing!"

"Your leg?"

I don't feel anything."

"I'll try a few more places and that will be all for today." Darrell was soon finished.

The days passed quickly as Carol and Darrel prepared for the big operation. I'La talked at length with Darrell about his surgery and told him about the healing power of the plants, vegetables and fruits that Adrian and GarGweth had been eating.

Darrell set up a lab with his microscope and studied for several more days before he operated on Esdra. As far as he could tell, from I'La's comments and Esdra's body functions, before and after the operation, the surgery was a success.

The only way they would know if the surgery was successful, was to wait and see what happened when her time came and she and Adrian mated.